TUACA TAN

FRANKI AMATO MYSTERIES BOOK 8

TRACI ANDRIGHETTI

Limoncello
Press

TUACA TAN

by

TRACI ANDRIGHETTI

***

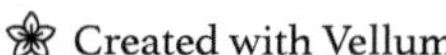 Created with Vellum

To my paraders in crime: Cherie Havard, Victoria Belue Schaefer, and Christina Vallery. Let the good times continue to roll—just not on another Mardi Gras krewe!

1

———————

"The Greasing of the Poles?" I asked, trying to wrap my mind around the slippery concept. "That's an actual event?"

Veronica looked up from her office laptop and shook blonde locks from her face. "I'm surprised you haven't heard of it, Franki. It's been the traditional kickoff for Mardi Gras weekend for over fifty years."

I shifted in the armchair in front of her desk. Growing up Catholic and with an old-school Sicilian nonna, I'd been raised with all sorts of traditions, some seriously weird, but greasing poles before Lent wasn't one of them. "When Glenda told me she'd been invited to compete, I assumed it was a stripping contest at Madame Moiselle's."

"Close. It's just down Bourbon Street at the Royal Sonesta Hotel, and it definitely gets bawdy. But it started as a way to keep paradegoers from climbing the balcony support poles for a better view."

"Ooh, *balcony* supports! They weren't one of the kinds of poles I was thinking of."

She cocked an eyebrow. "*One* of the kinds?"

"Don't give me that look." I kicked my legs over the side of the chair. "You know as well as I do that Mardi Gras weekend and our—I mean, *my*—ex-stripper landlady imply a couple of types of poles, and balcony supports isn't one of them."

"*Touché.*"

Both of my eyebrows cocked in reply. The French word meant "touched," which was a risqué choice considering the circumstances.

Veronica tapped her cell phone. "It starts at 10:00 a.m., so we need to leave in fifteen minutes to get close to the action."

The "action" was what gave me pause. "Before I commit, what will I be watching?"

"Glenda and three other local celebrities will compete for the title of Greasing Champion by smearing Vaseline on the poles at the hotel entrance. The contest is hosted by Moët, so the winner gets an engraved bottle of champagne."

"Poles, Vaseline, *and* champagne? How is this the first time Glenda's been invited?"

"I know. This event is perfect for her."

"Yeah, but not for me. Unless..." I sat upright, and my lips slid into a sly smile as though they'd been slathered with petroleum jelly.

"*Unless* what?"

"If Glenda wins, she'll be ecstatic, which means I can probably convince her to give me first right of refusal on tenants for your old apartment. I can*not* have the likes of Ruth Walker, Carnie Vaul, or Nadezhda Dmitriyeva living next door to me in the fourplex."

She chewed her lip. "Glenda's not one to turn down a dollar—"

"As indicated by her ex-profession," I quipped.

"Why don't you just move?"

"While I'm planning a wedding?" I shuddered. "No, thank you."

"That makes sense. But are you still paying Glenda an extra thousand a month to keep Nadezhda from renting the apartment upstairs?"

I pointed a defensive finger. "It's worth every cent to keep that penny-pinching, bikini-waxing, booze-peddling Communist out of the building."

Her head tilted. "You'd save a lot of money by moving in with Bradley. I know you're worried about your family's reaction, but you're thirty-two. They'd get over it."

My eyes rolled and dropped on her like a greased Glenda down a pole. "They'd have an easier time getting over a Muslim pope."

"You're probably right." She sniff-laughed and leaned back in her fuchsia leather chair. "Sometimes I miss the fourplex, but I love being married to Dirk and having my own home."

"I'm happy for you," I said. And I meant it, because her wedding week in Venice had gotten off to a dreadful start.

"Your turn next." She grinned and gave tiny claps. "How's the planning coming?"

"It's not."

Her smile faded. "Don't tell me the great date debacle is still going on?"

"No, I finally managed to talk Mom and Nonna down from the shock of finding out that our January eleventh wedding wasn't last month but next year." I refrained from adding that the experience had been almost as dreadful as her wedding week in Venice except that no one had died—so far.

"Then what's the problem? The location?"

"Yeah, Bradley's location." My lips pursed. "His crackerjack assistant—let me rephrase that—his cracker*wack* assistant keeps convincing him that he needs to go out of town to investigate a case. And you know why she's doing it?" I tapped my chest. "To keep him from me."

"She's doing it to help him solve fraud cases. Ruth's got a real head for crime—"

"And for all the perceived wrongs that have ever been done to her, which have evidently been committed solely by me."

Veronica typed something on her laptop and turned the screen so that I could see it. "Whatever she has a head for, it's working. According to this spreadsheet, in the two months she and Bradley have been at Private Chicks, they've increased our revenue by thirty percent. A large part of that has been Ruth's doing. If she keeps it up, I'll hire her myself."

I jerked as though Ruth had blasted me with her so-called Get Busy Buzzer. "Bite your evil, unclean tongue, Veronica Maggio Bogart."

Her look was stern as she turned the computer around. "Bottom line, you have to find a way to work with her."

"When she's doling out *Judge Judy* sentences for alleged office misbehavior and comparing our lunches to the skin conditions on *Dr. Pimple Popper*?"

Veronica's face faltered but returned to stern. "Ignore her."

"While she's buzzing that buzzer?"

"It's annoying, I agree. But it *has* been keeping everyone on task, which is part of that profit increase." She pulled a notebook from a drawer and tossed it on the desk. "Here's a solution for your Ruth issue."

"An exterminator manual?"

Her cornflower blue eyes turned midnight. "A gratitude journal."

I stared at the notebook as though it were *The Satanic Bible*. "How in the hell would that help?"

"It would shift your focus from negatives to positives, for example, from Ruth to your wedding."

"*Pff!* A crane couldn't shift my focus from Ruth 'Buzzi' Walker roosting at our reception desk."

"As your best friend, I'm asking you to try it."

I crossed my arms. "No."

"Then as your boss, I'm telling you to."

"Told you your tongue was evil and unclean." I swung my legs from the arm of the chair and stood. "I'll keep the gratitude journal, but don't expect results. Ruth is a black hole of negative that swallows everything positive in her vicinity."

I stalked down the hallway, and a blast from Ruth's Get Busy Buzzer had me gripping the doorjamb of my office to stay upright. When I recovered, I marched with clenched fists into the lobby and past the opposing couches to the reception desk. "Would you stop with the buzzer BS?"

Ruth raised her whiskered chin, tightening her turkey neck. She looked like an irate ostrich—with cat-eye glasses and a bun. "No can do, missy. The Get Busy Buzzer detected slacking."

"I wasn't slacking," I hissed. "I was talking to my boss."

She bit into a beignet. "Instead of sitting around chewing the fat," she said between chews, "why don't you rustle up some business?"

"Oh, so I should just go out and rustle up a homicide case to solve?"

"Shouldn't be hard. New Orleans has one of the highest murder rates in the country." Her eyes took on a skeptical squint. "Then again, I shouldn't expect you to find a case. I asked for a Santa-in-a-gondola ornament from Venice, and Franki Amato, ace PI, comes back with one made in Poland."

I threw up my arms. "How was I supposed to know the city of Murano glass sold Polish Christmas decorations?"

She removed her glasses. "The label."

My face turned as red as the scorned Santa's suit. Getting shown up by Ruth was more humiliating than getting your butt kicked by one of said Santa's elves, which hadn't happened to me personally but was something no one in The Big Easy could rule out.

The office door flew open, and David Savoie entered followed by Standish "The Vassal" Standifer. David waved spindly fingers. "Greetings, earthlings."

I frowned at my college-student coworkers' bandoliers, the combination tool belt and ammunition holder of the Wookiee Chewbacca from *Star Wars*. "Why are you guys still wearing those things? I thought the Intergalactic Krewe of Chewbacchus parade was canceled because of the hurricane."

David removed his faux-fur-lined bandolier and placed it on the corner desk. "The city gave us permission to reschedule. Now we get to walk on Mardi Gras day before an elite female krewe."

The Vassal nodded. "And the krewe is furious about it."

"Why?" I asked.

He clenched his slack jaw. "The most plausible explanation is discrimination against us ChewbacchanALIENs."

David flopped his lanky body into a chair. "Or they're worried about the krewe's history of pranks."

The mention of high jinks sent Ruth's eyes into slits. "What pranks?"

The Vassal pushed up his coke bottle glasses. "One year they staged an elaborate Big Foot hoax that caused controversy in the Sasquatch research community when the creature was revealed to be a Drunken Wookiee. Then they drew the ire of NASA by creating a website that claimed the Curiosity rover had located Mardi Gras beads on Mars and that the famous Martian 'face' was a Wookiee temple."

David doubled over in a fit of choked laughter. "The best one, though," he gasped out, "was when they announced that they were expanding the krewe from its Science Fiction theme to include Fantasy and Horror. Then, at their annual Alien Beach Party at Tipitina's, they organized a fake protest about the announcement by the Mystic Krewe of P.U.E.W.C."

"As in, 'puke?'" I repeated.

The Vassal slipped off his bandolier. "It's an acronym for 'People for the inclusion of Unicorns, Elves, and Whinebots in Chewbacchus.'"

Fake or no, the Krewe of P.U.E.W.C. was proof that an elf-whooping could happen in NOLA. "And *why* is that funny?"

His lens-enlarged eyes stared at me gobsmacked. "Because everyone knows that unicorns, elves, and whinebots will always be banned from Chewbacchus."

The dorky duo dissolved into snorts and honks.

"Welp, I haven't solved a homicide case," I said in a tone as dry as Ruth's ovaries, "but I've solved the mystery of why this elite female krewe is furious. They don't want a bunch of drunken Wookiee wannabes turning their classy parade into a Chewbacchanal."

The Vassal's nostrils flared. "Discrimination, as I suspected."

David shrugged. "What can you expect from the Krewe of Clotho?"

"Clotho?" Ruth tugged at her lace-collared cardigan. "As in cloth?"

"Indeed," The Vassal said. "Clotho was the spinner of the Moirai."

My index and pinky fingers pointed down in a *scongiuri* gesture my nonna had taught me to ward off bad luck. "Why would you say that word?"

"You mean," David scratched his temple, "the Greek name of the Three Fates?"

"Oh, I thought you said something else." I didn't tell them that I'd heard *morirai*, the Italian verb for "you will die." Uttering the word out loud was sure to tempt fate, which wasn't wise when the Three Fates were the topic of discussion.

The Vassal took a seat at his corner desk. "Ancient Greeks believed that the Moirai controlled one's destiny. Clotho spun the thread of life on her spindle, Lachesis measured its length, and Atropos cut it with her deadly shears."

Unease gnawed at my gut, and I flashed back to a homicide case I'd investigated at an old sugar plantation that had involved Atropos, the goddess of death.

"Ready, Franki?"

Veronica's voice snapped me out of a macabre memory. I shivered and grabbed my jacket from the coatrack. As I waited for her to exit before me, I heard a snip behind my back. I spun to face the reception desk.

Ruth's eyes glinted like the steel shears in her hand. "You had a loose thread."

My eyelids went low, and I slammed the office door on my way out. Ruth had pulled the thread stunt to fray my already tattered nerves. Nevertheless, as I followed Veronica down the three flights of stairs, the Three Fates weighed on my mind.

Call it a sixth sense or just plain instinct, but I had the sickening certainty that Clotho wouldn't be the only one of the Moirai parading at Mardi Gras.

"Is my outfit on point, Miss Ronnie?" Glenda shouted above the joyful jazz of the Original Hurricane Brass Band. She dropped into a lap-dance squat beneath the sign for Le Boozé, the Royal Sonesta Hotel's whiskey bar.

Veronica stepped back to take in her look. "Totally style worthy."

Smear worthy was more like it. She wore petroleum jelly

labels for pasties and a clear vinyl thong with a well-placed blue V—for Vaseline, naturally. And the accessories brought the greased getup together—her transparent PVC stripper shoes with a girl on a pole for the heels and a custom Fifi Mahony's fascinator with Stripper Barbie on a Bourbon Street sign pole that protruded from a Vaseline jar.

Glenda rose and flipped long, platinum hair highlighted with Vaseline-lid blue dye. "Times like these, I wish Bob Simpson hadn't retired from #strippercouture."

The former Texas lawyer had never struck me as a fashion designer, but he'd once convinced Glenda to wear an entire jumpsuit. And even though it had holes at the lady parts, it was still a notable improvement over her signature scanty stripper wear. "Why would you need Bob?"

"Do you really have to ask, sugar? He's the Shah of Shards, the Roi of Rhinestones. Why, he could've made fabric that looks like Vaseline." She pulled a Bourbon-Street-sign-pole cigarette holder with a king cake baby glued to it from her smearing ladder tray and took a frustrated puff. "I told you, Bob's the one who suggested the crystal droplets on Kim Kardashian's Met Gala 'wet dress.'"

Veronica's lips twitched. "We'll have to add King of Crystals to his titles."

"And Prince of Petroleum," I joked. But my gut quivered at the reference to the jelly, as though sensing danger. I tuned Glenda and Veronica out, not to mention the trombone blasting at my back, and scanned the crowd.

It was standing room only on Bourbon and on the balconies of the Royal Sonesta and Rick's Cabaret strip club across the street. Adding to the festivities were wild wigs, mainly from the two Mardi Gras dance troupes in attendance, The Merry Antoinettes in their powdered poufs and the Pussyfooters with their pink cotton-candy dos. Several women in sparkly opera gloves wore bouffant wigs decorated with Mardi Gras symbols—a purple one with a crown and feathers, a gold one with a fleur-de-lis and doubloons, and a green one with a mask and beads. The only exception was a group in crazy hats wearing t-shirts that said, "The Greasing of the Poles Fun Club from Switzerland."

A man in a tuxedo with a purple tie and green cummerbund exited the hotel with a gold tray holding a chalice full of petroleum jelly. With his free hand, he picked up a microphone, and the music stopped. "As your MC, I'd like to welcome you to the Greasing of the Poles. And we're talking about balcony poles, not people from Poland."

The audience laughed, but I didn't. The joke was spoiled by an image of Ruth's sour mug griping about that Polish Santa-in-a-gondola ornament.

The MC turned to the contestants. "Greasers, mount your ladders."

Glenda, who was competing under her stage name, Lorraine Lamour, waited while the others climbed purple ladders pre-equipped with Vaseline jars—a DJ in a Mardi Gras-colored pimp suit, a reality show star in a New Orleans Saints-themed tutu, and a fiftyish former federal prosecutor and failed mayoral candidate named Ken Lanier, who wore a brown suit and a leopard-spotted wig with a king cake crown. When they'd taken their smearing positions, Glenda, aka Lorraine, sashayed to the top of her ladder, licked her thin, lined lips, and ran her hand down the pole. "And this one's juuuust right."

The crowd went wild at the lusty Goldilocks reference, and Mardi Gras beads rained from the balconies.

The MC raised the chalice. "Let's take Ms. Lamour's cue and get to greasing."

The four contestants dipped their fingers into the jars, and

Glenda, not content to stay on her ladder, wrapped her legs around the pole and spanked it to apply the jelly.

"Get it, girl," a woman shouted.

Ken looked over his shoulder at Glenda and climbed onto his pole too.

Screams and whistles came from the audience.

After a minute, four judges raised paper fleurs-de-lis with the scores.

The MC turned to the crowd. "Looks like we have a tie between Ken Lanier and Lorraine Lamour. You know what this means, folks. A fifteen-second grease-off. But first, let's get these two some greased lightning!"

A woman wearing a hat topped with an overturned champagne bottle pouring into a glass gave Glenda one of two flutes of Moët on a tray, and the woman in the gold bouffant wig with the fleur-de-lis and doubloons handed Ken a creamy tan-colored drink.

"Chug! Chug! Chug!" the crowd chanted.

Glenda and Ken obliged. He squinted and pressed his forehead as though he'd gotten brain freeze from the frozen drink and wiped away a milk mustache with his sleeve.

Veronica looked up at Glenda. "You've got this!"

She hiked up her V thong and leaned down. "I'm gonna win me that engraved bottle of Moët. I've been greasing poles a lot longer than Ken has been greasing palms, and everyone knows Vaseline and *l'amour* go together."

My eyes flitted to the Le Boozé sign. After that questionable comment, I could use a Le Drinké.

The MC raised the chalice. "For the next fifteen seconds, 'grease' is the word!"

Ken ripped open his white button-down, revealing purple, green, and gold body paint on his hairy chest.

Several of the Merry Antoinettes literally flipped their wigs.

Glenda's eyes flashed, and using only her legs to grip the pole, she got to greasing—with her boobs.

The catcalls were deafening. Glenda had been stripping for so long that not only could she put on a serious pole show, she could also wrap her saddle bags around a pole and darn-near tie them in a bow.

"Put down your Vaseline," the MC cried. "It's time to crown the next Greasing Champion of The Big Greasy."

All eyes turned to the judges, who huddled in discussion.

Still perched on their poles, Glenda oozed Vaseline and confidence, but Ken seemed shaky.

"I'm not feeling so good," he mumbled.

That was obvious. His face had turned two of the Mardi Gras colors painted on his chest.

Ken dropped down the pole a notch and stopped with a jerk. Then he fell backwards and hung upside down before sliding head first to the ground with a thud and the crash of his drained drink glass.

A collective gasp arose from the audience, and Veronica and I made our way to his side.

I checked for a pulse, and one word came to mind—not "grease" or even "dead."

It was "Atropos."

2

———

"Officer, honey," Glenda huffed, so angry that Pole-Dancer Barbie shook atop her fascinator, "do I look like I need to kill a prosecutor to win a pole-greasing contest?" Before the policeman could respond, she gripped the pole and spread her skinny legs, displaying her V.

"Glenda needs to put a pole in it," I whispered to Veronica, "or she'll end up a suspect."

Veronica covered her mouth with her hand. "If she goes too far, I'll play the attorney card. But we don't know that Ken Lanier was murdered."

My eyes lowered to the cloth that covered Ken's dead body, and I thought of the goddess Clotho, who spun the thread of life. Atropos had cut his life short. *But was it natural causes? Or foul play?*

My gaze shifted to the shattered remnants of the glass the gold-wigged woman had handed him. It wouldn't hurt to ask some questions. "Stay with Glenda. I'm going to talk to the bartender."

I entered the Royal Sonesta's tan lobby and walked down a corridor to the entrance of Le Boozé.

The woman who'd served Glenda the champagne before the grease-off was crying in a fetal position in the bottom of a giant Moët glass. I sympathized because I'd been there—not in that specific glass but in the one in Glenda's living room.

A thirty-something bartender stood inside a rectangular-shaped bar surrounded by empty stools. He wore a Georgia Bulldogs cap and had an underbite that rivaled the school mascot's. "Bar's closed."

Fine with me. I wasn't willing to drink at Le Boozé after the grim greasing scene I'd witnessed.

He buffed the counter with a rag. "Cops shut us down on one of the best tipping days of the year, even though we didn't make that dead guy's drink."

That got my attention. "Do you know who did?"

"Some lady said the woman who gave it to him was holding it when she got here. The only one serving alcohol from the hotel was Sylvie, the champagne girl." He nodded in the direction of the giant Moët glass.

Sylvie popped from the bottom like a cork from a bottle. "I was supposed to serve Mr. Lanier champagne too, but that woman in the big gold wig beat me to him." She slid back to the glass bottom, bubbling in sobs. "Now I'm fiiirrred."

Glad everyone at the hotel has their priorities straight. "Out of curiosity, any idea what kind of drink it was?"

The bartender resumed buffing. "A dude who was standing next to the dead guy said he got a whiff of brandy from the glass, so my guess is a Brandy Alexander or a frozen southern milk punch."

"That punch is a local brunch drink, right?"

"Yeah, Brandy, Tuaca, cream, vanilla, and powdered sugar with nutmeg."

"Sounds heavenly."

He clamped his jaw shut, but his underbite was still visible.

Unsure whether he was bearing his teeth at me or just looked like that, I puckered. "Poor choice of words."

Veronica popped her head into the bar from the street entrance. "Glenda's free to go. She's going to walk back to the office with us so we can drive her home."

"I'm ready to head out," I said, walking toward her. "Ken's drink didn't come from the hotel."

A swarm of reporters buzzed outside the bar. The prosecutor's death was already big news in NOLA, and the way he died would take it national.

We made our way through the media mob and began weaving through the usual throngs of partiers on Bourbon. Given the naughty nature of the street, Glenda didn't stand out in her greasing getup, but a guy dressed as a cocktail mascot did —not because he was dressed as a drink but because Bourbon Street was the Dancing Hand Grenade's territory.

"I was thinking," Veronica pulled her Chanel bag higher on her shoulder, "it's possible that the woman who passed Ken the drink was a friend of his, and he died of a medical condition."

"Could be, Miss Ronnie." Glenda hiked up her V. "In my experience, quite a few men in their fifties die from heart attacks."

No need to ask what kind of experience that *was.* "For all we know, Ken mistook the woman in that gold fleur-de-lis wig for an employee of Moët or the hotel. But we can't rule out a crime. As a prosecutor, he would've had a lot of enemies."

"I'm inclined to think it *was* murder, sugar. A woman came by the fourplex this morning to see Miss Ronnie's apartment, and she predicted this would happen."

Veronica's eyes narrowed. "How so, Glenda?"

"She said I'd meet a slippery man who'd cause me trouble."

I snort-laughed. "That's hardly a prediction. Most women meet a man like that at one time or another."

"Child, don't I know it? But I didn't tell her I was competing in the greasing contest, so that 'slippery' is eerie."

"Is it?" I asked. "The *Times Picayune* probably had an article about the event and the contestants."

"They did, but she's a psychic, sugar, so she'd know these things. Why, she even knows you. Her name is Miss Chandra Toccato, the Crescent City Medium."

The name sent me reeling. I slid on some Mardi Gras beads, flailed my arms, and face-planted on the filthiest street in North America, both literally and figuratively.

"Oh, Franki!" Veronica stooped to help me up. "Are you okay?"

I wasn't. Not only had I fallen on a chicken foot in front of Marie Laveau's House of Voodoo, the beads I'd slipped on were decorated with crescent moons. Pain wracked my body, and my mind was seized by a primal hysteria, similar to a human in the grip of a lunar transition into a werewolf. "What the hell was Chandra doing looking at Veronica's old apartment?"

Glenda strut-turned onto St. Ann Street. "She needs a place to stay because she and her plumber man are on the outs."

"How?" I howled, causing a group of girls in iridescent tube tops to jump. "Lou barely speaks, and he does all the cooking. It's not possible to find fault with a man like that." Although, now that I thought about it, Lou *did* wear toe shoes, which constituted ten huge little-piggy drawbacks.

"You'll have to ask Miss Chandra, sugar. I don't want to discuss her private business."

"I'm not going to ask her anything, because you're *not* going to rent to her."

"Far be it from me to reject her application, Miss Franki. She said it meant a lot to her not to be alone in her time of woe."

"What about *my* time of woe?" I insisted, neglecting to point out that it had been ongoing since I'd hit puberty.

Glenda fired up her Bourbon Street sign pole cigarette holder and blew the smoke in my face. "Let me put it to you another way. Miss Chandra offered me more than the rent, not to mention a free French commode."

The smoke cleared, and my hopes for stopping a Chandra move-in were sunk, as in flushed. Because Glenda wasn't talking about a chest of drawers, she was talking about a custom toilet from Chandra and Lou's joint business, Crescent City Plumbing & Palmistry. "Don't do this to me, Glenda. Chandra and I have a history, and Lou might be related to Bradley through his grand-mother, which means that lunar lunatic could show up to my wedding and channel who knows what spirits. And I've got enough on my plate with my mom and nonna hounding me about getting married, not to mention Ruth buzzing at me at the office."

Veronica rubbed my back. "Look at the bright side, Franki. At least you know who you'll be dealing with."

"Yeah, a sham psychic. Every time her charm bracelet jingles, she somehow channels the murder victim of a case I'm working. You watch, Veronica. If Ken Lanier *was* murdered, his ghost will come to her, but only when I'm present."

My phone rang, and I pulled it from my hobo bag. "It's Bradley."

Veronica slid on a pair of sunglasses. "You'd better let him know about Ken Lanier."

I answered. "Hey, babe. Where are you?"

"New York, but I'm coming home tomorrow afternoon at four. Can you pick me up at the airport?"

"I'd love to. I need you here."

"I'm sorry, babe." His tone hinted at guilt. "I've been traveling so much lately."

"It's not that. It's...we just saw a prosecutor, Ken Lanier, die."

"What?" Bradley erupted in my ear. "How?"

He slid off a greased pole sounded kind of weird. "He was one of the contestants at the Greasing of the Poles. During the competition, he suddenly announced that he didn't feel well and then fell to the ground, dead."

"I can't believe it. He's the subject of the insurance fraud case I'm here investigating."

The investigation put a different spin on Ken's slide down the pole. I followed Veronica and Glenda onto Decatur Street and learned something else that put a new spin on the prosecutor's death—the three Mardi Gras-wigged women from the event had discarded their decorated dos on the street.

Veronica and I locked eyes, and I knew we had the same questions. *Why would three women ditch pristine custom wigs? And right after one of them had handed a drink to a man who'd up—make that down—and died?*

BLACK EYES SPIED on me in my kitchen, boring into my mind, willing me to do their bidding.

I pretended not to notice. Keeping my gaze on the anchovies dissolving in oil in the sauce pan, I calmly reached for the nearest item, a stainless steel pepper grinder.

A strangled growl rang out.

The grinder went still in mid-air, but my head jerked over my shoulder to my kitchen stalker. "What is it?"

My brindle Cairn terrier, Napoleon, had shifted his focus from me to the door, as though someone or something lurked outside our apartment.

Holding the grinder like a weapon, I entered the adjoining purple-red-and-gold brothel chic living room, courtesy of Glenda. Even the glass eyes on the bearskin rug seemed to be wary. I peered out the peephole overlooking the yard, but nothing was amiss. And Thibodeaux's, the bar across the street, was as dead as the neighboring cemetery.

Nevertheless, as I returned to the kitchen, my gut simmered like the anchovies and oil on the stove. I'd been on edge since the Greasing of the Poles, and my dog's behavior wasn't helping. Seeing Ken slide to his demise had been disturbing, but more unsettling was the queasy-uneasy sense that another dark event was looming.

"It's not like you're psychic," I said to myself. Then I shifted my weight on one leg. "Maybe that's what it is—the threat of psycho Chandra moving in to the fourplex."

Feeling as relieved as one could when their homelife was about to be uprooted by a mad medium and her simulated spirits, I pulled garlic from the spice cabinet.

A ship alarm blared, and I jumped.

It was the ringtone I'd selected for my family. Apparently, the looming dark event was a call from home.

I put the phone on speaker on the counter. "Hi, Mom."

"Francesca? It's your mother." She spoke, or rather shrilled, as though I wouldn't know her to drive home the fact that *she* was calling *me*, and not vice versa.

I considered shaking up the charade by pretending not to know her but feared it would result in more calls. "Hi again, Mom."

"What are you up to, dear?" she asked as though she had no agenda, which was as likely as her giving up trying to run my life for Lent.

"Making puttanesca sauce."

"Bradley's lucky to have a fiancée who can cook. Don't forget to add a teaspoon of sugar to neutralize the tomato acid."

"And-a *pepe di Caienna* for his-a weak digestion," Nonna rasped from another line in the house.

My lips tightened as I reached for a garlic press, ruing the day I'd told Nonna the white lie that Bradley took Cayenne pepper to help with a digestive issue, when, in fact, I was using it in a cockamamie witch spell that was supposed to get her and my mom to leave town. Now she was convinced that he had what she viewed as an emasculating condition. "The sauce is for me. Bradley's on a business trip."

Nonna harrumphed. "Forget-a the *pepe di Caienna*."

"And the sugar," my mother's tone was as acidic as the tomatoes, "since you'll be eating alone like the ladies of the evening the puttanesca sauce was named for."

I loaded a garlic clove into a press and squeezed the device as hard as my mom and nonna squeezed me. If only I could neutralize their acid with sugar.

My mother growled and tried to cover it with a throat clear. "Have you and Bradley looked at any wedding venues, at least?"

"They already got-a the ven-a-ue right-a there in-a New Orleans," Nonna shouted. "The Piazza d'Italia with-a the fancy red and-a green-a lights."

My gut went from a slow simmer to bubbling. Nonna continually pressed for a wedding at the American Italian Cultural Center's Disneyesque piazza. But with those lights shining on my white dress, I'd look like I'd worn the Italian flag to my wedding. "We still haven't decided on the city."

"You two had better hurry, Francesca. You're running out of time to book a place, unless—"

"A Houston wedding is out, Mom." The flattened garlic husk I pulled from the press would be me if I got married on my family's home turf.

"Then why don't we travel to some venues?" She used her cheer-faux tone to make it sound fun.

"While-a we look at-a ven-a-ues, maybe we look at-a some grooms-a too."

I shoved a can of San Marzano tomatoes into the electric

opener. I knew what that groom crack was about. "People travel for business, okay?"

"Your father didn't, dear. He's always with me, day after day, at home and at work."

The strain in my mother's voice spoke volumes about how well that togetherness was working out. "Ever since Bradley took the job at Private Chicks, I see him more than when he was president of Pontchartrain Bank."

My mom sighed, deflated. "Now if you could just see him at wedding venues."

I dumped the whole, peeled tomatoes into the pan and squeezed them until they popped.

"What's going on?" My dad erupted from somewhere in the house. "Bradley doesn't want to look at wedding venues?"

"Apparently not, Joe."

"No, sonny. Brad-a-ley leave-a town so he don't have-a to commit."

The sound my father emitted could've been mistaken for Lurch's signature groan on *The Addams Family*, but I knew it had come from his perpetually sick stomach rather than his throat. "Sounds like Bradley and I need to have a talk."

My gut was at a rolling boil. "Mom, please tell Dad not to talk to Bradley about our private business. He *does* want to look at venues—"

"Then why hasn't he, Francesca?"

There was no point in repeating that Bradley was on a business trip or that we hadn't settled on a city, so I rinsed my hands to get a rolling pin—but not to roll pasta dough. I needed it to put myself out of my misery. As I rummaged in a drawer, I spotted kitchen shears and thought of Atropos, who gave me an idea.

Cut the conversation short.

In Italian families, there was only one acceptable way to abruptly end a call. "My sauce is burning!"

My mother screamed like Janet Leigh in *Psycho*.

"*Madonna mia!*" Nonna beseeched the Virgin. "Save-a the sauce-a!"

"Is she burning sauce?" My dad boomed, his sick stomach no doubt in knots. "What the hell is she still doing on the phone?"

I gave a saucy smile and hung up. Humming a happy tune, I added capers and olives to the pan, lowered the heat, and headed for the zebra-striped chaise lounge.

Napoleon hopped up beside me. I gave him a scratch and grabbed my laptop to check for news of Ken Lanier's death. There was no new information, so I googled Atropos. Her name was Greek for "inflexible," but her Roman name was *Morta*, which meant "death" and "dead woman."

"The Italians sure have a knack for calling it like it is."

A knock at my front door rendered me corpselike, and Napoleon's ears went as stiff as coffins. A crazy thought crossed my mind. *Has Atropos come knocking?*

Or worse—Chandra Toccato?

I rose and crept toward the peephole. A hulking woman with a curtain of black hair, purple-and-gold smoky-eye makeup, and maroon-lined lips with tan matte lipstick made me take a step back.

Marcella from the American Italian Cultural Center?

"For a woman in her eighties," I muttered, "Nonna works fast." I opened the door. "Marcella. Hi."

She peered at me through her thick hair and lurched forward. "I'm sorry to stop by unannounced," she said in her oddly soft voice, "but it's urgent."

"Is the Piazza d'Italia that popular with brides?"

"Honey," she raised powdered eyebrows and tapped my wrist, "our red-and-green lights on a white dress make you look like a slice of bruschetta with tomatoes and basil. Need I say more?"

She kind of did because I wasn't grasping the appeal. "Before you launch into a piazza sales pitch, Bradley and I aren't getting married in New Orleans."

"You don't want to look like a tasty bite of bruschetta, that's your problem. Mine is that I have a friend who needs your help."

A woman who reminded me of Reese Witherspoon came forward in a getup that would've made me gasp if I didn't live downstairs from Glenda. She was small compared to Marcella's linebacker size, but her brown bouffant wig was huge—as were its eyes, nose, and bared fangs.

Napoleon growled.

I shushed him and ushered them in.

"*Mm.*" Marcella's Roman nose sniffed the air. "A red sauce. I'm surprised your fiancé can eat that with his weak digestion."

I'd forgotten Nonna had told her about Bradley's non-existent issue, but clearly she and Nonna never would.

Napoleon barked, and I scooped him up before he charged. "Sorry about my dog, but you have an animal on your head."

The woman ran her hands down her faux-fur mini dress that matched her knee-high boots and then smoothed her wig. "Yes, it's Mardi Gras season, and I'm a walking billboard for my business."

"Holiday taxidermy wear?" I asked, depositing Napoleon in my bedroom.

Marcella tittered. "She's a wigmaker."

"Wanda Wiggins." She shook my hand. "I pick a krewe and show them what I can do with their theme. Today it's Chewbacca for the Intergalactic Krewe of Chewbacchus."

No way I was telling David and The Vassal about Wanda's business. I already had an angry ostrich with a turkey neck in the office. I didn't need Wookiee wigs too. "You've got the perfect last name for a wigmaker."

"Wiggins is my brand. My real name is Wronka. That's Wonka with a *rr*."

The growling pronunciation comparison brought a loud librarian from my not-nearly-distant-enough Venetian past screaming to the present, which was all kinds of wronka.

Marcella sat in the purple armchair with the gold fringe, presumably because it matched her makeup. "Can I offer you something to drink?"

My non-smoky eyes darted left to right. "From...*my* kitchen?"

"We're imposing on *you*, silly." She pulled plastic wine glasses from her tote and began filling one from a spout hidden beneath a small flap at the corner. "It's a bag of Chianti in a bag. What's classier than that?"

My mouth couldn't answer. It was stuck in an open position because of what Wanda had pulled from a secret compartment in the bouffant portion of her Chewbacca wig—a small board with brie cheese and a knife.

Marcella handed me a glass, and I dumped wine into my open jaw and swallowed hard. "Wanda, I have to ask because of your wig, are you by any chance the woman who handed Ken Lanier the drink at the Greasing of the Poles?"

"No, but that's why Marcella brought me here." She unwrapped the package of brie. "Three of my Mardi Gras wigs were stolen from my shop last night, and then that prosecutor was murdered."

"You think your wigs had something to do with his death?" My tone implied that Wanda had flipped hers. "Also, how do you know it was murder?"

"Why else would anyone steal wigs and ditch them on a backstreet?"

I shrugged. "Because they didn't want to get caught with stolen wigs?"

She bared her teeth, and I put down my wine. Because of her Chewbacca wig, I thought I'd seen double.

Wanda rubbed her heart-shaped face. "Those women have money. They don't need to steal."

"What women?"

"I only know two of them. Claudine Denault, the one in the gold wig who handed Ken Lanier the drink, and Marie-Fleur Fontenot in the green. I recognized them from someone's cell phone video online."

Marcella raised her tote and topped off my glass. "I recognized them too. Wanda and I know Claudine and Marie-Fleur from when we went to private school together at the Ursuline Academy."

I was familiar with the Catholic girls' school because it was near the fourplex.

Wanda stood and paced in front of the fireplace, cutting a striking figure on the bearskin rug. "I got a scholarship to Ursuline for my senior year, and Claudine and Marie-Fleur never let me forget that I didn't belong. They also never let me forget that the boy they both had a crush on asked me on a date."

Marcella's smoky eyes fumed. "Those two were thick as thieves, and the expression fits them. They stole my Italianness when they Frenchified my name—Mar-SELL-a instead of Mar-CHELL-a."

I didn't ask why she still went by the Frenchified version. The pronunciation had taken me back to a case I'd investigated with three other sleuths that involved a *Charlene* with a *ch* as hard as her personality. "I was at the Greasing of the Poles, and even though Ken's death seems suspicious, I'm not convinced it was murder. Those wigs really stood out in the crowd, which is the last thing you'd want if you were going to kill a public figure."

Wanda grabbed the cheese knife and whacked off a hunk. "Not if it's the polar opposite of your usual look. They're all about sleek hair and neutral makeup because they're uppity society types."

"And you're positive those wigs were yours?"

Her crystal-blue eyes popped. "I'd know my own babies, wouldn't I? It takes me nine hours to make each one."

Even though Wanda appeared to be in her mid-forties like Marcella, I was pretty sure she didn't have children.

"But don't take my word for it." She bit into the cheese with her Chewbacca chompers. "My brand is stamped on the inside of the wigs, so the police called me in after someone found them in the street."

"That was my best friend, Veronica Maggio."

Marcella gasped. "Small world, isn't it? Veronica owns Private Chicks, where Franki works."

Wanda and her wig looked at me imploringly. "Claudine and Marie-Fleur set me up, and the police think I was one of the wig wearers. I need you to investigate this case before they haul me to jail."

My glass reminded me of the drink that had been handed to the prosecutor. I wished I'd taken a shard to have it tested for poison. "What reason would they have had to kill Ken Lanier?"

Marcella pulled back her hair. "You remember that I'm a Muff-a-lotta?"

I nodded. "It's hard to forget a Mardi Gras dance troupe named after a Sicilian sandwich, especially considering that the muffuletta launched my dad's deli career."

"Well, I told Wanda that last week when we were rehearsing our salami shimmy, I heard a rumor that Ken Lanier was going to open an investigation into their krewe for embezzling."

That was interesting considering that Bradley had connected the prosecutor himself to fraud.

Wanda returned to the chaise lounge. "We could investigate what Lanier was investigating by going undercover at their krewe brunch tomorrow."

I was confused by a few things, and one of them was Wanda's "we." But I decided to table that—along with the salami shimmy—in favor of the most pertinent question. "They have a Mardi Gras krewe?"

Wanda and Chewbacca nodded. "Claudine is captain and Marie-Fleur is treasurer of the Krewe of Clotho."

My stomach dropped like Ken Lanier from the pole. *Was the krewe a coincidence? Or had someone on Clotho cut the prosecutor's thread of life?*

3

———

A buzz blasted, and I jumped awake. "I'm not slacking, Ruth!"

The noxious noise had cleared the boxed-wine fog from my head, which led to a few realizations. It was Saturday, the buzz was from the alarm clock next to my canopy bed, and Bradley's buzzing assistant had not only invaded my life and my office, she'd infested my psyche and my apartment.

"I'm going to have to neutralize her," I growled, "and I don't care what Veronica says, a freaking gratitude journal is not the answer." I smacked the snooze button and rolled over.

Into brown fur with one eye, a semi-severed nose, and bared fangs.

Catapulting from the bed, I nearly screamed out my teeth.

Then I remembered—in the spirit of a true Chewbacchan-ALIEN, Wanda had drunk so much cheap Chianti that as she was leaving, she'd tossed her Chewbacca wig to me as though I were a paradegoer on Canal Street.

Napoleon sat beside the battered hairpiece on the fuchsia duvet, holding up a paw. He'd done his doggy duty and given the synthetic *Star Wars* varmint the death shake, but I hadn't given him his due praise.

"Good boy." I stepped into my slippers and threw on a robe. "Let's get you outside so you can do your business and hunt live critters with brown fur, like rats and psychics with bouffant bobs."

He bounded from the bed and followed me through the living room. I opened the front door, and a blue Mitsubishi Eclipse turned my world black, as though the moon had blocked the sun.

My hunting psychics remark had been a joke, but Chandra Toccato, fraud fortune-teller, was really moving in.

It wasn't the celestial-themed model of the car that told me it was her, or even the U-Haul trailer it was towing. The dead give-away was the car's custom paint job that rivaled the ones on her plumber husband's toilets. Emblazoned on the hood was Chandra's made-up moon-pie face and Boston-strong teased bob. Orbiting around her planet-like head were the various lunar phases.

Steeling myself for psychic schmatter—and the dark possibility that Chandra had discovered Lou might be related to Bradley—I stepped onto the porch.

As if on cue, Veronica's former apartment door opened. But the Chandra who exited had nothing on the one on the car. Her bob was flat, her face unpainted, and her signature paddle-shaped nails needed salon intervention. She was a little more Pillsbury Doughboyish than the last time I'd seen her, and instead of her usual solar system-themed clothing, she donned a gray sweatsuit and tennis shoes without even a hint of sheen or sparkle. But the most shocking change of all—she wasn't wearing her spirit-channeling charm bracelet.

Chandra stifled a yawn. "I didn't know you were home."

This from a woman who'd once predicted that I was outside her office before I even knocked.

Her squat body waddled down the driveway and opened a passenger door with a picture of her face inside a crystal ball. She retrieved a white half-moon-shaped handbag with three round cutouts resembling eyes and a nose, and a smattering of small oblong cutouts below them.

I pointed to her purse. "Is that supposed to be a crying ghost?"

Her face mimicked her handbag. "Are you trying to spook me, or something?" she boomed in her Boston accent. "You know I'm afraid of spirits."

I mentally thanked her and my lucky stars for the reminder. "Which is why it's not a good idea to move across the street from a cemetery. Are you sure you don't want to go home to Lou?"

A pudgy hand smoothed her hair. "Don't go blabbing this around, but I haven't heard from a spirit since Lou and I started having problems."

It was as though the moon had moved and the sun shone again. If Chandra had lost her spirit and *the* spirit, I was in the clear. Nevertheless, I wanted her gone. "That's another sign you should go home."

"Not a chance, sister." She slammed the car door. "Lou was never the same after the two of you took those cooking lessons at Bayou Cuisine."

Neither was I. That school taught its students recipes made from trash, insects, and roadkill, and I was still traumatized. "Are you talking about his cooking?"

"What cooking?" she huffed. "After he got to be the okra in the school's Gumbo Pot float last Mardi Gras, he never made another dish. He caught the parading bug and joined a krewe."

I wished she hadn't said "bug." It reminded me of the Creole

Cockroach I'd eaten in class that I'd thought was a spiced almond.

"Now he spends all of his time with his krewe buddies and almost none with me. So I said to myself, 'Chandra, you don't have to take that from him. You can give up on marriage like Franki and live next door to her at the singles' compound.'"

My tongue moved to my cheek to prevent me from going off on her for the backhanded inner dialogue. "Which krewe is it?"

"Commodus."

"You mean, Comus," I corrected, certain she was referring to New Orleans' oldest continually operating Mardi Gras organization.

She popped the trunk, and as the automated door rose, it revealed an upside down image of her disembodied head surrounded by tarot cards. "No, when the city passed the ordinance requiring parading krewes to reveal their members, Comus refused, so now they just have a ball." Her tiny mouth scrunched into a scowl. "Those krewes are so secretive, which is part of my issue with Lou. He started Commodus with his plumber buddies, and he never tells me what they're doing."

An image was starting to form of a giant toilet float full of krewe members brandishing toilet bowl scrubbers like swords and throwing toilet bowl cleaning tablets instead of plush toys or beads.

"Actually, I do know one thing they're doing. You know how the Rolling Elvi ride scooters? And the Laissez Boys ride motorized La-Z-Boy recliners?"

I saw where this was going—in the toilet, as I'd suspected. "I've seen them, yes."

"Well, Commodus is making motorized commodes to ride in the parade."

While I was glad to be wrong about the float, a procession of men sitting on johns was no better. As if to back me up on that,

Napoleon scratched frantically at the apartment door, trying to go in. "Sorry, but I've got to go."

"To the bathroom?"

I could see why she'd think that. "Eventually, but at the moment I have to find something tan to wear to a Mardi Gras krewe brunch."

"Oh, lord. Don't tell me you've joined a krewe too?"

I'd join Lou's commode krewe and parade on a pot if it would drive her from the fourplex. "Not yet, but I can't rule it out." My tone held a definite threat. "The brunch is part of an investigation."

"Homicide?"

Here we go. She's pumping me for info so she can conjure up a communication from beyond. "I'm not sure. A man died under suspicious circumstances, and his death could be connected to the Krewe of Clotho."

"That's weird. One of their board members approached me a few weeks ago about doing a quote unquote 'fun séance night event,'" she said, wiggling chipped paddle nails. "I informed them that there was nothing fun about séances."

Not if Chandra was conducting them. "Did you do it?"

"I'm a Cancer, remember? This moonchild wasn't in the mood." She pulled a suitcase from the trunk. "Plus, as the Crescent City Medium, I could hardly make a mockery of the spirit world."

"Nooo, you couldn't do that."

"But a strange thing happened. The woman asked for a tarot reading, so I drew three cards. Then she left before I could read them."

"Maybe she already knew what they meant."

She closed the trunk. "Could be. Whatever happened, it's just as well. I don't like to be the bearer of bad news."

I squashed a smirk. We both knew that her affinity for

spreading gloom was what had drawn her to the profession. "Just out of curiosity, what was the gist of the reading?"

She pulled the suitcase up the drive. "I can only remember two of the cards. One was Death—"

"Uh, that's probably why she left," I interrupted. "What was the other?"

"The Hanged Man."

"Gah, that's grim." I rubbed my neck, wondering whether the board member was one of the two women that Wanda had identified at the Greasing of the Poles. "So, she'll supposedly die by hanging?"

Chandra stopped at her door. "Nah, tarot cards are symbolic. They don't necessarily predict what's going to happen. They can also reflect what's going on in your life or even things you've done. And anyway, The Hanged Man isn't hanging by his neck. He's hanging by his ankle from a pole."

My spine went as straight as a Royal Sonesta balcony support. "A pole?"

"To represent the gallows." She went into her apartment and shut the door.

A heavy feeling settled in my chest. Chandra didn't seem like she was up to any psychic shenanigans, which made me uneasy about the tarot reading. The Death and Hanged Man cards certainly didn't make the case for Ken Lanier's murder. But because she'd drawn them for a Krewe of Clotho board member, I couldn't help but wonder whether they'd had a hand in the prosecutor's untimely pole dive.

"MAMMA MIA!" Marcella exclaimed from under the wide-brimmed hat she'd worn to obscure her identity. "That's Marie-

Fleur, one of the two Clotho board members who Frenchified my name in high school."

I sized up the forty-something bleached blonde behind the card table outside the Ernest N. Morial Convention Center banquet hall. "You took that crap from a woman whose name is Mary-Flower?"

Wanda hmphed. "Don't be fooled. She's a steel magnolia."

"And if she recognizes Wanda and me," Marcella said, "she'll turn Venus flytrap."

"We'd better go in." I led them behind the table to the entrance.

"Excuse me." Marie-Fleur turned in a tan chair that matched her ensemble and gave me a look that could have withered a sunflower. "The Krewe of Nyx brunch is tomorrow."

I blinked. "We're here for the Clotho empowerment brunch."

Marie-Fleur stared doubtfully at me—and at the too-short tan shift dress I'd reluctantly borrowed from Chandra. Then her icy blue eyes—made icier by a spray tan—flitted from Wanda's tight tan pencil skirt to her scoop neck blouse and landed on her tan beehive wig. With bees. And a honeycomb. From there her gaze traveled to Marcella's tan bodycon dress that emphasized her linebacker build. "I've already checked in everyone who registered. Did Josephine add you to the list?"

I had no idea who that was, but I nodded.

The frown on her lips was as thinly disguised as the dark eye circles under her concealer. "You'll have to pay again until I can talk to her. Write down your name and number and tell me which table level y'all purchased."

I wrote Ruth's contact info on a piece of paper. "We got the cheap seats."

Her exhale said, *Of course you did.* "That'll be two hundred dollars." She smoothed her sleek ponytail with a tan-gloved hand. "Each."

My chin retracted to my neck. The krewe didn't need to embezzle with prices like these. "This brunch had better last through dinner and breakfast tomorrow."

"She's joking," Wanda said in falsetto from behind me. She slid six C notes into my hand and leaned into my back. "Watch it," she warned under her breath, "or she'll think we're not krewe material and ask us to leave."

If the brunch cost had been coming from my pocket, I'd want to get rejected. I handed the money to Marie-Fleur and opened the banquet hall door.

The space was large enough to hold a rock concert. There was so much tan it looked like we'd fallen into a cappuccino. Despite the snobbery we'd encountered from Marie-Fleur, we weren't the only ones who weren't Clotho material. There was an air of superiority from the well-dressed women at tables near the front of the room and an air of desperation from the less-well-dressed in the back.

My gaze shifted to a couple of cops in a corner. *Why are they here? To investigate Ken Lanier's death?*

We found seats at a table in the rear. In keeping with the color scheme, the centerpieces consisted of stalks of wheat. Even the snacks were tan—breadsticks and cashews. I'd skipped breakfast for the event, so I was alarmed that I didn't see any food tables. I turned to Wanda. "Where's the buffet?"

"Clotho doesn't do all you can eat." She reached for a breadstick. "I'm shocked they have these carbs on the table."

Marcella leaned in, still hidden beneath her hat brim. "The spinners, as they call themselves, have to watch their figures to look like Grecian goddesses, which is ironic considering the vice president owns a praline company. We'll probably get a chicken breast and sauteed mushrooms."

My chin once again hit my neck, this time hard enough to bruise my esophagus, which wasn't good. I needed that to eat—

if we ever got any real food. "For two hundred dollars, there'd better be some bread with butter churned from gold."

A trumpet blared, and I jumped as though it was Ruth's Get Busy Buzzer.

The board members filed into the room like Miss America contestants—or rather Mrs., because they all appeared to be in their forties like Marie-Fleur. They had the same sleek bleached blonde ponytail and tan outfit, i.e., a silk blouse, fitted skirt, and gloves. The only deviation from their monochrome look was the blood-red soles of their tan Louboutins.

Three board members took their seats at a banquet table on a stage at the head of the room. Their names and titles appeared above them courtesy of a computer projector, as did the words *The Krewe of Clotho Court*.

I studied their faces, trying to identify any of them as the three Mardi Gras wig wearers from the Greasing of the Poles— and looking for a way to tell them apart.

Anaïs Monvoisin, president. Has the exotic features of a Bond Girl.

Honorine Ledet, vice president. With her pearls, definitely The Prep.

Marie-Fleur Fontenot, treasurer. A Paris Hilton-type It Girl.

A fourth Clotho clone entered who looked like a former Popular Girl from high school, but the years, and maybe the forbears of the two frosty mugs she carried, gave her the vaguely run-down look of a Party Girl. Based on the empty seat at the board table, she was Claudine Denault, captain.

"See what I mean about their style?" Wanda hissed. "It's impossible to match them to the women in my Mardi Gras wigs at the Royal Sonesta."

She was right about that. I watched Claudine hand a mug to Marie-Fleur before taking her seat, and like the room, the women were devoid of color. "We'll have to match facial features through social media pictures and video of the event."

Honorine handed a wad of cash to Marie-Fleur, who removed her gloves to count the bills and then took a long sip from the straw in her mug.

I thought of Ken Lanier's last swallow. "What are they drinking?"

Wanda bit off a hunk of her breadstick. "Frozen southern milk punch, Clotho's signature cocktail."

My blood ran as cold as the beverage. "You're kidding."

Marcella raised her hat brim. "Oh, no. Krewes take their booze seriously. The members of Rex only drink Ojen from Spain."

"What I meant was," I glanced around to make sure the other women at the table weren't listening, "that might've been the drink Ken Lanier had before he died."

"Did someone say drink?" A buxom waitress held up a tray of the frosted mugs. "Cuz I got just what y'all need—frozen southern milk punch at only twenty bucks a pop."

My hungry, thirsty mouth fell open. "*Only?* Drinks aren't included in the six hundred we paid for this brunch?"

The waitress opened her mouth, but Marcella waved her away and patted her tote to let Wanda and me know she had the drinks covered.

Captain Claudine rose and tapped a microphone. "Welcome to the empowerment brunch, spinners." She flashed a smile that exuded insincerity and silicone. "Before we get started, I'd like to thank the event organizers—the social committee, chaired by our president, Anaïs," she said, pronouncing the first part of the name *on* instead of *an*. "And the decorating committee, chaired by our VP, Honorine."

The audience stood and applauded, but I stayed seated.

Turning a room tan and throwing some wheat in vases was hardly worth the effort of an ovation.

The smile vanished from Claudine's face as though the silicone had suddenly been reabsorbed by her body. "Let's begin with some items of business. First, do not touch the centerpieces." Her gaze lasered in on those of us in the back. "If you so much as lay a finger on one, you'll be escorted out by New Orleans' finest, and your membership will be terminated."

I eyed the cops in the corner. "They brought in the police as *enforcers*?"

Wanda was wound so tight, the bees on her wig vibrated. "Welcome to Clotho."

"Right?" Marcella drawled. "If you're not careful, Franki, they'll change your name to Françoise."

Or to Ruth Walker, since I'd given Marie-Fleur her contact info.

Claudine pressed a fist to her Pilates-sculpted hip. "Second, we have events for the next three days, so stay organized. Tomorrow morning is costume and throw pickup at headquarters, and then we have our Murder Mystery Dinner at Muriel's restaurant in Jackson Square. On Monday at 6 p.m., you load your throws onto the floats in the parking lot across the street. We roll on Tuesday, Mardi Gras morning, after the Krewe of Zulu." Her eyes narrowed. "If you fail to wear a 1920s dress to the dinner or, God forbid, your costume to the parade, you'll be blackballed from Clotho."

A hush fell over the room, and I shifted in my seat. My borrowed dress was riding up, and this brunch was bumming me out.

Her silicone smile resurfaced. "Now, it's time to discuss our theme—empowerment. We're the largest all-female krewe in Louisiana history, and our waitlist is longer than the Krewe of Muses' entire membership roster. Why? Because New Orleans women know that Clotho has a secret." She paused to let that sink in and smolder. "We hold the keys to your success in this city."

Murmurs of agreement broke out across the room.

Claudine struck a power pose. "Success starts with investing in your look, which brings me to the hard work of the costume and parade committees, both of which are chaired by *moi*."

I leaned into Wanda's beehive, which was practically buzzing. "That's how they define empowerment? Your *appearance*?"

"What Captain Claudine isn't saying is that success is also dependent on your ancestry. The board members are all descended from Casket Girls. Ever hear of 'em?"

I'd not only heard of them, one of their descendants had almost killed me during an investigation. "Yeah, the women sent here by King Louis XV in the early 1700s to marry the city's settlers."

Marcella nodded. "People thought they were vampires because they were pale and emaciated from the long sea voyage and their trunks looked like coffins."

Now that she'd mentioned it, the Clotho Court reminded me of vampires—with spray tans.

Claudine held up a wad of tan fabric. "Because we're the most exkrewesive krewe in Louisiana, our parade costumes— this toga with a wreath headpiece and a gold half mask—were designed by none other than the King of Costumes, Bob Simpson."

A collective gasp was followed by squeals and hugs.

Wanda twisted a bee on her wig. "They could've done without the gold masks. They don't need them with all that Botox and fake tanning product."

I didn't comment. My face had frozen not only because of

that exkreweciating pun, but also because Glenda's favorite designer hadn't retired from fashion, as he'd told her.

Claudine raised a wooden rod with a disc on the end. "And, of course," she smiled, but the rest of her face didn't, "you'll want to accessorize with our spindle."

"Ooh," Marcella pressed her cheeks, "that looks like a fairy godmother wand wrapped in gold thread."

I straightened in my seat. "It looks like a weapon."

"In other exciting news," Claudine descended the stage steps, "we're holding a head wreath-decorating contest. The decorations have to reflect your float theme."

As she droned on, I understood why krewe members would risk arrest by touching the wheat centerpieces—they'd eat them to avoid starvation.

"My suggestion," Claudine strutted among the tables, "is to check out the decorative items we have on sale at our headquarters, because the float with the head wreaths that most accurately reflect the Clotho essence will ride after the court."

Screams of excitement erupted.

"Why is that good?" I shouted. "Do they throw food?"

Wanda glowered. "Supposedly, it ups your social standing."

Claudine approached our table, emitting a waft of Chanel No. 5. "To complete your look, don't forget your Clotho cosmetics." She stopped beside Marcella, who was still half-hidden beneath her hat. "This week we have a two-for-one deal on our tan lipliner."

Marcella's maroon-lined lips pursed.

Claudine proceeded to the rear of the room. "It's not too late to get our throw package, or buy another. And it's not just a *deal*, it's a *steal* at only two thousand dollars."

"It *is* a steal," I grumbled.

"Get your cash ready, ladies," Claudine sing-songed. "Our spindles are on sale for ninety-nine dollars, and it's time to unveil our new signature throw, available today only for ten dollars each." She held up a square of tan satin, and her silicone lips laid it on thick. "It's a Krewe of Clotho kerchief with our slogan, 'Be a spinner, and be a winner!'"

Women waved bills, and I couldn't fathom the reason. The kerchief slogan sounded like an advertisement for the roulette wheel at casino night.

As Anaïs and Honorine descended into the audience to gather the money, Claudine lit up like a Bourbon Street ATM on a Friday night. "Stand up and raise your glasses, ladies!" She twirled at the head of the room. "Spin and win!"

Women rose, held up their mugs, and spun like tops.

Marie-Fleur took another swallow from her straw and pushed up clumsily from the table. She half-raised her glass, semi-spun, and crumpled like a Clotho kerchief thrown from a float.

And she didn't get up.

While the rest of the Clotho Court collected cash, I dashed to the stage and took Marie-Fleur's pulse as Marcella and Wanda reached my side.

Wanda whipped out her phone and dialed 9-1-1.

Marcella removed her hat and pressed it to her chest. "What do you think happened, Franki?"

Judging from the melted look of Marie-Fleur's ice-blue eyes and her lifeless wrist, there was only one answer to that question. "She spun and lost."

4

———

"That brunch cop should find a new line of work," Wanda huffed, as we walked through the French Quarter to her wig shop. She stopped outside British Antiques LLC, pulled a hairpin from her bee hive, and in full view of the shop window, popped the balloon on their sale sign. "Marie-Fleur died, and did he show any compassion? Nope! Then he finds out Claudine handed her the frozen southern milk punch, and who does he question? Wanda Wronka!"

Marcella smirked beneath her hat brim. "So wrong."

It wasn't wrong—or wronka—but I didn't say that. Wanda was as mad as a hornet. Plus, I was busy trying to keep Chandra's too-short shift dress from riding up.

Wanda kicked a pavement menu outside the New Orleans Vampire Café. "He had no reason to suspect me, the jerk."

I had to speak up. It was one thing to anger the British, but quite another to rile the local vampire community. "No offense, but that cop *did* have a reason to suspect you—two, actually. First your wigs were worn at the Greasing of the Poles to commit what now looks like a probable poisoning, and then a woman dropped dead at a krewe event you attended. If I hadn't been with you at that brunch, I would've suspected you of poisoning Marie-Fleur."

Wanda stopped in front of an old brick building with a hanging sign that said *Wiggins Wigs*, spun on me with a venomous look, and whipped open a compartment in her hive.

Is she siccing bees *on me?*

In a rage, she pulled out a shop key, slammed her wig shut, and turned to the lock.

Storm—and swarm—averted, I zeroed in on the plywood covering a pane in the door. "Did the thieves break the glass?"

Wanda's stare was as pointed as her hairpin. "You mean, the Clotho board members?"

I sighed. Maybe the storm—and swarm—hadn't passed. "Look, I believe your story about the wigs. But now that two people have died, we need hard evidence that connects Claudine or Marie-Fleur to the wig theft if we're going to keep you out of jail."

She shoved open the door and gestured for Marcella and me to enter. Wanda smiled as Marcella passed, but when I walked by, she bared her teeth.

I was starting to gather that Wanda was a tad confrontational.

A quick glance around the Pepto-Bismol-pink shop told me Wiggins Wigged Out Wigs was a better name for the business. Like the Intergalactic Krewe of Chewbacchus wig she'd worn to my apartment, she had wigs for other Mardi Gras krewes—a red bob topped with a bedazzled high heel for the Krewe of Muses, a purple pixie with grapes and a bottle of wine for the Krewe of Bacchus, and gold curls with a gilded box for the Krewe of Pandora.

I paused before a black bouffant topped with a serving tray holding a muffuletta sandwich for the Muff-a-lottas.

Half of Marcella's head leaned from behind the wig. She

raised her hat brim, and her smoky eye gave me the stink-eye. "Move along, sister. I've got dibs on this one."

Apparently, Wanda was rubbing off on Marcella, which made me wonder whether that brunch cop and I should both find a new line of work.

I took a look around Wiggins Wigs. Apart from the broken door pane, nothing looked out of place—unless you counted the missing bodies of the mannequin heads that filled the room. "Just out of curiosity, do you sell any practical wigs?"

Wanda's fist slammed into her hip. "They're all practical. I design each one to do more than make you look good. They're functional too."

Marcella's lips slid into a grin as wide as her hat. "Like that Leaning Tower of Pizza wig you made me for last year's St. Joseph's Day parade."

"You mean, *Pisa*," I said, hoping for the sake of self-respecting Italian-Americans everywhere that she'd misspoken.

"No, *pizza*." Marcella gave a glossy grin. "I was in charge of bringing a dozen pies for the marching club, and thanks to Wanda's talent, I was able to stack the boxes on the wig." To demonstrate, Marcella removed her hat and held it at an angle. "For the entire route, anytime the marchers got hungry, they grabbed a slice from my head."

What's classier than that? I asked myself, mentally mimicking Marcella's signature question. Unexpectedly, an answer appeared—a wedding gown lit up in the colors of the Italian flag.

Shaking off the awful image, I moved to a display of period wigs. An elaborate brunette number caught my attention. It had interlaced braids and ropes of hair decorated with pearl pins, jewels, and gold ribbon. "What does this one do?"

"That's 'Renaissance Rapunzel.'" Wanda's voice held a note

of pride, as though she was speaking of her own daughter. "Those jewels on the hair clasps are poison pill compartments."

My eyes locked onto hers in shock. "What do the Marie Antoinette wigs do? Hide portable guillotines?" I pointed at the door. "You've got to get the weapon wigs out of here in case the police pay you a surprise visit."

Her chin revolted. "Caged wigs have been worn since Ancient Egypt and Rome. There's no crime in making them."

"True, but if you're the subject of a murder investigation, making wigs that hold poison is not a good look." I scanned the shop for any other egregious items. "By the way, were the stolen wigs caged?"

"Yes, to hold Mardi Gras essentials, like a flask, sunscreen, and aspirin, but they could've put other things in the compartments."

My Mardi Gras essentials were Nutella king cake, king cake French toast, and a king cake latte to wash them both down, but there was no point in having that discussion. The Clotho board members hadn't stolen Wanda's wigs to party. "Well, the police have the wigs now, so if there was something in them, they'll find it."

Marcella removed her hat. "I'll bet they hid the drink they gave to Ken Lanier in one of their wigs."

Another dubious supposition. "It was frozen, so they probably bought it at a bar near the Royal Sonesta. In fact, I need to get my associates on that." I pulled out my phone and sent a text instructing David and The Vassal to visit bars near the Greasing of the Poles hotel and find video of the event. Then I surveyed the shop again. "And they didn't leave behind any sort of evidence?"

Wanda glanced at the floor. "Nothing I could find."

"What about the police?"

"They called me to the station but never came to search the shop."

That didn't entirely surprise me. The New Orleans PD had more crimes than they could investigate, and they were usually short-staffed. I sat sideways in one of the three salon chairs facing a large mirror.

Wanda and Marcella followed suit, which was awkward because the chairs were bolted to the floor, so I had to look in the mirror to talk to them. "I know we went over this with the brunch cop, but can either of you think of any connection between Ken Lanier and Marie-Fleur?"

Marcella raised her hand. "Claudine handed them both a drink, and they died."

A couple of thoughts occurred to me. The first—it's a shame we didn't have a shard of either one of those drink glasses to analyze for poison. And second—Marcella had best stick to her work at the American Italian Cultural Center. "Um, I meant *before* their murders."

"Oh, sure." She pressed a finger to her cheek, and her powdered brows furrowed.

Wanda slouched in her chair and kicked her feet on the counter. "I don't know of any connection, but Marie-Fleur was the krewe treasurer. She could've discovered the embezzling and told Ken. Either that, or Marie-Fleur was embezzling and Claudine killed her for it."

"Not likely," I said. "Claudine would be a fool to risk going to prison for homicide if Marie-Fleur was doing the embezzling. She'd just let her get arrested—unless..."

Marcella's brows went up. "Unless what, Franki?"

"Marie-Fleur could prove Claudine was embezzling too, or that she had something to hide."

"Oohhhh, this is getting good. How do we find that out?"

I shrugged. "We join the krewe."

"Ha!" Wanda's head flew back with such force I thought her bees would flee the hive. "We fooled them at brunch, but we won't get away with that forever."

Marcella frowned. "She's right. They'd never let us join as ourselves. We don't have good breeding."

I didn't bother saying, *Speak for yourself*. My lack of breeding was fairly glaring.

My cell phone vibrated. *Private Chicks*.

"One sec. It's the office." I tapped *Answer*, and a blast of Ruth's Get Busy Buzzer made my ear vibrate like the bees on Wanda's wig.

"What're you doing boozing it up on Royal Street? Bradley's plane arrives in an hour."

Ruth's bellow had turned my ear buzz to a ring. "I'm at a wig shop, not a bar... Wait." My head jerked over my shoulder. "How do you know what street I'm on?"

"It's called Find My Friends, ace PI."

My teeth clenched. "You went into my phone?"

"With a password like 'Franki,' you were asking for it."

My face was the color of Marcella's eyeshadow. "What I was asking for was a password I could remember—and some damn privacy."

"I tell you what," Ruth's tone dripped disgust, "it's a good thing Veronica gave that gratitude journal to you and not Bradley. That poor man's got nothing to be thankful for with a vain, self-absorbed fiancé who's as fake as a Polish Santa-in-a-gondola ornament."

She would *drag Santa into this*. "That makes two of us," I hissed, throttling the phone as though it was her turkey neck. "As long as you're working for Bradley, I've got nothing to be thankful for either."

"Get off your vanity chair and get to the airport," she barked. "And remember, I'm tracking you, missy."

The line went dead, and I turned off Find My Friends.

Marcella's purple-shadowed eyes snuck a peek at Wanda before landing on me. "Everything okay?"

It wasn't, but I didn't want to go into the whole Ruth saga. It was longer than the Book of Ruth and not even close to uplifting. "That was Bradley's assistant, reminding me of something I need to do."

Wanda started. "Hey! The secretary."

My body stiffened. "I wouldn't call her that, if I were you. In her warped mind, she's judge and jury, and the entire Supreme Court."

"I meant that there was no secretary at the brunch, and all Mardi Gras krewes have them. They're an integral part of the board."

The significance was lost on me. "What does the secretary do?"

"Take meeting minutes and whatever else the board says."

Marcella nodded. "And the Clotho board wouldn't miss an opportunity to have a lackey to do their dirty work."

The missing secretary didn't seem relevant, but investigating crime had taught me that sometimes the evidence was what you didn't see. "I'll look into it, but right now I need to pick up my fiancé at the airport."

As I slid from my seat, Chandra's too-short dress rode up. I yanked down the hem and noticed that the bottom shelf of a black, floor-level display of wig toppers was uneven. I slid my fingers along the shelf edge and knocked something further underneath. "Fair warning, y'all—I'm going to bend over, and this dress isn't going to bend with me."

Their eyes locked onto the mirror.

Kneeling, I reached beneath the shelf and pulled out a square black cosmetic tube with a gold lid and entwined C's. "Anyone drop Chanel lipstick?"

"No," they replied in unison, still staring at the mirror.

I rose and pulled down the dress. "You can look now."

Marcella and Wanda turned.

"That's not lipstick," Marcella said. "It's refillable perfume spray for your purse."

I removed the lid and spritzed it.

Three sets of eyes darted back to the mirror.

Chanel No. 5.

The perfume Claudine wore at the brunch.

"*Two people are dead*?" Veronica's pitch hit a peak, piercing my ear through the phone receiver.

"Yeah," I shuddered and switched on the heater in my 1965 Mustang convertible, unsure whether my sudden chill was the effect of a cold front coming in or the murders. Then I peered through the windshield at the Baggage Claim doors to check for Bradley. "Atropos struck again."

"Who?"

"The Fate that cuts the thread of life."

"Have you been drinking? Ruth said you were at a bar."

My fingers tightened around the steering wheel, wishing they could get a grip on the old buzzer-buzzing buzzard. "No, I have *not* been drinking, even though that woman's doing her damnedest to drive me to it. But speaking of booze, Marie-Fleur was served the same drink as Ken Lanier, and by the same woman, Captain Claudine Denault."

"Seems like more than a coincidence. Do you think it was poison?"

"Let's put it this way, Glenda's heart attack theory is probably out."

A beefy airport security guard waved me on, but I played

dumb and raised my fingers in greeting. He frowned and turned his attention to a creepy Cadillac hearse with the license plate U R NEXT.

As well he should.

Come to think of it, I should pay attention to the dire death wagon too since I'd just mentioned murder and Atropos. I put my phone on speaker, placed it on the dashboard, and pointed my index and pinky fingers on both hands down in the *scongiuri* gesture. A hearse carrying a threat—and potentially a dead body—called for the double-fisted approach to warding off bad luck.

"Hmmm," Veronica dragged out the *m*, immersed in thought. "I just looked up 'frozen southern milk punch' and discovered that there's a rocks version."

"Is the recipe different?"

"Yeah, it doesn't have Tuaca like the frozen version."

The bartender at Le Boozé had mentioned the Italian liqueur, but I wasn't sure I'd ever had it. "Well, the Tuaca didn't kill Ken and Marie-Fleur, but whatever did was fast acting. By the way, I found a purse-spray bottle of Chanel No. 5 under a display at Wiggins Wigs, and it might be Claudine's."

"You think she poisoned it too?"

My head retracted, and I grabbed my nose. "I certainly hope not," I said, sounding like Neil Young with a head cold, "because I sniffed it."

"You're fine, Franki."

Must be nice to be so cavalier about my life. I had no such luxury with an aggressive corpse car in the vicinity.

"Any luck on figuring out who the third woman in the wig was?"

"Not yet." I scrutinized my nostrils in the rearview mirror for signs of poison-related discoloration. "My bet is either the Clotho president, Anaïs Monvoisin, or the VP, Honorine Ledet.

Tomorrow is costume and throw pickup at krewe headquarters, so I'm going to stop by and see what I can find out about the board and the embezzling Ken was allegedly investigating."

"Do you think their office will still be open after Marie-Fleur's death?"

"You know these Mardi Gras organizations, Veronica. The parade must go on come hell, highwater, or homicide."

"True dat," she said in local lingo.

I glanced again at Baggage Claim. "I'd better go. If Bradley doesn't come out soon, the airport will report me to Homeland Security."

"K. But don't get arrested. I'm in the middle of making beef bourguignon for Dirk, so I can't bail you out." She hung up.

I'd been joking about Homeland Security, but I wasn't sure Veronica had been about Dirk's dinner. "Good to know his beef bourguignon comes first. Definitely explains her blasé reaction to me potentially inhaling poison."

My gaze drifted back to my nose in the rearview mirror. Then I glanced at Baggage Claim. No sign of Bradley, but the security guard was staring me down and scowling.

Feigning a serious look, I averted my eyes to my phone as though I'd received an important message, and I googled information about Tuaca.

"The flavor has notes of Italian Brandy, vanilla spice, butterscotch...and Mediterranean citrus? Ugh. Figures." A Sicilian lemon tradition had wreaked havoc on my life, so it came as no surprise that a liqueur with Mediterranean citrus might be linked to murder.

Further down the page, I read that Tuaca was created in honor of Lorenzo de' Medici in Florence in the fifteenth century, which reminded me of Wanda's Renaissance Rapunzel wig and its poison pill holders.

Am I right to think that Ken and Marie-Fleur were poisoned? Or were their seeming deaths-by-drink a bizarre coincidence?

A black Mercedes G-Wagon with steel grille guards on the bumpers pulled in front of me and almost clipped my car.

"You cut it awfully close there, pal." I narrowed my eyes. The license plate was CSHCAR1 and a painted sign on the hatch had the slogan of a local car dealer, *Carl Cash Will Save You Money.* "Carl Cash almost had to *pay* me money for damage to my front end."

The security guard bared his teeth à la Wanda, so I glanced yet again at the doors to Baggage Claim.

Two Barbie doll doppelgangers exited in silky short sets, full-length furs, and thigh-high stiletto boots. They were so striking that I couldn't take my eyes off them, or their Gucci luggage.

The driver door of the G-Wagon opened, and from it emerged a forty-something male with the sallow skin of one who existed on a diet of cheeseburgers, fries, and Coke. He wasn't Carl Cash, because I'd seen him on TV commercials, so I figured the guy was an employee.

Curiosity prompted me to roll down my window and eavesdrop.

Sallow Skin nodded at the women, tugged at his waistband, and opened the rear passenger door.

"Tank you," Doll number 1 said and climbed into the backseat.

Doll number 2 nodded. "*Da.*"

I winced and rolled up my window. "The poor things sound like Nadezhda. Proof no one can have it all."

Luckily, the security guard was watching Sallow Skin load the Gucci luggage into the back of the G-Wagon, so I looked around for Bradley and saw the creepy hearse departing. "If I don't pick him up without incident, Ruth will haunt me for eternity."

I returned to my phone and without thinking googled "Ruth" instead of "poison." I snickered. "Basically a synonym."

The dictionary listed "Ruth" as a noun, but I didn't need to see the definition. As far as I was concerned, it meant *a destructive pest that burrows deep into the bodies and homes of those it infects and refuses to get the hell out.*

But, to pass the time, I scrolled down and found two definitions.

1. Compassion for the misery of another

2. Sorrow for one's own faults: remorse

A powerful force thrust me against the driver seat.

It took a moment to regain my bearings. When I did, I realized it wasn't the definitions of Ruth that had rocked my world—although they were earth-shatteringly wronka. The violent jolt had come from the G-Wagon backing into my Mustang.

My car lurched again as the driver pulled forward. I reached for my door handle, but the G-Wagon sped off.

With my bumper!

The breath left my lungs like air from a slashed tire. Then it returned in a surge as per gas from a fuel pump. "Hey! Bring that back!"

From the corner of my eye, I spotted Bradley exiting Baggage Claim.

But I didn't turn to greet him.

I hit the gas.

My tires spun out, leaving a stunned Bradley and a startled security guard in a gray cloud of acrid-smelling burned rubber.

"For your information," I lectured Sallow Skin, who clearly couldn't hear me as I raced after him, "this Mustang convertible is a 1965 classic, so the repairs for a ripped-off bumper will cost more than the rent on my apartment *and* my landlady, Glenda's, costume closet." I paused for dramatic effect. "And Carl Cash is going to pay every cent."

Several cars were between me and the G-Wagon, so I hunkered over the steering wheel and gunned the engine.

Sallow Skin must've seen me advancing because he gained speed.

"Go ahead, run," I growled, "but you won't get past the automatic gate arm at the parking attendant booth. And before you pay the fee, you'll be paying me." I threw back my head and gave a throaty laugh. "Put *that* slogan on your G-wagon, Carl Cash."

With the practiced calm of a Formula One driver, I caught up to the steel-grilled Mercedes, and the sparks coming from my dragging bumper only increased my rage—both at Sallow Skin and the Russian dolls.

"I know, I know," I raised my hand to stave off any protest from my more rational side, "the bumper incident isn't the stiletto-ed Slavs' fault. But, believe you me, the years of sparring with Nadezhda have taken a toll, kind of like a constant freaking IV drip of vodka on the brain." I ground my teeth and squinted. "And if those Russian Barbies are like their penny-pinching, bikini-waxing, booze-peddling Communist compatriot, they damn sure aren't telling Sallow Skin to pull over—or cough up the 'Carl cash' for my bumper."

The G-Wagon screeched to a halt in a booth.

I pulled behind it and leapt from the Mustang. "Excuse me," I shouted, storming the driver side. I stopped at Sallow Skin's tinted window and glared inside. "You *do* realize that you backed into my Mustang *and* took my bumper with you?"

He didn't even deign to look at me or the booth attendant. Staring straight ahead, he revved the engine, and the G-Wagon blew through the automatic gate arm, sending it flying.

But that wasn't the biggest shock.

Right before he sped off, I'd caught a glimpse of a passenger in the front seat, hiding behind black sunglasses and a visor.

Captain Claudine Denault.

5

———

"Thanks to your reckless G-Wagon driver," I said, trembling with repressed rage as I stood before a sales desk in the Carl Cash Cars dealership, "I lost my bumper *and* my Bradley."

The forty-something salesman, who appeared as unaffected by my anger as he was by the dead cockroach on the tile floor, leaned back in his chair. He contemplated me as he chewed a bite of honey-glazed biscuit like a cow chewing its cud.

"Aren't you going to say anything?" I semi-shouted.

His expression remained blank. "What's a bradley?"

"My fiancé, that's what—or who. And possibly my ex because of this dealership."

He swallowed and put down his Willie's Chicken Shack cup. "All I can say is, that must've been some Happy Hour."

A fresh round of rage prompted my fist to pound his desk, causing his Cajun fries to scatter. "For the last time, I have *not* been drinking."

"Now hold on a minute," he raised a brow and a chicken tender, "that's the first time I said it."

True. Technically, the Franki-is-drinking rumor had started with Ruth.

He eyed me, offended. "Also, I plan to eat these fries, so I'm gonna have to ask that you refrain from messin' them up."

"'Messing up' your *fries*?" I anger-air-quoted him. "Your driver 'messed up' my *car* and my *relationship*, and you're worried about how your *food's* arranged?"

"Everyone's got their priorities."

An enraged exhale rushed from my nostrils. "My priority was picking up my fiancé from the airport—that is, until your driver blew into Baggage Claim, snagged my bumper with his ridiculous steel grille, and took off. Naturally, I had to go after the guy, and when I went back for Bradley, he was gone. Now he won't answer my calls."

He pointed the chicken tender at me. "That right there's how you lost your Bradley—you left him behind like an old suitcase." He took a bite. "If I was him, I wouldn't take your calls neither."

An ostrich with cat-eye glasses and a tight bun popped into my head and screeched, "vain, self-absorbed fiancé." Then two hands lunged into the picture and wrung its turkey neck. "I want to speak to your manager."

"You're lookin' at him, and he's done talkin' to you." His tone was as flat as his gaze. "You'll have to speak to the owner, Carl. He's either on the lot or at the Service Center."

"Fine. But I'm not leaving Carl Cash Cars until my bumper's fixed." Tugging the hem of Chandra's too-short dress, I prepared to exit the main office. But before I did, I reached down with my free hand and gave his scattered Cajun fries a shuffle.

He pursed his lips, which was the most emotion I'd seen from him, and I stormed out.

The Service Center was at the far end of the lot, so I set off on the crumbling pavement and had two immediate regrets—

the brunch heels I was still wearing and the barrage of signs bearing slogans.

Carl Cash Will Save You Money!

Count Your Leftover Cash With Carl!

A Cash Car is Cash In The Bank!

"Honestly," I said to myself, "you couldn't pay me to buy a car from Carl Cash."

As I hobbled along, I kept one eye out for Carl and the other for Nadezhda. The dealership was on North Rampart down the street from her business, Lucky's Liquor and Waxing—or Vaxing, as Nadezhda pronounced it, and she was always looking for new ventures. A man named after money with a Service Center and a slogan was a perfect partner. When her late husband left her his liquor store slash life insurance company, she'd incorporated her waxing salon and changed the slogan from *Before you get your drink on, get your* affairs *in order* to *Before you get your drink on, get your* hairs *in order*. If she merged with Carl, she could expand the slogan to the catchy, albeit indirectly illicit, *Before you get your drink on, get your hairs and auto repairs in order*.

Midway down a row of cars, the automatic hatch of a Ford Escape popped open and began to rise. Two feet clad in snake-skin boots slid out followed by legs in money-green slacks.

My head whipped around looking for a camera.

This has to be a TV commercial.

The hatch completed its ascent, and the rest of Carl Cash slithered from the car.

With a lit cigar.

And a glittery gold cowboy hat with a band of dollar bills.

I was tempted to run to my mangled Mustang and race away. Obviously, I wanted my bumper fixed, but I'd been working in New Orleans long enough to know that Carl's emergence from a trunk didn't promise a sane encounter.

"Well, howdy there, little lady." Carl's beady eyes, as black as his dyed sideburns, locked onto me. And his smile stretched far on either side of his face, adding to his money-grubber, snake-oil salesman look. "What can I do you for?"

My nostrils flared. On top of his sleazy vibe, Carl had the vocabulary of an old cowboy and the voice of a carnival barker. Plus, his cigar smoke smelled like exhaust pipe fumes. "Your driver backed into my 1965 Mustang at the airport and took off with my bumper, so you can repair the damage free of charge."

"Driver?" he echoed through teeth clamped on the stinky cig. "I prefer to drive myself since I have my pick of so many fine machines." He gestured to the cars. "You could drive one too for a small down payment, which'll leave you cash in the bank to buy yourself something pretty."

Ever the salesman—and not a snake charmer. "Uh, I was talking about the guy who drives the Mercedes G-wagon. The one with your name all over it?"

Carl recoiled like a rattler about to strike, and his tongue flickered reptile-like from his mouth, as though ridding itself of a bad taste.

Is he reacting to the damage he's liable for?

Or the mention of that driver?

"Well, now," he patted his money-green lapel, "here at Carl Cash, we like to look on the bright side," he said as though I came from a place that didn't.

"The bright side of a broken-off bumper?"

He removed the cigar. "Most people would see it as a positive."

Admittedly, I could be a little negative, as Veronica had pointed out with the gratitude journal, but I was confident that I was in the majority in thinking a broken-off bumper was a bummer. "Under the circumstances, some negativity is warranted—"

"Warranty? Well, let me tell you, we guarantee all Carl Cash Cars for one year or two-hundred and sixty-five days."

"So, I didn't say warranty, and one year is *three*-hundred and sixty-five days."

"Negative and a nitpicker." He tsked and flicked a fleck of tobacco from his tongue. "Not a winning combination in a little woman."

My five-feet-ten inches—along with the three of the heels— rose up like the hatch on the Ford Escape. But before I could tell him off, he'd scooped my arm in his and pulled me toward the next row.

Carl's boots struck the pavement, and one foot dragged slightly, causing a rhythmic scrape. "I have a car that'll change your mind and your outlook."

"Whoa, there pardner." I wrangled my arm from his grip. "I'm not here to look at cars. I came to get mine fixed."

"I'd say 1965 is long past time for a trade-in. I'll sell you this little FIAT filly for a mere ten grand. Or," his serpentine smile resurfaced, "if you pay cash, I'll cut you a deal—only one hundred and ten hundred dollar bills."

The "little FIAT filly" was the Gucci collaboration, which reminded me of the Russian dolls' luggage—and my homicide case. I hit the brakes on my terse tone. "Listen, I don't want to pay anything, and especially not eleven thousand dollars when the price is ten. I just want my car fixed."

"Shame. I was saving the FIAT filly for my only daughter, Carly."

Carly? And Ruth called me *vain and self-absorbed.* "Then why sell it to me?"

He pulled a key fob from his suitcoat, and the headlights of a BMW came on. "Because I'm giving her that little beamer beauty instead." He beamed like the beamer's beamers. "Carly was invited to join a Mardi Gras krewe, so she needs a car that'll command respect and carry her throws."

Given that Captain Claudine was in Carl's G-Wagon, I had a feeling I knew which krewe Carly was joining. "I'm trying to get on a krewe myself. Clotho."

"Oh, they don't let just anybody join. It's exkrewesive." He gave a hearty belly laugh. "Get it?"

I did—the slight *and* the pun. The first time I'd heard that absurd term was from Claudine at the empowerment brunch, which further convinced me that she and Carl were connected. "How do you know about Clotho?"

"It's common knowledge that the more upstanding krewes have a strict vetting process." He removed his cigar and leaned in. "But I'll let you in on a little secret—I have insider information."

"Don't tell me you've joined an all-female Mardi Gras krewe?"

"Ha! Good one!" He slapped my back, and I tottered in my heels before regaining my balance.

The whack seemed like a warning—being in close proximity to Carl Cash and those in his orbit could be costly.

"In all seriousness now," he stuck the smelly cigar back into his mouth, "the board offered my Carly a prominent position."

Before he finished the brag, I knew exactly what the position was.

He gripped his money-green lapels and puffed out his chest. "Miss Carly Cash will be the next secretary of the Krewe of Clotho Court."

"Come on, Bradley." I pressed the phone to my ear as my mangled Mustang rattled through my neighborhood. "Pick up."

The call went to voicemail.

Frustrated, I tossed the phone on the passenger seat. I'd wanted to invite him for a romantic dinner to make up for the Baggage Claim debacle, but I'd once again be "eating alone like the ladies of the evening the puttanesca sauce was named for," to quote my mother. "How long can he stay mad about being left like luggage?"

The question was poorly timed since I was driving by the cemetery across the street from Glenda's fourplex. Not a good omen for my relationship status, so I flashed the scongiuri gesture—which I was doing a lot lately.

Also poorly timed—Chandra's psychic-psycho car and U-Haul trailer were blocking both spots on our driveway like a giant parade float.

My thoughts drifted to Mardi Gras, and the wheels of my mind turned like Clotho's spindle as I parked behind the trailer.

Carly Cash's secretary position on the krewe court was not a coincidence, and neither were the deaths of Ken Lanier and Marie-Fleur Fontenot. Something was up with the Clotho board, or what was left of them. "I've got to find out who the third woman in the wig was with Claudine and Marie-Fleur at the Greasing of the Poles."

Anaïs, the president?

Honorine, the VP?

Or Carly Cash, the new secretary?

I grabbed my phone from the passenger seat and googled Carl's daughter. Her image popped up, and I winced like I'd done when I heard the Nadezhda voices on the Russian dolls at the airport. "Oh, Jeez. She's a young Carl with red hair. Definitely not the stuff Clotho board members are made of."

Wondering how Carly had scored the Clotho invite, I climbed from the car.

Then I rushed back in.

And reclined my seat.

Either I'd sustained a concussion from the bumper incident, or there was a blow-up sex doll on the stripper pole in the middle of the yard—and four more straddling the balcony supports.

But there was no need to check my head for an injury. I'd been around the fourplex block a time or two, so I knew what I'd witnessed.

Glenda's Yardi Gras decorations.

Returning my seat to the upright position, I grimaced at what was clearly a stripper-clad sex-doll representation of the Greasing of the Poles. "I almost miss last year's jumbo cast of Glenda's breasts."

With a sigh, I climbed again from the car. "This day is enough to make me want to walk to the cemetery and lay down and die."

The door to the U-Haul creaked open, as if a ghost from one of the mausoleums across the street was offering me a portal.

I took several steps back—not because I believed the trailer was an entrance to the netherworld, but because inside sat a still-unkempt Chandra in a blue sweatsuit and silver moon boots—at a tiny table with a crystal ball.

"Have you been drinking, Franki?"

My eyelashes fluttered, which, admittedly, might've made it look like I *had* tossed back a few. "I have not." My tone was taut because I was tired of that question. "Have *you*?"

Her pudgy hand pressed her chest. "What would make you think that?"

"Oh, I don't know... Maybe it's because you're hanging out in a U-Haul with a crystal ball?"

"Since I refuse to go home to Lou, I had to set up an office somewhere."

I knew she was depressed, but this bordered on deranged. "Okay, but a trailer? In a driveway?"

Her eyes were icy. "Since I've lost the spirits, I'm summoning them from new places, and we *are* across the street from a bar and a cemetery."

She had me there. Drunks and the dead went hand in hand with summoning spirits.

"But it's just temporary." She sniffed. "Like the dress I loaned you, which, I see, you stretched out."

"Oh, sorry about that." I glanced at the elongated hem. "A spin in the dryer should snap it back into shape. It's too short, so I was pulling it down."

Her gaze lowered to my hips. "I meant, it's *wider*."

"*No*," I stressed, my patience wearing as thin as the fabric of the dress, "it's *longer*."

"It'll never fit around me now, so you keep it. It'll sag in the bottom."

My patience hung by a thread—that Atropos threatened to cut. "If anything, it'll be too *long*. But like I said, it'll shrink back *up* in the dryer."

Chandra scowled. "Just because you're upset about your relationship is no reason to take it out on me, or my dress." She ran ragged paddle nails through her half-teased bob. "I've got my own relationship problems."

My focus shifted from my bottom to Bradley. "How'd you know I was upset about my relationship?"

"I don't need this thing," she tapped the crystal ball, "to see that it's on the rocks."

Concern crept into my head—first about Bradley and then back to my backside. *Wait. Am I vain and self-absorbed?*

Chandra gave another sniff and rubbed her nose.

Of course I'm not, I thought. *Watch this.* I climbed into the trailer and sat on the footstool opposite Chandra. "Don't cry, okay?" I threw in a pat on her forearm. "You and Lou will work it out."

"I'm not crying, and this isn't about Lou." She exhaled, steamed. "For a PI, you're kind of clueless, you know that?"

My hands balled into fists. Empathy was hard when you had an unsympathetic subject like Chandra, but I was determined to show it. "So, why are you sniffling?"

"Because I keep smelling Chanel No. 5."

I froze. She couldn't know that I'd found the same perfume at Wiggins Wigs. "By any chance, was the Clotho board member you did the tarot reading for wearing Chanel No. 5?"

"Not that I remember."

"What about the third card you pulled for her—besides Death and The Hanged Man? Do you remember that?"

She massaged her temples. "How *can* I with this perfume headache? I'm sensitive to scents."

My eyes rolled like the inhabitants of the graves across the street. Chandra was sensitive to everything—except my feelings. Pulling out my phone, I googled Marie-Fleur Fontenot and held up her picture. "Is this the woman you did the reading for?"

Chandra's jaw dropped, and she gripped the table. "How'd you know? Can you see the past?"

"Uh, no, because *no one* can." I shoved my phone into my bag. "It's called investigative work."

She giggled and pressed pudgy fingers to her lips. "That's as funny as you having psychic intelligence." She bent over, the giggles now guffaws, and slammed her hand on the table. "What the hell was I *thinking*?"

My tongue parked on my back teeth. "So, *anyway*, her name is Marie-Fleur, and she was murdered at that brunch I attended this morning."

The laughter ceased, and Chandra went rigid.

I went rigid too, fearing she was about to channel a spirit.

Her moon-shaped face turned lunar white, and she keeled over onto her crystal ball.

"Chandra." I patted her back in case she'd fainted, which was proof of my empathy. Because, believe you me, it was tempting to leave her.

She rolled her head and batted me away. "Let me sleep."

Gladly. I could use the quiet to focus on the case.

In need of some air, I climbed from the U-Haul to wait for her to wake up.

Chandra's whiff of Chanel No. 5 was worrisome. Claudine wore it at the brunch, and now it seemed that Marie-Fleur might've worn it to the tarot card reading—because Chandra sure as heck wasn't psychic when it came to scents *or* spirits. "Nevertheless," I rubbed my chin, "it couldn't hurt to have Glenda put a clause in Chandra's rental contract that prohibits her from wearing her spirit-channeling charm bracelet around the fourplex and blabbing to tenants, i.e., me, about her spirit conversations."

Glenda burst onto the balcony, as if I'd mentally summoned her. She was dressed in a large white rag, the remnants of which were barely enough to cover her lady parts, and clutching a newspaper. "Have you seen this rag, Miss Franki?"

Is she talking about her outfit?

She sashay-stormed down the stairs in six-inch platform heels that said Dirty and Maid, respectively. "I took a break from cleaning my house to peruse the *Times Picayune*, and would you believe that a reporter ridiculed my Vaseline costume?"

What I struggled to believe was that she cleaned her house. "You know reporters. They write things to grab readers' attention."

Glenda lit a cigarette in a holder designed to look like a mini feather duster and blew out the smoke. "Well, he wouldn't have dared ridicule me if Bob Simpson had still been my stylist."

Oh, he would have, I thought.

Glenda pulled at a stray thread, and I silently begged her to stop. The thread reminded me of Atropos, whose lethal work I'd seen far too much of lately. And speaking of seeing lethal things, Glenda's outfit was literally hanging by said thread, which was another reason to let that sucker lie.

"The only thing to do, sugar, is call Bob and ask him to unretire. I don't care what his wife, Linda, says about him designing my #strippercouture."

If Glenda found out that he'd designed the Krewe of Clotho costumes, the situation could unravel quicker than her Dirty Maid outfit. "Why don't you let sleeping stylists lie?"

"I'm a local celebrity, Miss Franki. I can't have the entire town thinking I don't know how to dress myself."

Ironies abounded like the threads hanging from Glenda's rag outfit, but I couldn't focus on those. I had to go into damage-control mode. "Before you hear it from someone else, Bob didn't retire. Or, if he did, he came out of it. He designed this year's costume for the krewe of Clotho."

Glenda let out a cry and lunged at the stripper pole, shoving it with the strength of ten Dirty Maids.

It's concrete base tilted, and the pole—along with the sex doll—leaned like Marcella's Leaning Tower of Pizza wig. Finally, it fell.

And smashed the hood of my car!

The sex doll landed last, striking a wanton pose in my front seat.

My chest collapsed like my car hood, and my breath came out in rasps.

"What." *Wheeze.*

"Have." *Wheeze.*

"You." *Wheeze.*

"Done?!"

"Look at it this way, sugar." Glenda dragged off her cigarette. "Insurance will cover it, and the Mustang was already in sad shape."

It was the wrong time for a positive perspective. "Who are you?" I screamed. "Carl Cash from Carl Cash Cars?"

"Ooh, you should go see Carl," Chandra boomed behind me, waking up in the nick of time to weigh in on my misery. "Lou did the plumbing at his car lot, so I bet he'd cut you a deal on some new wheels. And you need them, not just because your car is trashed, but because you really should think about the image you're projecting with an old muscle car."

I shot a hard stare at Chandra's car with its images of her disembodied head surrounded by moons and tarot cards and then at her U-Haul office. And I threw up my hands in despair. *What is the* point *with these people?*

A truck sped past, and a newspaper flew from the window.

And nailed me in the forehead.

"What is *up* with this day?" I shouted at the heavens. "It's the evening, not the morning, and we don't even *get* the freaking paper."

"Nadezhda does," Chandra said. "She just started her subscription."

My head lowered, but my hands rose. And my fingers contorted into a clawing position. "Nadezhda. Doesn't. Live here."

Unfazed by my warning signs, Glenda stubbed out her cigarette with the toe of her Dirty shoe. "She will soon, sugar. Miss Nadezhda is leasing my costume closet."

I spun on my landlady like a stripper pole on a 1965 Mustang hood. "*Nyet* she isn't, because I'm paying you a grand a month to rent it."

"Yes, but your lease ends in two days."

"It doesn't end." My pitch skipped panic and went straight to hysteria. "I'm going month to month."

"Which means I'm free to lease to a long-term renter. And I did."

Long term?

Nadezhda?

My neighbor?

My contorted fingers pulled my hair, and I looked around for an outlet for the surge of frustration coursing through me. My gaze locked on the pole, but as I knew all too well, it had already been overturned—on my car. So, I picked up the *Times Picayune* and launched it at one of the balcony sex dolls.

The paper bounced off the doll and fell open on the ground, revealing a picture of Ken Lanier.

Chandra pointed to the headline. "*Late prosecutor murdered.*"

Duty called. I let go of my anger and picked up the paper. Apart from a bio, the article was mostly fluff—except for one brow-raising detail. Ken was survived by a daughter, Tiffany.

Who was the former secretary of the Krewe of Clotho Court.

6

———

"**G**oddesses aren't greedy! Goddesses aren't greedy!" A crowd of women chanted outside the Krewe of Clotho headquarters.

"What's this about?" I muttered, as I parked my mangled Mustang along Canal Street. I'd expected some women to bail on the krewe after Marie-Fleur's murder, but I didn't get the greed reference.

"Clotho are crooks!" a woman shouted into a bull horn.

"Refund our krewe dues," another yelled, "or we'll cram those ten-dollar kerchiefs down your throats!"

"And stick your spindles where the sun don't shine!" a third cried—too zealously.

Good thing I'm not a blonde like the board members. I removed the keys from the ignition and tossed them in my bag. *Those women are aggressive.*

My ship alarm ringtone blared.

"But not as aggressive as Mom and Nonna."

A black cloud rose from my engine, which didn't bode well for my car—or the call.

Bracing myself against the driver seat, I tapped *Answer.* "Hi, Mom."

"Francesca Lucia Amato!"

I froze like a kid with her hand in the biscotti jar. My mother was mad, and I knew it was bad because it was the first time since I'd left home that she hadn't started a call by introducing herself.

"Do I have to come down there?"

"No!" The word blew from my lips as though kicked from my gut. "Why?"

"Bradley said you left him at Baggage Claim. How could you abandon your fiancé like an old suitcase?"

Obviously, she'd talked to Bradley. But had she talked to the salesguy at Carl Cash Cars too? "A man backed into me and drove off with my bumper. What did you expect me to do?"

"Let your fiancé in the car, Francesca!"

That seemed to be the general consensus.

My parents' doorbell rang in the background.

She huffed. "Hold on."

Door-creaking followed, and voices erupted from the line. There were too many to make out what they were saying, but I recognized the cadence as Italian.

Irate Italian.

"Francesca?" she shrilled.

"Still here," I said, wondering why. "When did you talk to Bradley?"

"Fifteen minutes ago." Her tone was as hot as my fuming motor. "Since we couldn't get a wedding venue out of you, your nonna and I called him."

I slumped in my seat because I'd called him fifteen minutes ago, and he hadn't answered—and because the mob outside Clotho headquarters was getting as worked up as my mom and whoever had just arrived at her house. "So, a couple of things. One, please don't badger Bradley for wedding details. And two, getting me married is not a group effort."

"Given what happened at the airport, it most certainly is."

My gaze wandered to some homeless guys outside a liquor store next to the krewe headquarters. I could've used a swig of whatever they were drinking.

My mother snorted as though the weight of the world was on her shoulders. "Do you think I have time to straighten out your love life between my job at the deli, the housework, and your father's bad back?"

I straightened. "What happened to Dad's back?"

"Don't change the subject, Francesca. I haven't got time for that either."

A window of opportunity opened a crack. "I can tell. Sounds like quite a crowd at the house. Are you having another Canasta tournament?"

She gasped. "You think I could play cards during a crisis of this magnitude? That's the St. Mary's prayer group."

An alarm sounded in my head—church bells, to be specific —and I tugged at my turtleneck. "What're they doing there?"

"They're praying for your nonna. The poor woman collapsed when Bradley told her about the Baggage Claim incident. She's so weak she can hardly speak."

Panic gripped my chest. My mother had always regarded her mother-in-law as one step below a mob boss with whom she collaborated for one reason only—to get me a husband. If she was calling her a "poor woman," the situation must be grave. And it was all my fault for putting my bumper before Bradley. "Did you call a doctor?"

"She asked for a priest."

Frantic, I grabbed my keys from my bag. I had to get to Houston.

A blood-curdling scream erupted from the line. "*Forza, soldati! Siamo in guerra!*"

My lips curled, and I put the keys back. The Italian outburst had come from my allegedly too-weak-to-speak nonna, and the scream that preceded it wasn't pain. "For a woman at death's door, Nonna's lungs are pretty powerful. Somehow she managed a battle cry and, 'Onward, soldiers! We're at war!'"

"You know your nonna, dear," my mother said, chipper. "She's a fighter."

Indeed. One who would fight to her last breath to get me married—and use weapons, if necessary. "I don't know what y'all are up to down there, but let me remind you that my relationship with Bradley is *my* business."

"Let me remind *you* that we've all invested a lot of time and energy in this relationship. And believe me, getting you married is an actual battle. So we're calling in the troops."

"The troops?" I repeated. This so-called war was getting a bit too real.

"Besides the St. Mary's prayer group, everyone at the deli, and, when we get off this call, your nonna's friends in New Orleans."

My head lowered to the steering wheel—not in prayer but in fear. This could get ugly, as in elderly-Italian-nonne-descending-on-my-apartment ugly, and it wasn't like dealing with Chandra, Glenda, and soon Nadezhda was anything close to pretty. "Mom, I'm serious, this is between Bradley and me. Y'all stay out of it."

"I'm sorry, Francesca. You've left me no choice."

Concern crept into my chest. "What does that mean?"

"Brenda," my dad called from somewhere in the house.

"Oof! That man is running me so ragged I'll be the one with a bad back before long. Talk soon," she sing-songed.

"Mom—"

She'd already hung up.

And I imagined the fourplex surrounded by nonne from Texas and Louisiana, a Catholic army on a marriage mission. Instead of tanks, they'd drive FIATs like the one used to drive the Pope during his U.S. visit, and they'd all come armed with the same weapons—Bibles, rosaries, and Catholic guilt.

Exhausted at only nine a.m., I climbed from the car.

A muscle-bound man in a brown leather bomber jacket passed by, frowning and pressing a phone to his ear. "Get out my house, man." The order held a threat. "Nah, nah. Get your stuff, and get out my house."

For a split second, I considered chasing after him to get his number. He could come in handy when the Catholic cavalry showed up. But I got distracted by the angry mob of women, who were now swearing at their phones—and by the delicious fried smell coming from the Willie's Chicken Shack on the other side of the liquor store.

A bleached blonde in a snow-leopard coat looked up from her cell display. "If you're here for a refund, you can forget it. They're not canceling the parade. Captain Claudine just posted a video on the website. She's sobbing, not because a board member died at the brunch, but because we're asking for our money back in the 'face of a tragedy.'"

"Crocodile tears," a dirty blonde said.

"Clotho tears," a champagne blonde corrected. "It's all about the money with them. They nickel and dimed us, and now we won't get a cent back."

"More like ten and twentyed us," I couldn't help but comment. "That empowerment brunch was one long sales pitch."

A brassy blonde built like a kickboxer shoved a clipboard at me. "Sign the petition. Blondie here did some digging," she jerked an elbow at the woman in the snow-leopard coat, "and those spindles they forced us to buy are made by a company called Spinderella. Guess who owns it?"

I almost said "Blondie" because I couldn't get over the name. "Captain Claudine?"

"You got it, sister." She pointed a finger at me. "And I'll bet one of the board owns the company that makes those ten-dollar kerchiefs. We already know Honorine makes the pralines that come with our throw packages."

A platinum blonde poked her head into the group. "It's worse than that. One of them probably owns the float den on Architect Street."

It was too bad I couldn't enlist their help on the case. A mob of angry women could get to the bottom of anything.

The kickboxer tapped the clipboard. "You gonna sign that petition, or just hold it?"

The blondes lined up in formation, their brown eyebrows lowered.

If I didn't act fast, they'd turn on me like the Catholic cavalry, in this case, the Clotho cavalry. "The truth is, I'm not really a member. I'm a PI investigating—"

"Incoming," the kickboxer yelled. She wrapped her arms around my waist and lifted me from the ground.

"Hey!" I wriggled and shoved her shoulders. "Can we talk about this first?"

The brood of blondes gripped me in private places as they tilted me horizontally.

"Hands, ladies! Hands!" The next thing I knew, the angry mob was body-surfing me to the Clotho entrance.

Two sandy blondes shouldered open the door, and I was placed on my feet and pushed inside.

"Animals," a frosted blonde in a tan floor-length cardigan and heels snarled as she jabbed at them with a spindle. She closed the door, tossed the spindle on a throw display, and began pushing boxes marked *Costumes* in front of the opening.

With the spindle out of commission, I turned to survey the room. Clotho headquarters was the antithesis of seedy Canal Street. In fact, I wasn't even sure it was earth. It was as if I'd been transported to the mythical abode of the Greek gods on Mount Olympus. Beneath a sumptuous chandelier that lit up ceiling frescoes of the heavens, a larger-than-life sculpture of the goddess Clotho gazed at me from a pedestal. She was surrounded by gold filigreed wallpaper and white fur seating so fluffy it resembled clouds. At her feet were gleaming marble floors that evoked Olympus's snow-covered peak.

And that was just the lobby.

All I could think was, This décor cost some major krewe cash. If the mob outside gets a look at this place, Hades will freeze over.

The heavily made-up woman stepped in front of me, adjusting her tan silk top. She was at least seventy but had paid to look fifty-five. "Like I always say, a bleach job can't cover bad roots."

And plastic surgery can't cover aging, but I didn't dare say that after seeing her spindle-jousting skills. "Are you Josephine?"

Her surgically lifted brow didn't need to arch. "And you are?"

"Franki Amato. I went to the empowerment brunch, and Marie-Fleur said I should see you about my membership... before she was murdered."

She bristled. "Jumping the gun, aren't we?"

"Her death is suspicious. I know because I tried to help her."

"It could've been natural causes. After all, she was under considerable stress."

Interesting detail. "Why?"

Josephine averted false-eyelashed eyes to the window. "Is that your Mustang?"

Chandra's image comment echoed in my head. "I got into a couple of accidents, but I didn't cause them."

Her lasered lips pursed.

If the accidents made her unhappy, it was best not to tell her that my ex-stripper landlady did most of the damage with her front-yard stripper pole. "I went to Carl Cash Cars to discuss repairs, and he mentioned that his daughter Carly is taking over as krewe secretary."

She flushed and gritted her teeth, which was more of a reaction than she'd shown at the mention of Marie-Fleur's murder. "You're not a current member."

It was a statement, not a question. "I'm here to sign up."

She gave me a onceover so thorough she might have been scanning my DNA. "Is Amato your married name?"

"No, I'm engaged."

"And your mother's surname?"

I could see where this was going. "Pavan, also Italian."

"You do know that the American Italian Cultural Center parades for St. Joseph's Day?"

My pasta-kneaders curled into fists. I did, and I also knew that she didn't want me to join Clotho and that I would never celebrate St. Joseph's Day thanks to a certain Sicilian lemon tradition that had forever soured me on the fruit. "Yes, but judging from all the women outside demanding refunds, you have plenty of openings."

She inhaled and strolled to the window. "Never thought I'd see Clotho sisters turn on one another in their time of need, not in all my years as a go-between."

Josephine the Go-Between? "Is that a krewe title?"

"Naturally. I screen applicants to make sure they're of suitable ancestry."

"So that's what they mean by 'exkrewesive.'"

She turned to look at me. "It has to do with New Orleans

history. Because the city was founded by the French, we held balls in the style of the French Court, until Americans settled here and brought in the opera."

"You say 'we' as though you were there."

"Obviously, I wasn't," she snapped. "But I am descended from a Casket Girl."

"Like all the board members."

She averted her eyes to the window—as she'd done when I'd said Marie-Fleur was murdered—and took a seat behind a gilded desk. "The opera became the way for young women to debut in society. Then came the Civil War, and the New Orleans opera lost preeminence. That's when carnival organizations became the recognized vehicles for elegance."

"Why carnivals?"

She folded tan-manicured fingers in front of her chest. "Parading is a display of power. It dates to Greek and Roman times and was later adopted by royalty, the military, and even churches during the Middle Ages."

The churches also paraded in the present—when women left their fiancés at Baggage Claim. "So, Mardi Gras is a display of social power?"

"Of course. Each krewe makes a triumphal entry into the city. And membership comes with tremendous benefits, such as entry into other closed clubs, which, in turn, lead to important business contacts and marriage partners."

The latter was a great reason to never breathe a word to Mom and Nonna that I was joining Clotho. "So, Mardi Gras krewes are essentially Greek fraternities and sororities for adults."

She raised her suspiciously slender nose. "I prefer to think of them as membership societies that operate on a favor system."

All of which was secret, no doubt, as Chandra had lamented

about Lou's krewe. "Awesome. How about you do me a favor and sign me up?"

Josephine gripped the sides of the desk as though the question had provoked a stroke. "Under the inauspicious circumstances," she choked out, "we're going to open registration on our website—for this year only."

"Since I'm here," I paused to throw in a Cheshire-cat-style smile, "I'd like to register in person."

She scanned my hair and frowned. Then she put on a pair of readers and examined my skin.

Talk about being under a microscope.

"You'll have to bleach your hair or wear a wig."

My mind went to Wanda, but her wigs were out. "No problem."

"And use our Clotho cosmetics to brighten your skin and hide those pores."

"Mmm," was all I managed because I was clamping my lips shut.

Josephine locked eyes with me as she pulled a membership form from a drawer.

I reached for it.

She pulled it back.

Lunging forward, I grabbed the paper, tearing a corner.

She exhaled, aghast. "Proof you can't teach good breeding."

"Evidently," I replied with a look as sharp as her spindle. Then I took a pen from the desk and began filling out the application.

Minutes passed, and I heard weeping. I looked up from the paper. This woman was wearing my patience as thin as a Clotho-spun thread. "Everything okay?"

"All of my work has come to naught." She dabbed her eyes with a krewe kerchief.

With a deep inhale, I put down the pen. "You know, the

brunch theme was empowerment, but this experience is anything but."

She sniffled. "You're telling me."

Why am I getting labeled vain and self-absorbed when everyone else's priorities are off? I shoved the application toward her.

"Wait here. I need to enter your information into our database." Josephine rose, took the application as though it were a used tissue, and disappeared down a hallway.

And I texted Marcella and Wanda, telling them to come sign up for the krewe and urge women of every size, color, and ethnicity to do the same.

A man's scream brought me to the window.

"Lord a'mighty, ladies! Hands to yourself!" A chubby mailman fended off fingers with his mailbag. "Only my wife touches there!" He lowered his head and rushed the door as the unruly mob ripped at his uniform.

I felt for the guy, since I too had been felt up by the angry mob.

Mail came through a slot in the wall beside the door. A bill addressed to Marie-Fleur Fontenot.

As I stooped to pick it up, I spotted another envelope behind one of two gold columns flanking either side of the entryway. It was white, like the marble floor, so it had probably gone unnoticed.

Josephine hadn't returned, so I opened the bill and scanned the contents.

My eyes widened, and I tore into the second.

Then I dropped into a fluffy cloud chair.

A creditor was attempting to collect a half-million dollars that Marie-Fleur owed her black credit card.

And someone had sent her an anonymous letter in big, bold font threatening to tell her husband about her shopping addiction if she told Ken Lanier what she knew.

"WHAT DO you think you're doing?" Josephine the Go-Between bellowed not two feet from me.

I jerked down the anonymous letter, feeling the fear of the gods—the Greek Gods—in my gut and wondering how I hadn't heard her heels on the marble. As I stuffed the anonymous letter into my bag, I tried to come up with a cover in case her penetrating eyes had read the huge boldface font through the paper. "I was just reading a nasty note from my fiancé's assistant. She thinks she's Judge Judy, and she's always threatening me about some jobs I allegedly got her fired from. "

Josephine contemplated me, her face expressionless.

The flat look had to be paralysis from Botox and surgeries because my Ruth story was plausible. Impersonating a judge was a crime, and that wackjob wouldn't think twice about offing me for reporting her to a prosecutor.

"Your personal crisis is not my concern, but that chair is. It's reserved for krewe royalty."

I stood and fluffed the cloud.

Satisfied, she rummaged through the boxes at the door and produced a gold sack and a cosmetics compact. "Here's your krewe costume and the Clotho makeup. Don't forget the wig. I'll email your float assignment."

Anxious to exit krewe headquarters with the evidence, I shoved the items into my bag and headed for the barricaded door.

"No, ma'am." She grabbed my wrist. "Out the back."

Holding my tongue, I freed my arm. Obviously, she didn't want anyone seeing the Italian likes of me at krewe headquarters. And the only reason I didn't tell her off and leave out the front was the memory of the angry blonde mob assailing the mailman.

I stepped onto the street, and the door slammed behind me. I made the *vaffanculo* gesture even though Josephine was already inside. That Go-Between was really starting to get under my olive skin.

As I took the long way around the block to my mangled Mustang, I was grateful I'd escaped with the evidence. But I couldn't escape the questions that swirled in my head—or the odor of that Willie's fried chicken.

What did Marie-Fleur know?

And did she ever tell Ken?

If so, is that what got both of them killed?

And are those Willie's honey-glazed biscuits I smell?

"Hey, baby," a male voice said. "Bet you want some o' dis."

Scanning the street for the source of the come-on, I spotted him by a *Daiquiris and Cold Beer* sign inside Willie's Chicken Shack—in costume.

God, not another food mascot. A recent encounter with a dude in a crawdad suit had left a bad taste in my mouth, and this one had already made me bitter.

As I continued toward my car, I sized him up. He was shaped like a yellow test tube with tiny wings and had a small protruding belly so low that it was barely above his black-and-white Adidas. He wore giant white sunglasses, the red comb of a rooster, and a permanent sneer on his beak.

Clearly, a nefarious phallic figure.

The obnoxious mascot stepped into my path and raised two plastic drink-glass replicas of him. Then he pretended to guzzle them.

A chill passed through me like I'd shot-gunned a cold beer. It was worse than I'd thought.

He was a damn drink mascot.

My pace quickened. The French Quarter already had The Dancing Hand Grenade, and he was one too many.

"Come on, chick! You know you want some tasty chicken."

Truth be told, I'd been craving Willie's since I'd seen the salesguy eating it at Carl Cash Cars. But it was too early for lunch, and I needed to talk to Bradley and check out the float den the platinum blonde had mentioned. "If I were a 'chick,'" I said totally droll, "I wouldn't eat chicken."

"I don' know about dat. Like our slogan says, Willie's makes chicken so good you'll slap ya mama."

Of all the slogans I'd heard today, that was the most outrageous. "Trust me, nothing's that good."

He began to strut. "I am."

My jaw dropped. It was incredible that a guy wearing a rooster drink costume would think he was cock of the walk. "Awfully arrogant, aren't you?"

"Hell, yes. I'm a cocktail." He patted his abdomen. "You should try me."

I narrowed my eyes and read the writing on his costume.

Willie's COCKtail New Orleans Stiffest Drink. The *Willie's, tail,* and *New Orleans Stiffest Drink* were written horizontally, but the *C-O-C-K* was capitalized and written vertically, to call it out.

Okay, *that* was the most outrageous slogan of the day. It was stooping low—below the belt, as it were—to sell a drink. Plus, "New Orleans" was missing an apostrophe.

"I'll pass, thank you." I set off.

He followed me from the Chicken Shack to the liquor store, appropriately named Liquor Store.

I turned and shot him a lethal look. "You stalking me?"

"Nah, I'm going to get me a bottle. You got a problem wit dat?"

If the COCKtail wanted booze, it was none of my business. I turned again and felt a pat on my posterior. I pounced on the guy like a fox on a chicken. "Did you just touch my backside?"

"Lady, I'm a COCKtail. What did you expect?"

Given the capitalization of the first half of the word, I got what he was saying. Still, of all the things I expected a drink to do, that wasn't one of them. "Try that again, and I'll have rooster fricassee for dinner."

"Slow down, now!" He held up yellow, padded-gloved hands. "I'm a lover, not a cockfighter."

"So I gathered." I gave him a side-eye, and it struck me that something about the COCKtail seemed familiar. Then I remembered. He was near the Royal Sonesta, just before Ken Lanier was killed. "Didn't I see you at the Greasing of the Poles?"

He smoothed his red comb. "Maybe. I meet a lot o' people in my line of work."

I pointed at Clotho headquarters. "Have you met any of the Krewe of Clotho board members?"

"A few, but I cain't tell ya who. All o' dem blondes look alike."

Apparently, he was blind to their varying blonde shades, perhaps because of his shades. "What can you tell me about them?"

He hopped back. "What do you take me for? A snitch?"

For a cool, shades-wearing COCKtail, he was defensive. "No, a smart businessman."

"Dat's right," he bobbed his rooster head, "so I'm gonna need to get paid."

Since I was close to my car, I walked over and put my bag on the hood while I dug for my wallet.

"Damn, girl! You need a new ride. I know a guy who can fix you up. Carl Cash. Tell him the COCKtail sent ya."

This info could be worth a payoff. I handed him a twenty. "You know Carl?"

"Sho do. He's a regular." He held up his gloves. "Full disclosure, I get a percentage of sales I help facilitate."

"Why would a car dealer give a cocktail a kickback?"

He shrugged skinny shoulders. "He's a big fan of the COCKtail."

So many interpretations of that statement. "You ever seen him at krewe headquarters?"

"Once or twice." He cocked his head to highlight his sneer. "Carl likes tail."

It was a crass comment, but I expected no less from a guy who not only had "tail" in his name but had touched mine. "Can you elaborate?"

"Sometimes I deliver for Willie's, and I've seen a lot o' fine women at da dealership, coming and going in his cars."

Like Claudine and the Russian dolls. "What about the prosecutor who died at the Greasing of the Poles?"

"What about another Jackson?"

With a sneer that matched his, I deposited another twenty in his puffy palm.

"Lanier used to come 'round here, but always at night. I seen him wit one o' dem blondes from da krewe."

"Which one?"

"Like I said, dem blondes all look da same. But dis one wears Chanel No. 5."

Claudine.

Tires screeched, and an engine raced.

A blue Mercedes sped down Canal Street. The window lowered, and a man in a black mask threw something.

That crashed into my windshield!

In disbelief, I shouted and ran to get the license plate number, but the car careened around a corner. I glanced around for witnesses. The COCKtail had split, and Marcella and Wanda were pulling up in an old green K-Car wagon with the fake wood paneling and the words *Wiggins Wigs.*

Members of the blonde mob ran over.

"That criminal taped his license plate," the kickboxer said.

The bleached blonde pulled her snow-leopard coat closed. "Sorry about your Mustang." She eyed my shattered windshield. "I'll bet that iron was meant for the Clotho headquarters window."

Trembling, I leaned over my already battered hood. A note was taped to the iron. And it was definitely meant for me.

Kill the investigation, or die like the others.

7

———

"Please don't die." I rubbed the dashboard of my Mustang, already regretting the comment. Not only did it remind me of the death threat I'd just received, it conjured up the disembodied mannequin heads I'd seen in Wanda's wagon.

The Mustang lurched into the Private Chicks parking lot, and I switched off the engine. It groaned and spat another black cloud.

"My thoughts exactly."

Wanda and Marcella parked beside me, and as we exited our cars, my gaze traveled from the giant fruit wigs on the mannequins in the wagon to the primitive black-and-gold face painted on the coconut atop Wanda's yellow wig. "I take it that's your homage to the Zulu Social Aid & Pleasure Club?"

She fluffed the teased round wig, which matched her vintage Sixties wool skirt suit. "Their coconuts are the most sought-after throw at Mardi Gras." She gestured to the back of the wagon. "Those are my Personal Picnic wigs for spring. You'd be surprised at how much they can carry."

After seeing her pull a cheeseboard from the Chewbacchus

wig, I wouldn't. "Why don't you just put a picnic basket on them?"

"Too heavy. Plus, this way everyone can bring their own meal, which is perfect for people with food intolerances."

Wigs for dietary issues. Everyone's heard of those.

Marcella winked a black-and-gold smoky eyelid that complemented her trench coat. "Dibs on the tomato wig, Franki."

My hand went to my cheek. *Is it our Italian ethnicity that makes her think I'd want to wear a tomato and pizzas on my head? Or is there marinara on my face from the leftover pasta I ate for breakfast?*

We collected Willie's Chicken Shack bags and drinks from the wagon and began the three-story climb to the office.

"Thanks to the iron incident," Wanda said, "we didn't get a chance to tell you what we learned about Marie-Fleur."

Marcella slurped from her drink. "One of our old high school friends gave us the juice."

Judging from the tequila odor, the juice was in her cup. "Great. You can fill me in over lunch."

I stepped onto the third-floor landing and froze.

The Private Chicks door was ajar.

Motioning for Wanda and Marcella to stay in the stairwell, I stepped to the side of the door and pushed it open.

A figure dove behind one of the lobby couches, and my stomach dove too.

Is it the killer?

Wanda sprung onto the landing, pulled the coconut from her wig, and launched it at the intruder.

"Dear God!" a muffled male voice cried. "A tribble!"

Blocks sailed into the hallway—with Chewbacca faces.

My eyes rolled like the wheels of a parade float, and I pulled the door closed. Working with Sci-Fi-obsessed sophomores was so sophomoric. "False alarm, y'all. It's my colleagues, David and The Vassal."

Marcella picked up a bando block. "What are these, Franki?"

"I'm sure Wanda recognizes them. They're the signature throws of the Intergalactic Krewe of Chewbacchus. They use them to decorate their Chewbacca-inspired bandoliers, which are ammunition slash tool belts."

Wanda cracked a smile. "Since the IKoC is made of subkrewes, like Queer Eye for the Sci-Fi and the Krewe of Really Awesome Parodies, aka KRAP, they have their own individual throws too. Incidentally, KRAP hired me to do wigs for their theme this year, Dungeons & Drag Queens."

If Carnie Vaul were on that subkrewe, she'd throw barbs instead of beads. "Prepare yourselves. I'm going in." I gripped the door handle. "Hold your fire, or you're fired!"

We entered the office.

The Vassal crawled slack-jawed from beneath his corner desk, and David rose red-faced from behind the couch.

"Uh, sorry, ladies." David nodded at Marcella and Wanda. "We thought The Trouble with Tribbles subkrewe was trying to sabotage our bando-block decorating. Since we're on the Krewe of Klingons, we're engaged in an ongoing battle."

My policy was to stay out of their geek drama, but since they'd attacked a client, I needed more information. "What's this about?"

The Vassal straightened his coke-bottle glasses. "The Klingons wiped out the tribble species. Due to their prodigious reproductive capacity, they were an ecological menace." He turned alarmed eyes to Wanda. "They're born pregnant and reproduce every twelve hours. That's why I panicked when I thought one had invaded the office."

My brows bolted. "Um, say what?"

"You know, tribbles from *Star Trek*," he said, mistaking my sarcasm for confusion. "Scientific names Tribleustes ventricosus and Polygeminus grex?"

Unable to speak geek, I shook my head.

His lens-enlarged eyes grew wider. "They resemble coconuts?"

My jaw dropped at the utter nonsense, and The Vassal's slack-jaw dropped at my incomprehension.

We were locked in a slack-jaw-off.

"Apologies, boys." Wanda retrieved the coconut. "I didn't mean to cause any trouble with The Trouble with Tribbles." She snapped the fruit into her wig.

"Whoa!" David's eyes popped. "The coconut's detachable?"

"It's from my Weapon Wig line." She balled her fists. "You can't be too careful with a killer on the loose."

He flipped his bangs. "Yo, that's trippin'."

"Not as trippin' as my Chewbacchus version. Come see me at Wiggins' Wigs, and I'll give you both twenty percent off."

David high-fived The Vassal. "Rad!"

The correct term was *bad*. There was no telling what those two would store in their wigs, but I could guarantee it wouldn't be cheese. "Any luck with the Greasing of the Poles assignment?"

The Vassal sat at his corner desk. "We weren't able to find out where the frozen southern milk punch came from, but we've got two short clips from local news, and several from social media."

"Let's see them."

We gathered around his computer and watched the videos.

Marcella sighed. "Glenda's Vaseline outfit is glorious."

The *Times-Picayune* reporter didn't think so, but the people who filmed the videos did. The shots were all of Glenda's *V*. "We need a close-up of a woman in a purple bouffant Mardi Gras wig with a crown and feathers." I looked at David. "Try to get security footage from the Royal Sonesta. They'll have the whole event, and the audience will be facing the camera."

The Vassal saluted. "Aye aye, Captain."

"Franki," I corrected. I had no desire to be compared to a captain from The Starship Enterprise—or from a krewe of potential poisoners.

My phone rang.

"My landlady, probably calling about my car. I'm going to take it in my office." As I headed down the hall, I tapped *Answer*. "Hey, Glenda."

"I'm so glad I caught you, sugar. Miss Chandra's husband, Lou, is about to install your new commode. I told him it needs to match the black sink, and he said he could add decals. Any design requests?"

"Plain and a normal shape." I sat behind my desk and put the phone on speaker. "But if he can get me a toilet that runs better than my mangled Mustang, let me know."

"I'm sorry, Miss Franki. When you told me about Bob, I threw a tiny tantrum. Take it to the shop, and I'll file a claim under my homeowner's insurance."

"They'll cover my car?"

"When you have a claims adjuster who's a Madame Moiselle's VIP room regular, they will. Hang on, while I give Lou your instructions."

While I waited, I glanced at the gratitude journal and got annoyed. It was so much pressure to be thankful, and that was hard to do after receiving a death threat. But it was an order from my BFF boss, so I picked up a pen.

I'm grateful Glenda didn't throw a large *tantrum.*

I'm also glad she'll pay to fix my car.

Best of all, it's Saturday, so Ruth isn't in the office.

. . .

Grinning, I put down the pen. "Veronica was right. Jotting down some positives feels pretty good."

"All right, sugar," Glenda said, "the captain of the Krewe of Commodus says you're all set in the commode department. And since we're on the subject of krewes, I signed up for Clotho."

So much for gratitude. I closed the journal. "Is that a good idea?" I asked, envisioning Glenda running into Bob and trashing a parade float with a lamp post. "They're the subject of a murder investigation."

"I understand why you'd have reservations, but Bob gave up my #strippercouture to design a cheap #krewecostume, and a slight like that warrants a reply."

"You *did* reply, by smashing my hood and probably my engine."

"Yes, but I haven't replied to *Bob*, Miss Franki. I'm going to show him and good, not to mention that reporter from the *Times-Picayune*."

My eyelids lowered a notch at the word *show*, because this *was* Glenda. "How do you plan to show him, exactly? Or, *what*?"

"First I'm going to add some spice to his boring #krewecostume, and then I'm going to design my own line of #strippercouture called Hoochie Coochie Hot Couture. What do you think?"

I think, compared to Bob and the reporter, I got the short end of the stripper pole when you bashed my hood. "Uh, I don't know, Glenda. Sometimes the best response is silence. Also, the belly dance name gives me #stripper vibes but not #strippercouture."

She gave a huff that likely included a puff of smoke. "I have to respond, sugar. No one keeps Miss Glenda in a corner—she takes center stage. And I'm spelling my brand like Gucci and Pucci. Does that do it for you?"

Hucci Cucci? "Actually, yes."

"Fabulous. You Italians *do* know fashion."

Except when it came to wigs, apparently.

"I'll let you go, so I can get to sewing."

I'd always assumed she super-glued and stapled her outfits. "You sew?"

"Of course. My mother had me help make her Crawdad Queen costumes when I was small. And sewing's just like riding a pole. Once you learn how, you never forget."

An interesting twist on the bike analogy, but it worked.

Glenda hung up, and I returned to the lobby.

Wanda and Marcella sat on one of the couches with the food from Willie's Chicken Shack laid out on the coffee table in front of them—chicken tenders with Willie's Special Sauce, Cajun Sweet & Sour wings, honey-glazed biscuits, fries, and red beans and rice.

"Wow." I sat on the opposing couch. "I didn't realize you'd bought all of this."

Wanda's eyes sparkled like gold paint on the coconut. "Marcella was intoxicated by their mascot's charms."

Marcella tittered and flipped her hair curtain. "That COCKtail was fresh, wasn't he? He insisted I get drinks with the food, and since it's Saturday, I thought, 'Why not?' He picked the Williecolada for Wanda because of her coconut wig, the Hurricane Willie for you, Franki, because of the iron, and for me," she flushed, "Willie's Pink Passion."

The COCKtail had found an easy mark—or a date. "So, what were you going to tell me about Marie-Fleur?"

Wanda gulped from her glass. "Apparently, she was such a shopaholic that her husband put her on an allowance, which is saying a lot since the guy makes bank in oil. He threatened her with divorce if she didn't rein in the spending."

"Hm. Do you think he could've killed her?"

"Not unless he hired a hitman." She picked up a chicken

tender. "He's on his way home from a business trip in Saudi Arabia as we speak."

I bit into a soft, buttery biscuit—and resisted the urge to escape with the entire box. "What about Ken's daughter, Tiffany? Know anything about her?"

Marcella nodded as she nibbled on a wing. "A patron of the American Italian Cultural Center said she was estranged from Ken at the time of his death. She even legally dropped his last name. She just goes by 'Tiffany.' Can you imagine?"

I couldn't. The one-name thing always made me wonder how those people filled out online forms with required fields. "Any idea why they had a falling out?"

"Mm-hm," she said, mouth full. "Tiffany's the flighty artist type. Didn't finish school, lives on friends' couches. He wasn't happy about that."

That could make her hard to locate for questioning. "What about her mother? Where's she?"

Marcella's smoky eyes went soft. "The cemetery, poor thing."

That response prompted a swig from my Hurricane Willie, which was counterproductive. There was enough 151 rum in the drink to kill me. "If only we had a shard of glass from one of the drinks."

"Yeah." Wanda chewed a bite. "We could ID the poison and try to trace it."

Marcella lowered the wing, worried. "Where do we go from here, Franki?"

"To the float den for starters." I got up and paced in front of the window overlooking Decatur Street, and I spotted a black Mercedes entering the parking lot. Not Sallow Skin from the airport, but Bradley.

"My fiancé just pulled up, so I may have another answer." The *may* was because I wasn't sure whether he'd speak to me after the Baggage Claim debacle.

Marcella frowned at the food. "I'd tell you to take him some chicken, but it might upset his weak stomach."

It was a good thing Bradley hadn't heard that. Being left like an old suitcase was emasculating enough.

She gave a sly grin. "Want to give him some of my Willie's Pink Passion?"

"No, but thanks." If he was as mad as I suspected, it would take New Orleans' Stiffest Drink to soften him up—*with* the apostrophe. "Be back in a few."

Wanda stabbed her drink with the straw. "This Williecolada could use more coconut." She pointed to the one on her wig. "Got something I can use to puncture this thing?"

She wasn't kidding when she said her wigs were multi-functional. "Maybe an arrow from David and The Vassal's bowcaster?"

"Good idea."

As I exited the office, butterflies swirled in my stomach. Or maybe it was the Hurricane Willie. I descended the stairs and ran into Bradley on the second-floor landing.

Our eyes met.

He held up a box.

My hands went to my mouth.

He'd brought me a Gambino's king cake stuffed with Nutella.

"Bradley Hartmann, you're the most amazing man ever." I threw my arms around his neck and kissed him with the intensity of a combo Hurricane Willie and a Willie's Pink Passion.

He pulled back and flashed his dazzling smile. "Is that because you missed me or because of the rum you've been drinking?"

"The former." I gave him a sheepish look. "You're not mad that I went after my bumper?"

"Not after seeing your car in the parking lot." His blue eyes smiled. "What happened to the hood and windshield?"

"Glenda's stripper pole and," I glanced at him through my lashes and wrinkled my lips, "an iron with a death threat taped to it."

The smile left his mouth and his eyes. "Let's talk about this in my office."

"Okay, but I don't know much." I followed him upstairs.

He strode to the office across the hall from Private Chicks and opened the door.

And I jumped.

Ruth was on the other side, and she was so close I could almost feel the pricks of her chin whiskers.

"Well, if it isn't the ride reneger," she growl-drawled, the chains on her cat-eye glasses swinging, "and with booze on her breath."

Like I told Veronica, I thought in a growl-drawl that matched Ruth's, *gratitude journals don't work.*

"That's between Franki and me, Ruth," Bradley said as he entered the office. "And I've forgiven her as long as she lets me in the car next time."

Bradley and I exchanged a smile.

"On a more serious note," he said, "she's being threatened."

"Oh, dear." Ruth's face contorted with worry. "By whom?" She looked at Bradley, who'd turned to put the king cake on the coffee table, and then mouthed at me, *I'll get you for abandoning him at the airport.*

To which I reply-mouthed, *Try it, and I'll wring your turkey neck.*

Bradley turned around, and I forced a wide-eyed look. "The note told me to stop my investigation, so it has to be from Ken Lanier and Marie-Fleur Fontanot's killer. And if you ask me, that's either someone on the Krewe of Clotho board or Carl Cash."

"Carl?" Bradley rubbed his chin. "He and Ken are the

subjects of the insurance fraud case I was investigating in New York."

Stunned that Carl was also involved, I sank into a brown leather armchair—and opened the king cake box. It was no secret that I ate my feelings. "Can you tell me what it's about?"

Bradley sat on the arm of my chair. "Ken took a personal injury case involving a car Carl sold with an outstanding engine recall. The engine caught fire, and the buyer sustained burns and nerve damage. Carl claims Ken got a big payoff to lie about the extent of his client's injuries, and it wasn't the first time he'd been accused of accepting favors to throw a case."

The revelation reminded me of Glenda's "greased more palms" comment about Ken—and the black smoke coming from my own car engine. "Speaking of payoffs, Claudine and Honorine both own companies that are profiting off krewe members."

"That could be racketeering," Bradley said.

While I chewed on that comment, I shoved king cake into my mouth. Racketeering made me think of the Mafia and Gigi "The G-Man" Scalino, the spats-wearing former New Orleans mob boss who I sincerely hoped was still retired in Sicily.

Ruth leaned over and broke off a hunk of cake, and with it, a hunk of my heart. "Word around town is, those Clotho women are hyenas."

"Well," I closed the box to avoid a king cake catastrophe, "I met Carl today because his driver was the one who ripped off my bumper, and he's no better. The guy's a snake. He even looks like one."

"Personally," she ran her fingers over her cardigan-covered chest, "I find Carl attractive."

"Yuck, *how*?" I grimaced, grossed out. "He oozes sleaze."

"In a sexy, slithering way." She leered and bit into my cake.

My grimace turned gag. "TMI, Ruth. But you're not alone.

From what I hear, the snake gets around, and with beautiful women. I saw two of them getting into one of his cars at the airport with the Clotho captain."

She swallowed and reopened the king cake box. "They must be friends of his daughter."

"Why do you say that?" Bradley asked.

She stared at him over her reader rims. "Don't you know?"

"Know what?" I asked, taking advantage of her distraction to pull the box away from her cake-grubbing grasp.

"It's common knowledge around town." Ruth raised a brow. "Carl's a regular at Napoleon's Itch."

The gay bar on Bourbon Street?

"CAN you believe someone let the air out of my tires?" I squeezed a Styrofoam head in the back seat of Wanda's wig wagon. "When I find out who did it, heads are gonna roll."

Wanda took a sharp turn, and the mannequin heads in the back took a tumble. "It had to be the killer."

The head in my hands cracked, and I tossed it in the back to make it look like the turn was the culprit. "A killer who plays pranks?"

Marcella turned to face me from the front passenger seat. "You're getting too close, so they want to slow you down."

"They already accomplished that with the iron."

"Either way," Wanda's eyes met mine in the rearview mirror, "it was smart to have the Mustang towed to Carl Cash's service center."

"Yeah, but I'm not letting that crook fix anything except my bumper." I glared out the window at the brightly colored houses of the Faubourg Marigny neighborhood. "I just need to find out what Claudine and those Russian dolls were doing in one of his cars."

Wanda shot a side-eye at Marcella. "Well, we know they didn't fly to town for Carl's benefit since he scratches his itch at Napoleon's Itch."

Marcella snickered, and I scratched my neck. That bar name was suggestive in more ways than one. "Maybe Carl's just making money off the krewe with his cars."

"Makes sense." Wanda hooked another hard turn. "Those Russians could be krewe VIPs, or social media influencers."

I hoped they were the former. Now that Glenda's influencer quest had cost me a car, I had no interest in meeting more social media types. My life was already in danger, both from the killer and Wanda's driving.

Marcella opened the visor vanity mirror. "Maybe the Russians will be at the Murder Mystery Dinner tonight."

"Wait." I gripped the back of her seat. "The Krewe of Clotho is *still* doing the Murder Mystery Dinner?"

She shrugged. "They're having the parade."

"Yeah, but the dinner is different. I mean, what are we going to do? Solve the mystery of Marie-Fleur's murder?"

"You know the sentiment in New Orleans." She dabbed gold eyeshadow below her brow. "Mardi Gras must go on."

I'd said the same thing to Veronica earlier, but the dinner seemed so callous. And telling. The board didn't care about its own, or at least not about Marie-Fleur. *Why was that?*

"Here we are," Wanda said. "The 'Den of Goddesses.'" She pulled into a parking lot, and we got out of the wagon.

Marcella tightened the belt of her trench and put on her investigative face. "What are we looking for, Franki?"

"I don't know yet." I scanned the rusting, graffiti-covered warehouse. "But we need to check out the Clotho board's float."

"Shouldn't be hard to find," she said. "It probably has a huge spindle."

Wanda gave Marcella a stern stare. "If it does, don't touch it. Remember what happened to Sleeping Beauty."

Her smoky eyes flamed. "I'm willing to risk it. What single gal wouldn't sleep for a hundred years if she got to wake up to her prince?"

When she put it that way, it almost sounded enticing. Not the prince part, but the sleep. After the Hurricane Willie, I needed a lengthy nap.

As we approached the entrance, an enormous float on the other side of the building came into view. On the front was the torso of a huge Pinocchio—the lying wooden version—with giant pink flowers where his legs should've been.

"Oh!" Marcella pressed gold-polished nails to her cheeks. "Isn't he magnificent?"

Personally, I wasn't a fan of the puppet. "What's *he* doing here? Clotho is a Greek goddess krewe, and Josephine, their go-between, wasn't happy to have an Italian coming on board."

Marcella gazed at Pinocchio. "That's too bad. Reminds me of the Virgilians."

"Who were they?" Wanda asked.

"An Italian-American krewe named after the poet Virgil. They didn't parade, but they had lavish balls." She put a hand on her heart and gave a dreamy sigh. "For the first one in 1935, they did a Dante theme. The opera singer Marguerite Piazza dressed as Francesca da Rimini in a smoking-hot dress called the 'Flame of Hades.' We have it at the American Italian Cultural Center."

After a nighttime encounter in the Venetian lagoon with a bronze of Dante and Virgil journeying through Inferno in a gondola, I wasn't a fan of them either.

"Anyway, the Virgilians formed at a time when Italian-Americans weren't allowed to join other krewes. But their balls were so extravagant that invitations became highly coveted, and they came with a piece of themed jewelry." She whacked my arm. "How classy is that?"

That depended on what the jewelry depicted. "Why'd they break up?"

Her lips wrinkled. "Assimilation. Isn't that a kicker? By the time they had their last ball in 1964, Italians were allowed to join other krewes. It would've been nice if they'd stayed together and started parading."

Not if it meant riding on something like a Pinocchio head. "Speaking of parading, let's go find the Clotho board's float."

"Mind if we catch up?" Marcella held up her phone. "I'd like to get a few pics with Pinocchio and touch his nose."

"Nah, go ahead." From the sound of things, it was best if I left.

The door to the warehouse was unlocked, so I went inside. I set off through the vast space, passing an uninspired assortment of floats—a heart, a shield, a scepter. I stopped to admire a Medusa with writhing snakes. "Now *that's* what I'm talking about."

A loud crack sent me scurrying. Even though float decorations were made from a Styrofoam core, they were coated with pounds of papier-mâché, which could inflict major damage.

I headed deeper into the warehouse and felt as though I'd entered the belly of the beast. It was only one o'clock, but most of the lights were off, and there were few windows. Plus, between the Pinocchio outside and the gray metal of the warehouse, I couldn't help but feel I'd been swallowed by a giant whale.

Heels struck concrete somewhere in the building.

Anxiety gnawed at my gut—as did the fried food from Willie's Chicken Shack.

Is it Wanda and Marcella?

Or someone else?

Then I saw her—or it. A float adorned with an enormous bust of a golden-haired woman thirteen or so feet high, leaning forward like a ship's masthead. The same tan fabric as the Clotho krewe costume had been draped over her left shoulder to simulate a toga. Unlike the other floats, it was one story and resembled a cloud. Among the white fluff were thrones for each of the board members and a gold spindle wheel on an elevated platform at the rear.

With a spindle as big as a spear.

Wanda's Sleeping Beauty comment came to mind, but it didn't fit the case. The murder weapon wasn't a spindle, it was a poisoned mug of frozen southern milk punch. And there would be no prince for Marie-Fleur, because she wasn't asleep. She was dead. Not at the hands of Maleficent, but Atropos in the form of a Clotho board member.

Or a used car dealer.

Tapping shook me from my fairy tale musings.

No, *ticking*.

I walked around the nearby floats, searching for a clock or some other source of the sound. But I found nothing.

My text tone beeped.

I pulled my phone from my bag, hesitant to look at the display. It was most likely Marcella or Wanda, trying to find me. But I had my doubts.

What if it was the killer?

From inside the warehouse?

Chewing the inside of my cheek, I read the message. And a Hurricane Willie of emotions raged in my chest. "That go-between beyotch charged me for the two-thousand-dollar throw package?!"

I promptly googled the Krewe of Clotho to find the greedy

goddesses' number and pressed the phone to my ear. "Josephine's out of her freaking mind if she thinks I'm gonna pay two grand to throw crap at people."

While I waited for her to pick up, I stomped back to the Clotho float.

And smelled Chanel No. 5.

Claudine?

The ticking grew faster, and became a whir.

This time I knew where to look. My eyes darted to the rear of the float as the spindle detached from the wheel.

And flew straight at my chest.

8

____

To avoid a spindle to the chest, I threw my body to the concrete and heard a crack. *My ribs?*

"Wham!" a woman cried.

"Two for o, Wanda," Marcella marveled.

The coconut from her Zulu wig rolled up to me, its wide eyes and o-shaped mouth reflecting my sentiment.

Someone had spun the spindle wheel, and I had won.

For now.

Marcella used her linebacker build to heft me up in a single pull, sending tremors down my abdomen. "The spindle was coming straight at you, but Wanda knocked it off course with her coconut. When we were in high school, the kids called her Whamming Wanda for her deadly aim as a softball pitcher. If you came up to bat, and she didn't like you, *wham!*"

Wanda's sportsmanship was questionable, but her salesmanship wasn't. After the events of the day, I had half a mind to buy a weapon wig. "Thanks for your quick thinking out there."

"Never mind the kudos." Wanda scooped up the coconut, her pointed chin trembling with anger. "Who threw the spindle at you?"

"No one. The wheel started spinning, and it flew off."

She knelt and peered beneath the float. "It's under the cloud now, but someone set that wheel in motion."

Marcella shuddered. "Let's get you home, Franki."

She reached for my hand, which I yanked away to avoid another round of rib tremors. "We can't leave. I haven't inspected the float."

Bob Simpson strolled around the side of the cloud, and I blinked. Either I'd hit my head on the concrete, or he was wearing a tan Polo shirt and silky shorts with tan patent leather loafers.

Marcella shrieked. "He's armed!"

"Drop it," Wanda assumed a pitching position, "or I'll crack your coconut."

Bob's blue eyes bulged, and he raised the weapon. "My cordless glue gun?"

"Time!" I shouted in softballese. "He's with the krewe."

Wanda scrutinized Bob, tossing the coconut up and down in a threatening manner. "Did you just climb off that float? Because someone spun that wheel and launched the spindle at Franki."

"Dadgummit," he Texas-twanged. "I told Claudine that spindle was loose."

The three of us exchanged a look. The captain's name kept coming up, and in all the wrong scenarios.

"And if you must know," Bob yanked at his waistband, "I was in the Men's room. Enlarged prostate."

"Mound visit!" I signaled to Marcella to follow. I needed Wanda to cool it with the coconut and Bob to pipe down on the personal info.

Wanda stubbed the toe of her shoe on the floor, avoiding our gaze.

"Listen," I gave her back a pat, further proof of my empathy skills, "you were great out there. You saved me from the spindle *and* gave me something to write about in the gratitude journal Veronica's making me use, but the game is over."

"Gooood caaaall, Franki." Marcella pulled hair from her tan matte lips. "I have a gratitude journal, and I'm going to write that I touched Pinocchio's nose."

"Uh-huh," was all I could muster. Although, if touching a puppet's nose constituted a journal entry, I was golden. I could write that I was grateful for Wanda saving me from the spindle, and then fill the remaining pages with gratitude for every time my tongue touched Nutella. "Anyway, Bob is my landlady's ex #strippercouture designer, so I'll take over the questioning."

"You sure?" Wanda squeezed the coconut, still staring down Bob over my shoulder. "He seems shifty."

He *was* too normal for New Orleans—tan patent leather loafers excluded—but he didn't strike me as a killer. "Yeah, my ribs are sore, but if he gives me any trouble, I'll pop him in the old prostate." I punched her arm as a demonstration. "What I need is for you two to search all the floats in case the spinner is still in the building."

Marcella squealed and took Wanda's arm. "Let's start with Pinocchio. Who wouldn't want to hide on him?"

Wanda let Marcella drag her to the dreaded Disneyesque float, and I sauntered over to Bob, trying to figure out how to broach the subject of Glenda. "Sorry about the misunderstanding, but we didn't expect to see you at the float den."

"My hearing's not what it used to be. Can you speak a little louder?"

Clearly, Bob had no idea what it was like to grow up in an Italian family. "I said, I didn't expect to see you here."

Bob began gluing tan sequins to the white fabric overhanging the float. "I didn't expect to see me here either, but I've got to add a tan glint to this cloud. I'm known for my work with glue, and the Krewe of Clotho expects me to pull out all the stops."

I mentally added God of Glue to the long list of Bob's titles. "What I meant was, I thought you were retired."

"Oh, I was until the captain asked me to design this year's krewe costumes. It's such an honor to walk in the shoes of Mardi Gras costume giants like Anthony Colombo and his daughter, Susie Colombo Barocco, that I couldn't refuse."

I hadn't heard of them, but I was willing to bet they'd never worn tan patent leather loafers.

Bob paused to add a new glue stick to his gun. "What're you doing here? Are you on the krewe?"

"Yeah, in fact, I have the costume you designed." I pulled the gold sack from my purse and caught sight of the label. "Are you freaking kidding me?" I yanked the toga from the bag. "That godawful go-between gave me an XXL." I held up the scrap of fabric and gasped. "And it's the size of a Medium."

Bob took the costume. "No, it's an XXL. Clothing sizes are my business."

I snatched the tan toga from his hand and shoved it into my bag. "My business is tracking down criminals, and calling a Medium an XXL is a crime punishable by death."

He backed into the float and clambered on board, and his English Leather aftershave reminded me that I'd smelled Chanel No. 5. "You didn't see Captain Claudine around, did you?"

"Not today. But I'm supposed to meet the VP, Honorine, shortly."

I surveyed the area to make sure we were alone. "Can you keep something on the downlow?"

His eyes widened. "On the *floor*? I don't think it's been cleaned."

Questioning Bob was going to be hard. "Forget the floor. I'm investigating the deaths of Ken Lanier and Marie-Fleur Fontenot, and I was wondering if you'd noticed anything unusual in your dealings with the board members."

Bob glanced from side to side. "I do know something that isn't public knowledge. Ken wooed Claudine and asked her to go steady."

My jaw went slack. No wonder he hadn't understood the phrase "on the downlow." His language hadn't progressed past "Leave It To Beaver." "Gee, Bob. Did you see Ken and Claudine spoon, too?"

"Good grief, no." He held up his glue gun. "I'm not a Peeping Tom. However, I did see them have *quite* the spat."

Apparently, Bob hadn't gotten my hint that his lingo was Fifties TV show. "What about?"

He tapped his ear. "Couldn't hear a word."

"Any chance you're a lip reader?"

"Not without my glasses."

It wasn't Bob's fault, but he was frustrating. "Anything else you can tell me?"

"A few weeks ago, I ran into one of my former law partners." He dabbed glue onto the fabric. "And the scuttlebutt has it that Claudine broke it off with Ken, and he planned to get revenge by investigating Claudine for embezzling from the krewe coffers."

I didn't know what surprised me more—learning that Ken was investigating Claudine or hearing "scuttlebutt" used in a sentence. One thing I did know, Bob Simpson wasn't merely the God of Glue, he was also a gossip.

He climbed off the float, poured tan sequins into his hand, and blew them onto the glue. His smile gleamed like his handiwork, as he admired his design.

I hated to interrupt the Sultan of Sequins when he was

styling, but I had a case to solve. "Bob, I don't know how to break this to you, so I'm just going to say it. You're in danger, both from the murderer and from Glenda."

His smile faltered—and fell. "Does Glenda know I'm out of retirement?"

Not surprisingly, he was more concerned about my ex-stripper landlady than the killer. "Yep, because I told her."

Bob's cheeks turned red, and his nostrils flared as though he wanted to explode, but he couldn't because his lips were pressed together so tightly they were as white as the cloud float.

If I hadn't seen him that way once before, I would've thought he'd accidentally glued his lips shut. But no. He was so mad he couldn't speak, a phenomenon relatively unknown among my people. "Open your mouth, Bob. Let it out."

His lips stayed sealed.

"Glenda was going to find out about you, anyway. She joined the krewe."

His brows popped, and his lips followed suit. "Clotho?"

I nodded.

He paced the float den, his tan silky shorts and patent loafers gleaming. Then he stopped and put his hands his hips. "Well, at bottom, Glenda's a sensible woman."

"*Sensible*, Bob?" I blinked and gave my head a stunned shake. "I realize your eyesight and hearing are somewhat impaired, but are you *dead*?"

"Now, Franki, Glenda's prone to exaggeration—"

"I'll say she is," I snapped, cutting him off. "She used that stripper pole you set up for your front-yard photo shoot to bash the hood of my Mustang."

He sank onto the side of the cloud. "I can't have that. Linda and I recently redid our kitchen, and we need a new roof."

"You should've thought of that before you took the gig with

Clotho. When you agreed to design #strippercouture for Glenda, you signed a deal with the She-Stripper-Devil."

He grabbed a fancy fanny pack from the cloud and headed for the exit.

"Where are you going?"

"To move my car to an undisclosed location."

As he scurried away, I couldn't help but feel bad for the guy. Anyone who wore tan patent leather loafers didn't stand a chance against the likes of Glenda.

Turning my attention to the float, I climbed on board. A search of the fabric and seating turned up nothing. But one of the two pieces of wood that held the spindle had been cut by a saw blade. Since no one on Clotho could've known I was coming to the float den, I assumed the intended victim of the sabotage had initially been one of the board members.

But which one?

And how much damage could the spindle have done? Unless...

...it was poisoned!

I jumped down and crawled underneath the float to collect the spindle.

It was gone.

There was no way Bob could've taken it.

So who had?

Shocked, I scrambled from beneath the float.

And I screamed to high heaven.

Ruth Walker stood before me in a terrifying outfit—her cruise director uniform—a Safari vest, cargo shorts, long white socks, and Keds. There was one notable difference—apart from a turtleneck over her turkey neck—the Fun Meter badge she tormented people with was missing. If anything was worthy of a gratitude journal entry, that was it.

Her lips drew into a pucker, bringing her stubbly chin with them. "I'm surprised you're not at the bar."

Still shaken by the missing spindle, I assumed she was talking about Carl Cash's hangout. "You mean, Napoleon's Itch?"

"Any bar. Boozers can't be choosers."

My lips tightened on my teeth. I'd let my guard down in front of Ruth, which wasn't smart. The woman was ruthless, as in devoid of her name definitions. "For your information, I'm going there later but not to drink. I need to ask some questions related to the case."

"Uh-huh. Was that drink from Willie's Chicken Shack related to the case too?"

"Why are you here?" I huffed.

"The Krewe of Clotho called to collect their dues." She crossed her arms. "Seems someone gave them my name and phone number at the brunch yesterday."

My lips sealed as tightly as Bob's. We both knew that "someone" was me.

She plucked a hair from her vest that had somehow escaped the tight confines of her bun. "I got to chit-chatting with their go-between, Josephine, and mentioned that I was a former cruise director on the Steamboat Galliano. She offered me a position as the captain of float 24."

I collapsed onto the cloud, and a bizarre thing happened. Just like Bob with his anger affliction, I was so mad I couldn't speak. *First Glenda, now Ruth?* This Mardi Gras was miserable.

"What's the matter?" Ruth crowed. "Cat got your tongue?"

No, the turkey-necked ostrich did.

"Don't sit there like a bump on a log. These floats don't have numbers, and I need help finding mine."

A glimmer of opportunity to get rid of Ruth shone as brightly as the sequins Bob had glued. "The krewe decides the order based on the design, so you'll have to go to headquarters and get that information from Josephine. I tried calling her earlier, but she's not answering."

She bristled, as did her chin whiskers. "Do I look like I have time to run all over this damn town?"

"Honestly, yes."

"Well, I don't. Unlike you, I don't have all the livelong day to spin my wheels in bars, reneging on rides from the airport. I've got a float to inspect, and after that I need to get over to the Hotel Monteleone."

The ride-reneger comment deserved a comeback. "To stop by the Carousel Bar for a Pimm's Cup?"

She squinted, and her jaw cocked at an annoyed angle. "You've got booze on the brain, you know that?"

Another Bob attack loomed. Ruth had a way of turning the tables on me that was enraging. "Then why are you going to the hotel?"

"When I got here fifteen minutes ago, I saw something that makes me think there's some funny business going on with one of the board members. And we both know I won't join this krewe if there's foul play afoot."

I slid off the float. Ruth's arrival was within the timeframe that the spinner would have struck and snuck off with the spindle. "What did you see?"

"A blonde in sunglasses and a trench coat came out of the warehouse talking on a phone. I didn't get a look at her face, but I heard her say clear as a bell, 'I'm on the Clotho board with her, so tell her to get on the line *stat*.' Then she walked to the street and said to whoever got on the call, 'You keep your mouth shut, and I don't tell anyone what you've got going on at Hotel Monteleone.' After that—get this—a hearse pulled up, and she got in."

A chill settled in my chest.

Ruth shook her head. "Can you imagine?"

"I can—the license plate is U R NEXT."

"You saw it too?"

"At the airport behind the Carl Cash car with Captain Claudine that I told you and Bradley about." I ran my hand over my chin, trying to make sense of the revelation—and hoping it never grew whiskers like Ruth's. "She was there to pick up some gorgeous Russian women."

"WHAT ITCH CAN I scratch for ya?" The chubby redhead behind the bar slid a drink napkin in front of me.

And I slid back on my barstool. Napoleon's Itch had a wild reputation, but Wanda and Marcella had just dropped me off.

She stared at me, her face impassive. "I'm talking about a drink."

"Right." My face was probably as red as her hair.

"We like to play off the bar name when we take orders, but I should've asked what tickles your fancy."

My cheeks prickled at the old-fashioned expression. I had five or so years on her, but I was hardly Bob Simpson. "What do you suggest?"

"A buttery nipple or Sex on the Beach."

And she stared at me like I was a Boomer for thinking she'd come on to me. "How about something less sensual?"

She leaned an elbow on the bar. "We're known for our peanut butter and jelly shots and minty mojitos."

A liquid PB&J sounded revolting, but then again, Nutella in espresso was delish. "I'll go with the mojito."

"By the way," she pulled a glass from below the bar, "Napoleon's Itch does have a double meaning. It's a reference to his Russian campaign in 1812, which is why our sign out front shows Napoleon on horseback."

Once again, I was thinking sex but got something completely different.

She added mint to the glass. "Historians have proven that the French army wasn't defeated by the Russians, but by lice carrying typhus."

I scratched the back of my neck. The lice lesson was a lot to drop on me, especially before I'd had a drink.

As the redhead muddled mint leaves, I thought about the Russians—not the soldiers with lice, but the bombshells with the Gucci luggage. They weren't in New Orleans to scratch Carl's itch, so I had to find out what were they doing with Claudine in one of his cars—and how the creepy hearse was connected.

The hearse had left the airport before Sallow Skin and his Mercedes made off with my bumper, so there were two possibilities. Either the cars had arrived together, or someone in the hearse was surveilling Claudine.

And based on the conversation Ruth overheard, that someone was most likely another Clotho board member—who could be the killer.

One way or another, I had to talk to Anaïs, Honorine, and Carly at the Murder Mystery Dinner. In the meantime, I texted The Vassal and asked him to run a check on the U R NEXT license plate.

The redhead placed the mojito on my drink nap.

"Hey," I reached for the drink. "By any chance, did you work during the Greasing of the Poles?"

"Luckily, I was off."

I sipped the delicious minty concoction. "What about Carl Cash, the used car salesman. You ever wait on him?"

"Can't say I have."

She might know her lice history, but she doesn't know her long-time customers.

The redhead washed her hands and exited the bar, and I turned to check out Carl Cash's alleged hangout. Napoleon's Itch wasn't much to look at. Plain white walls, a few tables, and a grand total of six barstools. It was more or less a dive bar in the Bourbon Orleans Hotel.

I glanced out the entrance overlooking Bourbon Street.

A head retracted.

My gut went as cold as my iced drink. *Am I being watched?*

I stood and went to the street, but no one seemed suspicious—at least, not by French Quarter standards.

Returning to my barstool, I slugged from the mojito as thoughts rolled in my brain like mannequin heads in Wanda's wagon.

Did the killer follow me after the failed spindle attack?

Or was the peeper merely a curious passerby?

Napoleon's Itch was four short blocks from the Royal Sonesta, where Ken Lanier had his last cocktail. It was close enough to the Greasing of the Poles to get a frozen southern milk punch, but far enough away that the police might not suspect the location.

I'd asked David and The Vassal to find the bar where the drink had been made, but I was starting to wonder whether I'd found it myself.

A tall, slender male in a rainbow shirt with the words "Mr. Right" stepped behind the bar, smoothing his neatly trimmed brown hair. "Need anything, hon? Mr. Right is here to serve."

"I'm good on the drink—and on the Mr. Right. But did you work during the Greasing of the Poles?"

He rested his wrist on his forehead, and his brown eyes rolled skyward. "Lordy, yes. It was a zoo in here, and I'm talking actual animals."

My eyes strayed to the image of Napoleon's horse, but after learning about the lice, I didn't press for details. "Did Carl Cash, the used car salesman, come in?"

"Not that day. I'd remember, because he always sits at the bar watching our TV for hours, waiting for his boring commercials."

He took a cherry from the drink garnishes and tossed it into his mouth. "And he doesn't tip."

The cheap part was obvious because of Carl's cash obsession, but I added "narcissist" to his list of defects. Then I pulled out my phone and googled a video of the Greasing of the Poles. "Do you recognize the three bouffant Mardi Gras wigs?"

Mr. Right took my phone and enlarged the screen. "The purple one."

"You've seen it?"

"Yes, girrrl." His hand went to his heart, displaying five rainbow-polished nails. "You can't see it very well in this video, but the tiara on that wig is marvelous. Obviously, it can't compare to Princess Diana's Cambridge Lover's Knot." He fanned his eyes, waving away tears. "But what can?"

"Nothing," I said in all sincerity. I knew that tiara, and not only was it the best, no one had worn it better than Di.

"But, girrrl," he gripped the edge of the bar and his head flopped forward, "the woman who wore it was a POW."

"A prisoner of war?"

Mr. Right's head popped up like a cork. "No, a piece of work."

That fit the MO of a Clotho board member. "Did she pay with a credit card? Or tell you her name?"

"In regard to your first question, read the policy." He pointed to the *Cash Only* sign on the wall behind him. "As for the second, Mr. Right discourages all personal information from the clientele unless they're hot and buying him dinner."

After Bob's prostate comment, I should implement that policy myself. "This is a long shot, but do you remember the drink she ordered?"

He held up a hand. "I'm getting to that. I named the piece of work Miss Purple, after the wig, because that color is a *mood*, and she is it. Would you believe, she told me not to pour her drink too full so she could top it off with booze from home?"

I would, because this was New Orleans—and because the booze might've actually been poison intended for Ken Lanier.

"So I made the drink—"

"Sorry to interrupt, but what kind was it?"

His lashes lowered. "I haven't gotten to that part." He flicked his rainbow nails at my hands. "First I'm going to need you to place those palms on the bar and brace yourself."

Without hesitation, I laid my palms flat.

"So I serve Miss Purple the drink, and she says, 'It's too full.'" He opened his eyes zombie style, waiting for me to react to that shocker.

Keeping my palms firmly on the bar, I said, "That's outrageous. I'm always excited when I get a big pour."

"Girrrl, right? It stretches your drink dollars." He fluttered his lashes. "So I go, 'Just drink the excess. You paid for it.' And Miss Purple says, 'No, I can't,' because she's clearly the type who has things done for her. Of course, by this time, we've got a line out the door, and the customers are getting unruly. And I don't mean tear-my-clothes-to-shreds unruly, because Mr. Right enjoys that. I mean trash-the-bar unruly, like untamed animals."

"That's terrifying."

"Don't I know it?" He flicked his fingernails at my hands. "Pick up those palms now. Let's not exaggerate."

It was tempting to point out that he wasn't done with the story, but I didn't want to upset him before he'd spilled the drink name. "So what did you do?"

"I dumped some out. And then," he buried his face in his hands, "Miss Purple informs Mr. Right that he hasn't poured out enough."

In all fairness, that revelation deserved a bracing gesture because it was just too much, but again, I kept that to myself. "And what delicious drink was she wasting?"

His eyes went skyward. "Girrrl, that's the worst part. With all the chaos in the bar, Miss Purple wants me to find a bottle of Tuaca."

As soon as he mentioned the liqueur, I froze.

"Because she can't drink a regular Southern Milk Punch—oh, no. It's got to be the frozen version."

9

"Something's not right." I stood frozen in the darkness on my driveway, semi-regretting that the Uber driver had sped away. Actually, lots of things weren't right at the fourplex—the Yardi Gras decorations, Chandra's U-Haul office, the toilet with flames on top of Lou Toccato's plumbing truck, to name a few. But this was different.

Someone was lurking. I could feel it.

The death threat crashed my thoughts as the iron had my windshield.

Does the killer know where I live?

The lights were on at Thibodeaux's across the street, but it was Sunday night so business was dead. The cemetery was dead too.

But eyes were on me. I could feel them.

"Probably that creepy gargoyle on the mausoleum." I took a step and stopped.

Or is it Atropos waiting to cut the thread of my life?

"It's just my wild imagination." I headed up the driveway, and a breeze made the sex dolls bounce on the balcony poles. "Or it's those wild Yardi Gras decorations."

As I neared my front door, a figure crept from the shadows onto my porch.

My stomach seized. *That's no doll.*

The street light confirmed my conclusion. The creeper was thick in the middle.

Nadezhda?

No, she was round all over like a Russian nesting doll. Whoever this was carried all their weight in their belly.

Like a beer keg.

My hand went to my mouth. I knew that shape. This is why my mother apologized on the phone. She didn't send the Catholic Cavalry, she'd sent her best friend, Rosalie Artusi, to do her and my nonna's busybody bidding. But unlike their verbal arm-twisting, Rosalie was inclined to the physical version. And it didn't help that she resembled a cross between the late Chicago Bears coach, Mike Ditka, and the Le Boozé bartender with the underbite.

Trying to figure out a way around her, I leaned south.

Rosalie leaned with me.

I ran a yard or so north.

She did too.

"This is ridiculous, Rosalie. You need to get off my porch."

"As you wish." She barreled at me.

Given my already injured ribs, I turned and ran for Thibodeaux's.

My foot caught something, and I went flying.

That damn stripper pole.

My torso hit the grass first, and Rosalie landed on my back with the full force of her belly. *"Oompff!"*

She twisted my arms behind me, as per my description, and I gasped under her girth. The pain of the spindle incident was nothing compared to the damage rendered by Wrecking Ball Rosalie.

"Your mother sent me to set you straight. And what do you do? You turn gay." She bent my leg backward, shoving my foot toward my bottom.

"*Owww*," I howled, my cheek pressed in the grass. "My foot does not go there, okay? And no one *turns* gay."

"Then how do you explain flirting with that redhead at Napoleon's Itch?"

So Rosalie was the peeper, the creeper, and my keeper. "I wasn't flirting," I rasped. "I was investigating."

She dug an elbow into my back. "Are these sex dolls part of your investigation?"

"They're Glenda's. She thinks her likeness, and her body parts, are Mardi Gras decorations."

Rosalie released my leg. "Makes sense."

My gaze shot over my shoulder. "It does?"

"Yep. Works for me." She let go of my arms and lumbered to her feet.

If I hadn't been so enraged I would have asked her to explain. The logic of Glenda's decorations had escaped me for years.

The door to the U-Haul opened with a bang, and Chandra emerged all gussied up in a silver flapper dress and a rhinestone headband adorned with a glittery moon. "Can't a woman get some peace and quiet in her own home?"

"Of course," I pushed myself up and picked grass from my lips, "but you're in a U-Haul in a driveway."

She straightened her headpiece. "I can't go in my apartment. Lou's in there taking his sweet time installing a toilet."

My lips clamped shut. *Sweet* and *toilet* didn't belong in the same sentence.

"Chandra," Rosalie pleaded, her hands raised in prayer, "talk to him."

"*Puh!* After the way he behaved with that sex doll?"

My hands rose in prayer, and I begged God to stop this conversation.

Rosalie, who sprinkled gossip like Bob Simpson did sequins, grabbed my clasped hands. "One of the dolls fell off the balcony, and Lou almost tripped over his feet trying to pick it up. You should've seen the way he manhandled that thing while he was rehanging it."

Probably much the way she'd manhandled me.

Chandra stomped a silver sandal, setting off her flapper fringe. "I *knew* a Mardi Gras krewe would turn Lou into a womanizer."

"Let's not rush to judgement," I gushed, hoping to stave off a longer stay at the so-called singles' compound. "By the way, what's up with the Great Gatsby getup? A 1920s séance for a client?"

"No, but that reminds me, when Rosalie got here earlier, I smelled Chanel No. 5 again."

That was mystifying because Rosalie reeked of garlic and polyester.

"And then just like that," Chandra snapped her fingers, "I remembered why it reminded me of that poor woman, Marie-Fleur. During the tarot reading, she found Chanel No. 5 in her purse."

Has to be the one from Wanda's wig shop. "Was it a purse-sized tube?"

"Yes, like a lipstick. She said it wasn't hers."

Claudine could've planted it on Marie-Fleur to set her up for Ken Lanier's murder, but that didn't add up because Claudine herself had worn the perfume to the brunch—and then Marie-Fleur was killed. *What am I missing?*

"Go on, Chandra," Rosalie prodded, more in the know about my case than I was. "Tell her what else you remembered."

"This happened before I drew the third card."

"And you still don't remember what the card was?"

"No, but I'll keep trying. Right now I need to do my makeup." Chandra patted her huge hairdo. "I'm going to the Krewe of Clotho's Murder Mystery Dinner."

Rosalie might as well have bowled me over again. First Glenda, then Ruth, now Chandra. "Who the hell else is go—" I stopped before I finished that question. Better not to ask with Rosalie beside me. "Um, who told you the krewe was accepting new members?"

"Glenda," she said, offhanded.

Rosalie shot me a snide side-eye. "Chandra decided to join after Lou told Glenda about all of the pretty women who hang around his float den."

Groupies? For a krewe that celebrates toilets?

"I don't give a fig what Lou does." Chandra's tone was less than convinced. "I joined Clotho for the sisterhood."

"A warehouse full of plumbers." Rosalie elbowed my side. "Enticing, huh Franki?"

She was clearly testing my sexuality, but I refrained from comment. I envisioned a float den full of plumber cracks.

Her face grew serious. "Any of them single, Chandra? My two nieces are the spitting image of me, and they're looking for love matches."

Imagine that.

Chandra scowled and turned to me. "What are you wearing to the dinner?"

"No clue." I put my hands on my hips. "I've been so busy that I forgot about the Twenties theme."

She sniffed. "I'd lend you something, but," she lowered her gaze to my pelvis, "after you stretched out my dress, we both know you're too wide to wear my clothes."

"You mean, *too tall.*"

"No, Chandra's right." Rosalie sized up my backside. "Too wide."

"M-kay. I'm going in." I walked my too-wide backside to my front door and let Napoleon out.

He spotted Rosalie and made like Wanda's Chewbacchus wig. Then he ran to the stripper pole and hiked his leg.

"Good boy, Napoleon."

"You're praising that vicious mongrel?" Rosalie pointed at Napoleon as he darted past her to return inside. "He bared his teeth at me. I can't stay in the same apartment as him."

I wanted to say, *Which is one of the reasons I praised him*, but I focused on the more pressing matter. "Who said you're staying with me?"

"Your mother, that's who."

"Well, she doesn't live here." I went inside and slammed the door, which did nothing for my ribs. I marched to my bedroom, climbed onto the canopy bed, and called my parents.

"Hello?" my mother's shrill voice took a stab at innocence.

My hot breath resounded in the receiver.

"Who is this?" she demanded. "Are you a stalker?"

"Funny you should use that term." My tone was as cold as the hard ground I'd been pinned on by her BFF. "When I came home a few minutes ago, I had a stalker. Named Rosalie Artusi."

"Oh, Francesca. She's practically family."

"Then she can stay with you tonight, because she's not staying with me."

"I sent her to talk some sense into you—"

"And because I already have some sense, I'm sending her back."

"First, don't interrupt your mother. Second, I don't have time to come down there with your father and your nonna bedridden."

The Nonna news caught me off guard. "What's Nonna still doing in bed?"

"She's refusing to get up until you pick a wedding venue."

I flopped backwards onto the pillows.

"So I'm stuck here taking care of two invalids and the deli, and on top of all that, I have to keep the house spotless for the visitors. You should see the food. I've got enough meals in the freezer to last until summer."

Conflict raged in my chest. If my nonna got out of bed, she'd make my mother drive her to New Orleans, which was the last thing I needed. But on the other hand, she was in her eighties, and lying in bed wasn't good for her. "Make something up. Tell her the reception's at the Piazza d'Italia."

"I can't *lie* to her, Francesca."

A blatant lie. "You can, but you won't because the free food will stop."

"What's wrong with accepting a little help every now and then?" she snapped on the defensive. "I've certainly done more than my fair share of cooking for others, and Lord knows I could use the food with the way this family eats. There's no getting around it—we're a foodcentric people."

"That's a stereotype, Mom."

"Oh, really? And how many times have you thought about Nutella today?"

On the grounds that it might incriminate me, I refused to answer.

"You can't escape your roots, dear."

A hand-held bell rang somewhere in the house.

"Ooh. There goes your father again, wanting his rigatoni. I don't know where he got that damn bell, but if he rings it one more time, I'm going to shove it so far down his throat he'll never eat another piece of pasta. Talk soon," she sing-songed.

The call ended.

I tabled the talk of my father's murder in favor of my mother's roots comment. It reminded me of Josephine's crack about bleach jobs not being able to cover bad roots. *Was the go-between only referring to the angry mob? Or was she also referring to a board member's ancestry?*

"Something to investigate at the Murder Mystery Dinner."

My text tone sounded. A message from The Vassal.

No results for the U R NEXT license plate.

I massaged my temples. *Who the hell owned that hearse?*

Hell and the hearse reminded me that I had to send Rosalie packing in her Chrysler Pacifica. But first, I needed some aspirin. I hurt all over because of the spindle and stalker—and maybe the Willie's Hurricane and mojito. I went into the bathroom, and as I opened the medicine cabinet, the mirror reflected something horrific.

Spots.

As in a leopard-print toilet seat.

Despite my instructions to Glenda, the black toilet was not plain.

Gritting my teeth, I lowered the seat lid.

A big poop emoji smiled up at me.

Not only that, the tank had a giant decal of a jar of Nutella.

Which, I now noticed, was the same color as the poop emoji.

The words *sweet* and *toilet* had come back to haunt me.

Sinking onto the side of the clawfoot tub to digest this disgusting reality, I spotted another awful detail.

The flush handle was a silver spoon—shaped like a shovel.

"My mom might be right about our family being foodcentric, but this toilet is not my destiny, and neither is a wedding in an Italian flag dress in the Piazza d'Italia." I rose from the tub, determined to manifest my proclamations. Although, I *did* want to buy a set of those shovel spoons.

Rosalie barged into the bathroom. "I hope you like the toilet.

Lou left it plain, but I said you needed something to undo the French whorehouse décor."

Clenching my fists, I got in her face. "This toilet is revenge because I picked a Nutella spoon for a wedding favor instead of that awful pig with eyelashes and rose gold lipstick you tricked me into buying."

Her lips formed an *o* for outrage. "That pig *bomboniere* was adorable. And it held Jordan almonds, something your crappy Nutella spoon can't do."

A gasp escaped my lips. The phrase "crappy Nutella spoon" summed up my toilet—and confirmed my revenge suspicions. "That was the plan, because what wedding guest wants to eat Jordan almonds from a ceramic pig's bottom?"

Rosalie's face screwed up á la Mike Ditka's following a fumble. "Bridezilla rears her ugly head, just like when you disbanded my bomboniere committee."

"I'm only going to say this one more time," I said through my teeth, "I never approved any bomboniere committee, and I definitely don't approve of this toilet or you in my apartment."

Shoving past her, I stormed through my living room and out the door to Chandra's apartment. Without knocking, I marched inside to locate Lou.

The place was as sparse as the U-Haul trailer. A table, a chair, unpacked boxes.

Lou was in the bathroom, working with a crescent wrench, hunched over a toilet.

My eyes shot to the ceiling. "Mind if I interrupt?"

"Franki." Lou rose and pulled his pants over a beer belly that rivaled Rosalie's. He wore a Crescent City Plumbing & Palmistry uniform instead of his signature island shirt and shorts, but he stayed true to his toe shoes. He'd never gotten the memo that rubber gloves for feet were a trend for all of five seconds.

Lou swung his wrench in the direction of the toilet. "I made this full-moon model special for Chandra."

"I see that," I said, startled by its wide, circular shape. If Chandra could sit on that thing without falling in, it would prove I didn't stretch out her dress. "While we're on the subject, there was a mix-up with my toilet. Could you remove those decals?"

"Yup." He bounced forward on his toes. "I'll get right on it."

It was already 6 p.m. "After Mardi Gras is fine."

"After Mardi Gras," he repeated, sounding sad.

Genuine empathy flooded my chest. When the parades were over, he'd be forced to deal with life without Chandra, something he couldn't contemplate.

But, oh, I could.

"So how are you, Lou? The separation must be hard."

"It's tough, but I'm doing my part to get her back." He gestured at the toilet.

"Yyyeeesss." I smacked my lips. "Keep it up, because Chandra heard there were a lot of pretty women hanging around your krewe's float den, and she's so jealous she joined Clotho to keep an eye on you."

"Yeah?" His black brow popped up but promptly fell. "Truth is," he shoved his hands into his pockets, pushing his waistband close to the plumber precipice, "those women aren't groupies, or anything."

"Nooo." I feigned a shocked face.

He swiped his wrist under his nose. "Our warehouse is next to the Den of Goddesses, where Clotho keeps their floats."

Lou, a man of few words, had me spellbound. "Were the women blondes?"

"Not real ones."

"Well, not many are."

"Yup. Yup." Another toe-bounce. "Between us," he stole a

glance at me from beneath his lashes, "I think they're being paid. A buddy and I saw big bucks changing hands in the parking lot. He thinks the one handing out the cash is a Clotho board member, but we're not sure."

I was. What I didn't know was whether the money had anything to do with whatever was going down at the Hotel Monteleone.

"WELCOME to the House of Hucci Cucci." Glenda struck a pose in the doorway of her costume closet in what was clearly her Murder Mystery Dinner flapper costume, i.e., platinum art deco pasties and fringe—glued to her skin.

She ushered me in, and I knew better than to look back. I focused on an old Singer sewing machine in the middle of the clothing racks until she closed the door and came in. "Are you going to wear a headpiece?"

"Of course, Miss Franki. I made one, but given the time constraint, I had to pull my costume off the rack."

Off fabric *off the rack.*

"Feast your eyes on my first #strippercouture creation." She sashayed to a shelf that held her aptly named acsexories and picked up a headpiece that lay next to the Vaseline jar fascinator she'd worn to the Greasing of the Poles. "A rhinestone headband with peacock feathers, two of Bob's signature embellishments, protruding from one of my own—a bedazzled condom wrapper." She cocked her jaw and shimmied her fringe. "Because they don't call them the Roaring Twenties for nothing."

Apparently not. I held up Chandra's ex too-short shift dress that I'd stretched *down.* "You got any fringe or sequins I can glue on this thing? At the Clotho brunch, Claudine said anyone who didn't wear a 1920s costume would be blackballed from the krewe, and that can't happen before I've ID'd the killer."

She took a seat at the sewing machine. "You've come to the right #strippercouture house, sugar. Just give me a minute to put a few more stitches in a piece I'm creating."

There was no place for me to sit, so I stood next to the five-foot-tall go cup prop she'd used in her early performances—before she worked her way up to the giant champagne glass in her living room.

Glenda put on a pair of rhinestone readers, huddled over the Singer, and pressed a stripper platform with the word Cucci to the foot pedal. "If you tell anyone I wear glasses, Miss Franki," she said in a tone as pleasant and steady as the whir of the machine, "that damage I did to your Mustang will pale in comparison to what I do to you. Understood?"

"No questions on my end."

"Glad we've got that settled," she said, continuing to sew. "I take it you haven't identified the poison?"

"Not yet, but I think the frozen southern milk punch came from Napoleon's Itch, and the woman wearing the purple Mardi Gras wig we found in the street is the one who ordered it. The weird thing is, Ruth Walker said Carl Cash is a regular there, and I'm not sure whether that's relevant."

The machine stopped. "Oh, it's relevant. It explains why that old coonhound has never visited me in the VIP Room."

That wasn't what I'd meant by relevant, but I let it slide. Nor did I remind her that I'd been in the room to investigate a case, and Carl's sexuality wasn't the only reason for him to avoid it. There were trillions of others, as in germs.

Glenda pressed the foot pedal and resumed sewing. The needle was moving, but I didn't see fabric.

"What are you working on there?"

"An outfit for my Hucci Cucci line. This is the top."

That's why there's no fabric.

"By the way, sugar, what did you think of your commode?"

Where to start? "It's black, but far from plain."

She glanced up. "Well, I went to tell Lou your instructions and ran into your mother's friend. She said she'd handle it."

Oh, she did. And I'd handled her by forcing her into her Chrysler Pacifica and sending her back to Houston. "Lou's going to remove the decals, so no worries."

"That's a relief." She shook her head. "I already feel bad about telling Lou to take back Miss Nadezhda's commode, but I need this space until I get my fashion house up and running, so she can't move in."

My face was neutral, but in my mind, I was a majorette twirling a baton in a Mardi Gras parade as I led a brass band in a rousing rendition of "When the Saints Go Marching In."

Glenda turned the piece of seemingly non-existent fabric beneath the needle. "I wanted to make it work, but a snakeskin commode isn't right for the House of Hucci Cucci Hot Couture."

Personally, I'd taken the penny-pinching Communist for a metal-prison-toilet person, but the snakeskin brought me back to Carl Cash and Napoleon's Itch. I had to figure out why Miss Purple bought the frozen southern milk punch from Carl's favorite hangout. *Is it a coincidence?*

Or a setup?

And what does any of this have to do with the conversation Ruth overheard outside the float den? "Hey, have you heard anything around town about some 'funny business' at the Hotel Monteleone?"

She shot me a dead-serious stare. "No, sugar, but whatever it is, I want in on it."

I should've expected that reply.

Glenda snipped a stitch and raised the tiny object she'd been sewing—a beaded pastie that looked like a nipple. "Now then, let's get you ready for the krewe dinner." She rose from the machine. "Before I forget, have you seen Bob's Krewe of Clotho costume?"

"Yeah, it's super small."

"The size is fine. But, child, that design." She puckered and put her hands on her fringed flesh. "A tan toga and a wreath? Where's the style in that?"

She had a point. Bob had really underdone himself, especially compared to Glenda's Greasing of the Poles costume. "How are you planning to modify it?"

"That's a secret, Miss Franki." Her eyes went sly. "You'll have to wait until parade day for the big reveal."

Reveal *being the operative word.*

Or, is it secret?

I walked to the acsexories shelf and bent over to study the fascinator, looking for frozen southern milk punch splatter for testing. The hat was clean, so I peered into the Vaseline jar.

Straightening, I blinked and stooped again for a second look. Then I threw up my hands. "Show me the money!"

Glenda dropped into a crab position and pumped her pelvis.

I leapt back so high that I darn-near landed in the go cup. "Jeez, Glenda! I wasn't talking about me. I was using a profession-appropriate expression."

"I'm sorry, sugar," she rose on her Hucci Cucci heels, "but we strippers are a lot like soldiers. Certain words and phrases are orders that must be obeyed."

Strippers and soldiers? Evidently, Glenda and I both could use some work on our choice of words.

She flipped her hair. "Now, what were you talking about?"

I pointed at her fascinator. Stuck in the petroleum jelly that held Stripper Barbie's Bourbon Street sign pole was a curved shard of glass.

From Ken Lanier's frozen southern milk punch.

10

———

"Well, I'm sorry, Miss Franki." Glenda turned to look at me from the passenger seat of Nadezhda's silver Jaguar. "But I still say the discovery of that shard of glass called for twerking."

Even the memory of Glenda's sit bone connecting with my eye socket was painful. "Not on the sewing machine table." I pressed the raw steak Nadezhda had brought me to my face and winced. "I'm lucky I didn't get a retinal laceration from your fringe too. Either way, now I'm going to stick out at the dinner, when I need to blend in."

Nadezhda grunted in the front seat. "You alvays shtick out."

Ironic, coming from a walking matryoshka doll with spiked maroon hair and a missing eye tooth. I turned my unobstructed eye to Glenda. "Speaking of sticking out, why is Nadezhda your date for the Murder Mystery Dinner?"

"Technically, she's not, sugar. She signed up to drive one of the float tractors."

"*Da.* Zey get tips."

I would've rolled my good eye, but I was too afraid the

injured one would roll with it. "So, I guess that baggy gray shorts jumpsuit is your tractor uniform?"

"*Nyet. Prozodezhda.*"

"Whatever you said sounds like a combination of your name and Prozac, which I'm in favor of." We all knew she could use a mood regulator.

Glenda smirked. "It means 'production clothing.' It was the Soviet alternative to the flapper dress."

And a fine example of why Communism failed. I tossed the steak onto the butcher paper on the seat to get cleaned up.

Nadezhda flashed her tooth hole in the rearview mirror. "Careful vit zat beef. I bleach and bring back to store."

A checklist materialized in my mind. 1. Don't grocery shop at the same store as Nadezhda. 2. Get my car fixed ASAP.

Glenda lowered her window and lit a cigarette in a silver holder.

"Could you please not smoke while I'm in the back seat?" I asked, cleaning my hands with a bacterial wipe. "I'd rather not have a repeat of what happened the time you loaned me that hoop skirt."

"Vhy? Vat happen?"

Glenda exhaled smoke. "Oh, some ash from my cigarette burned a hole in the thing. Because it was Shore Week, all the wannabe pirates called it a porthole."

I dabbed my face with a clean wipe. "And they kept trying to look through it."

"Zat sound like fun time." Nadezhda pulled up on the side of Muriel's. "You get out. Ve go park."

Glenda leaned over the seat. "If you see Bob, sugar, tell him I'm coming."

"Easy, Glenda. We've already got two murders. We don't need another at the Murder Mystery Dinner."

"I'm not going to *kill* him, Miss Franki. Just teach him a style lesson."

The very thing I was afraid of. I exited the Jag and yanked down Chandra's ex too-short shift dress. I was a victim of her style lessons, and so was my Mustang. I had a black eye, and some of the staples she'd used to attach fringe to my dress were scratching my skin. And thanks to an impromptu V-neck she'd cut in the bodice, I looked more like a flasher than a flapper.

Pulling the V closed, I stared down the tarot card readers, mimes, and tourists watching from Jackson Square. Then I summoned my dignity and went inside the restaurant.

Wanda was on her cell phone, and Marcella was talking to a bored hostess.

"That's Marcella, as in Mar-CHELL-a," she said, reinforcing her Italianness. She spotted me, and her smoky eyes sparkled. "Holy cannoli, Franki! Bradley's going to love that dress. But that eye," she grimaced, "not so much."

"This is work, so I didn't invite him." I pointed to my shiner. "And this was an accident."

Marcella reached into her bucket bag. "Hang on. I've got my eyeshadow palette, so I can match it."

Super. I'd look like a Roaring Twenties raccoon.

"Too bad about Bradley." She spread shadow on my eyelid. "Muriel's is a great place for a wedding reception—that is, if the Piazza d'Italia is already booked. It has a 170-foot wraparound balcony with views of Jackson Square."

Wanda hung up her phone. "Franki's not here to look for a wedding venue. We've got to find the maniac who stole my wigs and set me up." She pointed to the star on her black satin headband. "My headpiece is a shuriken, in case we need ninja-style protection."

Marcella's eyes grew shifty as she slipped the palette into her bag. "And the feathers in my headband have spear tips."

And I was wigged out by Wanda's *wigs*. "Where are the board members?"

"Around here somewhere." Wanda led us into the main seating area. "They're all wearing mirrored tan Art Deco dresses and matching opera gloves, so you can't miss them."

I scanned the twelve-foot ceilings and a second-floor walkway overlooking an indoor courtyard. "This place is almost as big as the float warehouse."

Marcella nodded. "For most of the 1900s, Muriel's was Taormina's. The first floor was an Italian grocery store and the second was a pasta factory."

Great. The Axeman of New Orleans selected his victims from Italian grocery stores, and that wasn't comforting post-death threat crashing through my windshield. But I was disappointed I'd missed the pasta factory. "The brick walls look so old."

"This building has existed in some form or other since the city was founded in 1718. According to Muriel's website, the original owner was Jean Baptiste d'Estrehan, the royal treasurer of the French Louisiana colonies." She glanced at the ceiling. "There are lots of ghosts here. They even set a table for one in the stairwell."

I was glad Chandra hadn't arrived yet. The so-called psychic had a serious ghost phobia. "Did I miss anything?"

"Not really." Wanda sat at a table. "Claudine thanked Honorine for picking the Roaring Twenties flapper theme and for donating her pralines for dessert. She told us dinner starts at nine and said we could gamble for krewe throws and have one whole free drink from the bar. Woohoo."

Marcella sat her bag on the table and pulled out a wad of bills with an image of the goddess head. "Make sure you get some of this 'Clotho Cash' they handed out earlier."

The fake money caught me by surprise. *Is this what Lou saw the women receiving at the float den? Clotho Cash for the Murder Mystery Dinner?*

If not, why were they being paid?

"Remember my slogan," Carl Cash said to an audience of men, loud enough for the tarot card readers, mimes, and tourists outside to hear. "Carl Cash will save you money."

"Oh, daddy!" Carly giggled beside him in a shocking pink Great Gatsby dress that clashed with her red hair. "You're all work and no play!"

Not entirely true given his regular status at Napoleon's Itch.

Wanda growled. "How did Carl get his doppelganger daughter on the board?"

I had the same question. "Either Carl and Clotho are swapping favors—Carly for the use of his cars—or they were in cahoots against Ken Lanier, and Marie-Fleur got caught in the crossfire."

Marcella sat beside Wanda. "I resented Marie-Fleur for Frenchifying my name, but I didn't want her dead. What do we do, Franki?"

"You two find out where Carl and Carly were during the Greasing of the Poles, and see if anyone knows where Ken's daughter, Tiffany, is living."

"Got it," Wanda said.

"Also," I tapped my nostril, "keep a nose out for anyone wearing Chanel No. 5."

Marcella did a double-sniff. "On it."

I left the table and headed for the indoor courtyard. There was no sign of the Russian dolls from the airport, but Honorine mingled with a group of guests who were quite wealthy judging from their diamond jewelry.

Anaïs and Claudine were talking alone at a corner table.

I meandered across the room to eavesdrop.

Claudine bolted upright, her face taut. Anaïs grabbed her

wrist, but she yanked her arm free and stormed toward the back of the building.

Anaïs retrieved a purple-sequined Fendi baguette and rose from the table.

This was my opportunity to strike up a conversation. "Hi, I'm Franki—"

Her green eyes savaged me. "You want to talk," she raised her aquiline nose, "you'll have to get past my lawyers."

My chin retracted as she stomped to the hostess stand. That was aggressive.

"*Psst*. Franki."

My head swiveled. The male voice was close, but there was no one near me.

The leaves of a plant parted, and a hand waved me over.

As I approached, I made out Bob—in a tan velvet tuxedo with satin shoes.

"Is Glenda with you?" he asked from behind the leaves.

"She and Nadezhda are parking, and then they're coming for you. She's wearing a headpiece from her new #strippercouture line, Hucci Cucci Hot Couture. And if I were you, I'd gush about how fabulous it is."

His face emerged from the plant. "I'll have to see it first. By the way, did you know 'hoochie coochie' comes from the French *hochequeue*, 'to shake a tail?' It's the name of a small bird that shakes its tail feathers. In English, it's known as the Willie Wagtail."

I was going to call Bob Willie Wag*tongue* if he didn't stop yammering about birds. "Listen—"

"In fact, I've been working on a costume line with derriere feathers. I was thinking about combining 'hochequeue' with 'haute couture' and calling it 'hauche couchure.' It sounds so elegant."

Honestly, it was as clunky as prozodezhda.

"The idea came to me after I did a feather-bustle costume for the Rockettes, and one of them called me the 'Houdini of hoochie coochie.'"

The man refused to grasp the danger he was in. "You've got to listen to me, Bob. If you don't make like Houdini and disappear, Glenda will do the hoochie coochie on your hood *and* your head."

He paled and released the foliage, vanishing like the magician.

Resuming my search for Claudine, I walked to the antique wooden bar at the back of the restaurant and scanned the guests —a bunch of blondes and an Albert Einstein lookalike nursing a martini. She wasn't in the adjoining ladies room, either. Unless there was a secret doorway, the only other option was the kitchen. I sat at the end of the bar by the entrance and waited.

A burly bartender slid a bowl of spiced popcorn in front of me. "Be right with you."

"What a surprise to find you on a barstool," Ruth drawled behind me.

I spun to face her and wished I hadn't. Ruth wore a flimsy flapper dress with her hair down around her shoulders, and her breasts down around her waist. All the booze at Muriel's couldn't erase that visual. Nevertheless, I spun back to the bar and tried to flag down the bartender.

Ruth sucked her teeth. "Where's Bradley? You offer him a ride and renege?"

"Can't talk now. I'm working." I popped popcorn into my mouth.

"At a party?" She harrumphed. "You always were a Min on the Fun Meter, but this is pitiful."

"If I'm a Min, you're a Mis for Miserable."

She leaned an elbow on the bar and stuck her tongue in her cheek. "For your information, missy, that's not what the dermatologists in The Cotillion Room upstairs think. They said I could put the 'fun' in 'funeral.'"

"More like the 'fun' in 'fungus.'"

"Since you mentioned it, that popcorn you're eating looks just like the cauliflower warts on the big toe of a guy on *Dr. Pimple Popper*." She smacked her lips and spun on her Keds.

And I coughed and chugged Albert Einstein's glass of water. "Sorry," I grumbled, wiping my mouth. "But that woman belongs on the Krewe of Medusa, not Clotho."

He let out a chortle. "Clotho might be appropriate."

I eyed him, intrigued. "How so?"

"Alister La Roche," he twisted the wiry hair on his eyebrow, "professor of classical mythology." He released his brow and held out his hand for a shake.

The brow-hair twist didn't inspire a desire for physical contact, but I obliged to be polite. "I'm Franki. What did you mean about Clotho being appropriate?"

"The goddess wasn't a good sort." He picked up his martini and took a sip.

"How can that be? She spins the thread of life."

"Indeed." He used a toothpick to try to spear an olive in his glass. "However, she forced Aphrodite to sleep with other gods."

"Meh." I was unimpressed. "From what I remember of my college mythology course, Mount Olympus was a swinging place. Sleeping around was common."

"As well as murder." He stabbed the olive.

My body tensed. "Why would you mention that?"

"Because Clotho was a poisoner. She poisoned the Titan Typhon."

The room spun as though I'd taken another spin on my barstool. *Is someone invoking the goddess in deeds as well as name?* If so, the killer was mentally unstable, which made them even more dangerous.

To get my bearings, I slid from my barstool and went rigid.

Claudine was watching me through the kitchen door window.

THE KITCHEN DOOR BLEW OPEN, and Claudine came out, her expression as dark as her under-eye circles. "Out of my way."

"Wait." I hurried after her. "Can we talk?"

She stalked through the restaurant, ignoring me as I followed. She'd probably discovered I was a PI, which would also explain why Anaïs had threatened me with lawyers.

But does it explain the iron with the threatening note thrown into my windshield?

What about the one at Clotho headquarters that Marie-Fleur never received?

Claudine rounded a corner.

And I ran into a barrel.

In a brown flapper dress.

Rosalie scrunched her football-coach face. "So, I was on my way home, and I thought, 'Rosalie Artusi, why was Franki in such a hurry to get rid of you before the Murder Mystery Dinner?'"

"Did you tell yourself—first and last name—that it's because you're a pain," I heaved, clutching my ribs and trying to regain the breath she'd knocked from me, "both literally and figuratively?"

"AAANNNHHH!"

"What was that?"

Rosalie jerked, shocked. "The wrong-answer buzzer from *Family Feud*, my favorite show."

"How telling."

"Yeah, just like you sending me packing. You did that to keep me from finding out you didn't invite Bradley to the Murder Mystery Dinner." She tapped my still-breathless chest. "Are you on the prowl for a hot blonde krewe member?"

My head dropped back. Her single-mindedness was singular, exactly like my mom and nonna's.

Chandra waddled up. "Rosalie told me about you. And to think I worried you'd go after Lou now that he's single."

As if I would hitch myself to a lifetime of Lou's toe shoes. "Y'all want to know why I didn't invite Bradley? Because I'm working, so I can't spend time with him. And if I don't have time for my fiancé, I sure as hell don't have time for you."

Chandra gasped. "So rude."

"She's always had a mouth, Chandra." Rosalie shook her Mike-Ditka mug. "From the time she was little."

"Brace yourselves, because my mouth is about to go off again." I leaned forward for emphasis. "You're not staying with me, so you'd better find a hotel."

"No need." Rosalie cupped her bosom and gave it a hoist. "I'm staying with Chandra. She also loaned me this dress." She ran her hands down her barrel sides. "Incidentally, the flapper style flatters my figure."

Chandra gave her bouffant a bump. "And she won't stretch it out."

Not in the bottom, anyway. "Why's she staying with you? You hardly know her."

"I'm nice that way. I lent you a dress, didn't I? And you repaid me by stretching it out." She gave the dress a going-over. "And whoring it up."

"Down, Chandra. Down." It was a correction and a command.

"Yo, Franki." Wanda waved to me from the hostess stand.

"I've gotta go, and so do you." I took a few steps and turned.

"But for the record, Chandra, that full moon toilet Lou installed proves I didn't stretch out your dress."

She gaped and pressed paddle nails to her chest. "The gall!"

Wearing a crescent-moon smile, I went over to Wanda.

"No luck finding out where Tiffany lives," she whispered, "but I did learn that Carl was at the Royal Sonesta during the Greasing of the Poles."

That was major news. "Was Carly there too?"

"I haven't been able to talk to her yet. She's my next objective."

Marcella rushed up, glanced from side to side, and pulled her hair curtain over her matte lips. "No one's wearing Chanel No. 5. I've sniffed every guest."

Not exactly discreet, but I might've misled her with the nostril tap.

"Before I forget," Wanda touched my forearm, "I met your landlady and her friend. Nadezhda is so charming."

My body jolted as though Rosalie had barreled into me again. "That's not possible. Are you sure you met the right Russian?"

"Of course." Wanda raised her chin. "She reminds me of my Polish mother."

I had no idea what to make of that, but I wondered whether Wanda's need to wear weaponry was somehow connected.

Claudine emerged with a champagne flute from a cordoned-off hallway. She was scowling and holding her right glove, which looked wet, as did the bodice of her dress. Then she slipped through a nearby door.

"Marcella," I pointed to the hallway, "what's that roped-off area?"

She rubbed her biceps. "The old Carriageway. It's rumored to be as haunted as the restaurant."

"Haunted?" Chandra shrieked, her phasmophobia in high gear.

I should've known she was eavesdropping.

"You hadn't heard?" Marcella flipped her hair. "Inside the door Claudine entered is a stairwell with a table set for the ghost of one of the building's former owners, Pierre Antoine Lepardi Jourdan."

Chandra did an imitation of her weird white handbag with the three round cutouts. "G-g-ghosts?"

"Mm-hm," Marcella hummed. "In the early 1800s, he lost this house in a poker game and took his life. But don't worry. He doesn't usually hang out at his table."

"Why not?" I asked, my tone facetious. "Does he prefer the bar?"

"Uh," her maroon-lined lips parted, "not when they leave him two glasses of red wine on the table and a basket of bread."

I shrugged. "Maybe he's into hard liquor and bar snacks."

"Don't be ridiculous, Franki. He's French-Italian."

She had a point. Both were notorious bread and wine cultures.

Marcella's smoky eyes glowed. "Jourdan's ghost is usually in the séance lounge upstairs. But he doesn't appear as a person— just a glimmer of sparkly light."

"Very disco. I'll be sure to say hello if I see him." I headed for the stairwell. "I'm going to try to talk to Claudine."

I opened the door and was greeted by the chanting of Gregorian monks. Beside the dark wood stairs was a nook with the infamous ghost table. Muriel's management had decorated the area with a blood-red curtain and an old floral chandelier. They'd also put a framed card on the table introducing patrons to Pierre Antoine Lepardi Jourdan.

Rosalie barged in with Chandra in tow. "That chanting is spooky."

I hadn't expected them to follow, and it was all I could do not to grab both of the ghost's glasses of wine and chug them. "That's the idea."

"Do we have to go up?" Chandra gripped my arm.

"As a matter of fact," I pried her paddle nails from my flesh, "you don't."

Rosalie, who'd already sampled the ghost's bread, looked at me and frowned. "I'm not letting you go upstairs alone."

"Oh? Afraid I'll hook up with a lesbian ghost?"

She exhaled and dropped a side-eye on Chandra. "There she goes with the mouth again." Then she heaved her head in my direction. "We both know your mother would kill me if I let something happen to you before she gets a grandchild."

Right. After that, I was expendable—a mythical time I'd been waiting for since I'd reached the so-called "marrying age."

"Fine, but stay out of my way."

I began climbing the stairs.

A pair of arms wrapped around my waist.

"Chandra," I extricated myself, "I'm not going to have a repeat of what happened at that plantation home."

I went up another step.

She latched onto me again.

Frustrated, I looked over my shoulder.

Rosalie had latched onto her.

"This is not a Conga line, all right?" I removed Chandra and pushed past them to the bottom of the stairs. "You two go first, and I'll follow."

"Coward," Rosalie said. Then she shoved Chandra up the stairs.

"Dear Gahd. Dear Gahd. Dear Gahd," Chandra said with each step.

Despite the monks' chanting and the medium's chattering, I heard a clatter outside the door and peered out.

Anaïs had knocked over one of the brass rope posts cordoning off the Carriageway. She looked behind her and proceeded down the hallway.

I tiptoed to the rope.

Anaïs exited onto the street.

On a whim, I entered the Carriageway. An unlit kerosene lamp hung from the ceiling, and flickering white candles on floor stands lined the centuries-old brick walls. My heels made scratching sounds as I walked the length of the paved stone floor and looked out a window.

Sallow Skin, the guy who'd ripped off my bumper at the airport, was holding open the door of a black BMW.

Anaïs got in.

He closed the door and returned to the driver seat.

The car sped away, but I caught the license plate—CSHCAR2.

What's going on with this guy and Carl Cash's cars?

Turning to head back, I saw Honorine wringing her gloved hands and staring at the overturned brass rope post. "Is everything okay?"

"Oh," she raised a hand to her updo but lowered it. "These events are stressful."

Honorine didn't pick up the post, so I did. "Yes, especially when one of your friends has been murdered."

Her diamond-shaped face convulsed, but she regained her composure. "I can't discuss that." Her voice was hushed, almost frightened. "It's not...wise."

My pulse picked up. "Why? Are you in danger?"

"Not here." She checked for bystanders. "Be at my house at noon tomorrow. 1134 Royal." She rushed into the restaurant.

Finally, I was going to get to talk to a board member. With any luck, I'd be able to question Claudine too.

I returned to the stairwell and ran up the steps, exiting onto the walkway overlooking the indoor courtyard. The chanting of the Gregorian monks was even louder on the second floor. The fact that I hadn't heard it downstairs was a testament to the size of the restaurant.

Hooking a left, I entered a hallway with gold-leaf wallpaper. I kept an eye out while I walked, not for Jourdan's ghost or even the killer, but for Ruth Walker and the dermatologists.

I exited onto the balcony. It was empty, and the view was haunting. A hazy mist surrounded a full moon the size of Chandra's toilet seat. St. Louis Cathedral was deceptively close to Muriel's. Its three iron Gothic spires seemed to stab the night, and the white stucco glowed in the moonlight, ghostlike.

My cue to leave. I retraced my steps to the walkway and turned right.

The chanting of the Gregorian monks grew louder. I passed a wrought-iron-gated room with a table surrounded by racks of wine bottles and entered a lounge bathed in red light with matching velvet rococo furniture and a painting of Marie Antoinette.

The source of the chanting came from an adjoining room, also aglow in red lighting. I stepped inside. "Must be the séance lounge."

To my right were two upright Egyptian mummy sarcophagi on either side of a small couch. The lounge was decorated with animal print furniture and plush brocade pillows, gilded mirrors, and silk floor lamps. On the walls were an old French poster and disturbing porcelain masks peeking from folds of draped cloth. Heavy red drapes in the middle of the room were closed, presumably for a séance.

I didn't believe in ghosts, but there was something creepy about the place.

Knocking erupted, and I glanced around, bewildered.

A ghost from beyond wanting to chat?

The sound was coming from one of the sarcophagi.

A mummy?

The fringe on my dress shook as my hand inched toward the gold pharaoh. I counted to three, opened the lid, and jumped back.

"Bob?"

He emerged and wiped sweat from his brow with a tan satin kerchief. "Glenda locked me inside after I mentioned that I was the Houdini of Hucci Cucci. She said, 'Let's see you do an escape trick,' and shoved me in."

"If I were you, I wouldn't mention that nickname around Glenda again. And if you do, I'd go with something humbler than Houdini."

"It's not like I pick the nicknames myself. I earn them based on my many talents."

Clearly, Bob wouldn't be taking the humble route. "Ohhh-kay then, next time make sure there aren't any trunks or lock boxes lying around."

"You bet your bottom dollar I will." Bob tucked the kerchief into his tux pocket. "At any rate, I'm glad you came along."

"Yeah, well, this isn't going to be an entry in my gratitude journal. I almost had a heart attack."

"Me too." He adjusted his bowtie. "I heard a woman scream a few minutes ago."

Chandra and Rosalie.

Where are they?

On autopilot, my body turned to the other sarcophagus. I wrenched open the lid, and my heart stopped.

Chandra was inside, eyes open. But she was stiff.

Mummified.

"Chandra, snap out of it!" I pulled her out. "How did you get in there?"

Her eyes stared straight ahead. "The devil."

Bob threw up his hands. "It was Glenda."

"This is Glenda's new tenant, Bob, so I seriously doubt that." I turned back to the mad medium and gave her a shake. "Chandra, who is the devil?"

"The third tarot card." Her speech was slow, entranced. "I remembered."

And I remembered the other two cards—The Hanged Man and Death.

A queasy sensation swirled in my belly. "Where's Rosalie?"

"The picture on the card," Chandra said, still in shock. "It's the devil holding a fiery torch and sitting on top of a black door. At his feet, a man and a woman are chained to that door by the neck."

Bob gripped her shoulders. "Is it me and Glenda? Dear God, how can I ever break free?"

"Calm down, Bob. Jeez." I used my arm to propel him backwards. "If anyone, the chained man and woman represent Ken Lanier and Marie-Fleur. Now help me—"

I stopped before I could say *find Rosalie.*

Because the séance lounge had been partitioned.

What's behind those curtains?

Or who?

As I gripped the blood-red curtains, a deathly fear gripped me. A cry came from my throat as I threw them open.

Claudine Denault sat in a red velvet armchair, beneath a painting of a woman playing the harpsichord at the French court. In front of her was a small table with a crystal ball, and next to it was her wet right glove. Her eyes were closed, but she wasn't communing with any spirits.

She was dead.

11

"A murder at a Murder Mystery Dinner." Veronica came from the office hallway with a Mr. Coffee pot and carried it to the lobby couch where I was laying. "It's unbelievable."

"It was unbelievable *before* Claudine's murder." I removed the ice pack from my black eye and sat up reluctantly, not only because of my bruised ribs, but because it was barely eight a.m., which was too early to be vertical. "After Marie-Fleur died, the Clotho board should've had the decency to cancel."

She poured coffee into the "Be nice to the PI" mug I'd bought as a message to Ruth—that clearly hadn't worked—and sat on the opposing couch. "And the police never found Claudine's champagne glass?"

"Not even after a thorough search. And none of the waiters working the private dining rooms saw her, so they didn't take it."

"If only Chandra had gotten a glimpse of the killer."

I dumped Baileys Caramel creamer into my coffee, fervently wishing they made a Nutella or King Cake version. "She was pushed into the sarcophagus from behind as soon as she went into the lounge. She managed to turn around before the lid closed but not in time to see the culprit."

Veronica poured herself a cup and put the pot on the coffee table. "Didn't you say Rosalie was with her? Surely she saw something."

"She did." I flashed a wry-lipped look. "A private dining room full of potentially eligible dermatologists for her doppelganger nieces. Ruth was on the prowl in there too." I angry-stirred my coffee. "Neither one of them made it to the séance lounge until after I found Claudine."

"That's too bad." Veronica sipped from her mug. "What are your next steps?"

"First, I'm going to Carl Cash Cars to check on my car—and Carl. Then I meet with Honorine at noon, and after that I'll try to find Ken Lanier's daughter, Tiffany. Most importantly," I pulled a plastic baggie from my purse, "I have to get this shard from Ken Lanier's glass to a forensics lab."

Veronica's jaw dropped, and her mug almost followed.

"Inside the Vaseline jar on Glenda's fascinator," I answered before she asked. "Know where I can get a quick analysis?"

"The quickest I know of is a couple of weeks, but I'll make some calls and see if I can get a faster turnaround time. Then I'm joining the Krewe of Clotho."

"Veronica—"

She held up a hand. "I'm well aware that you can handle this on your own. But when multiple murders are involved, I want to be with my best friend."

A swell in my chest threatened to flood my eyes. I missed having her as my neighbor, and just hanging out. "Having you on the case would be great."

Veronica squeezed my hand. "It'll be like old times. You and I on the case."

"And who knows?" I spread my arms in mock wonder. "As

long as Ruth isn't our float captain, we might even have some fun this Mardi Gras."

"She's not that bad, Franki."

"*Ha!*" I slapped my thighs to drive home the disbelief. "I don't know who The Devil represents on the tarot card Chandra drew during Marie-Fleur's reading, but I'll tell you this—if she'd drawn that card for me, The Devil would be Ruth. That demon woman's got me and Bradley chained to hell's door by our necks."

The door to Private Chicks opened, and Ruth entered, dowdy, dour, and devilish.

"Speak of The Devil tarot card," I said.

She slid on her cat-eye glasses. "What are you yammering on about that's not work related?"

"An ironic question when you consider that last night I was investigating a homicide while you were dallying with dermatologists." I raised my mug and took a suggestive sip.

Ruth stiffened and raised an index finger. "First of all, thanks to my so-called 'dallying,' I'm getting a suspicious-looking mole removed from my left breast scot-free." Her stance relaxed, and her jaw cocked at a jaunty angle. "Between us, I suspect the doctor wants to take a peek at both—the mole and the boob."

"Hm." Veronica's brow lowered. "I'm sorry to hear that."

I was too. The sip had soured in my mouth.

"And second," Ruth returned to her rigid posture and raised another finger like a Girl Scout reciting the Promise, "I put in extra hours at the Hotel Monteleone yesterday."

For once she had my interest. "Did you find out anything?"

"Certainly." Her eyelids rose to haughty heights. "I've got skills too, you know."

She did, just not the kind she thought.

Veronica looked from Ruth to me. "What's going on at the hotel?"

Ruth's stubbly chin drew up, smug. "The President of Clotho is staying there."

"Anaïs?" I put down my mug. "What makes you think that?"

"The front desk couldn't find a reservation in her name, but she was hanging around the Carousel Lounge. And right before the Murder Mystery dinner, she disappeared for twenty minutes and came back in her flapper dress. No way she went home and changed in that time."

Veronica shrugged. "She could've been staying with a friend. But so what if she has a room there? Lots of locals stay in hotels during Mardi Gras so they don't have to drive."

"Sure," I leaned back against the couch cushions, "but Ruth overheard a Clotho board member threatening another on the phone, saying she'd expose what she's up to at the Hotel Monteleone."

"The little devil had her back to me," Ruth growled, "so I don't know who she is."

Her choice of words brought The Devil card front and center. Whoever was on the phone outside the float den was probably the killer, and the fact that she climbed into a hearse with a U R NEXT license plate seemed to prove it.

But am I next?

"Yoohoo, Franki." Veronica waved her hand. "Happy Hour at the Monteleone?"

I shook my head, casting off my concerns. "That'll be one of the more enjoyable tasks on my to-do list."

Ruth eyed the clock and grabbed some papers from her desk. "As fun as it's been showing you up, Ace PI, I've got a to-do list of my own to get to in Bradley's office before float-loading begins tonight."

"Ugh." I put my face in my hands. "I forgot about that."

Ruth blasted the Get Busy Buzzer, and I jumped, jostling my ribs.

"Get off your behind and find the murderer," she shouted on her way out.

Clutching my side, I pushed up from the couch. "Ruth's lucky she left, or I wouldn't have to look for the murderer, because that would be me."

"Franki," Veronica's tone held a warning and worry, "what are you going to do?"

"What you told me to do—keep a gratitude journal." I grabbed the blasted buzzer, tossed it on the floor, and stomped on it. Then, with a flourish, I opened the door and threw it down the stairwell. "There. Now I have something to write about."

A corner of her mouth rose. "Well, I *am* glad to hear you're using the journal."

"You know, I can honestly say that it's been helpful."

As I returned to the couch, the door flew open halfway, but a hand stopped it from slamming into the wall.

Veronica sighed. "David."

He tiptoed in, followed by The Vassal. "Sorry," he said, sheepish, "I'm kinda wound up because we almost got hit by a tiny UFO in the stairwell just now."

My lips wrinkled, repressing a laugh. "Maybe it was a mini Star Trek Enterprise, checking for those pesky tribbles."

"Uh, no." His eyes shifted to The Vassal, as though I was the geek. "It looked like a Learning Resources toy I had when I was a kid."

I'd never heard of such a thing, which explained why he was a computer whiz, and I wasn't. On the flip side, neither one of them had figured out that the UFO was Ruth's buzzer.

The Vassal removed his backpack. "We're still trying to get the Royal Sonesta video of the Greasing of the Poles. We requested it from their security team, but they have to get the approval of hotel management."

"If they refuse, hack into their computer system."

He pushed up his glasses. "I would enjoy that immensely."

"Question for you." I retrieved the plastic bag from the table. "Know anyone at Tulane who could test this glass shard today for traces of poison?"

"Um," David flipped his bangs to the side, "a fellow ChewbacchanALIEN could probably do it. He's a grad student in Chemistry."

The Vassal nodded. "He owes us a favor."

"That settles it," I gushed before he could elaborate. I had no desire to know what kind of favors ChewbacchanALIENs did for one another. "Guard that shard with your lives."

David took the bag and stuffed it into his backpack. "No one's going to mess with us. We have our Chewbacchus bowcasters."

That's exactly why they're going to mess with you, I thought, but I kept my mouth shut. "I need to get going." I grabbed my jacket from the coatrack. "Text me if you run into any issues."

As I headed downstairs, one of my ribs ached with each step. I got to the street, and my foot flew out from under me. Flailing my arms, I fell onto my tailbone. A jolt went up my spine, and I went flat.

The pain knocked the breath from me, and my sight.

When the darkness cleared, I rolled my head to one side and saw the culprit.

Ruth's busted Get Busy Buzzer.

I turned to the sky.

Why?

"Aw, hon." A thirtyish blonde in a purple bullet bra and orange fuzzy coat leaned over me with a Hand Grenade. "I've been flat on my back in the Quarter more times than I can count."

"Girl, me *too*." A brunette in a fishnet dress and faux fur wrap came into my line of vision. She huffed out a boozy breath and hiked the strap of her bag over her shoulder. "Let's get you up."

I wasn't sure whether they'd ended up on their backs from falling down drunk or from their profession, but I let them slide their arms around me and pull me up. "Appreciate it, ladies."

"You be careful, hon." Purple Bullet Bra shot me a look as pointed as her triple D cups. "It's rough out here."

I was well aware. Pressing my hand to my lower back, I took a couple of steps and clenched my teeth. My coccyx was crying.

Bradley rounded the corner, and concern flickered across his face. "Franki, are you all right?" He put his arm around my waist. "What happened to your eye?"

"Uh..." I had so many injuries that I had to think back. "Glenda's sit bone."

His head cocked, as though he couldn't quite figure that one out. "First your car, now this. What's going on between you two?"

"Her ex #strippercouture designer, Bob Simpson."

Bradley smirked. "Am I to assume that Bob's the reason we haven't looked for a wedding venue?"

"What?" I asked, before I realized he was joking—and maybe a tad hurt. "No, I—"

"Hey, so I've been thinking." His other arm slid around my waist, and he looked into my eyes. "Since you went to college in Austin, how about The Driskill? We could go this weekend. Get away."

"I'd love that." I caressed his cheek. "But the way this case is going, I'm afraid to leave town. Wanda could be in danger, and maybe Marcella."

His kissed my forehead. "I have a confession to make—I heard about Claudine on the news this morning and wanted to get you out of town. Are you any closer to solving this thing?"

Sighing, I rested my head on his chest. "I'm working on it.

I'm on my way to Carl Cash Cars to check on my Mustang and ask him some questions."

"That's funny. As I was driving here just now, I passed Carl and a couple of blondes in mink coats."

My head popped up. That sounded like the Russians from the airport. "Where did you see them?"

"Going into Nadezhda's place."

Lucky's Liquor and Waxing?

"SHAKE DAT BOOTY, BABY," a young guy yelled from a speeding Corvette.

"No one asked for your input," I shouted, squeezing the strap of my hobo bag. *Jerk.* So rude to comment on a woman's body, especially when it reminded her, i.e. me, of Chandra's stretched-down shift dress.

Hiking my bag over my shoulder, I continued up North Rampart Street, wishing I'd taken Bradley up on his offer of a ride. As it turned out, you couldn't walk off a tailbone injury. From the way I was swinging my hips, you'd have thought I was dancing the Hoochie Coochie.

Finally, I arrived at the two-story liquor store slash apartment Nadezhda had inherited from her late husband. The wooden building leaned harder to the right than the last time I'd seen it, but the blue paint was still peeling. The only change was that the Lucky's Liquor and Life Insurance sign had been replaced with a new one.

Lucky's Liquor and Vaxing.

"You'd think the sign maker would've said something." Although, maybe they'd assumed Nadezhda sold booze and vaccinations.

I opened the glass door, and a bell rang.

Despite the new sign, the interior of Lucky's was the same. Dingy and cramped with a maze of aisles with liquor stacked almost to the low ceiling. But I *did* detect a whiff of cheap perfume among the familiar stench of mold and sour milk.

Is it from the Russian dolls?

I made my way to the cash register and found a cardboard note on the counter.

You vait. I vax in back.

"God. No wonder the store is empty." My head turned to the door to the backroom where Nadezhda did her waxing. *Surely Carl isn't in there with the women.*

Not wanting to know but needing to find out, I tiptoed to the door and pressed my ear to the wood.

Silence.

A scream.

My hand went to my mouth, but my mind to another body part.

Angry Russian ensued—in a voice not unlike Nadezhda's Natasha-from-*Rocky-and-Bullwinkle* version.

At least one of the dolls was in there, but I could hardly crash a waxing session.

The bell over the door rang.

A security mirror in the corner showed a fortyish male in an Atlanta Falcons cap, a Miami Dolphins shirt, and a New Orleans Saints jacket.

While I waited for the Russians, I browsed the soda and snacks area for Hubig's pies, a local favorite that had recently returned after a ten-year absence. But it was as though I'd entered an alternate universe. Cucumber Sprite. Lay's sour cream and white mushroom potato chips. Snickers with sunflower seeds. "What's next?" I muttered. "Cabbage-flavored Doritos?"

The fickle football fan entered my aisle, grooving to a silent tune. He saw me and stopped dead. "You lookin' for dem Hubig's pies?"

His intuition was uncanny. "How could you know that?"

"Your body language. It's all de*jected.*"

Granted, I *was* in sad shape from the injuries, which might've made me seem depressed. *But was my body language so explicit that it said I wanted a fried hand pie?*

"I got my ice cream all ready, and I ain't even got me a Hubig's yet. Dem pies come in, and dey gone." He pointed a bag of beef jerky at me, and his eyes widened. "You got ta *git* here."

"Uh, I'll do better next time."

He gave a wary nod, as though doubting my pie commitment, and resumed shopping.

A door opened and shut, so I rushed to the cash register.

Nadezhda was at the counter in a silver sequin snake-print dress and gray smock with her company slogan. "Vhat you vant?"

Before I could answer, the Russian dolls emerged from the backroom in furs and white silky lingerie. As they strutted to the counter in thigh-high boots, their stares were colder than a Siberian snowstorm.

The taller of the two handed a wad of cash to Nadezhda, who shoved it into her bra instead of the register. Rapid-fire Russian ensued between the women. It sounded angry, but I didn't need to be Fickle Football Fan to read their relaxed body language.

In the midst of their chatter, I made out the word *sissy.* "You're sisters?"

"Nyet." The tall doll sneered. "Her is sissy." She raised her nightie and pointed to her very bare lady part.

She might as well have thrown a bowl of cold borscht in my face.

The three Russians erupted in Kalashnikov rounds of laughter. Then they each picked up a cardboard box full of liquor and left.

But I stood statue-like, not because I'd been flashed, but because they'd actually come in for liquor and waxing.

Nadezhda leaned an elbow on the counter. "You vant vax?"

"No, I want to know who those women are. And did you catch why they're in town? Or where they're staying?"

She sucked her eyetooth hole. "Vhat you buy?"

The penny-pinching, sissy-waxing, Cucumber-Sprite-peddling Communist was also an extortionist. I scanned the bottles on the shelf behind me, picked Tuaca, and handed her a twenty. "Okay, so who are they?"

"Sasha."

"Both of them?"

"Da."

"Did they mention the Krewe of Clotho or Mardi Gras?"

"Nyet."

From the sound of things, the price of the Tuaca didn't warrant multi-word sentences. "Well, I saw them at the airport with a Clotho board member who died last night, so I need to find out everything I can about them."

"Zey not killers. Zey whores."

The response wasn't a surprise. "How do you know?"

"Come on. You a man."

My fingers wrapped around the neck of the Tuaca bottle—as opposed to hers. "Get this through your thick, maroon-spiked head, I'm a woman, tall and somewhat big boned. And if it comes up in a conversation with Chandra, I didn't stretch out her damn shift dress. I stretched it down."

"*Hyeh!* You hang noodles on ears."

"What is that? An ethnic slur? Or a Russian expression?"

Fickle Football Fan grooved to the counter with the beef

jerky and a soda. "She's translating literally. We say, 'you're pulling my leg.'"

He wasn't only a body language expert, he knew the Russian language too. And because he'd joined the discussion, I side-stepped the issue of my gender and focused on the Russians. "Maybe the Sashas are pushers instead of prostitutes."

"Zen vhy get vax?"

Fickle Football Fan jutted out his lower lip. "Could be a personal preference."

I considered telling him to butt out, but in light of the Hubig's pie incident, I valued his insight. "What did they buy? Matrioshka vodka?"

Nadezhda's eyes narrowed to the width of a nail file. "Zat a stereotype."

"Hate to say it," Fickle Football Fan tucked his chin, "but she's right about dat."

"Fine. Then what kind of alcohol was it?"

She tugged at a maroon hair spike. "Matrioshka vodka."

"Go figure." I smacked my lips and deposited the Tuaca on the counter, in case I was tempted to turn it into a weapon for a future Wanda wig. "Did they say what they were going to do with all that vodka?"

"Have party at Monteleone."

"Oh, yeah. Dey whores." Fickle Football Fan's face fell, and he hung his head. "Ladies, let me rephrase dat. I shoulda said 'hookers.' De high-class type."

Judging from the flashing I'd received, not so much. But even if the Russian dolls *were* prostitutes, that didn't explain their connection to Claudine. Or to a used car salesman. "What happened to Carl Cash, the man they were with? Bradley drove by and saw him with the Sashas."

"He leave. But offer sveet deal on used van."

"Hey, now." Fickle Football Fan leaned in. "You think I could get a sweet deal on a used Mercedes?"

Despite his choices in football teams, I liked the guy. But I drew the line at letting him hone in on my twenty, because Nadezhda could bleed me dry faster than the Krewe of Clotho. "Um, excuse me," I huffed, brows hiked, "if you're going to ask her questions, you have to buy something the same way I did."

"Cain't argue wit dat logic." He pulled a few dollar bills and a handful of change from his pocket and began counting it.

I picked up the Tuaca. "Nadezhda, what do you know about this liqueur?"

Fickle Football Fan eyed the bottle. "It's made by the Sazerac Company. Their headquarters is here in Metairie."

"No, I mean, does it cause any adverse reactions when mixed with medication?"

"Vat zis look like?" Nadezhda gestured to a liquor shelf. "Pharmacy?"

In my defense, the "vaxing" on the sign lent itself to one. "No, but—"

"Booze is poison. You not know zat?"

Fickle Football Fan held up his soda. "Why d'you think I'm gettin' dis Cucumber Sprite?"

I had no way to answer that question. Not only was soda unhealthy, Sprite with cucumber was inexplicable.

But I had an idea how to answer the one about the Russian dolls' involvement with Carl Cash. The problem was, it was going to cost me.

More than I'd paid Josephine the Go-Between for the throw package.

And maybe my life.

12

———————

Nadezhda's Jaguar veered to the right, jolted, and bounced, knocking my battered body around the trunk like a spare tire.

"Where are we going?" I shouted into my cell phone. "Carl Cash Cars is straight down the street."

"Too many traffic," Nadezhda replied from her phone inside the Jag. "I take shortcut."

Most people would complain about the traffic, but she sounded as content as a comrade at a vodka and caviar party, which furthered my suspicion that she was taking me for a ride —in both senses of the phrase. "How is there a shortcut when the dealership is a block away?"

"I drive in park."

"As in, Louis Armstrong Park?"

"Vhat you tink? I drive vit car in Park gear?"

My mood turned as black as the trunk. This ride from hell was already no walk in the proverbial park, and her sarcastic tone didn't help. "Vhat I tink is, you're going to get arrested before I even make it onto the car lot. And per our agreement, you have to help me sneak into Carl's office, or the deal is off."

"No vorry. I handle pigs. I make *kholodets*."

My gut lurched at the mention of the Russian meat gelatin. I wasn't sure what she was getting at by bringing up the dreadful dish, but I *was* sure it rattled my already frayed nerves. Even though she denied it, I still suspected that her pigs' feet kholodets had killed her husband, Lucky.

The car hit a bump, and I hit my head, which was par for the course. Using my feet and arms, I braced myself for more trunk turbulence and a serious case of carpet burn. I regretted asking for Nadezhda's help infiltrating Carl Cash Cars, both for my well-being and that of my wallet. The penny-pinching Communist had extorted a down payment on a van for Lucky's, which, like the two-thousand dollar throw package, was a hefty expense I couldn't pass on to Wanda.

The car wrenched left, bounced hard a couple of times, and jerked to a stop.

Jaguar is a misnomer. This car rides like a dinosaur.

"Ve here." Nadezhda's voice had turned conspiratorial, as if we were plotting a break-in at the Pentagon rather than a used car dealership. "Remember, keep tail up like gun."

All I could think of was my injured tailbone, and the only person it was capable of hurting was me. "Is that Russian for 'keep your chin up' with a weapon thrown in?'"

"It mean, 'stay positive.' Vhy you so violent?"

"Oh, and 'keep your tail up like a gun' isn't?"

She made a spitting sound and hung up.

Hopefully, she'd spat out the window. Either way, the trunk was looking better and better.

The Jag's engine shut off.

Motionless, I waited for Nadezhda to enact our plan to lead Carl to the far end of the lot, near the Service Center.

My phone vibrated.

A text from Rosalie.

I'm sending these to your poor mother. She has a right to know.

"Right to know about what?" I scrolled down.

My head rose up, and my stomach seized as though I'd eaten a platter of kholodets—the original version made with the severed head of a sheep with newly brushed teeth.

The "these" Rosalie referred to were two pictures.

One of me in the arms of the scantily clad women who'd helped me up outside Private Chicks.

And the other of me staring at what was underneath the Russian doll's skirt.

My head dropped back and hit a tire iron. Biting my lip to keep from crying out, I rubbed my skull. All the bumps and bruises I'd sustained in this case would be nothing compared to the verbal concussion I'd get from my mom and nonna when they saw the sexy snapshots.

How I'd missed Rosalie tailing me was a mystery. The Wrecking Ball wasn't exactly subtle. Or small. But regardless, I had to stop her from sending those pictures.

My fingers began typing a plea.

"We meet again, little lady."

Carl's voice slid down my spine like a viper, and I dropped the phone. My eyelids squeezed shut, and I prayed he hadn't heard the thump.

"Da. I come for sveet deal."

"My salesmen are busy with other customers, so I get to show you these beauties all by my lonesome. I'm one lucky fella."

My eyes opened and took a hard roll. Carl was hard to stomach, so I was glad Nadezhda had to deal with him. And it was a lucky break that she was wearing snake print. Carl might not be into women, but the serpent was his spirit animal, and Nadezhda was nothing if not reptilian.

The Jaguar door opened and slammed.

"I vant van. Vit slogan."

"I'm fond of a fine slogan myself," Carl drawled. "And Carl Cash can certainly save you pennies on the van and the paint job."

Pennies? Is that the so-called 'sveet deal?' I'd say this for Carl—he was an honest con man. And his emphasis on pennies was further proof that he and Nadezhda would make perfect business partners. In fact, the "waxing" in Nadezhda's business name lent itself to the human body and automotive vehicles.

"Let's mosey over to a little Volkswagen vixen over yonder."

My tongue stuck out to make way for vomit.

Heels struck the pavement with a rhythmic scrape.

Carl's snakeskin cowboy boots.

The footsteps faded, and I grasped a rope we'd tied to the inside of the trunk lid. Then I pressed the emergency release and let the lid open a few inches. No one was around, so I climbed out, mentally thanking Carl for popping out of a trunk during my previous visit to the lot. If the scheme succeeded, I owed it to him.

I opened the door to the showroom. The salesman wasn't at his desk, but the cockroach still was. I tiptoed past the desk to a tiled hallway. Carl's office was obvious from the nameplate—Head Honcho.

The door was unlocked, so I slipped inside. The room was small but furnished with a supersized desk and chair, probably a reflection of the overinflated ego of their owner. Sunlight streamed through a window, lighting up pictures on the walls. Almost all of them featured Carl with a cigar and, despite what the COCKtail had said about all the fine women frequenting the dealership, lots of men. Customers, maybe.

Or maybe not.

Starting with the desk, I opened the drawer. Pens, a Hubig's pie, and a pistol.

What would Fickle Football Fan say about my body language now?

In a desk cabinet, I found a stack of *GQ* magazines, which Carl undoubtedly bought only for the articles, and a legal-sized Manila envelope with dates penciled on the front. I looked inside, and my eyes popped.

Tens of thousands of dollars.

Cash from car customers? I pulled out a stack of bills, and a few fluttered to the floor. All hundreds.

And a Clotho Cash note.

How'd you get in the envelope? I knelt to pick it up. The goddess on the front of the fake money meant one thing. The krewe had paid Carl for something.

The cars and driver?

The Russian dolls' services?

Drugs?

Or something I hadn't yet thought of?

Heels hit the tile hallway—with a slow scrape.

Carl.

Adrenaline flooded my body.

There was nowhere to hide.

I shoved the envelope into the cabinet and opened a window. Already out of time, I threw myself out, torso first. My foot caught on the windowsill, and I landed on my shoulder, swallowing a shout.

This case wasn't merely costing me, it was killing me.

Leaving the window up, I limp-ran around the corner to the Jaguar. With my good arm, I popped the trunk, climbed in, and pulled it closed.

And breathed a sigh of relief.

Until I heard the heels and the scrape.

Coming toward the Jaguar.

Closer.

And closer.

Until the footsteps stopped at the trunk.

My lungs ceased to breathe.

"Funny how you found Claudine's body." Carl's drawl spread through the trunk like venom through veins. "You've got a knack for that."

Silence ensued, but no heel scrape.

Carl hadn't left.

Is he going to open the trunk?

More importantly, does he have his pistol?

"But a word to the wise, Ms. Amato—I wouldn't find another."

"Where *were* you when Carl was threatening me?" I shouted the second Nadezhda opened the trunk outside Willie's Chicken Shack.

"Don't make scene," she said as I stepped onto the sidewalk.

"How is that possible right now?" Although, a woman with a black eye emerging from a trunk was probably not an uncommon sight on Canal Street. Case in point, not a single Willie's customer even looked up from their chicken tenders. "You haven't answered my question."

"I sign van contract." Her lips slid into a satisfied sneer. "Got sveet deal."

"Let me guess, you saved pennies."

"Da. You pay only two tousand dollar."

"*Two tousand dollar?*" My stomach joined the long list of my aches and pains. "We agreed a grand, max."

She pulled a Tic-Tac box from her bra. "I make double payment. Get free mints."

The penny-pinching Communist spent an extra grand of my money for free mints?

"You mean *I* get free mints." I tried to pry the box from her fingers, but she had the steel grip of a Soviet revolutionary's clenched fist. And I had a sore shoulder and wrecked ribs.

She flashed her eyetooth hole. "You veak."

"I'm injured."

"I give vone."

"So generous." Nevertheless, I took the two-thousand-dollar Tic-Tac because I had a bad taste in my mouth. "All I know is, Carl Cash had better fix my bumper."

Nadezhda scowled at the trash and cigarette butts littering the sidewalk. "Vhy you vant to come here?" She caught sight of the liquor store, and her spikes shot up. "You go to rival for booze?"

"No, I've got to see a rooster about a snake."

"Sound like crazy English expression."

The Russian was one to talk.

Before I went into Willie's to find the COCKtail, I checked my phone to see if Rosalie had replied to my text.

And I swayed like the drunks outside the Liquor Store.

When Carl's serpentine voice interrupted my texting, I stopped at *Rosalie, do* instead of *Rosalie, don't.*

And somehow I'd sent the message.

Now I was certain she'd texted those suggestive pictures to my mother, whose silence was screaming.

The COCKtail danced out of Willie's doing a pelvic-thrust move.

We all got the word play with his name and the "New Orleans Stiffest Drink" on his costume, but seriously?

Nadezhda pointed. "No fair. Liquor Store guy have free Villie's mascot."

"What are you whining about? You got my two-thousand-dollar Tic Tacs."

"I vant mascot."

For a Communist, she was surprisingly greedy. "What of? A woman with bikini wax strips holding a booze bottle?"

"Nyet. Matrioshka for vodka. But zat not bad idea."

To be honest, neither was a matrioshka mascot.

"I go inside. Give Liquor Store guy piece of mind."

The poor man had no idea what he was in for. Nadezhda was a live wire in a Molotov cocktail.

A couple of young women passed by in strappy heels and miniskirts.

The COCKtail made like his slogan. "*Mm, mm, mm.* Here chicky, chicky."

This rooster was cocky. At least the Dancing Hand Grenade didn't talk.

He started popping, a funky street dance that made his rooster comb vibrate.

It was almost time for me to head to Honorine's, so I went over to the dirty drink. "I don't have time to dance, so I'll get to the point—I need everything you didn't tell me about Carl Cash, starting with the fine women."

"Aw, *fff!*" He flapped his arms and kicked a black-and-white Adidas. "You a cop?"

"A PI, and three people are dead, so don't yank my tail, *capisci?*"

"The COCKtail takes tail very serious." He touched his giant shades. "And after de scare you gave me, I'm a bit parched. If I'm gonna talk, I'm gonna need me a bottle o' whiskey to wet my throat."

And I was going to need me a part-time job to cover the costs of this case. I handed him a twenty. "Now spill."

"Let's make it a double."

Hot air whooshed from my nose as I handed him another bill. The COCKtail needed to lay off the booze.

"Awrite, so last week when I was making a delivery to de dealership, a Cash Car pulled up, and a woman in de back handed Carl an envelope o' cash."

I was willing to bet the two-thousand-dollar Tic Tacs that it was the envelope I'd found in Carl's desk. "Did you see the money?"

"No, but he gave me a tip from dat envelope. A Franklin too."

"And you don't know what it was for?"

"I'm a casual COCKtail, hence de shades. I don't ask no questions. But I seen her before, one o' dem lookalike blondes leaving from Clotho headquarters over dere."

Probably a board member. "She wasn't Russian, was she?"

"How should I know? We didn't have no conversation."

It was hard to believe him with that nefarious sneer plastered on his beak, but to his credit, he'd told me about the envelope. "Have you ever seen a hearse around here or at the dealership?"

"A hearse?" His padded yellow hand made the sign of the cross.

"You're Catholic?"

"Yes, ma'am. You're looking at a Catholic COCKtail. You got a problem wit dat?"

"Actually, I do. That drink is red wine, not a phallic-shaped rooster full of vodka."

"God don't judge."

He might if he saw the COCKtail's costume. "Do you know whether Carl or the woman have any business at the Hotel Monteleone?"

"If dey do, it ain't none of mine. Now I got to go. I got a job to do, and I can't be seen talkin' to no PI."

More like he had booze to buy.

The raunchy rooster strutted toward a group of women in feather boas. "Yo, chicks! Wanna be part of my flock?"

The COCKtail was a male chauvinist, but I had to admire his confidence.

My phone vibrated. The number to my parents' deli.

I'd sooner join the COCKtail's flock than answer that call. Besides, I needed to tell Nadezhda I was leaving. I headed toward the Liquor Store and caught Josephine the Go-Between sneaking around the corner. She wore a headscarf and dark sunglasses with a trench coat, possibly to evade protesters.

Or someone else?

"Hey, Josephine." I jogged over to her.

She gripped her lapels and continued walking. "I don't have time to chat. If you need help with something, call the office."

"Actually, I wanted to ask if you have a last-known address for Ken Lanier's daughter, Tiffany?"

The Go-Between stopped and got in my face. "Even if I were willing to give you that information, which I'm not, it wouldn't do you any good. That flake moves from house to house like a trashy vagabond."

"That's harsh. She's a human being."

"Life is harsh." Josephine huffed the word, lingering on the *sh*. And for a brief moment, the rage on her heavily made-up face belied all the work she'd done to hide her age. "The world of Mardi Gras krewes is no different."

"Not everyone can be born into the elite social circle of the Clotho board."

The anger disappeared from her mouth, and her brows knit, as much as they could post surgical lift.

"What's going on, Josephine? If you can't tell me, go to the police."

She squeezed my wrist with the force of someone much younger than her seventy-something years. "You listen to me.

Where there is big money, lives are at stake. If you want to save yours, quit the krewe and stick to your own kind."

"Is that a threat?"

Josephine cast my wrist aside. "Free advice."

So she said. But as I watched her leave, I was certain it was the second time I'd been threatened that day.

Nadezhda came out of the Liquor Store, and a couple of young thug types pointed at her maroon spikes and howled.

She spat through her eyetooth hole at their feet.

They scattered.

Nadezhda rolled up to me looking very matrioshka mascot, except for the silver sequin snakeskin print. "You tank me. I do favor."

After the double-down-payment incident at the dealership, I doubted the favor would make my gratitude journal. "What? You opened a store credit account in my name?"

"Nyet. But not bad idea."

Also not a bad idea to keep my mouth shut.

"I ask Liquor Store guy about Tuaca."

My nostrils flared, smelling a setup—and some delicious Willie's biscuits. "What'd he say?"

"He tink like me. All liquor is poison."

And there you have it.

Her eyes narrowed to reptilian slits. "Most poison when guy in hearse buy."

My body went as cold as a corpse. The airport, the float den, and a liquor store—to get a liqueur used in the krewe's signature drink. I had to find out what was going on with that funeral coach, and there was one man who could help.

At a City of the Dead.

"Can you drop me off at the Saint Cecilia Cemetery?"

"Vhat for?"

"I have to see a man about a hearse."

~

"HIDEY-HO, FRANKI." The crypt keeper popped out of a mausoleum.

And I almost fell over and died right there at the cemetery. The shock of seeing a live human come from a crypt was too much, as was his merry demeanor. Apart from his long-sleeved shirt and cargo shorts, he reminded me of the Santa-on-a-gondola ornament I'd gotten Ruth in Venice—a jolly strapping St. Nick complete with beard, but in an entirely unexpected environment. "Hey there, Phil."

He pulled the mausoleum door closed with a bang. "It's been an eternity since we've seen you at Saint Cecilia."

The "eternity" reference wasn't comforting, especially because the mausoleum was topped with a sculpture of an enormous crouching skeleton that beckoned to the living with a bony hand. And neither was the "we" because he was talking about the cemetery residents. "Yeah, I don't have much business here."

He flashed a toothy grin. "Not yet."

I'd set myself up for that macabre message.

"Care to join me for a bite?" Phil retrieved a pick axe from the side of the tomb.

Unnerving. "Gosh, I can't," I said, and it was true. My stomach had slammed shut along with that mausoleum door.

"You sure? I have aged ricotta and *sanguinaccio*."

The mention of the Italian blood sausage drained the blood from my face. "You go ahead. But if you don't mind working on your break, I'd like to pick your brain—" My eyes went to the axe. "I mean, ask you something."

"I'd be delighted. Please, follow me to the office."

We walked along one of the mausoleum walls that enclosed the cemetery, and I focused my gaze on the pathway. I knew from my last visit that rotting coffins—and their residents—were occasionally visible behind the walls' deteriorating doors. But I did notice that a *For Sale by Owner* sign had been removed from a crumbling crypt. "I see this one sold."

Phil looked over his shoulder. "No, but we got a renter." His eyes sparkled Santa style. "A ten-year lease."

I had questions about that, but I didn't want the answers.

We arrived at the caretaker building. Phil opened the door, bowed, and gestured for me to enter, still holding the pick axe. "Ladies first."

With grim resignation, I went in and took a seat in a rickety chair that might've been made from coffin wood. His "office" was the size of the mausoleum he'd exited and no less uninviting. The décor was a fusion of armory and antique bookstore with taxidermy touches to complete the look.

He sat at a desk and rolled up his sleeves, revealing a tattoo of a cat in pajamas that went with the bees on his exposed knees. "I see you're engaged. Who's the lucky stiff? Wesley Sullivan?"

My stomach lurched. I could have laid down and died at the reference to my old nemesis—and the expression. "The detective passed away."

"Sorry to hear that. Where's he buried?"

"I'm not sure." I said, neglecting to explain that the detective was technically missing.

"Don't watch much news, I'm afraid. This job is 24/7, so I'm usually here with the residents of Saint Cecilia. And their lips are sealed as tightly as their tombs." He whacked off a slice of blood sausage.

And I almost leapt from my skin.

"Sure I can't tempt you with a bite? Made this myself from a critter rooting around the graves. I relocated him a few times, but he kept coming back, the little devil."

I shuddered—for so many reasons. But the mention of the devil shook me hardest. The Satanic figure recalled Detective Sullivan, the tarot card Chandra had drawn for Marie-Fleur, and the *chevals-diable* grave grasshoppers Phil told me about the first time I'd come to Saint Cecilia.

"Are you all right, Franki? You're as pale as a corpse."

My hand went to my face, and I imagined the bony version on the mausoleum skeleton. "Oh, spaced out for a second."

"Anyways, can't say I blame the critter for returning. Who could give this up?"

My lips mustered a jerk. A smile was asking too much.

"So what's the reason for your visit? Are you in the market for a burial site? If so, we've got a darling crypt coming open soon."

"As tempting as that is," I said, "I'm not here to shop. I came to ask if you could help me find the owner of an old hearse with unregistered plates, U R NEXT."

Phil rose. "You never know, do you?"

I shook my head. Not with a death threat hanging over me— and a creepy crypt keeper with a cleaver and a penchant for blood sausage and taxidermy.

He pulled a book from a shelf and returned to his seat. "Any idea of the make and model?"

"Maybe the 1960s? It has S-shaped scrolls where rear side windows would be."

"Landau bars, a decorative nod to the mid-18th century German carriage of the same name." He twisted his moustache. "A touch of Old-World funerary elegance."

"Y-yes."

"My personal favorite is the 1970 Cadillac Superior Crown Sovereign Funeral Coach." He opened the book and tapped a picture. "It came in a color called 'Romanade gold' and the top was black crinkle." He kissed his fingertips. "*Bellissimo!*"

Phil's enthusiasm was not contagious.

"Although," he closed the book with a jarring *thwack*, "the 1959 Cadillac Miller-Meteor hearse is the most iconic thanks to the Ecto-1 in *Ghostbusters*, though it was an ambulance version. Sure beats the pompous modern coaches, like the Rolls-Royce Phantom Hearse B12. Made entirely from aluminum, and the coffin compartment has high luminescence LEDs. *Pshaw!*"

The hearse *did* sound too funeral disco, but it would've been perfect for the sparkly ghost at Muriel's séance room. "So, how can I find out who owns the one I saw?"

"There are quite a few makes and models, but there aren't many hearses around town." He pressed a finger to his lips. "Let me call my buddy, Carl."

My body tensed. "Carl Cash, the used car salesman?"

"Heavens no."

"Ah, okay." I relaxed.

"Carl Goings, a cemetery recovery consultant."

My muscles contracted all over again. "Uh, a what?"

"He sorts flood-tossed graves, scattered coffins, floating mausoleums. Built an app that tracks those suckers wherever they travel."

With a name like Goings, he was the guy to do it.

"These days we just slap a barcode on the coffins and scan them like groceries at the supermarket. Completely revolutionized the identification of the frequent floaters by the bayou."

My jaw dropped, but I promptly shut it. *Cemetery dust.*

Phil whacked off another sanguinaccio slice. "Sure beats the old way of opening up the coffins to look for a golf club or gold tooth to identify the resident."

My legs stood, wanting to run. "Let's call your friend."

"Delighted to." Phil chewed the sausage and rummaged through some items on his desk. "I seem to have left my phone in the crypt." He stood. "Wait here."

Definitely. He left, and I sat as still as a tombstone. But my eyes hopped around looking for those grave grasshoppers.

And tomb-rooting critters.

My gaze wandered to the bookshelf. I vaguely remembered some of the volumes—anatomy, embalming, and zombies. But there was a new addition—*Daily Gratitude for the Graveyard Keeper*.

"Maybe that's how Phil stays so cheery," I said under my breath. I really ought to take the gratitude journal more seriously.

A cuckoo erupted from a clock striking eleven.

Make that a raven.

And I knew what my next gratitude entry would be. *I'm grateful I don't work, or reside, at Saint Cecilia.*

The door flew open.

"Eureka," Phil shouted, his face alight like a funeral pyre.

If I didn't leave the cemetery soon, I *would* reside in it.

Permanently.

Barring a flood, of course.

"Carl says a friend sold his 1960 Cadillac Eureka Hearse to a young man from Texas not three weeks ago. Paid thirty grand, cash."

Apparently, I'd gotten off cheap with the two-thousand-dollar Tic Tacs.

Phil returned to his desk. "Said it had a pristine black vinyl bench, brand new curtains, and a chrome-finished casket-loading table. The guy got a deal."

Highly debatable. "Did Mr. Goings tell you who the buyer was?"

"Travis. Couldn't recall his surname, unfortunately."

Travis from Texas. Probably ten percent of the males in the state.

"Apparently quite a braggart, though."

"Let me guess. He's a hunter who plans to fill the hearse with deer."

"No, nothing about himself." Phil picked up the cleaver and sliced a stray thread from his shorts.

And Atropos made a cutting appearance.

"Young Travis said his sister is quite rich and powerful." He put down the cleaver and stroked his beard. "On the board of some Mardi Gras krewe, as if that were a big deal."

It *was* a big deal.

Because Travis's sister was the killer.

13

———————

"Anaïs said you're a private investigator."

Honorine's greeting was as unexpected as the décor of her French Quarter home. The double parlor's red velvet furniture and leopard print curtains bore a striking resemblance to Glenda's brothel chic, which was at complete odds with the Clotho VP's preppy blonde ponytail and tweed skirt. I sank into an ornate gold chair beside the couch where she sat and suppressed a brow-raise at the erotic nude painting over the fireplace. "That explains why she threatened me with lawyers when I tried to talk to her at the dinner last night."

"Yes, she had you investigated."

"Why?"

Honorine picked a thread from her cream sweater. "You tell me."

Not a warm welcome, but I'd had worse. "It was probably something I said or did when I tried to help Marie-Fleur at the brunch. Unfortunately, I was also at the Greasing of the Poles, and I think that there's a connection between the death of Ken Lanier and those of Marie-Fleur and Claudine."

Her demeanor softened. "I suspect the same."

"Do you have any idea who killed them?"

"Ken was a prosecutor, so any number of people could've had it out for him. As for Marie-Fleur and Claudine, I was hoping you'd discovered the connection." Her hand went to her heart. "I'm devastated. And frightened."

Me too, thanks in no small part to the flying iron and rogue spindle. "Do you know where I can find Ken's daughter, Tiffany?"

"No, she's a drifter. Stays with friends. But I heard she had Ken cremated."

That was news. I wondered whether the police had identified the poison.

A petite maid entered with tea service. She wasn't the one who'd come to the door or the one who'd taken my coat. She placed a tray with a tin of Mariage Frères French Afternoon tea and cucumber finger sandwiches on the gilt coffee table.

Honorine's fox-slanted eyes met mine. "Is almond milk all right? I'm lactose intolerant, so that's all I have."

Professor La Roche's words at the Murder Mystery Dinner echoed in my mind.

Clotho was a poisoner.

Still, there were so many maids in the house. *Surely I'm safe?* "I take my tea black, thanks."

While the maid poured a cup, I scanned the parlor and saw a flash of brown outside a window overlooking the side of the house.

A squirrel?

No, the top of a head.

My jaw tightened.

Rosalie, trying to get more shock pics for my mother.

Honorine dabbed her nose with a Clotho kerchief. "Sorry, it's allergies. I'm also scent intolerant, and one of my maids brought scented laundry detergent into the house. I can't wear perfume, either."

A crash shattered the calm.

The maid pressed her palm to her cheek as she stared, mortified, at a broken teacup she'd knocked from the tray. "I'm sorry, Miss."

Had she seen the head? If so, I could claim Rosalie is my stalker. A smile threatened to erupt at an obviously inopportune moment.

I could have Rosalie arrested.

"That was expensive china, Lety." Honorine's face was none too forgiving.

"Yes, Miss." The maid, flushed, picked up the pieces and hurried from the room.

"Since you brought up perfume," I said, to break the awkward tension, "does Anaïs wear Chanel No. 5?"

"Yes, she always says it covers all transgressions."

That was a surprise. I never got near Anaïs at the brunch, but she hadn't worn perfume at the Murder Mystery Dinner.

Honorine's features drooped, morphing into melancholy. "Marie-Fleur was always buying some floral scent, like rose or gardenia, but Claudine only wore Jasmin Rouge by Tom Ford."

"You mean, Chanel No. 5? She was wearing it at the brunch."

"Oh, that's right." Honorine shook her head. "She borrowed it from Anaïs because she'd forgotten hers. I remember now because Anaïs had a new bottle, still in the package."

Because she was the one with Claudine and Marie-Fleur inside Wanda's wig shop, and she'd lost the purse-sized version when they stole the wigs?

The maid returned with a teacup decorated with violets.

My mind flashed to the purple-sequined Fendi baguette that Anaïs had carried at the dinner. "Was Anaïs with Claudine and Marie-Fleur at the Greasing of the Poles? In a purple wig?"

"This is the first I'm hearing of any of them being there. I was home working on krewe business."

"Were your maids here too?"

Her eyes darted to Lety, who was pouring her cup. "They had the day off."

Honorine didn't have an alibi.

To be on the safe side, I reached for her teacup and glanced out the window.

Nothing.

Probably an animal. "Do you or Anaïs have a brother named Travis?"

"Anaïs might." She picked up her cup. "She doesn't talk about her family."

"Would Josephine know?"

"You've met her?" She eyed me as she sipped the tea.

"When I joined the krewe. I thought it was so interesting that even your go-between is the descendant of a Casket Girl."

She returned the cup to the tray. "Josephine mentioned that?"

"Yeah, but she didn't seem convinced that you all have Casket Girl ancestors."

Her fox eyes turned deer caught in the headlights. "Really? Because she vets every board member. Krewe members too—at least, until the awful events of the past couple of days."

Movement caught my attention.

The top half of the head had re-emerged from below the window.

With a wine bottle and a corkscrew on either side?

That's not Rosalie.

It's Wanda in a wig.

She must've seen me entering the house. Hopefully she was looking out for me and not here for a confrontation. She was screwy, like that corkscrew above her ear. "Is there any chance

Josephine was wrong about one of you? I mean, how many people can prove they're descended from a Casket Girl?"

Honorine's head practically rolled. "Surely you're not doubting my ancestry? The women of my family have been making pralines since the Casket Girls arrived in New Orleans."

"No, no," I gushed. "I've heard of your praline company. But what do pralines have to do with the Casket Girls?"

She relaxed and reached for a sandwich. "The girls were shipped here to be wives for the colonists. But until they were married, they were in the care of the Ursuline nuns in the old convent here in the Quarter. And part of their domestic education involved the art of making pralines. The nuns were the ones who originally brought the recipe from France in 1727."

"Wow. I had no idea."

Her nose rose a fraction. "All upstanding New Orleans women made pralines."

"Are you saying that praline-making was an indication of ancestry?"

"Yes, and in some circles, it still is."

I picked up a finger sandwich that had been underneath Honorine's—just in case. As I popped it into my mouth, I caught a glimpse of Wanda, who glared and detached the wine bottle from her wig.

My body tensed. *Is she going to throw it through the window?* "So, uh, while we're on the subject, is Carly Cash descended from a Casket Girl?"

Honorine's laugh was as dry as the bread I was chewing. "If anything, that father of hers is descended from a Correction Girl. You can't escape your roots."

Exactly what Josephine had said. "That name is familiar. Who were they again?"

"The Correction Girls immigrated to New Orleans after the Casket Girls. Word got back to France that the conditions in the colony were far worse than the Casket Girls had been led to believe, so no respectable women would agree to immigrate after that. Also, the colonists were so rough that a lot of the women either fled into the swamp or flat refused to marry them, which is saying something when you think that in those days a girl of twenty-five was forced to wear an old-maid outfit."

A fit of coughing burst from my lungs.

"Oh, gosh, you're choking." She handed me my cup. "Drink some tea to wash down the food."

I nodded and took a sip, but the block in my throat wasn't the bread. It was surprised outrage that my nonna had treated me like an old maid from the age of sixteen when French women had until twenty-five. I put down my cup, as bitter as the black tea. "Just out of curiosity, what was the outfit?"

"A bonnet with ribbons tied under the chin and a plain sack dress."

Sounded like Nadezhda's prozodezhda.

My phone vibrated, and I smirked at the screen. My parents' deli.

As if on cue.

My mom and nonna channeled spinster talk like Chandra used to channel spirits.

Honorine cleared her throat. "Do you need to take that?"

"Definitely not." I dropped my phone into my bag and peeked at Wanda.

The wine bottle was tipped. The thing had wine in it, and Wanda was enjoying a swig. I envied her. The French Afternoon tea we were drinking tasted like vanilla and cardboard. "You were saying about the Correction Girls?"

"Well, King Louis XIV ended up forcing female prisoners from La Salpêtrière, a Paris house of correction, to come to the colony."

"Hence the nickname."

"Exactly. A lot of them were sick and malnourished, some had venereal disease, and others were just plain dangerous. Before they could be shipped to New Orleans, the king had them chained and marched across France as a crime deterrent. Some revolted and were shot, but most died on the marches and on the voyage. The ones who survived were tough, and through the years, their descendants started passing them off as Casket Girls."

Regardless of what the Correction Girls had done to end up in prison, it was a tragic story. And I shared Honorine's respect for those who'd lived to tell about the brutal treatment.

Speaking of brutal, Wanda was twisting the tip of the corkscrew at her temple.

Why couldn't I ever have a normal client? "Since we're talking about the Cash family, Claudine was in one of Carl Cash's cars picking up a couple of Russian women from the airport, and Anaïs left the dinner in a Cash car. There's also a creepy hearse going around town that seems to be connected to the krewe. What's going on with the cars and the women?"

"You'll have to take that up with Anaïs, since she's the president. But..."

"What?"

Honorine fidgeted with the tip of her ponytail. "Anaïs is hard to track down. She disappears for days at a time, doesn't answer her phone." She glanced at me and smirked. "She's a writer."

Oh, swell. Everyone knows writers are addicts and maniacs. "Does her writing have anything to do with why she stayed at the Hotel Monteleone last night? Like, maybe a writer retreat?"

"I didn't realize she had. I wonder if she used her pen name, Anna Monahan instead of Anaïs Monvoisin."

That might explain why the Hotel Monteleone had no record of her reservation. "What does she write?"

"She's working on a psychological thriller."

So was Wanda based on the way she was stabbing the corkscrew at the window. I knew there was something wronka with that wigmaker. I turned my attention back to Honorine. "Psychological thrillers sometimes have an unreliable narrator, right?"

Honorine peeled off the top of a finger sandwich.

As well she should. That bread was so stale it could've been a bone from the Saint Cecilia Cemetery.

"Yes, from what I've gathered, the main character often has an addiction or mental illness that makes them unstable." She peeled a cucumber from her sandwich. "The thing that worries me is that this book has changed Anaïs. At least, I think that's what's going on. She's been drinking and...distant." She dropped her deconstructed sandwich onto the tray.

"Is something wrong?"

Honorine looked at the floor. "It's just that I stumbled across the first few pages of the manuscript in her office at Clotho headquarters, and it's about an all-female Mardi Gras krewe."

I shrugged, feigning indifference. I didn't want to seem too eager for whatever she was about to add in case it scared her off. "As they say, write what you know."

"That's just it." Her fox eyes shifted to mine. "What does Anaïs know about a woman who murders members of a Mardi Gras krewe?"

Valid question, which begged two more. *Is the plot a red herring?*

Or a red flag?

~

"OVER HERE." A hand with a bracelet of grapes beckoned from a side street.

I glanced at Honorine's house to make sure I wasn't being watched. Then I rounded the corner and found Wanda.

Wearing a barrel.

No wonder I'd mistaken her for Rosalie. "What's up with the wine wear and the weird window antics?"

"I'm on the Krewe of Cork, and today on our French Quarter walk, I see you going into Honorine's." Her pointy chin rose. "What did you think I was going to do? Leave you for dead?"

My stance softened. "I appreciate the concern, but you need to let me do the job you're paying me for."

Wanda put her hands on her barrel hips. "The two Clotho board members I went to high school with stole my wigs to kill a guy, and now they're dead. I'm not going to wait around to see if I'm next. Or you, for that matter."

"Look, I understand, okay? But I don't think you're the killer's intended scapegoat."

"Why not?"

A group of partiers passed wearing enough beads to stock a parade float, so I waited until they were out of earshot. "You have no connection to Ken Lanier. Something bigger's going on here."

"That may be, but it was a bad idea to go into the den of a potential she-wolf alone." She tugged at a cork earring. "I hope you didn't drink or eat anything."

Fear flitted across my chest—and a touch of hypochondria. "Honorine's got a house full of maids," I said, more for my benefit than Wanda's. "No way she'd kill me in front of them. If anything, she was using me."

"So, Honorine's the killer?" Wanda ripped the corkscrew from her wig and took a step toward the house.

"Slow your roll, wine barrel." I pulled her back by the wine spigot. "It's too soon to say who's behind the murders. Honorine claimed to want reassurance that I was on the killer's trail, but I can't rule out the possibility that she was pumping me for information and setting up Anaïs. And Anaïs has lawyered up, so she's definitely on my suspect list."

Wanda reattached the corkscrew. "One of those two is the poisoner. Or both."

"Don't forget Carl Cash. He might be an accomplice."

"Hopefully, we'll learn something at float-loading tonight. Meet me and Marcella at the American Italian Cultural Center at six, when she gets off work, so we can go together." She tucked her thumbs under the shoulder straps that held up her barrel. "Now I've got to catch up with my krewe. This is a marketing opportunity."

I assumed that she was talking about her wigs until she turned to leave, and I read the back of her barrel.

Wiggins Wigs and Winery.

Not a bad business idea. I could already hear the slogan, *While you get your wig on, get your wine on too.* In fact, Wanda might be a better business partner for Nadezhda than Carl Cash.

It was only two o'clock, so I had several hours to kill before meeting Veronica for Happy Hour at the Hotel Monteleone. I headed up Royal Street, trying to figure out my next stop. The most pressing task was to identify the poison so I could try to link it to the killer.

Where to start?

A woman in a Saints jersey and matching black-and-gold tutu walked by, and Fickle Football Fan grooved into my mind. I could try the Sazerac Company he mentioned when I'd asked Nadezhda about adverse reactions associated with Tuaca and medication.

My head shot up.

The Historical Pharmacy Museum. It was a block away on Chartres, and it had a library and archives that dated to the founding of New Orleans. Clotho was a poisoner, and it was entirely possible that the Casket and Correction Girls had been poisoners too. Maybe they'd passed down a poisoning technique to their daughters and granddaughters.

Like an old praline recipe.

I turned down a side street and shivered. Ursulines Avenue, named after the nuns in charge of the Casket Girls.

A sign that I'm on the right path?

Squeals and laughter erupted.

The Krewe of Bosom Buddies & Breast Friends was coming toward me. As their name suggested, the female walking krewe and their men were all about boobs. And between Glenda and her Yardi Gras decorations, I'd seen enough of those to last me a lifetime. Scratch that.

An eternity.

As I hurried toward Chartres, I was intercepted by a sixty-something man with two balloons strapped to his chest. He handed me a black headband with a tiny tiger-striped hat and patted my breast. Stunned, I looked down and saw a sticker of the moon with the words *I'll send you to the moon.*

Normally, I would have sent *him* to the moon for a stunt like that, but I was too excited. I mean, the hat *was* faux tiger print.

I slipped on the hat and joined the tourists and day drinkers making their way through the Quarter. But I kept an eye out for Rosalie and other maniacs riding in Carl Cash cars or hearses. While I was at it, I checked Find My Friends on my phone to make sure Ruth Walker hadn't turned it on again.

She had.

How does she freaking do it?

"There has to be a way to deactivate Ruth," I muttered, turning off the feature.

The pharmacy museum sign was up ahead. It was shaped like a mortar and pestle and said *Le Pharmacie Française,* possibly to harken back to its French colonial origins. A display window featured ornate glass bottles filled with colorful liquid. According to local legend, the place was haunted by a former pharmacist who performed sadistic experiments on his patients. But from the outside, it looked like a cute place to spend an afternoon.

The double green door opened to a narrow hallway. No one was at the ticket stand, so I went outside to a quaint brick courtyard. It was pretty with lush greenery, a lamp post, and an old fountain. One of many wonderful French Quarter secrets.

Battered doors opened into the old pharmacy. Unlike the building's charming exterior, the inside was dark and foreboding. Wall-to-wall antique cabinets made of stained wood with intricate carvings held shelves of glass bottles filled with herbs and powders. Everything was covered in dust, some of which could've been centuries-old medicine, i.e. poison.

Holding my hand over my nose and mouth, I strolled past pills, salves, even voodoo potions and spells for luck, which didn't bode well for the patients. I gave a wide berth to a white porcelain jar with LEECHES in bold black letters and browsed a glass case with awful-looking contraptions. The names on the exhibit labels were no less horrific. *DeLee's Uterine Packing Forceps, Simpson's Perforator, Spiral Placenta Curette, Blunt Hook & Crochet?*

Had to be the sources of the sadistic experiments.

"Have you seen Wathen's Uterine Dilator?"

I turned to see who'd spoken.

It was an aging male in a drab white lab coat who looked like he'd been hitting the poisoned medicine cabinet. He had untamed gray hair, a gray sunken face, and watery eyes tinged with insanity. If I didn't know better, I'd say I was face to face with the ghost of the evil pharmacist.

His mouth stretched into a wide grin. "As the information

card says, the blades of the dilator are sharply corrugated to keep the instrument from slipping out of the uterus."

My head felt faint.

But my legs were clamped tight.

My phone vibrated.

Speaking of torture devices, it was my mother calling from the deli, her radar probably sensing that I'd just lost my desire to ever bear children.

"Excuse me for a second." I returned to the courtyard. The Pharmacy Museum was as good a place as any to swallow the bitter pill of my mother's reaction to Rosalie's shock pics.

"Hi, Mom."

"Francesca? It's your mother, dear."

She sounded too cheerful for a woman who'd seen Rosalie's alleged incriminating photos. But her tone was the one she used when she wanted to convince me to do something.

Is it to swear off women?

"Why aren't you at home, Mom? Are Dad and Nonna better?"

"Your father is. Your nonna's still in bed, but I just learned something that will not only get her up, it will have her dancing the tarantella."

This was baffling. The only things that would make my octogenarian nonna dance the Sicilian folk dance were me wearing a wedding ring and a grandbambino, one of which wasn't going to take place for almost a year, and the other might never happen now that I'd seen those uterine torture devices. "So, what is it?"

"You remember Mrs. Salvato from my Canasta group?"

I didn't, but I wanted to avoid a long-winded reminder. "Uh-huh."

"Well, she and her husband paid a fortune for a wedding venue and catering for their daughter, Laura, who isn't going to use it."

That was a scenario I couldn't have envisioned. If I got a free wedding, my nonna would not only dance the tarantella, she'd throw in the jitterbug and maybe even breakdance. "Did Laura call off the engagement, or something?"

"The groom ran off with the wedding planner. Isn't it marvelous?"

"Uh, not for Laura."

"Honestly, Francesca," she drawled, as though I was a downer for not seeing how the cheating scandal was a positive, "could you look at the bright side for once? The Salvatos don't want their money to go to waste, so they're offering you an all-expenses-paid reception at The Tuscan Courtyard."

Despite the dark circumstances, the "Tuscan" piqued my interest. And even though I knew it was a longshot, I had to ask. "Is that, by any chance, in Tuscany?"

"No, dear. Texas City!"

So that was the reason for her convincing tone. Texas City was home to oil refineries with a noxious smell and the odd leak, spill, or deadly explosion. Pretty much the anti-Tuscany. Not to mention that with family and friends like ours, Bradley and I didn't need to add any risk to our wedding. "That's not what Bradley and I have in mind."

"Then what *do* you have in mind, pray tell?"

Not a jilted bride's venue and menu. "Mom, I'm working. I need to run."

"Fine, but call me back *today*, either here at the deli or on our landline. I've lost my cell phone." She hung up.

The black oil-emissions cloud hanging over my head began to dissolve, and a ray of sunlight came through. If my mom didn't find her phone, and I deleted the pictures from Rosalie's, crisis averted.

Next stop, the fourplex.

My mouth twisted into a smile-smirk. It was my turn to tackle the Wrecking Ball.

I went back inside the museum.

The ghostly pharmacist clasped his hands behind his back. "Pardon the indiscretion, but I overheard your conversation. If you're in the market for a wedding venue, Le Pharmacie Française is popular with brides."

If I had to choose, I'd take my chances on Texas City. I couldn't fathom why any woman in her right mind would marry at the museum, unless she wanted to show her husband, family, and friends why she intended to remain childless. "Good to know. I'll tell my fiancé."

"You might also mention that Le Pharmacie Française is on the National Register of Historic Places."

My face remained expressionless even though I'd noted an alarming pattern—he spat when he pronounced an *f* sound in French.

He gestured with a veiny hand. "This room has been preserved intact since Louis J. Dufilho, Jr. became the first man in the United States to pass a pharmacy licensing examination in 1816. Before that, anyone could apprentice for six months and then mix medication without any regulation."

It was a wonder anyone survived the era. "There must've been a lot of poisonings."

"Most certainly. If you're interested in poison, you'll want to see the bottles in cobalt blue glass. We also have a common poison antidote from the eighteenth century." He pointed to what looked like a grayish lump of clay with hair. "A fur ball from a goat's stomach."

Nausea gripped *my* stomach. If I'd been poisoned, I would've let myself die before eating that.

He stepped behind a counter with an old cash register. "Is there any particular poison you'd like to see?"

"Actually, I was wondering if there's a link between poison and the French colonists, specifically, the women."

"It's possible given 'The French School of Poisoners,' or *les empoisonneurs*, as they were known."

Casually, I wiped my face because a second alarming pattern had emerged—the spittle was more projectile when he pronounced a French *p*. "There was a *poison school*?"

"No, not a building. It was a group of women who practiced the Dark Arts. By the late 1500s there were around thirty thousand poisoners in France."

Dang. The whole freaking country was suspect. "Any idea how many there were in 1718 when New Orleans was founded?"

He scratched a brow. "Far fewer, I would imagine. *L'affaire des poisons* had a cooling effect on the poisoners."

And his spit had a cooling effect on my cheek. "What was that?"

"*L'affaire des poisons*?"

"Yes," I said drily—to hint that my face wasn't.

"One of the biggest scandals in French history. Between 1677 and 1682, some four hundred members of the aristocracy were arrested for poisoning and witchcraft."

"Why the aristocracy?" I asked, leaning against the counter.

"They were under the influence of a cunning fortune teller called *La Voisin*. Her most famous client was Madame de Montespan."

Again, I wiped my face—and moved down the counter. "Who was she?"

"An aristocrat who'd set her sights on King Louis XIV. She had La Voisin celebrate a black mass to win his love, and it appeared to work. She became the king's official royal mistress. When he lost interest in her, she conspired to have him poisoned."

"So how did these poisoners do it? With food? Or in drinks?"

"Both, but poison doesn't have to be consumed orally. One can be poisoned through skin contact."

My hands retracted from the counter, and I wiped them on my pants. "Is there any evidence in your archives that French poisoners immigrated to New Orleans?"

"That's impossible because they would have been too old. In 1718, the only women arriving from France were young brides-to-be for the colonists."

Made sense since a twenty-five-year-old woman was considered a spinster. But some of the Casket and Correction Girls could have been descendants of the French poisoners. "What happened to La Voisin?"

"She was tried and burned at the stake in 1680. She never revealed the names of her clients, but her daughter, Marguerite, did in court."

His French seemed to have settled down, so I moved closer. "Any chance you have their names in your archive?"

"I'm afraid we don't have that information. All I can tell you is that Marguerite testified against Madame de Montespan."

A spit mist fell upon my face, and I let it lie. After all, I'd practically asked for it.

"When the king learned his former mistress was a poisoner, he made the rest of the trial secret. There's no further record of Marguerite Monvoisin."

My eyes locked onto his. "Monvoisin? I thought you said 'La Voisin.'"

"A nickname. La Voisin's real name was Catherine Monvoisin."

My skin tingled as though I'd been poisoned. Anaïs had the same last name as France's most infamous poisoner.

14

———

"Vassal, I have names for you." I glanced at my sixty-something Uber driver, Hal, to see if he was listening to my phone conversation. He was fiddling with the knob to the heater, so I figured he wasn't. "Honorine Ledet—I also need her maiden name—and Anaïs Monvoisin."

"Noted," The Vassal said. "Who else?"

"Try Anaïs's pen name, Anna Monahan."

"Oh? Does she write Sci Fi?"

The hope in his tone was predictable. "Psychological thrillers, and since she's working on her debut novel, I'm worried this could be a case of life imitating art."

Hal's eyes gravitated to the rearview mirror—and squinted.

Mine gravitated toward the intact fried pot pie from the Turkey and the Wolf restaurant on the front passenger seat. I'd been craving a fried pie since I'd failed to find a Hubig's hand pie at Lucky's Liquor and Vaxing. And the only thing I'd eaten for lunch was the lousy finger sandwich at Honorine's, so I was hungry like the wolf. Plus, I smelled turkey.

And butter.

The Vassal breathed into the receiver. "That reminds me of a romantic thriller author I heard about who murdered her husband."

"Yeah," I switched the phone to my other ear, "except that there have been three murders and counting."

Hal's brown eyes popped.

I attempted a reassuring smile, but there was nothing reassuring about the case. Or the fact that the fried pot pie was getting cold.

Hal's gaze returned to the road, and he turned onto Maple Street.

"Anyone else, Franki?" The Vassal asked.

"I got a tip that one of the women I mentioned might have a brother named Travis. Can you check on that?"

"Certainly. Who is your source?"

"The cemetery caretaker I told you about a while back." I looked out the window of the white Kia. "The one who does taxidermy and makes sausage from animals he finds roaming the tombs."

Hal gagged, hunched over the steering wheel, and accelerated.

"Ah, yes." The Vassal cleared his throat. "What prompted you to consult him?"

"A hunch that he could help me track down the owner of that creepy hearse I keep seeing with the U R NEXT license plate—"

The Kia screeched to a stop in front of Thibodeaux's. Hal shut off the engine and bolted from the car.

"Gotta go, Vassal." I hung up and opened the door. "Hey! Where are you going?"

"Lady," Hal ran a hand through thinning hair, "after that phone call, I need a drink." He yanked open the door to Thibodeaux's and went inside.

Served him right for eavesdropping. I exited the car and

went to the front passenger side. There was no reason to leave a perfectly good fried pot pie in the car.

Or its tarragon-buttermilk dipping sauce.

I added the cost of the pie to Hal's tip before setting off across the street.

Rosalie's Chrysler Pacifica was in the driveway, and this time I was grateful because it meant that I still had a chance to get her phone and the photos. "Something to add to the gratitude journal."

Chandra was upstairs on Glenda's balcony in a navy velvet jumpsuit with rhinestone stars, removing the last of the Yardi Gras decorations. The other dolls lay in a pile on the lawn.

I bit into the fried pot pie, and the buttery flaky crust was so sublime that I lost myself in a food-induced daze and stumbled over the stripper pole still lying in the yard.

Chandra made a disgusted sound. "Have you been drinking?"

If I hadn't quasi-tripped, I would've resented the question. "Not alcohol, but I'm drunk on this fried pot pie."

"Lou used to make a chicken version with white wine, but his lobster pot pie with sherry cream sauce was the best." Her moon-pie face turned from waxing to warring. "Then he worked on that vampire case with you and started the Krewe of Commodus." She cut the doll loose from the balcony.

Based on the way Chandra stomped down the stairs, I thought it best to change the subject. "Does Glenda know you're taking down her decorations?"

"No, and she won't, either. What I have to say to Lou will only take a few minutes. I'll have them back up before she and Nadezhda get back from the automotive store."

"Glenda's not trying to buy a new hood and windshield for my Mustang, is she?"

"I doubt it. She said she needed car parts for an outfit she's designing for her Hucci Cucci line."

That statement would sound strange to the average person, but those who knew Glenda were well aware that she could do a lot with grilles, spark plugs, and rearview mirrors. "Out of curiosity, why'd you take the dolls down if you're just going to put them up again?"

"Lou's on his way over to talk about our relationship, and I don't want a repeat of the manhandling incident." She punted the doll to the pile with the others.

"Interesting." I took another bite. "I thought you didn't 'give a fig about Lou.'"

Her cheeks tinged with pink, and she fumbled with her bouffant bob. "As far as I'm concerned, we're through. I just don't want him to embarrass me again." Chandra eyed my chest. "Speaking of embarrassing, why do you have that moon sticker on your breast?"

My eyes lowered. I'd forgotten to take the damn thing off. "Uh, because it reminds me of your toilet seat."

"Hardy har har."

"Yeah, I'm on a roll—a toilet paper roll." As soon as I uttered the corny pun, I looked at the fried pot pie. *Is there booze in this thing?*

Chandra grabbed two dolls by the hands. "Can I store these in your apartment?"

"Why don't you put them in the U-Haul?"

"That's where I'm meeting Lou."

"What's wrong with your apartment?"

"I can't be near a bedroom when I meet that man. Who can resist his sex appeal?" She took a step back. "Well, except for *you*, that is."

Yeah, and it wasn't for the reason she thought. I liked Lou, but his beer belly, Hawaiian shirts, and toe shoes didn't exactly evoke animal magnetism. Not like the fried pot pie.

"Plus," she gestured to her front door, "Rosalie's inside."

"Then you're safe. She'll kill any desire you have for men and life in general."

Chandra's tiny mouth pursed. "Is that what happened to you?"

Another question I would have resented if it didn't contain a grain of truth—about life, not men. "What happened to me is busybody Italian women and the Catholic Church."

"Oh! God!" Chandra stumbled backwards and hit the railing, and her arm shot up.

Alarmed, I looked behind me and then at her wrist—no charm bracelet, but something was up. "Are you channeling a spirit?"

She straightened and bumped her bob, annoyed. "I told you, I haven't spoken to a spirit since my split with Lou. I was trying to regain my balance."

"Then what was that about?"

"When you mentioned the church, I remembered something from the Murder Mystery Dinner last night. As I was being pushed inside that awful sarcophagus, I heard Claudine say 'devil' and then something else that was muffled."

"Is that how you remembered that the third tarot card you drew for Marie-Fleur was The Devil?"

She nodded. "I must've forgotten it from the shock."

Claudine might have called the killer a devil, which wasn't exactly a clue. Although, the use of the word was odd given the tarot card. "Did you smell any perfume in the séance room?"

"No, I didn't. I'm still trying to figure out the reason the killer went in there. If they'd already poisoned Claudine's champagne, why go to the crime scene?"

"To make sure she was actually dead and take the glass. Whoever it was obviously hadn't expected to find you in there."

"I guess." Chandra looked at her watch. "Lou will be here any minute. I'd better get to the U-Haul."

"All right, but," I gave a salacious wink, "don't close the doors."

Her eyelids lowered. "Just hide the dolls, okay?"

"Happy to." I smiled to myself. A plan had materialized in my head like one of Chandra's channeled spirits. I was indeed on a roll.

I finished the last of the fried pot pie and lined up the dolls one after the other in front of Chandra's door. Then I ducked around the corner from her porch and called Rosalie.

"Franki?" she practically shouted.

"Yeah, uh…" I suppressed a giggle. "This is awkward, but I need a favor."

"Oh, suuure. You're ungrateful until you need something."

"I'm sorry about that. I've been working on being more appreciative with a gratitude journal Veronica gave me." Which was true. "This is something I need you to keep quiet. It's, uh, compromising."

"You can count on me to keep your secret."

A bald-faced lie, not only because she had the biggest mouth in Texas, but also because she was so loud I could hear her outside—without my phone. "Yeah, that's why I called you. My Mustang's still in the shop, and I lost my wallet dancing at a club. Can you pick me up?"

"What club?"

"It's a pop-up called…GrrlSpot."

"I knew it," she hissed under her breath.

"What's that?" I asked, but I'd heard her loud and clear.

"I said, 'I'll do it.' You hold tight, and I'll be right there."

Grinning like The Grinch, I hung up and got my camera ready.

The door flew open, and Rosalie's foot bounced off a sex doll. She tripped and fell face forward into the pile, and her purse went flying. She raised her head. "Wha—What the hell is this?"

After snapping shock pics of my own, I scooped up her purse and fished out her phone. "I shouldn't have to explain a set-up to you, but I do need to explain this—If you set me up again, these sex-doll orgy photos, which I just emailed to myself, go to your husband and the entire congregation of St. Mary's Church in Houston. We clear?"

Rosalie's face resembled a tomato about to explode. "*Crystal.* What are you going to do with my phone?"

"Put it in that Nutella poop toilet you decorated for me."

She found her footing among the silicone. "No, you don't."

"Ah, ah, ah." I pointed to a picture on my display, and she went as limp as the dolls.

Euphoric, I entered my apartment, patted Napoleon, and marched into the bathroom where I deposited her phone in the toilet. I pushed down the shovel-spoon handle and watched the water swirl around it. "Rosalie Artusi, down."

My eyes met their reflection in the mirror. "Next up, Ruth Walker."

An awful sound made the hair on the back of my neck stand up.

Screaming?

No, tires screeching. *Hal?*

I did take his fried pot pie—and the dipping sauce.

Dashing from the bathroom, Napoleon ducked under the zebra chaise lounge, and I drew the gold drapes in my living room.

My hand went to my I'll-send-you-to-the-moon sticker.

The hearse was in the cemetery across the street, gunning the engine so hard that smoke surrounded the mausoleums.

A frightening sight.

From the corner of my eye, I saw a commotion outside Thibodeaux's.

Hal had fainted.

And it was easy to understand why. The driver wore a black hood. Like an executioner.

Or the Grim Reaper.

Swallowing my fear, I went to the door. I had to find out who was driving the hearse—and make sure Hal was all right. It was the least I could do after I'd eaten his fried pot pie.

I opened the door and ran behind Rosalie's Chrysler Pacifica, in case the hooded demon was armed, and peered around the trunk.

He blared the horn, and red lights illuminated the U R NEXT license plate.

Another threat.

The engine raced, the tires peeled out, and the hearse sped from the cemetery.

BRADLEY STOPPED the Mercedes in front of the windows to the Carousel Bar and Lounge. His blue eyes gazed at me from beneath his lashes. "You sure you want to do this after the hearse incident?"

"I'll be fine. I'm meeting Veronica, and you know the bar is always packed."

"Okay, but I'm not going to let you stay alone tonight. There've been too many threats, and now the hearse driver knows where you live."

His concern was sexy—as was the way he'd rushed over to

my apartment to rescue me. I leaned in and gave him a kiss that reflected the depths of my appreciation.

When we came up for air, he rested his forehead against mine. "You know, the Hotel Monteleone is a great place for a wedding reception."

And a far cry from the Historical Pharmacy Museum. "Are you saying you want to get married in New Orleans?"

"I'm saying I'll marry you anywhere."

"Bradley Hartmann, you're making it really hard for me to leave this car."

"Baby, that's the idea." He raised my chin and went in for another kiss.

Seriously considering ditching the happy hour, I opened one eye and peered at the bar. What I saw made me change my mind —and it wasn't the crowd staring in Bradley's car window. I pulled back. "I'd better get inside. Veronica needs me."

Reluctantly, he released me. "Meet me at the office after float-loading. I'll be there late."

"Can't wait." I gave him a peck and dashed from the car, glaring at our audience.

The doorman opened the hotel door, and I climbed the steps to the crowded lobby and hooked a right. As I entered the dark hallway to the Carousel, I flashed back to the first case I'd worked with Veronica. Like now, it was during Mardi Gras. I'd confronted a killer in the adjoining lounge down the steps from the rotating bar. And unbeknownst to me at the time, I'd crossed paths with another murderer—in a crawdad costume.

Steeling myself, I stepped into the bar.

The Russian dolls were at the carousel, laughing with men in expensive suits. But I turned my attention to the lounge—and a blonde with huge teased hair in a short leopard dress and a Cookie Monster-colored fur coat. I went down the steps and walked up behind her. "Uh, Veronica?"

She spun around. "Verushka, darlink." She winked a heavily purple-shadowed eye and sipped from a Cosmopolitan. "You vant good time?"

I sat in the love seat across from hers. "If I did, I would've stayed in Bradley's Mercedes out front."

She snickered.

Is she snockered? "What are you doing down here?"

Veronica reached for some peanuts on the coffee table between us. "The Russians made it clear I was encroaching on their territory, so I thought I'd work the lounge. But before I left the bar, a man in a nice suit asked if I was with the Krewe. I said yes, and he asked me to do him a favor. When I asked what he wanted, he walked away like I had a virus."

"That's weird."

"I know. However, this look did get me a tip from the reception clerk, after I had a drink with him."

My mouth cocked in a semi-smile. "How'd you get rid of him?"

"Easy. I told him I was into women."

"That's what Rosalie told my mother about me—with phony photos."

Veronica's palms smacked her cheeks, and she lay down on the love seat.

"Don't panic," I said, although it was too late for that. "My Mom lost her phone before she saw the pictures, and I flushed Rosalie's before I came here."

"Oh, Franki." Veronica sat up. "If your Mom finds that phone..."

I grabbed a handful of peanuts. I'd been raised from birth to eat in times of stress. "So what was the tip?"

"Anna Monahan is staying at the hotel."

My jaw dropped—and I loaded it with nuts. "How'd you know Anaïs's pen name?"

"The Vassal. I was at the office when you called. How'd it go with Honorine?"

"She's a little too helpful. They're always the freaking murderer on *Dateline*. But, then you consider Anaïs writing a psychological thriller. I'm telling you, mystery and thriller authors are nuts, total psychos who spend their days plotting to kill people."

Veronica raised her glass. "*And* she lawyered up."

"She also has the same last name as a seventeenth-century French poisoner."

"Ooh. We might have our killer. She's definitely behind a prostitution ring."

I shivered. "This is crazy."

"What is?"

"A Classics professor I met at the Murder Mystery Dinner said the goddess Clotho was not only a poisoner, she also forced Aphrodite to sleep with other gods, like a madam."

Veronica glanced over her shoulder at the bar. "Life imitating mythology."

But who is Clotho in this scenario?

And the gods?

I surveyed the unattached men at the carousel bar. I didn't know about Clotho, but the gods were businessmen with money.

Nadezhda entered, followed by Glenda in a silver ribbon she'd wrapped around her body like a package—from pubic bone to left shoulder and tied in a bow across the breasts.

"God, what are they doing here?" I breathed.

"My bad. I asked Glenda to lend me these shoes," she leaned back and kicked up six-inch platinum stripper heels, "and when she and Nadezhda dropped them by the office, I filled them in on the happy-hour plan."

"I'll take care of them. You keep an eye on the bar."

Nadezhda, who'd expanded her reptile-wear into velvet crocodile, scowled as I approached. "You vant drink?"

The offer caught me by surprise. "Yeah, I'll take a Prosecco."

"I take two tventy."

My eyes went from her outstretched palm to her greedy gaze. "Why am *I* paying for the drinks?"

"It not my case. You pay expense."

"Expense? You're not part of this."

Glenda pulled me by the wrist to a corner table. "Miss Ronnie told us about the sting operation, sugar. Since the krewe wants Russians, Miss Nadezhda has offered her services as a lure."

A *HA* burst from my lungs, and I added a *CK* to make it sound like a hard throat clear. I clamped my mouth shut to prevent another laugh mishap. But the next *HA* made my lips flutter. Before I knew it, my lips were flapping like Mr. Ed's, the talking horse my nonna watched on reruns.

Then I gave up, and gave in to the laughter.

With those maroon spikes, Nadezhda made a babushka look like a bombshell.

"You no get drink," she snapped and stomped to the bar.

"Now, Miss Franki." Glenda tsked. "That was rude."

Wiping tears from my eyes, I gave one last belly laugh. "In all fairness, you should've given me a heads-up. These are high-class hookers. No one's going to pay top dollar for that penny-pinching Communist. Plus, the Sashas met her today at Lucky's when they were loading up on vodka. They know she's not a prostitute."

"They're her people, sugar, so she can come up with an explanation. And if my example has proven anything, it's that you shouldn't count out us low-budget gals."

Money and class weren't the issue. It was Nadezhda's dragon demeanor and crocodile smile—sans eyetooth.

"By the way," Glenda spread her arms, "you haven't said anything about my first official designer creation." She pointed to the ribbon, which had fuchsia rhinestones that spelled HU and CCI on either breast, and then she did a three-sixty to show me CU and CCI written in matching body paint on either buttock cheek. "Coochie dressed all hoochie. Plain and simple."

It was. And far more comfortable than brake-line tubing.

One of the Russian dolls, aka Short Sasha, stood and led a man from the bar by his necktie.

Her intention was clear, but I had to confirm my suspicions—and escape the horrors of a Nadezhda pre-mating ritual. "Duty calls. Be right back."

Rather than follow Short Sasha and her john from the bar, I went the opposite direction to the Criollo restaurant entrance midway through the lounge and exited into the lobby. The pair was enroute to the gift shop at the other side of the hotel.

My phone vibrated. *David.*

Trailing them at a distance, I tapped *Answer.* "Please tell me you got the Royal Sonesta video."

"Not yet. I'm calling because the Chem student from Chewbacchus has the toxicology results on the glass shard, but he won't discuss them over the phone."

"Why not?"

"He, uh, likes to recreate fake bombs and stuff from Sixties Sci-Fi shows, only his are real, so he's got an FBI file."

That was explosive news, but FBI file or no, I needed those results. "When can we see him?"

"Tonight after seven."

There went some time with Bradley. "Fine," I ground out, as Short Sasha and her john went down the hallway to the elevators and the parking garage. "Can you pick me up from float-loading at seven thirty? It's at the parking lot across from the Convention Center."

"Totally. But when you meet him, be chill and don't say anything about his face."

I pictured a body with a tribble from *Star Trek* for a head. But I'd seen stranger things on Bourbon Street. "You got it."

The pair turned toward the elevator, and I hung up.

There was no reason to follow them to the room—it was obvious what they were going to do. What wasn't clear—why Clotho would run a prostitution ring, and who knew about it besides Claudine and Anaïs. *Is this the information the anonymous-letter writer was telling Marie-Fleur to keep quiet?*

Since Ken Lanier dated Claudine, he'd probably known about the "funny business at the Hotel Monteleone," to quote Ruth, and it could've been the reason he wanted to investigate the krewe.

But what about Honorine? Does she know about it too?

My mind turning like a carousel, I returned to the bar.

Tall Sasha was still looking cozy with her businessman. Nadezhda was drinking a Moscow Mule and checking her maroon spikes, looking about as inviting as a bag of borscht-flavored potato chips.

A Mardi Gras dance troop began filing past me into the bar and lounge, lining the walls for an impromptu performance. It was the Pussyfooters, who'd been at the Greasing of the Poles. They wore their signature pink-and-orange-striped corsets with matching layered ruffle skirts and white boots, which they'd paired with pink wigs and little hats.

A drunk guy leaning against the wall with a near-empty Hurricane slid to my side. "The Puthyfoossers. Some name, ishn't it?"

I shot him a side-eyed smirk.

His brows rose a couple of times before one stayed put. "So many connotashions."

"None of which I plan on discussing with you." I marched down the steps and sat with Veronica.

Glenda kicked a fuchsia stripper shoe with the word *Mama* on the heel. "I was just telling Miss Ronnie that the Pussyfooters are my favorite dance troop. Their tagline is 'Majorettes from the Mothership.'"

Sounded like a group from the Intergalactic Krewe of Chewbacchus. "What does pussyfooting have to do with majorettes?"

"It means to walk stealthily and furtively like a cat, sugar."

Another word with a surprise meaning, like those Ruth name definitions. "I thought it was a double entendre for 'screwing around,' which is what the Sashas are doing."

Glenda's face grew serious. "Make no mistake, Miss Franki, those Sashas are stealthy and furtive."

"Da, like Siberian tiger," Veronica said in her Verushka voice and drained her Cosmopolitan.

Probably not a good idea to let her continue with the vodka.

Nadezhda took a seat next to Glenda and scowled at the bar.

Glenda patted her shoulder. "What's wrong, Miss Nadezhda?"

"A man ask for favor. I say, 'you pay,' and he valk avay. Zen he leave vit Big Sasha. Veirdo."

The HA threatened to erupt again, but it died in my lungs. "That's it." I looked at Veronica. "The favor—a guy asked you for one too."

"Yeah," she straightened, "but what does it mean?"

I motioned for everyone to huddle. We all leaned in and abruptly leaned back—Glenda's breasts had broken free of their bow.

She chuckled and stuffed them back in line. "Wardrobe malfunction."

I'd often wondered what that would look like for her. "Anyway," I whispered, "Josephine the Go-Between said Mardi Gras krewes are based on the favor system, and that's what this is. Prostitution based on favors."

"Vat? Zey not get money?"

It figured the cheap Commie would focus on cash. "The Krewe of Clotho accepted favors from these men, probably sponsorship and access to other donors in the business community, and this is how they thank them. By buying them exotic women."

"Not Carl Cash, apparently." Glenda tightened the ribbon. "He'd rather hook up at Napoleon's Itch than the Carousel Bar."

"Right," I said, "but he's still getting in on the action by lending his cars to the operation. He gets a cut and probably a kickback. Nadezhda helped me sneak into his office, and I saw an envelope stuffed with cash that had dates."

Now that Glenda's girls were strapped in, she reached for her champagne. "What do you plan to do next, Miss Franki?"

"Tonight I go see David and The Vassal's chemist friend about the glass shard, and then I have to find Ken Lanier's daughter, Tiffany."

Veronica chewed the cherry stem from her drink. "Good move. She's bound to know something."

"Let's hope." I scanned their worried eyes—and Nadezhda's resting Russian face. "Because, before this is all over, Atropos is going to cut someone else's life short."

15

"Veronica, so good to see you," Marcella gushed as she let us inside the American Italian Cultural Center. She pressed a hand to the breast of her shimmery black jumpsuit and stuck out her tongue. "And, mamma mia! *Love* the eye makeup."

She would. Her bright blue smoky eyes rivaled the late Tammy Faye Baker's.

"Wanda has a migraine," she said, locking the door behind us, "so she'll meet us at the float."

Veronica rubbed her forehead. "I know the feeling. Too many Cosmopolitans."

Marcella's maroon-lined lips pursed. "Wanda's culprit was the wine on the Krewe of Cork walk."

I didn't say anything, but the culprit could've been the bottle and corkscrew she'd carried on her head. "You ready to go, Marcella?"

"I need to finish one thing. Follow me, girls, and you'll see the new-and-improved Center." She clasped her hands, barely containing her excitement. "After years of planning, our third-floor exhibit finally tells the accurate story of Italian immigrants from their arrival in New Orleans to the present."

As we followed her up the stairs to the third floor, I wondered what the inaccurate story of Italian immigrants was. But I'd sooner eat spaghetti with ketchup sauce than ask. Marcella was likely to launch into a college-level course on Italian-American history that would make us miss float-loading and all of Mardi Gras.

She led us through the exhibit to a wax figure of a mother superior with her hands pressed in prayer.

Rather than the stern look I associated with nuns from my Sunday School days, her wax brow was permanently furrowed with concern. "Who's your friend, Marcella?"

"If only! Wouldn't it be great to be friends with a saint?"

I was going to say that I already was, but Veronica wasn't looking too saintly in her slutty makeup and sex-worker garb. Plus, she was splayed out rather provocatively on a display dedicated to legendary New Orleans' grocer Merrill Ferrara.

"She's St. Frances Xavier Cabrini, the patron saint of immigrants, but most people know her as Mother Cabrini. She came to New Orleans with six sisters in 1892, a year after the eleven Sicilians were lynched, and the population had been decimated by Yellow Fever."

No wonder the woman looked worried.

Marcella pushed back Mother Cabrini's veil. "First she opened an orphanage and school for Italian children in the French Quarter, and then she started a convent and orphanage on Esplanade that's now Cabrini High School." Her eyes filled with longing. "I wish I'd gone there instead of the Ursuline Academy. They would've known my name is Mar-CHELL-a."

I wish she had too so we wouldn't have to keep hearing about her name drama.

"Before I forget, Franki," she raised her hair curtain, "an old high school friend whose daughter knew Tiffany came into the Center this morning. She heard through the grapevine that Tiffany had Ken Lanier cremated."

"Yeah, I heard that too."

Marcella retrieved her wine tote from a shelf. I thought she was going to offer us a go cup after the grapevine comment, but she pulled out an eyeshadow palette.

"Well," she studied the makeup shades, "I have a hunch that Tiffany will process with the Société de Saint Anne."

"What's that?" I asked. "A religious group?"

"A walking krewe of artsy types. On Mardi Gras morning, they walk from the Bywater neighborhood to the Mississippi River at ten a.m. to dump the ashes of their loved ones in the water. That way they can live in the spirit of the holiday for eternity."

Veronica, who'd not only found a rolling pin but was rolling it on the top of her head, looked up at me. "That sounds like something Tiffany might do. She doesn't seem the type to organize a funeral for Ken."

This Mardi Gras was already tragic enough without a mass ash-spreading ceremony, but I had to talk to Tiffany. "I'll check it out, but we're supposed to be on the float before ten."

Marcella dabbed brown shadow on one of Mother Cabrini's eyes. "We'll be waiting in a line of floats until we roll at noon, so it's not a big deal if you board late."

I was so shocked to see her making up the sister saint that I barely heard what she'd said. "Do you think eyeshadow is a good idea? I mean, she is a mother superior."

Marcella looked surprised. "She might be a nun, but she's not dead."

"Actually, she is."

"Dead is no excuse for this complexion." She gestured to the nun's cheek. "It's so waxy."

I scratched my neck. "Because she's a wax figure."

"Well, Mother Cabrini deserves to look more human, and I know just the thing." She spread gold eyeshadow over the brown. "A neutral smoky eye that'll accentuate her habit."

Something told me the *inaccurate* history of Italian immigrants was creeping back into the exhibit.

Marcella stood back to admire her handiwork. "*Bellissima!*"

The real reason for Mother Cabrini's concern became clear. Not only was she Marcella's unwilling fashion victim, the eyeshadow combined with her wax complexion made her look like she'd contracted Yellow Fever.

"Before we head out," Marcella slung her wine tote over her shoulder, "there's something I want to show you, Franki."

"Marguerite Piazza's Flame of Hades dress?"

"No, that's right over there." She pointed to a red-sequined number with huge flames coming from the shoulders and the attached headpiece.

The gown was so extravagant that if the fashion kingdom saw it, they'd abolish Bob Simpson's Sequin Sultanate.

She winked. "Now follow me."

I helped Veronica up and headed to the stairwell as concerned as Mother Cabrini. After seeing a nun get a smoky eye, I couldn't fathom what Marcella had in store for me.

She led us downstairs to a rather plain white room on the second floor with columns in the middle, a wood floor, and various dining tables. "We've turned this into a venue overlooking the Piazza D'Italia. It's called the Renaissance Room, and it would be a wonderful place to have your reception dinner before dancing the tarantella with your paisans in the piazza."

I forced a smile but said nothing. I'd been rendered speechless by a mental image of myself in an Italian-flag-colored wedding dress, courtesy of the piazza's red and green neon lights, and Wanda's Renaissance Rapunzel wig with the poison pill compartments. The look would never come to pass, but if somehow it did, those compartments had better be filled with the poison pills.

Veronica took a seat, and I went to the window—not to gaze at the garishly colored Postmodern piazza that *Architecture Magazine* had compared to a Hurricane cocktail, but to check for the hooded hearse driver and any other delinquents.

A thirty-something male sat near the piazza fountain, a shallow pool formed by arcs of water that were spat onto the pavement by the disembodied faces of the architect himself. First he removed his shoes, then his socks.

Odd behavior given the chilly weather, but hardly criminal.

Marcella sighed. "It's hard to tear yourself away from that piazza view, isn't it?"

"Uh-huh," I agreed, watching the guy remove his sweatshirt.

Then his jeans.

And boxers?

"Any case updates, Franki?" Marcella asked.

I glanced at her over my shoulder. "Uh, yeah. The killer might be the descendent of a Correction Girl rather than a Casket Girl. And after my visit to the Historical Pharmacy Museum, I think she could also be the descendent of a notorious poisoner named Catherine Monvoisin."

Mouth in an *o*, she placed her hand on the wall. "That's Anaïs's last name."

"Exactly. And evidently this Catherine woman is linked to a French school of poisoners from the late 1500s."

Marcella's lips slid from the *o* to a dash, and her hand moved from the wall to her linebacker hip. "Can we talk about how tired I am of the French always getting the credit?"

Here we go again with the Frenchified name. "We *are* in a former French colony."

"And no one will let us forget it. My name is MAR-CHELL-A. MARCHEEELLLAAA," she shouted as Brando did *Stella*.

Veronica pressed her temples. "No need to shout," she hummed in a fake cheery tone reminiscent of my mother's. "We're on your side of the ethnic name debate."

Marcella's smoky eyes sparked. "I know. But, let's get something straight—the French School of Poisoners was influenced by the Italian School of Poisoners," she paused and rummaged in her wine tote, "and I can prove it."

I admired her ethnic pride, but like so many others around me lately, she needed a priority check.

As Marcella typed on her phone, I looked down at the fountain.

Now Naked Guy had a bar of soap.

Irish Spring.

I considered telling Marcella what was happening, but she was already worked up. And the scene wasn't all that uncommon in The Big Easy. In fact, it reminded me of the time I'd seen a guy bleach his hair in a bucket smack in the middle of Bourbon Street.

"Here's the article." Marcella's tone held the *umph* of triumph. "It says the Borgia's systematic use of poisons like *cantarella* in the late 1400s gave rise to the Italian School of Poisoners. So there you have it. We were first."

I turned around. "What's cantarella?"

"No one knows, but the symptoms were similar to arsenic poisoning. The Borgias tested it on animals and later the poor. They dumped the bodies in the Tiber River."

Yeah, not a good look for our people—much like a naked guy bathing in the Piazza D'Italia fountain.

Marcella scrolled on her phone. "The Borgias killed so many cardinals that cantarella was nicknamed the 'liquor of succession,' and the expression 'tasting the cup of the Borgias' became a euphemism for death."

The liquor and cup references stole my attention from the public bathing spectacle. "Since Tuaca is in frozen southern milk punch, I've been wondering whether it played a role in the murders. And it was created in honor of Lorenzo de' Medici."

"Oh, well," she rolled her eyes as she shoved her phone into her wine tote, "speaking of famous Catherines and the French, Catherine de' Medici, Lorenzo's granddaughter, showed France how poisoning was done in the mid-1500s."

Marcella was a walking encyclopedia of Italian poisoners, which was probably something she should keep to herself until the case was solved.

"She was betrothed to King Henry II of France, and when she moved to Marseille for the wedding, she brought her personal perfumer from Florence. Incidentally, Florence was the first place to perfume clothes as well as skin, because Italy was the cradle of Western Civilization. And what's more civilized than perfume?"

"Or classier?" I added in keeping with Marcella's style of conversation.

"Catherine introduced perfumed gloves to the French court. They were called 'sweet gloves,' and they became a total status symbol. By the way, they were perfumed because animal poo was used in the tanning process."

A detail I could have done without.

"Then, get this," Marcella cocked a powdered brow, "her sweet gloves became the subject of a murder investigation."

A detail I could do with. "How so?"

"A rumor started going around the palace that Catherine had used the gloves to kill the Queen of Navarre since she opposed a strategic marriage between their children." She put a hand on her hip and leaned in. "The Queen was Protestant and didn't want her son marrying one of us Catholics. Don't even get me started on that."

Veronica shot me a pleading look and shook her head.

"Okay, I won't." I held up my hands. "But are you saying Catherine poisoned her own gloves to kill the queen?"

"The exterior. And, yes, that's what the French thought." Marcella's gaze smoldered like her smoky eyes—and Mother Cabrini's. "But they accused Catherine of all kinds of evil things. Truth is, they never accepted her because she was Italian. The French always believed we were masters of the Dark Arts."

Made sense since the Italian School of Poisoners came first —and because I was related to my Mom and Nonna.

But Catherine de' Medici's story also raised questions—e.g., were the Clotho board members' gloves merely part of their costume? Or did they serve a more sinister purpose?

More importantly, was I focusing on the wrong country and era?

Based on what I'd heard, the murders of Ken, Marie-Fleur, and Claudine might not have been inspired by Greek goddesses or French poisoners.

But is it possible that the crimes are rooted in the Italian Renaissance?

~

"FLOAT 24?" The blood drained from my face as I stared at the Clotho parade information email. "That's the one Ruth Walker was looking for at the warehouse."

Thunder rumbled, and lightning lit up the Convention Center parking lot. It was a scene from a horror movie—not the weather, but the float assignment.

Marcella checked her phone and squealed. "Wanda and I are on the same float."

Pain crossed Veronica's face. "Me too."

"At least we're together," I said, because I was going to need lots of shoulders to cry on—or hold me back when I tried to push Ruth off the moving float. "Any idea which one is ours?"

Marcella scanned the floats lining the rear of the lot. "When they bring them from the warehouse, they park them in the order they'll leave for the parade. The Clotho board's is first."

I located the sequined cloud with the goddess masthead, thrones, and spindle wheel and began counting. When I got to twenty-four, my blood raged back to my face. "Freaking Pinocchio?" My shout echoed across the lot, and possibly the entire Warehouse Arts District. "Is this some kind of joke?"

Women loading throw bags onto floats stopped to stare.

I didn't care.

Getting assigned to Pinocchio with Float Captain Ruth was more upsetting than my close encounters with the flying iron and the rogue spindle combined. "Can someone please tell me the purpose of a lying Italian puppet in a Greek goddess parade?"

Veronica eyed Pinocchio's pole nose. "He *is* out of place."

"No, no," Marcella said. "I see the connection." She held up a hand, inviting us to share her vision. "Clotho spins the thread of life, and Pinocchio turns into a real live boy."

"Too bad he's a character," I grumbled. "Atropos can't cut his thread."

Veronica laughed. "Ow," she frowned, "that hurt my head."

"O-M-G!" Marcella gripped Veronica's arm. "You just reminded me—our head wreaths." She clasped her hands à la Mother Cabrini. "What I wouldn't give for them to have a tiny Jiminy Cricket."

If they did, I'd step on that insect—just like the delinquent Pinocchio did in the original novel. "Come on. Let's get this float-loading over with."

We trudged across the lot in silence—until a clap of thunder made us all shriek.

The dark clouds didn't bode well for the parade tomorrow. *But what about this Mardi Gras did?*

The duffel bags of throws we'd ordered were in a huge pile, as though a dump truck had backed up to the float and unloaded. I lifted one. "Wow, this thing feels like it has boulders instead of beads."

Marcella stooped and examined a tag on a bag. "Our names are on them. The krewe email says we get two each."

"Hang on." My weight shifted to my back leg. "I paid two grand for two duffel bags of plastic and plush toys, *and* I have to ride on a pink-flowered Pinocchio? The Krewe of Clotho should pay *me* to parade."

Ruth's head appeared over the edge of the float's upper deck. "Just be glad we're not riding on a cheap Santa-on-a-gondola ornament from Poland."

I should've known the battle axe was on board, waiting to make Mardi Gras more miserable. "That makes zero sense."

"Exactly. Because that ornament should've been made in Venice."

"Ruth, there's no correlation between this float and your ornament, so stop trying to force one."

Marcella raised a hand. "I see the connection. There's a book about Pinocchio's adventures in Venice."

I studied her for a long moment. "Put a cork in it, Marcella."

She mimed inserting a cork between her maroon-lined lips.

Chandra trudged up in her navy velvet jumpsuit with a subdued Rosalie. "No bickering, please. I have such a headache."

Veronica spread out supine on the mountain of throw bags. "What Chandra said."

With this krewe, I was going to get a headache too. I turned to Rosalie. "Why aren't you on the road to Houston?"

"Because I signed up to parade with Chandra. How do you think I got an invite to the Murder Mystery Dinner?"

Could this Mardi Gras get any worse?

Thunder clapped overhead.

There's my answer. "I assumed you were Chandra's plus one."

Chandra sniffed. "Don't get your hopes up, Franki. Just because Lou and I are separated doesn't mean I'm bisexual."

My immediate thought was, *I would sooner walk Pinocchio's nose like a plank.*

"Speaking of Lou," Chandra smoothed her bouffant bob, "he tried to convince me to leave the singles' compound and come home. He thinks all he has to do is ask, but he's going to have to work harder than that."

"Atta girl, Miss Chandra." Glenda strutted up beside me and took a drag off a cigarette holder that was made from some sort of antenna.

My gaze dropped, and my jaw with it. She'd already assembled an entire outfit from her auto parts store visit—two car-horn buttons for pasties, a seat belt around her waist, and a thong made from wiring and a Ferrari hood badge. She didn't need to turn around for me to know she had a tail light in the rear.

"Now *that*, sugar," she tapped my lowered chin, "is the kind of reaction I expect from Bob Simpson when he sees my Hucci Cucci Hot Couture."

Couture wasn't the word.

It was *Carture*.

Ruth came down a ladder on the side of the float in her cruise director uniform. "We need to go over a few items of business." She pulled a clipboard that said Krewe Director from under her arm and slipped on her cat-eye readers. "One, be at the float in costume at six a.m. sharp tomorrow."

Groans erupted from the group.

"Shut it, slackers." She glared over her glasses rim. "Two, we need a catchy float-krewe name. The krewe on the float with the shimmering goddess picked The Blingtastic Babes."

I raised my hand. "How about The Pathetic Puppets?"

"Terrible suggestion."

"Okay then," I said, "The Judgmental Geppettos."

Ruth poked her tongue into her cheek. "Since no one has a serious proposal, I hereby name us The Spinner Winners."

My hand shot back up. "If you want serious—The Raving Ruths."

Her turkey neck wobbled, as did the chains on her readers. "Any more guff out of you, missy, and you're off the krewe."

If I didn't have to investigate, I would've taken her up on that.

"Number three on the list," Ruth consulted the clipboard, "tip the float driver."

Nadezhda flashed a homicidal grin, the closest she could get to a pleasant smile. "I take cash, Venmo, PayPal, Apple Pay, credit card and piggy bank. No check in case you crook."

A smirk slid across my lips. Her pronunciation of payment forms was flawless.

"Lastly, and most importantly," Ruth pulled papers from the clipboard with a snap, "you have to buy me a float captain gift." She handed each of us a sheet. "I've compiled my preferred gift options."

My eyes popped at the pricy list. "A leather couch? A widescreen TV? You'll be lucky to get movie tickets."

"Note the large print." Ruth pointed to the top and bottom of the page.

. . .

*DO NOT LET FRANKI AMATO, NOTORIOUS SKINFLINT
AND KNOCKOFF SHOPPER, PICK MY GIFT.*

I COULDN'T BLAME her for the disclaimer—at least, not for the
knockoff part. "If you didn't want me involved in the gift, you
shouldn't have picked me to ride on Pinocchio."

"For the record," Ruth waved the clipboard at the float, "I
thought *you* were the reason I was assigned to this juvenile
delinquent puppet."

Marcella mimed removing the cork. "Five of us here are Italian-American. Maybe we've been ethnically profiled!"

If we had, Josephine the Go-Between was behind it. But my
guess was that we'd been relegated to the puppet because of our
lack of social connections.

Rosalie picked up a throw bag. "Regardless of how we got
Pinocchio, I want to clarify something—he was a good boy." Her
beady eyes zeroed in on me. "His problem was getting mixed up
with the wrong crowd."

I held up my phone to remind her of those pictures I'd taken
of her face down in Glenda's Yardi Gras decorations, in case she
was thinking of resurrecting the lesbian business.

Chandra picked at a paddle nail. "I think Rosalie is referring
to unsavory types who frequent cooking schools and Mardi Gras
krewes."

"I concur, Miss Chandra." Glenda stepped on her cigarette
with a side-mirror-heeled shoe. "Bob Simpson turned bad when
he hooked up with the Krewe of Clotho."

Bad?

Bob?

I didn't know how I'd ended up on this float of fools, but I
wanted off. Careful not to wake a now napping Veronica, I
grabbed one of my throw bags from the pile and dragged it up

the ladder, trying to ignore the shoulder pain from my fall outside Carl Cash's office window.

The float was a wooden structure so primitive that it looked like Geppetto had built it in his workshop back in the 1800s. To my right was a port-a-potty-style bathroom. To my left was a ladder to the upper level and standing-room only with hooks on the railing for harnesses—which would render riders trapped if the float collapsed. "This is certainly in keeping with the Pinocchio theme."

Chandra climbed onto the float with Rosalie in tow. "Ruth said we're upstairs."

"Of course we are." I hoisted the duffel bag over my aching shoulder and began climbing the ladder. The bag was so heavy that it slid to my waist, so I powered through the opening and got jammed midway. I yanked and pulled, but the bag wouldn't budge.

Neither would I.

"Can you hurry?" Chandra huffed from below. "We need to get home and get some sleep."

"Yeah," a no-longer-subdued Rosalie bellowed, "we need our beauty rest."

There was so much I could've said in reply, but I limited myself to, "I'm stuck, all right?"

"Did you hear that, Rosalie?" Chandra asked. "And yet she still says she didn't stretch out my dress."

My chest swelled, which wasn't helping my situation. "It's the *bag*, Chandra, *not* my bottom."

"Hold on, Franki," Rosalie bellowed. "I'll get your bottom through the hole."

That sounded more ominous than the coming storm. "No need—"

She ramrodded my behind with what had to be her shoulder. The bag popped like Marcella's mimed cork, while my torso and hands slid forward on the second floor, picking up some serious pre-real-boy-Pinocchio splinters.

It was lucky for Rosalie and Ruth both that Louisiana law mandated float harnesses. Otherwise, I might've been responsible for more Mardi Gras murders.

My body and ego smarting from the blow, I pulled myself up and picked wood from my palms.

"Over here, Bob!"

A car horn honked—from the float.

Glenda was near Pinocchio's head, pressing one of her pastie horns and waving at Bob who was passing by below.

Bob continued walking.

She honked again.

"Don't mess with him, Glenda." I dragged my throw bag to a harness hook where she stood. "The man knows his way around a glue gun. I saw him attaching sequins to the Clotho cloud float."

"Glued sequins?" she shouted. "Lordy, what happened to you, Bob?"

He turned, taking her bait. "That's what the board asked for, Glenda."

She put a hand on her hip. "Like you taught me, the client doesn't know best."

"Well, the Sazerac Company is Clotho's biggest sponsor, and they were so impressed with my work that they asked me to do the honor of christening the board members' float tomorrow with a bottle of Tuaca."

I leaned over the rail. "Why Tuaca?"

"It's an ingredient in the krewe's signature drink, and I'm a local celebrity."

Glenda struck a pose. "So am I."

"Don't forget," Bob adjusted his tan silk collar, "I'm a designer."

"So am I. You're looking at one of the debut outfits in my launch of Hucci Cucci Hot Couture, the best #strippercouture in town," Glenda said, tooting her own horn—not either of the ones on her chest, but her figurative horn.

Bob chuckled and shoved his hands into his tan cashmere pants' pockets. "I guess that remains to be seen."

"See this, Bob!" Glenda spun and mooned him with her lit-up tail light.

He gasped, either offended or impressed.

Rather than hear—or watch—anymore of this nonsense, I went to get my other throw bag. I was surprised the Clotho board would allow a male to christen an all-female krewe float. But as I'd witnessed at the Hotel Monteleone, they were wont to do men extreme favors.

Outside the float, Wanda tottered toward me in a short white frock that resembled Nadezhda's prozodezhda. "Sorry, I'm late. I drank a tad too much at the Krewe of Cork."

I looked at the Sixties-style nurse hat on her teased blonde wig. "Is there a krewe for nurses?"

"What?" She touched her hair. "No, I wear this wig when I have to go out with a headache." She pulled up the hat and pulled out an aspirin bottle.

"I could use some of those for my shoulder. You wouldn't happen to have any antacids in there too?" I rested a hand on my belly. The fried pot pie from Turkey and the Wolf was wreaking revenge for being stolen from Hal the Uber driver.

"Sure do. I keep this medicine chest wig fully stocked." Wanda handed me a couple of tablets. "Any case updates?"

"Ask Marcella to fill you in. I need to load my throw bag before David picks me up to meet a chemist about the poison." I popped the antacids and grabbed my duffel bag.

Then I dropped it in shock.

A hand, palm up, was sticking out from beneath the pile.

And the fingers were twitching.

Fear—or agita—gripped my gut. "Wanda! Someone's under the bags!"

She jumped into action.

"Someone call 9-1-1!" I shouted as Wanda and I heaved bags.

Veronica bolted upright from her nap, saw the hand, and made the call. Then she joined the effort to save whoever was under the pile.

After we'd moved a dozen or so bags, a heavily made-up face emerged.

"Josephine!" I pulled a bag from her torso. "Who did this?"

Her lasered lips parted. "On... On..."

Wanda knelt and started CPR, putting her nurse-hat wig to work.

And she kept going even after Josephine's heart had stopped.

The others gathered around and watched in silence, waiting for paramedics, while I tried to make sense of yet another senseless murder.

Because it *was* murder. Josephine hadn't crawled underneath those bags. Someone had done this to her.

But why had she come to float 24?

More importantly, what had she meant by "on"?

Or who?

My palms went clammy as an answer came to me.

She'd been trying to say Honorine or Anaïs.

16

———————

What kind of case have I gotten myself into? My eyes darted to David and The Vassal in the front seat of his blue Toyota. *And them?*

I rested my elbows on their seatbacks and spotted a thread hanging from my sleeve. But the thought of Atropos cutting the thread of life prevented me from pulling it. After four murders in as many days, I was hanging on to my life—and said thread—with all I'd got.

David stopped at a red light and looked at me in the rearview mirror. "It's so insane that the cops didn't shut down the Krewe of Clotho."

"I know. But as far as they're concerned, Josephine's death was an accident, at least until they talk to the company that delivered the throw bags and get an autopsy. There's no way any of that will happen before we parade tomorrow."

The Vassal tugged at the top button of his long-sleeved shirt. "With so many deaths, you'd think the city would require the krewe to hire trained security for its riders, instead of the usual volunteers."

"Right? It makes me wonder whether our police and politicians are benefitting from Clotho's hotel "favor" system. Because this case has all the markings of a spree killer."

David cracked his knuckles. "Who's trying to silence people."

The light turned green, and he hit the gas, causing a Darth Vader bobblehead on the dashboard to shake.

It reminded me of Baron Samedi, the voodoo loa of the dead.

And the hooded driver.

Sliding low in my seat, I peered out the back window to make sure we weren't being followed by the creepy hearse—or a Clotho board member. "Vassal, did you find out whether Anaïs or Honorine have a brother?"

"Honestly, I wasn't able to find information on either of them through the usual channels. I'm looking into whether they have social media accounts under false names."

I shifted to accommodate my smarting tailbone. "Call me with what you find out, no matter what time it is. If we can link one of them to a brother named Travis, we have our Mardi Gras murderer."

"By the way," David said, "bad news on the Greasing of the Poles video. The cops confiscated it from the Royal Sonesta."

"Dead ends at every turn. And dead bodies." I ran my hand through my hair. "Your chemist friend had better know the name of the poison. It might be the only way to identify the killer."

The Vassal pushed up his glasses. "His name is Andy, and he's extremely thorough. If poison was inside Ken Lanier's glass, he found it."

David pulled in front of a house in the artsy Marigny neighborhood and shut off the engine.

My eyes had to be pulling my leg. The shotgun-style residence was a doppelganger for Wanda's Chewbacchus wig. Awnings over the two windows had been made to look like eyelids, and one over the front door resembled a mouth complete with teeth. To complete the Wookiee look, a black plastic nose was just above the door, and brown plastic streamers hung from the roof to simulate fur. "Those are some serious Yardi Gras decorations."

The Vassal turned in his seat. "They're not decorations. His house is art."

"This isn't art, Vassal," I chided as I exited the car. "It's a crime scene. An innocent building has been murdered."

"Franki, wait." David climbed from the driver seat. "Remember not to say anything about Andy's face."

Exhausted from his face-fretting, I headed up the walkway. "Would you mind telling me what it is I'm not supposed to comment on?"

"When he was in high school, he tried to make an exploding pen with silver, and it blew up and tattooed his skin."

I snorted. "That's nothing. When I worked the strip club case, I saw a guy with the whites of his eyes tattooed black." I let David go around me to the front door. "Instead of worrying about his face tattoo, let's go back to his bomb hobby. Any chance this place is booby trapped? Or there's a forgotten explosive lying around somewhere?"

"Totally." David pressed the doorbell, and I didn't know what scared me more—his answer or the Chewbacca roar that came from inside the house.

The Vassal's eyes were larger than usual behind his thick lenses. "Watch for trip wires, infrared light, and freshly dug holes."

Holes? In the house floor? That was more terrifying than the roar doorbell.

The door opened, and Andy stood there, staring.

I tried not to stare back, but it wasn't easy. Put a funnel on his head, and you had the Tin Man.

"You must be Franki."

"Hi," I said, resisting the surprisingly strong urge to add, "ho, Silver!"

His eyes narrowed as he gestured for us to enter.

After checking for landmines, I stepped into a long hallway. I'd expected a hoarder of *Star Wars* memorabilia or, at the very least, comic books. But what I saw was unexpected. The walls were lined with shadow boxes that featured real food.

David pointed to a potato chip with a dark spot. "Andy collects food that looks like stuff. Most of them are obvious, but if you can't tell what something is, check out his labels."

The dark spot vaguely resembled Mother Cabrini, but the label said it was the Grim Reaper. Below it was a Cornflake in the shape of Florida, a French Fry that looked like the Statue of Liberty, and a Cheeto that was the spitting image of Jesus, hence the "Cheesus" label. "Do you have anything with the Virgin Mary? She's always showing up on food."

Andy pointed to the opposite wall. "Not yet, but I've got toast with Nicolas Cage in *Moonstruck*. See his wooden hand?"

I squinted to study the browning pattern of the bread. I sort of did.

"Follow me to the back." Andy squeezed past us. He might've been a ChewbacchanALIEN, but he was shaped like Jabba the Hutt. Or, if I had to compare him to food, frozen yogurt on a cone.

He led us to a midnight-blue room with a twin bed and a desk topped with a large platter of tenders from Willie's Chicken Shack.

The delicious fried smell beckoned to my empty stomach, which replied with a roar as loud as the Chewbacca doorbell. Wanda's antacids had taken care of the damage done by the fried pot pie from Turkey and the Wolf, and now I was as hungry as a wolf. And a turkey. I needed to get this meeting over with before I ate Nic Cage and his wooden hand. "Looking for food shapes in those chicken tenders?"

"Nah." Andy scratched his sandy blonde head, revealing a peach scalp. "It's my dinner."

"I'm super late for dinner with my fiancé." I forced a sheepish smile. "I don't suppose you could spare a tender?"

His silver face went as hard as sterling. "I don't share my food."

My brow arched. Like the Tin Man, Andy didn't have a heart.

"Wait here while I get your glass." He picked up a chicken tender, as if to spite me, but I lost my appetite.

The tender was shaped like the Polish Santa-on-a-gondola ornament I got Ruth in Venice.

Andy slipped through an adjoining door.

And I turned to face my colleagues. "You could've warned me that he looked like a *Wizard of Oz* character."

David blinked. "Is that, like, a heavy metal opera?"

"No, let me guess." The Vassal pressed a finger to his lips and squinted. "You mean a Marvel character, like the Silver Surfer?"

"Duuude." David pointed at The Vassal. "Or the Silver Centurion in *Iron Man*!"

Andy closed the door behind him with a bang. He looked angry about the silver references, but not as angry as I felt. I had barely more than a decade on David and The Vassal, so there was no way they hadn't heard of *The Wizard of Oz*.

"Here's the shard." Andy shoved a plastic baggie at me. "Don't take it out of the plastic. That thing's covered in nicotine."

I took the bag and eyed the shard. "Ken Lanier drank nicotine?"

"No, it's on the outside of the glass."

David's hands shot up as he moved back. "Whoa."

"'Whoa' what?" I looked from his pale face to Andy's silver

one. "Ken wasn't smoking when he took the drink, and neither was the woman who handed it to him."

He shook his head. "This isn't trace nicotine from a cigarette. It's liquid nicotine, probably from an e-cigarette cartridge. It's been painted on the outside of the glass."

"But why?" I stared at the shard. "What would that do?"

"Skin absorbs it, and with that much on the glass, it would be fatal in minutes."

My jaw mimicked The Vassal's, which was already extra slack. The ghostly pharmacist had told me that poisoning could occur through skin contact. And if the victims weren't drinking the poison but touching it, that raised critical questions.

Did the killer poison all the victims' glasses and wear gloves as protection?

Or, since there was no glass near Josephine's body, was literally anything a potential murder weapon?

"WANT US TO ESCORT YOU, FRANKI?" David eyed me from the rearview mirror in front of Private Chicks.

The Vassal turned in the passenger seat and laid a warrior look on me through his coke-bottle lenses. "We have our bowcasters, which shoot arrows."

"Very chivalrous—or Chewbaccalrous—but I'll be fine. The stairwell lights are on, and Bradley's still here." I gestured to his Mercedes in the lot. "I know it's late, but try to track down social media accounts for Honorine and Anaïs before we parade tomorrow, or anything else that'll lead me to a brother named Travis."

David nodded. "We're on it."

"Thanks. I'll work on figuring out who bought the nicotine, and where." I exited the car and slammed the door.

A lone purple glove on the sidewalk near the stairwell made me think of Miss Purple, the woman in the bouffant Mardi Gras wig who'd bought Ken Lanier his last drink from Napoleon's Itch. And one detail no longer made sense—asking the bartender, Mr. Right, to pour out so much of the liquid. After all, the nicotine hadn't been added to the drink, but coated on the glass.

As I climbed the stairs, I replayed the murders in my mind, focusing on the gloves—or lack thereof.

A gloved Claudine in a gold Mardi Gras wig hands a glass to Ken at the Greasing of the Poles, and he drops dead off a balcony support.

A gloved Claudine hands a glass to Marie-Fleur at the empowerment brunch, and she removes her gloves to count money, continuing to sip from her drink.

A gloveless Claudine holds a champagne flute at the Murder Mystery Dinner and dies in the séance room.

And a gloveless Josephine dies beneath the throw bags outside Pinocchio.

A couple of things were clear. One, Josephine's murder was most likely unplanned, possibly because she'd come to the float to tell me something. And two, the Clotho board members wore gloves to protect their hands, so the Catherine de' Medici story about poisoned sweet gloves no longer seemed relevant.

But what about the Tuaca?

Somehow the Renaissance liqueur was part of the killing spree. It wasn't a coincidence that Travis, the hooded hearse driver and brother of the killer, had bought a bottle at the Liquor Store. *But what is he going to do with it?*

There was also the fact that the Sazerac Company was hosting a float christening with a bottle of its Tuaca rather than champagne. *What role does that play in the case?*

My phone rang.

I stepped onto the third-floor landing and pulled my phone from my bag.

My mother at midnight on a Monday?

A horrifying realization hit me like a liqueur bottle. I hadn't heard a ship alarm.

Because she's calling from her cell phone.

"Holy mother of de' Medici." My hand went to my mouth. "She's seen Rosalie's fake incriminating pictures."

Out of nowhere I heard "Tubular Bells," the haunting piano motif from *The Exorcist*.

I spun to look behind me.

"Of *course* the stairwell is empty," I whispered. "Your mother's in Houston with your bedridden nonna." I paused. "Appropriate soundtrack, though. Because now that she's seen those pictures, you're going to need an exorcist to get the devil out of her."

The Devil.

I spun again to check for the killer—and my mother.

My head joined my aching ribs and eye and tailbone and shoulder. This case was already too much, and now I had family drama brewing.

A devil's brew.

I needed Bradley.

And dinner.

With a sigh, I knocked on his office door, hoping he'd gotten takeout. I was so famished I would've polished off the stale food in Andy the chemist's shadow boxes, including Cheesus, however sacrilegious.

Bradley didn't answer.

"It's Franki. Open up." I jiggled the knob.

Locked.

The nape of my neck tingled.

I spun once again.

"Mom?"

No one was behind me. I would've heard them on the old wooden stairs.

So why am I on edge?

My gaze shot across the landing to the Private Chicks door.

Slowly, I walked to it and gripped the handle.

Open.

Is Bradley in here?

My gaze shot over my shoulder.

That purple glove outside on the sidewalk.

The same color as Anaïs's sequined Fendi baguette.

My head jerked back to Bradley's office. I raised my phone and called him.

Voicemail.

Has he been abducted?

Or worse?

My gut churned as I pulled a nail file from my bag and jimmied his lock. I got inside and checked the floor, afraid of what I would find.

Everything was in order.

Pounding descended the stairs.

Footsteps!

My gut went down with them. "Oh, God. Someone was inside Private Chicks."

I closed Bradley's door and dashed downstairs to the street.

Deserted.

I ran around the corner.

A group of teens were riding bikes, but no one else was in sight. Whoever had been in the office had escaped.

My phone rang in my hand.

My mother. Again.

Panicked, I gazed at the lights in the office.

Is Bradley up there after all?

Maybe injured?

Or...?

With my heart racing in my throat—and freaking "Tubular Bells" back in my head—I sprinted up the three flights of stairs and burst into the lobby, then the hallway. I stopped abruptly at the kitchenette.

Someone was face down on the two-top table, but Bradley didn't have a bun.

"Ruth!" I threw my phone on the table and carefully lifted her head by her whiskered chin. Her eyes were closed, and she had a dried brown substance around her mouth.

Blood?

"Wake up, Ruth!" I shook her. "Snap out of it!" As much as I disliked her, I didn't want her to die. Just go away. Someplace far. Like Venice, where she could get an authentic Murano-glass Santa-on-a-gondola ornament.

Her eyelids fluttered, and a moan escaped her lips.

"Come on, Ruth!" I patted her cheeks. "You're a krewe director. You have a float to captain tomorrow morning."

She opened her eyes. Her lined face drew up, possibly to underscore the seriousness of her charge, but she didn't utter a word.

Which, honestly, was nice.

She tried to lay down her head.

"Ruth, you have to stay awake. You've might've been poisoned."

"Yeah," she struggled to sit upright, "I have."

"Did you see who did this?"

Her head bobbed. "You."

My cheek-pats remained gentle, but it was hard. "No, there was an intruder."

She stiffened. "There was?"

"Yes, so this is one problem you can't blame on me."

"Fair enough."

My brows rose. The nicotine must've reached her brain.

"Technically," she stuck out her tongue, "it *was* your leftover Nutella king cake that sent me into this food coma."

My king cake? The one I'd hidden to keep her from eating? My fingers folded into fists. I couldn't worry about a cake with Bradley missing, but she'd pay for this later. Gambino's Bakery was outside of town, and I didn't have a car. And king cake season ended on Mardi Gras Day—tomorrow. "Where's Bradley?"

"He went to get dinner from VooDoo Tavern & PoBoys."

My heart fell to the floor. The tavern was around the corner. He could've run into the intruder. "Stay here, and don't touch anything in case it's poisoned." I grabbed my phone. "I'll explain when I get back."

Frantic, I called Bradley as I ran through the lobby.

"Hey, babe," he answered, totally normal.

Relief flooded over me, and tears threatened to spill.

"Sorry I didn't answer before. I was ordering us some dinner."

My eyes squeezed shut. "Tell me you're still at the VooDoo Tavern."

"I am. Why?

Relieved, I took a moment to breathe. "A few minutes ago, an intruder fled the office."

"Are you all right?" The concern in his tone was palpable. "And Ruth?"

"We're both fine," I said, although that term was tough to use in regard to Ruth.

"I'm on my way."

"No, don't leave the food! I mean, stay where you are for a while longer until we know it's safe." I hoped he hadn't heard the fierce stomach growl that had preceded the clarification.

"Franki, I'll be fine. Just make sure the door is locked until I get there."

"Okay, but don't touch anything, not even the doorknob." I grabbed a Post-It from the reception desk and turned the bolt. "It could be poisoned."

He exhaled, stunned. "It's going to be all right. I love you."

"I love you too, so be careful because, contrary to what my mother thinks, I can't wait to marry you."

"What?" He sounded more concerned than when I'd told him about the intruder.

"Uh, I'll explain later." I hung up.

What on earth prompted me to say that?

I sighed and headed toward my office. As I passed the kitchenette, my phone rang. One glance at the display, and I pressed *Decline.*

Ruth was at the sink, wiping her face with a wad of paper towels. "Was that Bradley calling back? He could be in trouble."

"Relax. It was my mom, and she's going to keep calling."

"Then why don't you answer?"

Maybe it was the seriousness of the situation, but I decided to be honest. "Because her friend, Rosalie, made her think I'm into women."

"Well I'll be damned." She slapped her thigh. "You're not only a ride reneger, you're a reception reneger too."

My mouth didn't deign to respond, but my eyelids did. "I'm going to check the rest of the office. You call Veronica and let her know what happened."

I took one step down the hallway.

And stopped cold.

A spindle protruded from my door, which was ajar. "Ruth," I called, "did you open my office door?"

"I've been unconscious in the kitchenette, remember?"

The killer had been in my office, which was almost as creepy as when Ruth moved in over Christmas.

In case the handle had been doused with nicotine, I kicked the door open.

Everything was as I'd left it.

Except one thing.

My gratitude journal was open in the middle of my desk.

Calmly, I walked around to my chair, careful not to touch anything.

The intruder had left me a message—handwritten in purple ink.

If you and your fiancé have anything to be grateful for, it's that his assistant was in the office. But rest assured, this is your last Mardi Gras.

Ruth hovered in the doorway, wearing her cat-eye readers and holding the wad of paper towels. "Find something?"

"A threat to Bradley and me."

Her glasses chains started swinging. "How dare they."

We were in agreement about that, even though I suspected her outrage was reserved for Bradley. But, like her, I wasn't worried about me at the moment. The killer had made a huge mistake in threatening Bradley.

I walked over to Ruth, snatched the paper towels from her hand, and used them to rip the page from the journal and wad it up.

"What'd you do that for?" Ruth's turkey neck trembled. "Aren't you going to give that to the police?"

"Not a chance." I dropped the crumpled paper and paper towels into my bag. "That would deprive me of the pleasure of cramming it down the killer's throat."

17

"Hey, babe," Bradley called from my living room. "Can you come here for a sec?"

"I'll bet he's got a surprise for you," I whispered to my reflection in the bathroom mirror. Giddy with excitement, I switched off the light and went to find out what my fiancé was up to.

But Bradley was nowhere to be found, and my front door was wide open. *Did Napoleon run into the cemetery again?*

"That Cairn terror," I grumbled. "He only pulls this stunt in the dead of night."

I stepped onto the porch. A thick fog had rolled in, so I couldn't see a thing, not even Thibodeaux's bar across the street.

Odd.

A pair of headlights came on, illuminating the swirling gray fog.

And Chandra's U-Haul.

Chanel No. 5 was in the air.

The Clotho killer was here.

An engine raced, and the creepy Cadillac hearse pulled up

with its glowing red U R NEXT license plate. The door opened, and a force pushed me in.

To a coffin.

I spun to find the culprit.

Ruth Walker leaned into the doorway, her chin whiskers as sharp as spindles. "Time to pay for your sins, you ride-and-reception reneger."

I didn't respond. I'd sooner let the hearse driver take me to hell than plead with a woman who didn't fit her name definitions.

She ran her fingers over the door, and the paint turned from black to Romanade gold. "At least the ride will be smoother than a Polish Santa-on-a-gondola ornament."

"I told you," I ground out, "that makes no sense!"

The hooded driver threw back his head and laughed. The hood fell off, revealing silver skin, a liquid black mouth—*and Wanda's Chewbacchus wig?*

What kind of devil car am I in?

The hearse set in motion, and high luminescence LEDs lit up the aluminum coffin compartment.

My cheeks grew hot. Not because I was sweating my destiny, but because I was in the disco Phantom Hearse B12 Phil had told me about.

The funeral coach lurched to and fro, and the ride seemed eternal. *Where is the driver taking me? To Baron Samedi?*

We came to a stop.

The underworld?

I peered from the coffin.

No, the damned Pinocchio float.

The de-hooded driver pulled me from the coffin with the strength of Chewbacca, threw me over his shoulder, and carried me up the ladder.

Screaming, I pounded his back. *Pink fur?*

Bradley was on board, gagged and chained to the bathroom door.

But it was no longer a bathroom.

It was a portal to hell.

Bile bubbled into my throat. *Are we in The Devil tarot card Chandra drew for Marie-Fleur?*

A handcuff snapped shut on my wrist, and I stared horrified at my captor—an old woman in a black mourning dress with a matching handbag. "Nonna?"

"Eh!" She shrugged. "We gotta get-a you two to the altar one-a way or another."

"*Satan's* altar?" I shrieked.

An evil laugh erupted above my head, emitting a blast of fiery hot air.

Has to be my mother.

I looked up, and sure enough. She sat over the door, surrounded by fire, in horns, a tail, and Marguerite Piazza's Flame of Hades dress. "That's right, Francesca. Your nonna made a deal with the devil—me." She laughed, causing her forked tongue to bounce. "Now I get exclusive rights to plan your wedding."

"Mom, we're not getting married in Texas City!"

Her tail waved off the notion. "That Santa-on-a-gondola ornament has sailed."

My head retracted. "What does that even *mean*?"

"It means you and Bradley are getting married at the deli, and your brother Anthony will officiate."

Bradley's eyes bulged as he moaned through the cloth gag, and I understood the reason. Given my brother's affected New Jersey-Italian accent and the location, we might as well have Tony Soprano do the honors at a butcher shop.

A balcony support rose from the flames with Rosalie clinging to it like a stripper to a pole. She held up a pig bomboniere with lipstick, false eyelashes, heels and a feather boa, and gave it a shake. Jordan almonds rained from its bottom.

Marcella materialized on a second balcony support. "How classy is that?"

My mom cackled and raised a bottle of Tuaca. "Here's to the happy couple."

"Happy? We're in hell!" Perspiration broke out on my upper lip. "Release us from these chains."

"Not on your lives," she bellowed in a devil voice. She poured Tuaca on the fire, and it roared, devouring Rosalie and Marcella. Then she hurled the bottle at my head.

I caught it but realized too late that it had been coated with nicotine. I looked at my gloveless hand in horror and dropped the bottle, which morphed into a Willie's COCKtail glass and splashed Lord knows what on my cheeks.

My eyes fluttered open.

Standing over me was my mother—holding a cup from my bathroom. "Sorry to douse you in water, dear, but you've been writhing around in that bed and wouldn't wake up. And you feel hot."

I was still sleep-dazed, but one thing was clear. I'd awakened from a nightmare to a nightmare.

Wiping my face with the sheet, I exhaled. "If I'm hot, it's because you've been holding my feet to the fire over this wedding."

"What are you talking about?" she shrill-drawled. "For your information, I stopped your nonna from bringing an exorcist." She gestured to the bathroom. "But now that I've seen what you did to your toilet, I think I should've let her."

My head rolled toward the clock on the nightstand. Five-thirty a.m. After I'd refused her calls over Rosalie's fake incriminating photos, Brenda Amato had loaded my nonna into the Ford Taurus and driven all night to get here.

Happy Mardi Gras!

Yawning, I pulled myself onto my elbows. "That toilet was your best friend's doing—the one you sent to keep me in line?"

"A lot of good it did."

"You just made my point."

My mom returned the cup to the bathroom counter. "Rosalie said this case is taking all of your time. You've got to wrap it up and pick a wedding venue."

"Um, identifying a homicidal maniac doesn't work like that."

She gave a stiff smile and patted my arm. "That's why we're here, dear."

Before I could delve deeper into that troubling statement, I heard car doors slamming.

Lots of them.

I cocked my head. "Who's that?"

"The nonne."

Madonna mia. The Catholic Cavalry had come after all. I flopped onto my pillow.

Then I shot up. "Where's Bradley?"

"Having a chat with Father John. Your nonna and I thought some pre-marital counseling was in order."

Bradley had proposed to me on Mardi Gras the year before. *How did we go from that bliss to this bottomless pit?*

Now that I thought about it, my Devil tarot card nightmare hadn't been that far off.

My bedroom door opened, and I screamed.

A mini hearse driver in a Chewbacchus wig entered.

No, wait. It was Chandra in a black trench.

She pushed her brown bouffant bob from her eyes. "I don't know what's going on at the singles' compound this morning, but my Mitsubishi is blocked in, and we need to get to the float."

Glenda hopped into the room, bound in chef aprons with strange bluish lights shining through the bodice. "The

Lilliputians have done it again, Miss Franki. Not only have they put me in these straitjackets, they did the same to my Yardi Gras decorations."

Rosalie rushed in. "Still working on the parking, but the good news is, everyone's confirmed for the Krewe of Clotho."

"Wonderful." My mother gave my arm another pat. "See there, Francesca? Like I said, we'll help you find the killer."

It was fitting that I had to search for Tiffany among the mourners of the Société de Saint Anne. I didn't have any ashes to dump into the river, but I was definitely in mourning.

Nonna shuffled in, clutching her handbag. "It's-a worse than-a we thought, Brenda. Brad-a-ley told-a Father John they haven't look-ed at a ven-a-ue, and-a Franki doesn't have-a any tomatoes."

"Why do you need tomatoes, Nonna?"

She blanched and crossed herself, as though the question were a form of blasphemy.

"Sauce, Francesca!" my mother cried. "Or don't you want your guests to eat?"

Guests? They were intruders, like Ruth and the killer in my office.

My phone vibrated on the nightstand.

The Vassal.

"Everybody out!" I rose from the bed and shooed them to the door.

My mother scowled. "What about the venue?"

"And my Mitsubishi?"

"And the Lilliputians, sugar?"

"And-a the tomatoes?"

It took all of my strength, but I managed to shove the lot of them into the living room. "Rosalie can help with all of that. She's got serious control skills."

Rosalie covered her mouth and leaned in to my mother, but "Bridezilla" was audible.

My nonna raised her fist. "I told-a you, Brenda! We need-a the exorcist."

"If you call one, Nonna, let me know. I have some possessed people in the house." I slammed the door.

Then I got back into bed and answered my phone. "Hey, Vassal. Quick question. Is there a Chewbacca with pink fur?"

"The Pink Wookiee. You haven't heard of him?"

No, but somehow my subconscious had. I couldn't decide whether that warranted a dream analyst or a psychoanalyst. Probably both. "Forget I asked. Have you found out whether Honorine or Anaïs has a brother?"

"No, but I have learned that Anaïs Monvoisin is an assumed name. Her birth name is Anna Moyer."

So, she wasn't the descendant of the notorious French poisoner, Catherine Monvoisin. "Maybe that's why Josephine the Go-Between came to the float, to tell me that Anaïs isn't a Casket Girl. She's a fraud."

"Potentially. But I discovered one other interesting detail. Her parents own a smoke shop in Opelousas."

Nicotine.

"IT'S SO HAAARD," a plump, sixtyish woman wailed. She pressed her blue-and-green wizard hat to her head. "How will I go on?"

I'd been asking myself the same thing. Given my litany of injuries, it had been an especially long walk from the Bywater neighborhood to the Société de Saint Anne's ash-spreading spot at the Mississippi River. And I still hadn't found Ken Lanier's daughter, Tiffany.

As I adjusted the shoulder of my too-tight Krewe of Clotho toga, I spotted a box under the woman's arm and realized she was grieving. "I'm sorry for your loss. Maybe counseling will help?"

"How? It won't bring my Jerry back."

I winced. Sounded like she'd lost her husband, or maybe a son.

"Oh, Jerry." She hugged the box. "You were the best gerbil."

"Jerry was a *gerbil*?"

Her chubby face drooped. "Now you understand my pain."

I'm pretty sure my face was blank. "So, I guess that's Gerry with a *g*?"

"Short for Gerald." She sniffled and opened the box to retrieve a baggie with a few tablespoons of ashes.

Mixed with aqua blue glitter.

Wind whipped over the water, which was concerning given what was about to happen. I didn't want to wear Gerry.

Or inhale him.

Leaving her to mourn, I slipped into the crowd. Hundreds of people had processed to the river with the bohemian krewe. Most wore wild costumes, and many played instruments. Fortunately, not all of them held ashes.

As I continued along the river's edge, a fishy odor assailed my nostrils, which conjured up unpleasant images given the nature of the ceremony and the expression "fish food." Even worse, women with crab nets decorated with colorful streamers were dipping them in the water and flicking them at the crowd, anointing us. No ashes had yet been spread, but the droplets reminded me of the spittle of that ghostly pharmacist.

God only knows what was in it.

"Vicky need a picky?" a middle-aged woman in a tiara and silver fairy wings asked in baby talk. She stooped to pick up a small mass of brown fur on a leash.

The dog growled and snapped.

She snatched back her hand and looked at me. "Victor—I call him Vicky—doesn't like to cross certain streets, or go around some corners. He also doesn't like various kinds of sidewalks and models of cars. And he really doesn't appreciate leaf blowers and noisy construction sites."

Vicky was maybe fifteen pounds and looked like a cross between a guinea pig and Wanda's Chewbacchus wig. "He sounds...picky."

"Oh, don't say that. It's his safe word."

"His *safe* word?"

"For me to pick him up." She beamed at the dog. "Because Vicky's tricky."

He stuck out the tip of his tongue, which was adorable.

Despite myself, I knelt to pet his head.

As my hand approached, Vicky rose up on his back feet, his front arms dangling, and swayed from side to side like Axl Rose dancing to "Sweet Child o' Mine." He sounded like Axl too—a cross between a vibrato growl and a nasal whine.

"No bitey, Vicky," the woman admonished. "Just licky." She lowered her hand, and Tricky Vicky latched onto her finger.

And drew blood.

Time to move on. That mongrel was more terrifying than the hooded hearse driver and my nightmare devil mother.

Scanning the people who'd assembled on the riverbank to spread ashes, I saw a young woman with pink hair sitting alone. She wore a faded Free Brittany t-Shirt, a red tulle skirt, and black Chuck Taylor high tops, and beside her was an urn that I sensed held the remains of Ken Lanier. "Tiffany?"

Steely gray eyes met mine, as did a pair of Martian eyes protruding from her hair. "And you are?"

"A PI. I'd like to talk to you about your father's death."

She gazed at the river. "Judging from your black eye and tan toga, you're on the Krewe of Clotho."

A snort escaped my nostrils. Even though the black eye was caused by Glenda's sit bone, I definitely felt as though I'd been battered by the krewe. "I'm investigating members of the board who broke into my client's wig shop."

"Wiggins Wigs, I know the place."

Judging from her hairdo, she did.

She sniffed. "And I know the board."

I crouched beside her. "I heard you were the krewe secretary, until Carly Cash replaced you."

Tiffany leaned back on her hands. "Carly and her reprehensible father led a campaign against me to up their social standing."

"And not because of the personal injury case your dad represented involving one of Carl's cars?"

She shook her head. "Carl hated my father for that, but I don't think he had anything to do with his murder, if that's what you're getting at. Carl's too smart to get mixed up in anything that'll cost him money."

Good to know since the snake still had my car.

"Besides, Anaïs is the one who replaced me with Carly."

My ears pricked up. "Why would she do that?"

"Evidently she wanted something in exchange."

The use of his cars? Or something more? "Who do you think killed your father?"

"At first I suspected the captain, Claudine Denault." She frowned at the urn. "My father and I had a falling out over their relationship. She was dishonest, like the rest of them, and he knew it."

"Yeah, but I heard he wanted to investigate her."

She shot me a hard look. "To get revenge. Claudine left him for a woman."

I was glad Rosalie hadn't known that. The chubby redhead at Napoleon's Itch had been enough to send her into full wrecking-ball mode. "Who was the woman? Another board member?"

"No, a Russian, but I don't know her name."

I got an image of Nadezhda sucking her eyetooth hole. *Has to be one of the Sashas.* "I found an anonymous letter at Clotho headquarters threatening Marie-Fleur if she told your father what she knew. Any idea what that might be?"

"Could be anything. They all had secrets."

The wind picked up, which was bad news. Two shirtless men in Spandex pants were pouring ashes into the river right next to me.

My nostrils clamped shut.

"I'm coming, Gerry!"

I recognized the voice of the gerbil woman and turned.

Just as she threw herself into the mighty Mississip.

For a split second, I was tempted to join her. After all, my mom and nonna were not only in town, they were on my Mardi Gras krewe.

But of course I was joking.

Sort of.

The woman wasn't kidding, though. She hadn't come up.

A soulful sigh escaped my lips. Somehow, I'd known my journey with the Société de Saint Anne would come to this. I waded into the river, reached underwater, and used brute force to lift her up.

Because there was no way in Hades that I was dunking my head in a liquid graveyard.

She sputtered and gasped but didn't struggle.

Two of the women with crab nets came to help.

"Come on, dear," one said, leading her away. "Let's get you dry."

Tiffany looked up at me and scrunched her nose. "That was nice of you."

I squeezed tan water—and Gerry—from my tan toga. "You were saying? About the Clotho board members' secrets?"

"Oh, I just meant that none of them are who they say they are. They're frauds."

Anaïs certainly was. I thought about Josephine's silence following my comment about all of the board members being Casket Girls. "Care to elaborate?"

"They were good at keeping secrets and covering their tracks, for themselves and one another." She rested her hand on the urn.

And the hearse driver reared his hooded head. "Do you know if Honorine or Anaïs have a brother?"

"They never talked about their families, but my father once said Honorine's origins are humbler than she lets on. Despite her rich act, she married money."

I knew Anaïs, aka Anna Moyer, had humble origins, as in the family smoke shop. "What about Anaïs? How'd she come into cash?"

"She married a construction magnate, then got a divorce and a small fortune."

"Did you know she's an aspiring writer of psychological thrillers?"

"I'm not surprised." She rose and picked up the remains of her father, evidently done with my questions. "Anaïs took great pains to keep this a secret, but before she got married, she worked at Crescent City Books in the Quarter. So she had plenty of time to research how to write."

And to research poisons.

~

YOU'RE OUT OF TIME, *Franki.*

A toxic thought given the threats I'd received, but that wasn't how I'd meant it. It was almost 11:30, and the Krewe of Clotho paraded at noon. And yet instead of heading to the Pinocchio float, I was race-walking through the French Quarter to Crescent City Books.

The instant Tiffany mentioned the used bookstore, I knew I had to go. The name reminded me of Chandra Toccato's cockamamie psychic moniker, the Crescent City Medium. And even though I was convinced Chandra was a con artist, somehow she'd helped me solve cases.

Would someone at the bookstore do the same?

It was a long shot, but I had to check it out. And there was no time like the present to ID a killer, particularly when more lives could hang in the balance.

Hang, *Franki?*

Really?

The word recalled Ken Lanier upside down on the balcony support and The Hanged Man tarot card Chandra had drawn for Marie-Fleur. Not to mention, Glenda's godawful Yardi Gras decorations—that were now wearing chef's aprons.

I picked up my pace, weaving through partiers, huffing and puffing.

Pew! Also toxic—the fish smell coming from my Clotho costume. Not even Chanel No. 5 would cover the odor. But no matter. During Mardi Gras in New Orleans, it wasn't weird to see a woman in a bedraggled tan toga that smelled like dead fish.

The Death tarot card flashed in my head.

Then The Devil card.

Is Anaïs the spree killer?

All indications pointed to her, but I needed concrete proof. Thanks to vaping, one didn't need to have a smoke shop in the family to get a hold of pure nicotine. And a purple-sequined Fendi bag certainly didn't link Anaïs to the purple Mardi Gras wig.

No, Honorine could be the killer too.

Without video of Miss Purple's face at the Greasing of the Poles, I couldn't be sure who the spree killer was. What I was sure of—either Anaïs or Honorine was trying to frame the other for the murders.

And while it was possible that no one else was going to die, I couldn't rule out another victim, maybe even during the parade.

But who would it be?

A member of the Krewe of Clotho who wasn't on my radar?

Or Bradley and me?

I rounded a corner onto Chartres Street and yanked open the door to Crescent City Books, wishing I hadn't seen *Grimm's Complete Fairy Tales* in the window.

For a French Quarter establishment, the bookstore was unremarkable. A glass storefront, plain white walls, and musty-smelling books stacked everywhere.

A cat walked along a glass case that served as a counter. Behind it sat a woman in a white knit cardigan and Mardi Gras beads who looked as old and yellow as the books she was selling.

"Hi." I adjusted my shoulder fabric, attempting to look dignified. "I'm an acquaintance of Anna Moyer. She used to work here?"

The cat's eyes narrowed.

"Ah, yes." Her gaze mimicked her pet's. "I remember Anna."

"She recommended a book to me, but I've already forgotten the title. It's about poisons—I, uh...I'm thinking about writing a mystery."

A paw batted at my breast.

Does this cat know I'm lying? Then I put two and two together —the fish smell from my dip in the river.

The woman clapped at the cat. "Isabel, go to your chair."

Isabel sat and licked her paw.

The woman picked up a pair of rhinestone cat-eye readers that rivaled Ruth's—and Isabel's feline stare. "I know the book. Anna was always reading it."

Hope soared through my chest. "Do you still have it?"

"She took it with her."

My hope nose-dived into the Mississippi. "So you don't have a copy?"

"I have several." She slid on the readers. "It's out of print, but it's still the gold standard for authors who want to use poison in their plots." She smiled and pushed from her chair. "Or anyone else, really. Follow me."

After that last comment, I wasn't sure I wanted to. But I needed to follow the book lead, wherever it went, so I followed her stooped frame.

And Isabel followed me.

The woman's knobby fingers pulled a book from a shelf. "*Deadly Doses: A writer's guide to poisons.*"

I knew writers were addicts and maniacs. "Mind if I look through it?"

"Take your time." She walked away.

I exited the shelf and sat in a chair.

Isabel leapt into my lap.

"Shoo, cat."

She batted at my thigh.

Apparently, this was her chair. I rose and flipped to the Index. I found nicotine and went to the first page referenced.

My eyes skimmed the text.

A discussion of Italian poisons, including the Borgia's cantarella, and how the French word *Italien* became synonymous with *empoisonneur*.

My hand went to my cheek, both from the surprise at seeing that particular topic on a page about nicotine—and because I could almost feel that ghostly pharmacist spitting on me.

The next line mentioned none other than Catherine de' Medici.

Further down the page, La Voisin, aka Catherine Monvoisin.

My hands trembled. These weren't coincidences. I'd found something—at the very least, the origin of Anaïs's assumed surname, Monvoisin. But to link her to the murders, I needed the nicotine.

Nudging Isabel from the chair, I took a seat.

And I scoured the page, word for word.

The cat batted the hem of my toga, and I let her. She was annoying, but she was no Tricky Vicky.

Nerves on edge, I came to a mention of Catherine de' Medici's notorious *parfumeurs* and a list of her enemies that they allegedly helped her to poison.

I stopped at the story of the Cardinal of Lorraine.

And my heart seemed to do the same.

Because the Cardinal died after handling gold coins—treated with nicotine.

18

———

My nerves were wound as tight as thread on a spindle as I walked across the convention center parking lot in my bedraggled, too-tight toga, holding my ribs with one hand and rubbing my tailbone with the other. The case was coming to a head, I could feel it. But I had no idea what that meant.

Another death?

An arrest?

Something I couldn't predict?

Pinocchio came into view, and the answer hit me like Geppetto's hammer.

A float captained by Ruth "Ruthless" Walker teeming with the likes of Chandra, my mom, Rosalie, Sicilian nonne—*and sassy drag queens?*

"This Mardi Gras is *murder*," I muttered.

Nevertheless, I began climbing the ladder to the first level, hoping to slip to the top of the float unnoticed by one notoriously cranky queen.

But it wasn't meant to be.

With each rung, more of the hopeless reality awaiting me

emerged. Big feet squeezed into strappy Roman sandals, a wide togaed torso with a "Miss Campy Clotho" sash, and a block head in a blonde wig with spools for curlers.

Carnie Vaul's gold-glossed lips pursed. "Look what the cat dragged in, hours after we were supposed to be on board."

There was no way to counter that comment. I was late and covered in gerbil. "I had to question a witness. It couldn't wait."

"*Mm-hm.*" Her tone had turned hard. "Meanwhile, *we* had to."

My gaze strayed to the queens behind her, who were hard at work unwrapping individually packaged items from their throw bags. If it hadn't been for them, I would've recommended that Campy-Clotho Carnie go take a hike with KRAP on their Dungeons & Drag Queens walk with Chewbacchus.

The bathroom door opened, and Glenda sauntered out looking like the Blue Fairy from *Pinocchio: The Stripper Version*. Rather than full fabric, she'd opted for a smattering of gold threads, gilded leaves over her privates, and blue lights, which explained the glow I'd noticed coming through the aprons the nonne had covered her with at my apartment.

"There you are, Miss Franki. I forgot to mention that I invited Miss Carnie, since we had spaces to fill."

It took effort, but I limited my response to a nod. I would've sooner recruited a rider from New Orleans' Central Lockup, like the skin slougher who'd used me as a pillow the time I spent my birthday in the slammer.

"Over here." Carnie beckoned to a queen wearing what could only be described as a luxury-lunacy look. Not only had she bedazzled her toga with Chanel's double-C logo and cubic zirconias, she'd turned her eyebrows into her eyelid creases, drawn fake eyebrows above them, and used rhinestones for eyeshadow with inch-long, painted-on eyelashes. Most eye-catching, she wore a wide-brimmed hat topped with a cuckoo clock that reminded me of the one in Phil's office at the Saint Cecelia Cemetery.

"Miss Glenda—and Franki," Carnie grunted, "this is my dear friend, Coocoo Chanel. Miss Coocoo wears everything Chanel, and she's practically a scholar of the brand."

Coocoo fixed Glenda and me with her crazy-expensive stare. "*Enchanté.*"

I extended my hand for a shake, but Campy-Clotho Carnie shoved me away. "Girl, what is that scent you're wearing? *Poisson?*"

The joke was clear—the French word for *fish* instead of the perfume Poison—but I definitely didn't laugh. "A woman with the Société de Saint Anne went into the river, and I had to help her."

"Need I remind you," Carnie thundered, spools shaking, "that riding on a Mardi Gras float is an hourslong journey, all downwind?"

"That's why I'm upstairs, and you're down here." I attempted a dignified look by tossing my damp toga fabric over my shoulder. "But it has nothing to do with my smell, and everything to do with your hot air."

Carnie gasped and flailed her arms, literally taken aback.

Poor Coocoo had to catch her.

Glenda dropped into a stripper squat to unwrap her throws. "I hope you know your scent isn't the reason I'm riding downstairs, sugar. It's to avoid another clothing confrontation with The Lilliputians."

"I don't blame you, Miss Glenda," Carnie butted in. "A woman's style can't be repressed, although Franki's river-rat style should be."

"It's river-*gerbil*," I corrected.

Carnie was so shaken one of her wig spools fell to the deck.

Glenda hung Mardi Gras beads with boobs on the throw

hooks that lined the float. "Speaking of scent and style, Miss Franki, have you seen Bob Simpson?"

"No. Why?"

"I want him to see my Hucci Cucci Hot Couture version of his tired tan toga."

Carnie clasped her hands. "Love the name, Miss Glenda. The hoochie coochie was performed at carnivals."

A carnie queen *would* bring that up. "Just out of curiosity, what do the blue lights have to do with Clotho?"

"Well, sugar," Glenda ripped the wrapping from a penis plushie package, "I envision her as a morning nymph, so they symbolize drops of dew."

Except that the dewdrops were practically the size of headlights.

She pointed the decidedly non-child-friendly throw at me. "One way or another, Bob's going to see this costume. If I have to, I'll climb onto Pinocchio's nose and put on a show."

Given his nose's similarity to a pole, we all knew she'd do that regardless.

Coocoo laid her mad-money stare on Glenda. "You're going to make Pinocchio a real boy."

"You mean," Carnie smirked, spinning the stray spool, "a real *man*."

On that note, I started climbing the ladder to the top deck.

Once again, I hoped to avoid one rider in particular.

But no such luck.

Rung by rung, another dejecting reality appeared. Long, narrow feet in white Keds, a togaed torso with a clipboard, and a lined, frowning face in a blonde Cleopatra-style wig.

"It's about damn time you showed up," Ruth snapped with a crack of her clipboard. "Chewbacchus and Commodus are already on the parade route, and we're due to line up any minute."

I shrugged. "Perfect timing, then."

She glared at me over the rim of her cat-eyes. "For a ride and reception reneger."

"Clearly, I'm on the ride, Ruth." I gestured to Pinocchio's innards. "And I won't miss my own reception."

"I'll believe that when I see it." Ruth spun on her Keds.

She wouldn't see it, because she wouldn't be there—even if I married at the Historical Pharmacy Museum and had a chance to go all Borgia on her.

Ruth went to the helm behind Pinocchio's enormous head, where Wanda, Marcella, and Veronica had saved me a spot. In the middle of the float were Chandra, Rosalie, and my mother, and Nonna was in the rear with the nonne. Everyone wore the Krewe of Clotho tan togas except the nonne, who were in Catholic Cavalry black—in rosaries instead of Mardi Gras beads.

But all donned the same blonde Cleopatra wig as Ruth.

Those in togas unwrapped their Clotho throws, while those in mourning dress sorted pasta, tomatoes, and garlic—the Italian answer to the St. Patrick's Day parade's potatoes, cabbage, and onions.

"Franki," Nonna's black eyes met mine from beneath blonde bangs, "we got it all-a planned. We throw-a the pasta and-a garlic to the people, and-a we use-a the tomatoes on-a the killer."

Santina Messina, nonna's longtime friend who sat in a chair, picked up a tomato and did a mock demonstration.

"Thanks, Nonna." I hugged her. "But I thought the tomatoes were for the sauce."

"Eh." She turned up her palms. "It's-a Mardi Gras. We get-a the takeout."

My head spun like a Clotho spindle. In her eighty-plus years, my nonna had never uttered a more sacrilegious comment.

"Francesca," my mother tapped me on the shoulder.

"YeaAAAAHHH"! I reply-screamed as I turned.

Like Mother Cabrini, my mom had either had a run-in with Marcella's eyeshadow palette, or she'd made up her eyes like Elizabeth Taylor's in *Cleopatra* to go with the wig.

"Try to stay calm, dear," she said, mistaking my fear of her appearance for fear of the killer. She pointed to Rosalie and Chandra. "We're going to stand guard in the middle, and we have better weapons than tomatoes."

Chandra two-fisted Clotho spindles. "Anyone makes a wrong move, and I'll clock 'em with one 'o these. Boston strong!"

Rosalie stared at me, silent.

But I wasn't convinced that my fake incriminating pics of her cavorting with Glenda's Yardi Gras decorations could restrain her inner wrecking ball.

As we faced off, my gaze strayed to her throw station to check for the pig bomboniere, in case she planned to sprinkle Jordan almonds to trip the killer.

Her gaze strayed too.

I lunged for her throw bag but stopped.

Whistling and catcalling had erupted on the drag deck below.

"That man-servant lewk is giving me life," a queen yelled.

"It's for the gods," another shouted.

"Love the Mount Olympus outfit, Bradley honey," Glenda drawled. "Shows off your buff arms and legs."

Uh-oh. I leaned over the side of the float.

Bradley was below, slightly pink-cheeked, in a tan one-piece tank-top-mini-man-skirt combo that almost revealed his other pink cheeks. "Hey, babe. I signed up for krewe security."

"Awww," my mother grabbed my wrist right as I was about to blow him a kiss. "Isn't that romantic, Francesca? He's looking out for you."

"*Madonna mia!*" Nonna clutched her sagging jowls. "Some-a-one had-a better look-a out-a for his-a pants. He's-a naked out-a there."

"Forget the pants," Chandra announced in a warning tone, "someone had better look out for Franki's toga. Her backside is really straining the fabric, and those seams are about to blow."

Carnie's head emerged from the float and turned to stare up at me. "Gurl, find a cover-up. No one wants to see your seafood platter, much less fresh out o' the river."

"Yep." I smacked my lips. "No chance at romance with this krewe."

With cheeks hotter than Bradley's, I straightened and checked my costume. The seams *were* in sad shape, but there was no way I was going to tell Chandra that the toga had been too small to start with after she'd accused me of stretching out her ex too-short shift dress. "It must've shrunk after it got wet."

"Oh?" She pressed a paddle nail to her lips. "Is that what happened to the dress I lent you too?"

I glanced over the side, but not at Bradley. The truth was, I was semi-considering shoving Chandra off the float. "Say that one more time, and I'll show everyone the photos I took of your full-moon-sized toilet seat."

She gasped, stepped backwards, and fell on her lunar lump.

Chandra Toccato, down. Next up, still have to get Ruth Walker.

As if summoned, Ruth goose-stepped toward me. "No fighting with fellow riders, and no flirting with security. They've all got a job to do, and so do you."

She got zero argument from me. The sooner I did my job, the sooner I'd be free of this Mardi Gras madness. I waded through grocery and throw bags toward my station at the helm but stopped short at a disturbing sight.

Maroon spikes emerged from the ladder, then Nadezhda. "Vhen I get tips?"

It came as no surprise that she was worrying about her money when I was focused on a killer. "Tips are at the end, *if* you do a good job."

"Sissy," she hissed.

My head snapped back. *Did she mean the Russian word, as in the Big-Sasha-raising-her-skirt version? Or does she still think I'm a man?*

She'd already descended the ladder, so I couldn't ask her. But either way, no tip from me.

Ruth produced a microphone, and the upper float deck gave a collective groan.

"Attention riders," she tapped the mic, "I'll be expecting my float captain gift at the same time you tip the tractor driver."

As far as I was concerned, she'd be waiting until the Mississippi froze over.

The tractor engine started.

"Throw stations, everyone," Ruth commanded at enhanced volume. "And put on your harnesses and masks."

Veronica moved a throw bag to make room for me. "Did you find Tiffany?"

"Yeah, and it was quite an experience. Let me get ready, and I'll fill you in."

Wanda held out a wig. "I made the four of us weapon attachments." She held up a Clotho spindle that had a sharpened end like the one in my office door. "You insert it into a holder under the hair, and pull it out as needed."

While Wanda gathered my hair in a net, I pulled the spindle from the wig. It sounded like the unsheathing of a sword.

Marcella's gold smoky eyes glinted. "Now that you're here, Franki, I can finally unveil our float wreaths. We didn't have anyone on our committee, so I stayed up all night putting them together."

"That was nice," I said, as Wanda took the wig and pulled it onto my head.

"Oh, it was my pleasure." Marcella opened the lid of a large box and produced a wreath that stank of spray paint. But the odor was the least offensive thing about it. There were fairy wings on either side, a Jiminy Cricket cutout glued on the front, and below it was a long (lying) Pinocchio nose made from a drumstick.

Wanda's wigs aside, I couldn't think of a more ridiculous set of objects to wear on my head. And it took everything I had not to fulfill my vow to rip the cricket off the wreath and stomp on him. "That's... Wow, Marcella."

"I know, right? If I'd gotten them done in time to enter the wreath contest to ride after the board members' float, we would've won. These wreaths definitely capture the Clotho essence, if I do say so myself."

Regardless of when the wreaths got done, the only way we were riding second was to cut.

She placed the wreath on my head, stood back, and clasped her hands. "Positively ethereal. And that blue glitter you're wearing is a nice touch."

A nice touch of Gerry.

The float began to move, and it was a good thing we had to wear harnesses. Nadezhda was obviously in a hurry to get her tip money. And like the wooden boy he was, Pinocchio swayed and creaked under the weight of the riders and throws. But as much as I disliked the puppet, I had to admit that he rode a lot smoother than my mangled Mustang.

"I'd better unwrap some throws, even though I don't know how much throwing I can do with this shoulder." I crouched and whacked the drumstick nose on the side of the float, knocking the wreath and weapon wig flying.

It was going to be a long parade.

For so many reasons.

Veronica retrieved the items. "Let me help you." She reassembled the Cleopatra-Pinocchio ensemble on my head. "Before I forget, we're getting a new office security system."

Wanda turned. "Did something happen?"

I nodded. "The killer broke in, stabbed a spindle in my door, and wrote a threat in my gratitude journal." I shot a scowl at Veronica. "Told you those journals were bad."

My BFF put her hands on her hips. "In their defense, murderers don't usually write threats in them. Now what did Tiffany have to say?"

"Basically," I sat on a throw bag to pad my tailbone, "everyone on the Clotho board has secrets."

Marcella rubbed her hands. "Gossip fest! Spill the tea, Franki."

"It's not like she gave me the list," I said, unwrapping some beads, "but we already know about Marie-Fleur's shopping debt, Claudine's embezzling, and Anaïs's prostitution ring. Tiffany did say that Honorine came from a poor family, and apparently Anaïs did too. Her biggest revelation was that Anaïs used to work at a bookstore in the Quarter."

Wanda frowned. "Why do we care?"

"Because I stopped by there this morning, and according to her former employer, this was her favorite read." I pulled the copy of *Deadly Doses* from my bag and opened it to the incriminating page.

Veronica took the book, and Wanda and Marcella looked over her shoulder. Then Ruth joined in.

One by one, with jaws set, their eyes moved from the page to me.

Veronica returned the book. "This doesn't look good for Anaïs."

"Especially not when you consider what The Vassal told

me." I slipped *Deadly Doses* into my purse. "Anaïs Monvoisin is really Anna Moyer, and her family owns a smoke shop."

Marcella sucked in her breath. "The nicotine!"

Wanda unsheathed her wig spindle. "I'll get her for setting me up."

"Slow your roll, parade float." I pointed a bead package at her. "If Anaïs is trying to set up anyone, it's Honorine. So put that weapon away before someone gets stabbed."

Chin out, Wanda sheathed her spindle.

"We do have to be on high alert." I hung the beads on a throw hook. "And once we're on the parade route, I'm going to give Nadezhda a chance to earn her tips."

"How so?" Veronica asked.

"I'm going to have her put the pedal to the metal and move us from float twenty-four to float two."

Ruth held the microphone to her mouth. "Nothing doing, route reneger. We're not bucking float order on my watch."

I didn't object to the new nickname, because it was the first legitimate renege version I'd earned. "We have to keep an eye on Anaïs, Ruth. And this way, when the media is getting shots of the Clotho float, yours will be right behind it, basking in the celebratory glory."

She stroked her ostrich stubble. "I do deserve it. But I give the mutiny orders."

"Of course. Just get me behind that float."

Marcella beamed. "I guess it doesn't matter that I didn't finish the wreaths in time to enter the contest. We're still going to ride second!"

But not to up our social standing, I thought. *We're going to unmask a murderer.*

The nonne began shouting and throwing tomatoes.

Tensing, I rose and scanned the area, expecting the hearse. It was a vehicle, all right, parked in a corner of the parking lot. But it bore no similarity to a funeral coach.

Wanda gripped the railing. "Why are they attacking that leprechaun float from the St. Patrick's Day parade? It's not even going to roll today."

"I'll tell you." Marcella's nostrils flared. "The Irish stole the leprechaun from the Italians. The word comes from the Latin *lupercus*, the name of a Roman god in charge of protecting flocks and his mischievous male cult members."

I'd never heard that before. But her reaction reminded me of the conversation we'd had about the Italians being the first to create a School of Poisoners. I didn't know which was worse—being the origin of deadly poisons or of wee bearded man fairies.

My phone rang, and I fished it from my bag.

"Who is it?" Veronica asked.

I held up my phone. "A telemarketer from Sicily Island, Louisiana."

"Where's that?"

My gaze shifted to the nonne, who were still pelting the leprechaun. "Right here on Pinocchio."

She chuckled but quickly grimaced and pressed her temples. Evidently, she was paying for yesterday's Cosmopolitans.

"Boohoo, Franki!" Carnie shouted from the deck below. "Boohoo!"

Mouth cocked, I leaned over the side of the float and saw her staring up. "I believe that's 'yoohoo?'"

"Not when I smell you it isn't. Makes me cry every time." She doubled over the railing and dissolved into a fit of laughter.

And I repressed a different kind of fit. "What do you want, Carnie?"

She stood and wiped her eyes for dramatic effect. "We're short a few wreaths."

Marcella looked at me. "I must've miscounted. Can you help me bring the box downstairs?"

Needless to say, I would've rather taken another dip in the Gerry-infested river than descend into the den of that drag, Carnie, but I could hardly refuse to help.

Begrudgingly, I went down the ladder, and Marcella lowered the box.

Carnie covered her nose. "Miss Coocoo, please do us all a favor and spritz Miss Fishy Franki with some of your Chanel No. 5."

I ignored Carnie but gave the perfume my full attention. I put the box down and followed Coocoo to her station at the far end of the float. I didn't want a spritz, just information. "Carnie mentioned that you know a lot about Chanel."

"I am cuckoo for the brand," she said, touching her hat.

Silently, I willed the bird not to pop from the clock. After the raven, Gerry, and Tricky Vicky, I was done with unexpected animals. "What can you tell me about Chanel No. 5?"

She grabbed a gold classic-flap handbag. "Coco Chanel created it in 1921 to celebrate the liberated spirit of flappers in the Roaring Twenties. Before then, there were only two types of perfume, a single garden flower for respectable women, and musk or jasmine for the others."

Honorine had mentioned that Marie-Fleur preferred a flower scent, and Claudine wore Jasmin Rouge. *Was it significant?* "Do you happen to know why the number five is in the perfume name?"

"Why yes. Coco thought it was a mystical number, the pure embodiment of a thing. From the age of twelve, she was raised by French nuns in a convent orphanage, and the paths that led to its cathedral were created in circular patterns repeating the number five." Coocoo paused and pulled a bottle of Chanel No. 5 from her bag. "Also, when the perfume was in production, she was given numbered samples to choose from, and she picked the fifth vial."

The story reminded me of the Casket Girls at the old Ursuline convent.

Coocoo held up the iconic bottle. "Now close your eyes and whisper, All roads lead to Paris."

"You mean, Rome."

"Not when you're in New Orleans, *chère*."

I closed my eyes but stayed silent while Coocoo spritzed. I didn't dare betray my ancestral motherland in case word got back to Marcella. And also, my stomach was lurching.

The tractor was speeding along a backstreet to the start of the parade route, causing the float to jerk violently. But that wasn't what was upsetting my gut. The source of my sickness was a series of nagging—and nauseating—thoughts.

Or themes.

Chanel No. 5.

The Roaring Twenties.

French nuns caring for girls in a convent orphanage.

The number five.

Worst of all, I was beginning to think I'd been all wrong about the killer. But there was one thing I no longer doubted.

Atropos had indeed come to Mardi Gras. And if I didn't figure out who she was, a fifth person would die.

19

"What's the hold-up, Float Captain?" I glared at Ruth without lifting my head from the throw-bag bed I'd assembled on top of Pinocchio. "We've been waiting to turn onto the parade route for almost three hours."

"That's how long it takes when you're on float 24 behind two other krewes." She unfurled an old-fashioned nautical spyglass and squinted into it like a seasoned seafarer. "The Clotho board hasn't even started rolling."

Which meant we were all safe for the time being—or so I hoped. "Well, I could've walked the freaking route by now."

She retracted the spyglass with a snap. "And if I were a ride reneger like you, I could've kicked you to the curb by now too."

Ruth was raining on my Mardi Gras parade, but I kept my mouth shut. The woman was capable of awful retaliations, including making me wear a fun meter while buzzing her Get Busy Buzzer to force me to feign more fun. And there was no enjoyment on Pinocchio at the moment.

Even though it was February, the sun beat down on the upper deck, and I hadn't worn sunscreen. Adding to my misery, despite the penis plushies I'd borrowed from Glenda to pad my ribs and tailbone, my throw-bag bed was exacerbating my injuries.

I wasn't the only one despairing. Except for the nonne, who were skilled in the arts of waiting and suffering, all the riders were getting tired.

And drunk on Jell-O shots.

So far I'd avoided the dessert drinks because I had to keep my wits about me, but my willpower was waning. The box lunch we'd been given was wearing off, and my only other option was to try to cook one of the nonne's bags of pasta with my bottle of water, which, given how hot it had gotten, might've worked.

After a couple of hours.

I rolled onto my side. "How many Jell-O shots did you make, Marcella?"

She pulled back her Cleopatra hair. "Oh, I didn't make them. The nonne did."

My head shot up. Jell-O shots were a staple on Mardi Gras floats because there was no chance of spills, but I didn't know the nonne knew about them.

Or made them.

Veronica's text-tone beeped, and she raised her head from her throw-bag recliner. "It's David. When Chewbacchus is done parading, he and Standish will head this way."

That would've been an entry in my gratitude journal—if the killer hadn't ruined it for me. None of us had a clue how things would go down when Clotho started rolling, so we could use the help.

Veronica rose. "Time for some hair of the dog. What flavors do we have left?"

Marcella leaned forward on the throw-bag couch she shared with a napping Wanda and opened the cooler. "All three. Aperol spritz, peach Bellini, and Limoncello."

Limoncello Jell-O had a ring to it. But given my lemon history, I'd almost rather have a frozen southern milk punch.

Chandra waddle-waded through the throw bags and sucked a shot.

The sight of her chewing made my stomach growl. I returned to my back, and my tailbone sent a jolt up my spine. Come to think of it, the shots were essentially lunch and pain killers rolled into one. *Win-win.* "Veronica, can you grab me a couple of spritzes?"

"Speaking of spritzes," Chandra frowned and sniffed the air, "after your dip in the river, did you go swimming in Chanel No. 5?"

"Chandra's got a point, Francesca," my mother said from her throw-bag litter. "You overdid it with the perfume."

I didn't know how anyone could smell me over Rosalie's garlic and polyester odor and the nonne's mothball-and-church-incense scent. "You can all thank Carnie and Coocoo Chanel for that."

Veronica brought me the Jell-O, and I popped a much-needed shot.

Chandra stopped midway enroute to her throw station, gasped, and clutched her heart. "Damn! I shouldn't admit this, but I'd like a piece of that smokin' hot bod."

I followed her gaze.

To Bradley. Who, incidentally, was looking mighty muscular in his tan Mount Olympus costume.

Rising up, I swallowed my Jell-O spritz. "Uh, slow down there, Singles'-Compound Chandra, because that smokin' hot bod and I are picking a wedding venue when this case is over."

Her moon face turned as hot as the sun, and she came for me—paddle nails out.

I shoved her back. "What's the matter with you?"

"So that's what the Chanel No. 5 is about." She poked me in

the bruised ribs. "I knew I shouldn't have fallen for that lesbian story. It was all a front so you could make a play for Lou."

"Make a *what* for Lou?"

"You heard me." She twisted my bruised eyelid.

"Hey!" I gripped her wrist. "No one does that in a fight."

Ruth used the mic to whack our biceps. "And no one cat-fights on my float."

Chandra and I glowered at one another, massaging our arms and wounded pride.

Rosalie giggled behind me.

My head whipped around, but she was smoothing her Mike Ditka mustache. I turned back to Chandra. "What does Lou have to do with this, anyway? You were lusting after Bradley."

"No, I wasn't. I was lusting after my husband."

I took another look. Lo and behold, Lou was behind Bradley. I must've been blinded by my fiancé's muscles because there was no other explanation for how I could've missed the king of the Krewe of Commodus. Lou was copping a pose on a flaming toilet that had been bolted onto a wooden platform with wheels and an engine. His arms were outstretched to reach the high Harley Davidson handlebars mounted on a pole in front of the pot.

He'd obviously come to show off his hot rod—and 'smokin' hot bod'—to Chandra.

As if to prove my point, Lou puffed out his plumber-shirt-clad chest and raced the engine. Then he turned on his toe shoes and flushed his toilet. Smoke rose from the lid, and fire came from the sides.

"Hooo!" Carnie wailed on the deck below. "That's what I call bathroom realness after a fried oyster po-boy from Domilise's!"

"Mr. Plumber Man," another queen shouted, "I'll help you clear your pipes."

"John, honey," a third called, "I'll be your ho after the parade tonight."

Chandra's cheeks flamed, matching the toilet's heat. But she wasn't angry or even embarrassed about the drag queens' commentary. No. Lou had lit her desire fire.

More Commodus members descended on the street, toilets twirling and zipping around, except for one who rode a urinal in the shape of opened red lips and teeth with the slogan "potty mouth."

No sooner had the krewe arrived than they turned back, returning to the parade route with Lou in the lead and brandishing the standard plumber equipment—plungers, pipe wrenches, and sagging pants that revealed their cracks.

Chandra dropped onto a throw bag and dabbed perspiration with her toga fabric. "That man is too sexy on that toilet."

My hunger pangs extinguished like the flames from Lou's commode. Just like *sweet* and *toilet*, *sexy* and *toilet* didn't go together either.

Someone tapped me on the back. I turned and gave a shout. I still couldn't get used to my mom in her Liz Taylor-Cleopatra makeup.

"Francesca, your nonna and I are relieved to hear you're picking a wedding venue. Will that be tonight when the parade is over? Mardi Gras *is* the anniversary of Bradley's first proposal, and with the wedding ten months away, venues are filling up."

Nonna jutted out her bottom lip. "Franki, me and-a the girls have-a been-a talkin." She pointed to the octogenarians in Catholic black behind her. "You can have-a the reception in-a Santina's back-a-yard or on-a the patio at-a Mandina's restaurant."

Not a chance in inferno, I thought. Santina's lecherous son, Bruno, still lived at home, and Mandina's was the site of a former Italian grocery store with a possible link to The Axeman of New

Orleans. Compared to those options, Texas City during a refinery leak would be idyllic.

"And-a don't-a forget," Nonna held up two fingers, "you got a couple-a Italian churches in-a New Orleans for the wedding, Our Lady of-a Guadalupe or St.-a Mary's."

My face was impassive, but inside I was dying. The former was the Old Mortuary Chapel, given its history as a burial chapel for victims of yellow fever, and the latter was the Old Ursuline Convent, which housed the Casket Girls and their alleged vampire-coffin hope chests. *I'd be better off getting the ghostly pharmacist to marry me in front of the uterine torture device case at the Historical Pharmacy Museum.*

Marcella catapulted from her throw-bag couch. "I've been thinking, Franki, and we can do the whole shebang at the American Italian Cultural Center—get you hitched in the Renaissance Room, and then party in the piazza."

My mother's egregiously blue eyelids fluttered. "Or you could get married at home in Houston, dear, and celebrate at the deli."

Rosalie fluffed her stache. "Unless...you don't want to get married."

I held up my phone.

And she held up her hands. "But, we all know that's nonsense, right?" She forced a laugh. "Who wouldn't want to marry that hunk of man, Bradley? I know I do."

It was my turn to giggle.

The tractor engine roared, and the float began to move.

My attention turned to Ruth. She'd been popping a lot of Jell-O shots, which explained her undone bun and the slipping shoulder of her toga. "You know those shots are alcoholic."

"And you know I don't drink. I'm having the lemonade."

"That's Limoncello, which definitely isn't just lemon juice and sugar."

She eyed a shot in her hand. "Well, it *is* Mardi Gras. No harm in letting loose."

There *was* harm, and plenty of it. If Ruth got any looser, we'd see the suspicious-looking mole on her left breast that the dermatologist wanted to check out.

Pinocchio began to move, and we turned from S. Claiborne onto Napoleon Avenue, the start of the parade route.

Throngs of people lined the streets, adults on foot and in lawn chairs, and kids on traditional Mardi Gras ladders. All of them held up their arms and shouted for throws.

Chewing a shot, I stayed low and scanned the area for the hearse. The hooded driver had targeted me before, so I had every reason to believe he was lurking on a side street, keeping me in his deadly sights.

It was comforting to see first responders on patrol—except for a fireman smoking a cigarette.

Only in New Orleans.

Between the crowds and the narrow street, there was no way to cut around the floats in front of us. I had to figure out how to get to the Clotho board's float.

Wait. Nadezhda! If I was a route reneger, she was a route renegade. "Float Captain Ruth, tell Nadezhda to pass St. Charles and head to Prytania Street. That's the only way we'll catch the Clotho float."

Our fearless leader produced a walkie talkie. "Captain to Commie, come in."

I moved close to hear Nadezhda's reply.

Ruth turned, and the Pinocchio noses on our wreaths locked like swords, as did our eyes.

"Do you mind?" she drawled.

I couldn't step back fast enough. Her boozy Jell-O shot breath was horrendous.

She pressed the walkie talkie button. "Captain to Commie. Do you copy?"

"Da."

"The correct term is 'affirmative.'"

"Da."

Apparently, Nadezhda wasn't as skilled in the pronunciation of radio lingo as she was in payment forms.

Ruth gave a frustrated snort and lowered the walkie talkie. "I should've expected as much from a Commie bikini waxer and hooch store owner." She raised the radio to her lips. "Change of route. Go to Prytania and catch Clotho. 10-10."

The tractor came to an abrupt stop, as did Pinocchio. We all lurched, and Wanda fell off the couch.

"Nyet! I no sweat like whore in Orthodox Church for ten ten dollar!"

Ruth pursed her lips. "10-10 is radio code for 'transmission complete,' not 'ten ten-dollar bills.' And don't sweat it, Commie. We've got forty riders on this float. If everyone pitches in a twenty, you'll net a cool eight hundred."

Nadezhda leapt from the tractor. She unscrewed the gas cap, pulled a bottle of Matrioshka vodka from her snakeskin bag, and poured it in the tank.

Wanda whistled. "Woohoo, Nadezhda! That'll get us where we need to go."

And then some, I thought. *That Matrioshka vodka was pure rocket fuel.*

Nadezhda hopped behind the wheel, and the tractor engine roared like a Russian fighter jet. Pinocchio zipped from the line, blew through the blockade at the main parade route on St. Charles, and hooked a hard left onto Prytania.

The people on the street seemed shocked. Either they weren't expecting a float, or they weren't expecting us. A pink-flowered Pinocchio full of black-garbed grandmas and drag queens in drab tan was wild even by New Orleans standards.

Marcella looked at Ruth. "How are we going to get around this traffic?"

"Never fear. Your captain is here." She shot a triumphant brow arch in my direction, pulled a brand new Get Busy Buzzer from the bosom of her toga, and blasted it into the microphone.

As annoyed as I was to see another buzzer, to Ruth's credit, people and cars began moving out of our way. "Where do you think we should tell Nadezhda to cut back over to the parade route?"

"At Gallier Hall."

Veronica blinked. "The former City Hall building?"

"Yes," Ruth unfurled the spyglass and squinted through it, "the Clotho float is going to stop there for a spindle wheel ceremony."

"Why there?" I glanced at Wanda and Marcella, who seemed as surprised by the ceremony news as Veronica and I were. "That's near the end of the parade."

Ruth closed the spyglass and gave the buzzer another buzz. "Gallier Hall's had a traditional place of honor during Mardi Gras since the 1800s. They set up those viewing galleries out front so Mardi Gras royalty can watch the parades and marching bands."

"Not only that," Wanda said, "the mayor always stands on the steps to toast the kings of the Krewe of Rex and the Zulu Social Aid & Pleasure Club."

"The mayor?" I sank onto my throw-bag bed. I wasn't sure what the ceremony was about, but after I'd almost been hit with the flying spindle at the float warehouse, I knew it wasn't good. Clotho obviously wanted to make a big statement.

And without a doubt, so did the killer.

But was the mayor the intended victim?

THE POUNDING of marching band drums matched my pulse. I moved from my throw-bag bed to Marcella's couch to confer with the girls—not the octogenarians, but the thirty-somethings. "Can y'all think of any reason the killer would target the mayor?"

Veronica chewed a nail. "She *is* a woman." Her eyes darted to Wanda. "Maybe she has some connection to the krewe?"

"I seriously doubt that." Wanda put her hands on her hips. "If Clotho had the mayor in their pocket, we would have heard aaall about it at the empowerment brunch."

Marcella reached for a peach Bellini. "And I would've heard something at the American Italian Cultural Center because the mayor is a big supporter of our work. If you ask me, either Anaïs or Honorine is going to kill the other."

"Mark my words," I paused to make sure they actually did, "whichever one of them committed the murders plans to frame the other to avoid prison. And the best way to do that is to kill someone else today with all of New Orleans watching."

Marcella's gold-shadowed eyes searched mine. "But if the mayor isn't the next victim, who is it?"

"She *did* threaten Bradley and me..."

Whamming Wanda rotated her shoulder, warming up her softball pitching arm. "Neither one of you is anywhere near her."

That didn't mean anything.

Or did it?

I tried to think, but the screaming of the crowds was deafening, and we weren't even on the parade route. The problem was, we couldn't get there. A sea of cars had flooded Prytania Street, so the float was at a standstill. "We need Ruth to get back on her buzzer and clear this traffic."

There was another problem. Float Captain Ruth was under the influence of the Limoncello Jell-O and an audience that screamed the Mardi Gras battle cry, "Show us your tits!" She was lowering her toga top, flashing people on the street.

Stressed out and grossed out, I marched over to her. "Could you please keep those covered? My nonna is on board."

"Get used to it, Miss Priss. The word 'carnival' is Latin for "farewell to flesh."

"Uh, that's because eating meat was forbidden during Lent. So how about we all stop saying hello to your flesh?"

"Prude!" She popped another Jell-O shot.

Which wasn't a positive sign.

Chandra pulled me aside. "We've got to do something about her," she whisper-huffed. "She's acting like a hussy, and after the way Lou behaved with Glenda's Yardi Gras doll decorations, he doesn't need to see any real breasts."

My eyes turned like the wheels of Pinocchio. If Chandra was worried about her husband being attracted to Ruth Buzzi Hussey's knockers, there was nothing I could do to help her. "I can't deal with this right now, okay? I've got a murderer to contend with."

Chandra's tiny mouth puckered, and she poked my ribs.

"Listen, Boston Strong," I snarled. "Keep doing that, and you'll meet the might of Houston and Austin Strong combined."

She flipped her Cleopatra hair—and her middle finger—on the way back to her throw station.

Ruth picked up her mic and turned to the upper deck. "Let's get in the Mardi Gras spirit, Spinner Winners!" She dropped her toga top and did a Glenda-style shimmy. "*Laissez les bons temps rouler!*"

My stomach churned. The good times weren't the only things rolling on Pinocchio.

Italian prayer erupted from the far end of the float as the

Catholic Cavalry crossed themselves and clicked rosary beads. Meanwhile, a red-faced Rosalie held a suspiciously quiet huddle with Chandra and my mother.

"Someone has to do something," I muttered. I ripped the mic from Ruth's hand, picked up the buzzer, and blasted the blasted thing.

Cars began to move, and Nadezhda hit the vodka-gas. Pinocchio lurched forward, and so did Ruth.

Over the side of the float!

We all gaped over the railing.

Our float captain hung by her harness.

A little voice told me to look at Rosalie, who was creeping away from Ruth's throw station. Her beady eyes attempted innocence, but we both knew what had happened. She'd wrecking-balled Ruth.

"Wheee!" Our fearless, topless leader swung back and forth. "Everybody, now! Show us your tits!"

Angry Italian flew from the nonne's mouths just as Ruth had flown from the float.

Carnie's head emerged from the lower deck, and her face raged up at me. "Don't just stand there, Miss Fishy Franki. Reel in Float Captain Uncouth!"

Veronica grabbed my arm. "She's right. We've got to pull her up."

To make a point, my eyes locked onto Marcella, who was, after all, the one built like a linebacker.

Wanda reached for the rope, but Chandra stopped her. "No, leave her."

What I was about to say made me sadder than when I'd first boarded the float. "We can't let Ruth hang there, Chandra."

"Why not? She's having fun, and it'll keep her out of our hair."

"Yeah, but once we get on the parade route, she'll scare the children."

Chandra pointed to her head. "Have you even *seen* our wreaths?"

There was no arguing with that. Jiminy Cricket, fairy wings, and a lying Pinocchio nose protruding from leaves were every bit as terrifying as Half-Nude Ruth. But now that Chandra had mentioned the annoying cricket, I ripped him off my wreath and stomped on him.

"Mitts off my breasts, savages!" Ruth shouted. "Only the dermatologist can touch these puppies—when he checks that suspicious-looking mole."

Cringing at the "puppies" comparison, I reluctantly peered over the railing. The drag queens were pulling Float Captain Uncouth into the lower deck. "What're you going to do with her?"

"Lock her in the damn bathroom," Carnie barked. "Someone's got to have some balls around here."

No way I was touching that one with so many queens on board. I chewed my lower lip, debating whether to intervene in Ruth's abduction—until I remembered she'd eaten my leftover Nutella king cake.

Ruth Walker, down.

Next up, the killer.

Grabbing the microphone and buzzer, I tried again to clear the traffic.

Glenda strutted up and struck a pose in her Blue Fairy number and stripper Roman sandals. "You should see Miss Ruth fighting those queens, sugar. She's a wildcat."

"You mean, a wild *bird*—a hybrid ostrich-turkey."

Glenda reached into her toga and pulled out a cigarette holder. "I'm gonna need a smoke after that scene."

"Whoa, not on the float. Pinocchio will burn like matchsticks."

"Fine, Miss Franki. I'll just have a nicotine fit. But while I do, you need to take over the float captain duties and tell Miss Nadezhda to hurry. We've got to get to Gallier Hall before Bob does the christening. Otherwise, he'll leave without seeing my outfit."

"The Clotho float christening? That was at the start of the parade."

"No, sugar. I read in this morning's paper that it's before some silly spindle ceremony at the old City Hall."

I'd never heard of a christening near the *end* of an event. And I didn't like the sound of it. Or maybe it was Glenda's reference to nicotine that bothered me.

"Look, Franki!" Veronica held up her phone. "I found a livestream of the parade. The Clotho float is halfway to the Hall."

"Let me see if Bob's on the float, Miss Ronnie." Glenda took the phone and zoomed in on the screen. "There he is..." The lines on her forehead deepened, and her inch-long lashes blinked. "*With Devil Child?*"

The name made my nerves sizzle. "Who?"

"One of the women on the Clotho cloud float. She was a stripper who called herself 'Devil Child' in the early 2000s. I can't think of her real name, but she always wore red sequins when she performed."

Images flashed through my brain.

The Devil tarot card.

The Flame of Hades dress.

Aaand, my mother with Bradley and me chained to Hell's door.

I looked over Glenda's shoulder and watched Anaïs and Honorine wave from their thrones while Bob stood near the rear of the float. "Which one is Devil Child?"

But before Glenda pointed to the woman, I knew.

Honorine.

Glenda smirked. "She once said the devil wore Chanel, not Prada, to explain why she wouldn't take the stage without a spritz of Chanel No. 5."

A crash from the past echoed in my ears. The teacup the maid dropped after Honorine had claimed to be scent intolerant.

Glenda typed something into Veronica's phone. "That's right! Her name is Dana Devlin."

"How did you find that out?" I gushed. "What did you just search?"

"The crime she committed against a client—attempted murder."

Murder?

Veronica looked from me to Glenda. "Why isn't she incarcerated?"

"An attorney got her off on a technicality. She was supposed to be retried, but she disappeared and, apparently, changed her identity."

It was all starting to fit.

Like a glove.

Pacing the upper deck, I ran through the facts. "Honorine was the woman in the purple Mardi Gras wig. She planted the Chanel No. 5 at your wig shop, Wanda, and told me it belonged to Anaïs. But Anaïs wasn't at your shop, or at the Greasing of the Poles."

Wanda scrunched her nose. "Okay," her tone was hesitant, "but you saw Claudine give Ken Lanier the frozen southern milk punch."

"Yes, after Honorine bought it at Napoleon's Itch and poisoned the glass. She's lactose intolerant, so she made the bartender pour a bunch out rather than drinking it herself to make sure none of the liquid spilled down the side, because that would've caused the nicotine to penetrate her glove before she handed the drink to Claudine to give to Ken."

Marcella's brow wrinkled. "What about the empowerment brunch, though? I saw Claudine give the frozen southern milk punch to Marie-Fleur."

"That's just it. Marie-Fleur wasn't poisoned by the glass. Honorine knew Marie-Fleur would be wearing gloves when she took the drink, so she put nicotine on the money she handed her. Of course, Marie-Fleur took off her gloves to count it." I stopped pacing and stared at the girls. "So, Honorine poisoned her the same way Catherine De' Medici poisoned the Cardinal of Lorraine."

Veronica flopped onto her throw-bag recliner. "What about the Murder Mystery Dinner at Muriel's?"

I leaned against the railing. "None of us saw Honorine give Claudine the poisoned champagne flute. All we know is that Claudine carried it with her bare hand because someone or something got her right glove wet. But, Honorine passed by the Carriageway after Claudine died, which is right by the stairs to the séance room. That explains why no one found the flute and why she wouldn't pick up the brass rope post Anaïs had just knocked over as she was leaving the restaurant."

Glenda fiddled with a blue light on her chest. "Excuse the interruption, sugar. But what does a rope post have to do with Claudine's murder?"

"Honorine probably didn't see who knocked the post over, but she might've thought it was Claudine—who had nicotine on her right hand. Honorine knew she also had nicotine on her gloves from handling the champagne flute. Now that I think about it, I remember she reached for her hair and stopped. So even though she was staring at the post, wringing her gloved hands, she didn't pick it up because she would've left traces of nicotine. And that could've gotten her convicted."

Chandra gasped. "That's why Claudine said 'devil' before she died."

I nodded. "And the other word you couldn't make out was 'child.'" Obviously, Claudine knew about Honorine's past, and I'm sure Marie-Fleur did too since she and Claudine have been close since high school. Either Claudine or Marie-Fleur or both told Ken Lanier. And Josephine the Go-Between definitely knew, which is what got her buried beneath the throw bags. Honorine poisoned the others while framing Anaïs for the spree killings. I'm betting Honorine's husband has no idea who she really is."

Marcella applauded. "Way to solve a case, Franki! Just like Marisa Tomei's character in *My Cousin Vinny*."

"Uh, not really. Her character was a hairstylist, mechanic, and pool hustler?"

My mom threw her arms around me. "This is wonderful, dear. Now you can pick a wedding venue."

Nonna and the nonne danced a jig—that was disturbingly leprechaunish.

But I couldn't celebrate.

Honorine was still free.

And she had a fifth victim on her hit list—one I hadn't identified.

Glenda returned the phone to Veronica. "I'm surprised you and Miss Franki didn't hear about the Devil Child case while you were at school. It was a major news story."

Veronica and I exchanged a puzzled look. Then I turned to Glenda. "We didn't go to college here. We were in Austin."

"That's where Dana tried to murder her client. Some bigshot lawyer with connections to the Capitol."

A lawyer from Austin?

The hair on my neck went rigid. "Honorine's next target is Bob!"

20

———

"You've got to save Bob, Miss Franki," Glenda shouted over the screaming paradegoers from her perch on Pinocchio's nose—which put a whole new spin on the Blue Fairy's relationship with the puppet.

"We're trying," I yelled as I rummaged through Ruth's things alongside Veronica, Marcella, and Wanda, desperate to find the walkie talkie or the microphone to communicate with Nadezhda. "Why don't you come down and help us look for the radio? It's not safe up there."

"Nonsense. I've got my Mighty Grip, and someone needs to be the lookout."

Glenda wasn't fooling anyone. If she'd brought her pole-dancing powder, she was on that nose to do a number.

Chandra strode over with Rosalie and my mother, not to help, but to hover. "Why would Honorine kill our costume designer?"

I sifted through a throw bag. "He used to be a lawyer in Austin, so he probably recognized her from the attempted murder trial and slipped up somehow."

"Hmm," Rosalie hummed, dubious. "How's she going to do him in with all these people watching?"

"A bottle of Tuaca."

"Brenda," she shot a look of disapproval at my mother, "your daughter's been hitting the sauce again, and I don't mean marinara."

My eyes rolled, even though I *did* have those Jell-O shots. "I know what I'm talking about, Rosalie. During the christening ceremony, Honorine is going to switch the bottle from the Sazerac Company with one the hearse driver, aka her brother, Travis, bought at a liquor store by Clotho headquarters."

My mom removed her gold mask, giving us all another look at her Liz Taylor-Cleopatra eyeshadow. "Why would she do that, dear?"

"She coated the bottle with nicotine. It's fatal if the skin absorbs too much."

The nonne began emptying pasta bags to cover their hands.

Veronica raised the walkie talkie. "Found one of them!"

Grateful for an exit from the conversation, I practically ripped the radio from her grasp. "Franki to Commie, come in."

"Nyet. You not captain."

"That's 'negative,' and if you want your tips, you'll do what I say."

"I need raise."

"Ha! You already soaked me for a two-thousand-dollar van down payment."

"And you got free Tic Tac."

If I wasn't so frantic to find Bob, I would've hurled the walkie talkie at her maroon spikes. "Either get this float to the parade route, or kiss your tips *da svidania*."

The tractor roared to life. Pinocchio ploughed past parade-goers, made a couple of hair-raising turns, and emerged onto St. Charles.

In the middle of giant tribbles?

Wanda cupped her hands around her mouth. "We've gone too far, Franki. We're in the Intergalactic Krewe of Chewbacchus."

Right. The Trouble with Tribbles subkrewe that David and The Vassal had been battling since joining the Krewe of Klingons. For a second there, I was worried.

My college-aged colleagues ran up wearing Wanda's Chewbacchus wigs and carrying their Wookiee weapons. They ripped bando blocks from their bandoliers and pelted the tribbles. The nonne and queens joined in, launching tomatoes and silicone bra inserts.

Evidently, the Krewe of Klingons wasn't the only group that disliked the prolific *Star Trek* creatures.

The tribbles responded by throwing miniature versions of themselves, and the parade route descended into chaos.

As the drunken revelry of the Chewbacchanal degenerated further into drunken weaponry, I pressed the Walkie Talkie button. "Franki to Commie, go to Gallier Hall."

The tractor took off and turned onto a side street.

Pinocchio jolted to a stop.

Gasps and screams erupted from our float.

"*Un carro funebre,*" Nonna shouted.

It was indeed a funeral coach—the creepy hearse with the U R NEXT license plate. The driver's hood was down, and his face sent a shiver from the base of my neck to my tailbone.

A skull with skin stretched over it.

"Not today, Satan," Carnie bellowed. "Not today!"

The queens unleashed a flurry of platform shoes.

Wanda passed out spindles to Marcella, Veronica, and me, while the nonne got out their garlic. Rosalie, Chandra, and my mother threw the tarted up pig bomboniere.

As mad as I was that the Wrecking Ball had brought the

garish wedding favors, I appreciated the damage they were doing to the hearse hood. The thing was in worse shape than my Mustang after Glenda's stripper pole smashed it.

David and The Vassal came around the corner wielding their bowcasters. They pulled hard on the strings, but didn't have the strength to actually shoot arrows.

The hearse driver revved the engine.

Which spelled doom.

"Glenda," I unlatched my harness, "get back on deck." I put a foot on the railing and extended my hand to help her climb down.

Tires squealed, and the hearse slammed into the side of Pinocchio.

The smell of burned rubber filled the air—as I flew through it.

And landed in...*pink fur?*

I lifted my head, and a Pink Wookiee stared back at me. "I really have to see a specialist about my nightmares."

"Way to stick the landing, sugar," Glenda shouted, still astride Pinocchio's nose.

And I did it without Mighty Grip.

The hearse driver threw the car into reverse, and the Pink Wookiee threw *me.*

Pain shot up my spine as I landed on the street, tailbone first. "You're obviously not a hero like your brown twin!"

The hearse came gunning.

Terrified, I flipped onto my hands and knees. An arm circled my waist and scooped me up as the hearse crashed into a balcony support.

My savior wasn't the cowardly Pink Wookiee, it was Lou on his flaming toilet. He drove me to the float.

"Thank you, Lou."

"Aw, Franki." He turned as pink as the Wookiee and fiddled with a plunger. "It was nothing."

Carnie came down the ladder and pulled me off the pot. "We've got to go. That hearse hooligan took off on foot." She turned to Nadezhda. "Get us to the Hall," she yelled in her man voice. "We've got a score to settle."

The tractor took off.

Carnie, much like Rosalie, didn't need a mic or a walkie talkie.

The queens wept and wailed as they tried to put their looks back together, and Carnie began to pace. "We're all worked up. Bob's creating some costumes for a drag brunch show we're putting together. If anything happens to him, we'll have to call it off. How can we possibly replace the Sultan of Sequins, the Guru of Glitter, the Roi of Rhinestones?"

"Miss Carnie," Glenda shouted from above, "don't forget the Shah of Shards!"

Still a little stunned, I gripped the ladder to the upper deck. "Based on his work this Mardi Gras, you could add the King of Crystals, the Prince of Petroleum, and the God of Glue to Bob's title list."

Coocoo fainted, and a crowd of queens gathered around her.

Carnie's face turned as red as one of her spool threads. "See what you did?"

From the bathroom, Ruth broke into a verse of "Whiskey River" by Willie Nelson. Judging from her nasal twang and slurred words, the queens had locked her in there with Jell-O shots.

Suddenly, the upper deck krewe seemed normal. I climbed the ladder to rejoin my people.

Mom and Nonna hugged me, and the nonne applauded.

Chandra sniffed, clearly miffed. "Oh, so *now* you can walk *and* climb ladders—after you needed to be rescued by Lou."

There was no point in telling her that a plumber on a motorized toilet wasn't my idea of a knight in shining armor. Mine was an ex-banker-turned-financial-crimes-investigator in an ancient Greek miniskirt.

I clapped to get everyone's attention. "We need to find the microphone before we get to Gallier Hall. It might be the only way to warn Bob about the nicotine."

Everyone began searching.

Pinocchio turned onto St. Charles, and the viewing galleries went silent.

"Wow," Wanda smoothed her wig. "We're not cut from the same cloth as the Clotho board, but I didn't think we looked that bad."

She hadn't seen the drag queens post-hearse accident.

The cheering resumed, and I scoped out the scene. The mayor stood on the steps of Gallier Hall with its enormous fluted Ionic columns, gazing at the float. Bob was on board near the ladder, while Anaïs and Honorine sat on their thrones watching a man I didn't recognize near the Clotho goddess masthead.

My gaze shifted back to the two remaining members of the Clotho board. Both women wore opera gloves.

"Keep searching," I shouted. "We're almost out of time."

And so is Bob.

The unfamiliar man raised a microphone. "The Sazerac Company is delighted to present an honorary bottle of Tuaca to the President of the Krewe of Clotho, Anaïs Monvoisin."

There were cheers and a few catcalls as Anaïs accepted the bottle, raised it high, and passed it to Honorine.

Veronica nudged me. "She's going to make the switch."

I judged the distance between Pinocchio and the goddess float. There was no way to get to it in time, not even on Lou's flaming toilet.

Is Bob going to die?

The Sazerac Company rep passed the microphone to Honorine.

"Ninety-nine Jell-O's with hooch on the wall, ninety-nine Jell-O's with hooooch..."

But the singer wasn't Honorine.

"Ruth's got the microphone!" I hurried down the ladder and heard Honorine greet the spectators.

Carnie and Coocoo were already in the bathroom, scuffling with Ruth, who was wearing Carnie's spool wig and Coocoo's clock hat.

"Yikes," I muttered but went in.

"As the Vice President of Clotho," Honorine said, her voice loud and clear in the bathroom as I struggled to wrest the mic from Ruth, "I have the honor of passing the Tuaca bottle to our amazing costume designer, Bob Simpson, to christen the goddess Clotho. Before I do, I'm going to cover the neck of the bottle with one of our signature throws to protect his talented hands. It's a satin kerchief with our slogan, 'Be a spinner, and be a winner!'"

Ruth grabbed a lock of my hair and twisted my bruised eyelid—the thing I told Chandra no one did during a fight. A set of teeth came at me and diverted to Ruth's wrist. Ruth dropped the mic, but not my hair. And Carnie refused to release her wrist.

Escaping the bathroom minus a hunk of hair but with the mic, I leaned over the rail in time to see Honorine pick up a Tuaca bottle as Bob walked toward her. "Bob, stop! Don't go any closer!"

He kept walking.

Carnie groaned. "He can't hear you over the crowd."

The queens began to scream, and the nonne prayed.

There was only one thing to do. I tapped the mic repeatedly

on the rail until the crowd went silent, and I raised it to my mouth. "Honorine poisoned that bottle, Bob. Do not touch it!"

"Don't touch the Tuaca!" erupted from those in the viewing galleries.

Bob raised his hands and backed away.

Honorine stood as still as the Clotho masthead as Anaïs and Bob swiftly deboarded the float.

Even though Bob was safe, I pressed on because police were in attendance. "Honorine Ledet isn't the descendent of a Casket Girl or the founder of a praline company. She's an ex-stripper named Dana Devlin who skipped out on a retrial for attempted murder in Texas. Then she killed Ken Lanier, Marie-Fleur Fontenot, Claudine Denault, and Josephine, uh, Go Between to stop them from telling everyone who and what she really is."

Two officers approached the float ladder.

Travis blew from the crowd, hopped on the tractor, and put it in drive.

"Follow that float, Commie," I shouted into the mic.

Nadezhda hit the vodka-gas, but the engine gave an odd sputter.

And seemed to sing?

Thanks to the Matrioshka vodka, the tractor was as tanked as Ruth.

I pulled a piece of paper from my bag and stabbed it onto my wreath nose. Then I descended the ladder to a commode—commandeered by Bradley, who stood at the handle bars.

Carnie puckered. "Go catch that killer. But I *will* joke about your ride later."

Certain of that, I nodded and sat on the toilet, which was an uncomfortable sensation in public.

"You sure you want to do this?" Bradley asked over his shoulder. "The police have radioed for squad cars."

"Honorine only needs a few minutes to get away. She's disappeared before. She'll do it again." What I didn't say was that if she and her hearse-driver brother escaped, it would be our funeral.

Bradley sped after the Clotho float, and I looked behind us, holding my wreath. As I suspected, we were flanked by Lou and his team of toilets.

St. Charles was closed to traffic during Mardi Gras. Nevertheless, Travis couldn't speed because of the occasional car illegally crossing at an intersection.

But not for long. St. Charles went to Interstate 10.

Bradley pulled up alongside the cloud. "Be careful, babe."

"Count on it. We've still got to pick a wedding venue." I gave him a quick kiss and slid the wreath onto my arm. Then, holding the flush handle, I stepped onto the toilet platform. Watching the asphalt zip by between me and the float, I jumped forward and latched onto the ladder.

And I willed Atropos away as I clung to the rungs for dear life.

Carefully, I began the climb, expecting Honorine to appear and stomp on my fingers. But she didn't. I made it onto the float and found her sitting on her throne, staring stone-faced at the road ahead. "Hi, Honorine. Or should I call you Dana?"

She stood and swung the Tuaca bottle.

I ducked and backed up, which was difficult on a moving float.

"You know what they say," she grimaced and took another swing, "it's bad luck if the bottle doesn't break at a christening."

I slid the wreath from my arm and held it up to fend off direct contact with the poison. "Your luck has already run out. The police are on their way, and they'll have no trouble catching a tractor."

"This one tops out at 87 miles per hour. They won't catch me before I make good on my threat to take you out. You were right about me not having a Casket Girl ancestor, but I *am* the descendant of a Correction Girl."

Another swing of the Tuaca.

And another step back. "You're living proof that you can't escape your roots."

"If it wasn't for Claudine and Marie-Fleur, I would have."

"Because Claudine broke up with Ken, and he planned to investigate her and the krewe as revenge. And y'all have too many secrets to let that happen."

She went as still as the Clotho masthead.

And I kept talking to buy time. "Claudine's embezzling and racketeering, Marie-Fleur's secret shopping addiction, Anaïs's prostitution ring, and your stripper past."

"Go on." Honorine motioned with the bottle for me to continue.

"So you all hatched a plan to kill him. The others thought it would end with his death, never realizing you had a plan of your own—to kill everyone except Anaïs, so you could frame her. But, tell me, what makes you so sure Anaïs won't tell everyone about your dancing days?"

Her mouth rose in a half smile. "Simple. She doesn't know. Claudine's the one who dug up the dirt on me and blabbed it to Marie-Fleur. But unbeknownst to Claudine, her best friend traded my identity for a free divorce."

That jived with what Wanda had heard about Marie-Fleur's husband threatening to divorce her, but it didn't quite make sense. "If Marie-Fleur needed Ken Lanier's help with a divorce, why would she help kill him?"

"She made the deal with Ken before we all met to discuss how to stop his investigation into the krewe. When we settled on the solution, Marie-Fleur was too afraid to tell us what she'd done. The only way I found out was when the bastard tried to blackmail me, which made poisoning him especially sweet."

I grimaced. The word *sweet* didn't go with *poisoning*, either.

Sirens wailed in the distance.

"Intermission's over." Honorine swung the bottle.

And I leapt back, wondering how much room I had left on the float.

Which was picking up speed.

Disappointment crossed Honorine's brow. "It's a shame that Marie-Fleur betrayed me, because I like Anaïs."

"And yet you're framing her."

Honorine's eyes flashed fire, a glimpse of her inner devil, and she swung again. "Anaïs made herself an easy target with her psychological thrillers and a poison book she carries with her."

Deadly Doses.

She jabbed the bottle at me.

l deflected contact with the wreath.

Her expression was determined—and devilish. "And I can't go to prison because I have a social reputation to uphold and a praline company to run."

The woman's priorities were as off as she was.

The sirens were closer.

But my back was against the railing. "Tell your brother to stop. This float's about to be surrounded by cops."

"One way or another, I'll get away." She flashed a smile so evil it could only be described as Satanic. "Then I'll finish off your fiancé too."

Rage flooded my chest. I pulled the paper from Pinocchio's nose and shoved her threat into her mouth, as I'd vowed to Ruth to do. "Eat your words, Dana. That's the note you left in my gratitude journal."

She gagged and pulled out the paper. Then she kicked me hard into the railing.

Tailbone pain blinded me for a second. When the haze cleared, she was raising the Tuaca over her head.

Be a spinner, and be a winner, I thought as I spun and leapt the railing onto the back of the Clotho masthead. I was one with the goddess, clinging to the thread of life with my arms and legs.

"Swerve, Travis!" Honorine screamed. "Knock her off!"

The tractor serpentined, and the float followed. The motion slung me from Clotho's back to her breast.

If I let go, I'd be run over—by multiple wheels.

Police lights were visible.

Honorine slung her leg over the rail, still holding the bottle.

This Mardi Gras was a hellscape. But I couldn't let the anniversary of Bradley's proposal be forever marred by a murder.

Mine.

She leaned forward with the Tuaca.

I wasn't sure whether she was going to beat me with the bottle or rub it on my skin. Nevertheless, I released my legs and hung by my arms to put more distance between us. I wouldn't be able to hold this position for long, especially if we swerved or hit a bump. I looked down, and my gut plummeted, along with my hope.

We were on the highway.

As I gazed at the road, contemplating whether I could propel myself to one side and survive a fall at eighty-plus miles per hour, wig hair whipped my face.

How is Wanda's weapon wig still on my head?

Must be the weight of the...

My eyes popped.

Then, hanging from my left arm, I unsheathed the spindle and stabbed it into Honorine's bicep.

Shock shot across her face, and she let go of the Tuaca.

And the rail.

The bottle crashed on the highway.

So did Honorine.

21

———

"Thank you again for coming to my rescue, Bradley." I wrapped my arms around his neck in the middle of I-10 and held him tight, but I didn't mention that he was the second man to catch me that day—or maybe the first since the other was a pink humanoid alien from the *Star Wars* universe. "You're my knight in shining Mount Olympus miniskirt wear."

"You should thank Lou." He buried his face in my neck and kissed my hair. "His flaming toilet can really cruise on the highway."

I mentally thanked the king of the Krewe of Commodus for not trying to rescue me a second time. If he had, I would've died today—at the hands of Chandra and one of Lou's pipe wrenches.

Still in Bradley's arms, my gaze locked on Travis, who hung his head in the back of a squad car. I couldn't wait for him to be taken away like Honorine, who'd left in an ambulance minutes before. With one Devlin bound for jail and the other incapacitated by broken bones, I hoped it was the last I'd ever see of the devious duo. Fortunately, the police had already taken Anaïs into custody.

Bradley pulled back and took me by the hand. "Come on. Marcella's expecting us at an impromptu Mardi Gras party she's throwing at the Piazza d'Italia."

"I don't know, Bradley. My whole body hurts, and I'm exhausted."

"Everyone from the float will be there." He arched a brow. "And your mom and nonna are getting Venezia pizza and pizzelle with gelato from Angelo Broccato's."

Per usual, talk of carbs and sugar brought my stomach to life. We *were* mere minutes away from the American Italian Cultural Center, and it was only six p.m. on the biggest holiday in New Orleans. "Okay, but no pralines."

"At the Piazza d'Italia? Sacrilege!"

My lips curled into a smile, and I straddled the flaming toilet.

As we sped down the highway, I realized that even Lou's motorized commode rode better than my mangled Mustang. And oddly enough, if it had looked like the Nutella-jar version in my bathroom, I would've liked it even better.

But only as a vehicle. I promised myself that I would manifest the two proclamations I'd made about my destiny after I'd confronted Rosalie in my bathroom. I had a feeling I was going to go back on one of those proclamations, since I was an occasional reneger. But not the one about redoing the toilet. That Nutella poop theme was a no-go.

When we arrived at the piazza, the Pinocchio float was parked out front, along with around thirty toilets. The columns glowed red and green, and live accordion music filled the street.

Bradley and I entered, and everyone applauded.

Veronica threw her arms around me. "I'm so glad to see you, Franki."

"Me too." Despite my injured ribs and shoulder, I hugged her hard.

Wanda was behind Veronica, still in her krewe wig. "I've got to hand it to you, girl. You got me off the police suspect list, and we all had fun in the process."

Not so much, I thought, *particularly at the end there.*

"Excuse us, Wanda." Bradley put his hands on my shoulders. "I need to get Franki off her feet." He steered me to a table near the fountain and pulled out a chair.

I'd barely sat down when Glenda sashayed over with Carnie and Coocoo, who'd recovered their respective spool wig and cuckoo clock hat from a ripped Ruth.

"Miss Franki," Glenda's blue lights glowed beneath a red gingham table cloth courtesy of the Italian couture house Non-Naughty Nonne, "you did NOLA proud. You rid the city of an awful woman who valued her social standing over people. Now maybe the victims' families can find some peace in seeing her brought to justice."

I wanted nothing less.

Carnie pursed. "Even though it pains me, Franki, I have to give you kudos, both for your crime-solving skills and your fiancé-finding skills. When you rode off with Bradley on the back of that toilet, I thought, 'Never has hugging the porcelain god seemed so appealing.'"

My lips twisted into a smile. That joke was worth the wait.

Coocoo looked at me with her insane-money stare. "I agree, Miss Franki. When I saw your fiancé drive up on that commode, my cuckoo almost flew the coop."

I glanced at her battered wide-brimmed hat. "You mean, the clock?"

"No, the coop."

Best not to probe that comment further.

Glenda lit a cigarette. "Anyhoo, you won't be surprised to

learn that Bob loves my version of the Clotho toga. But for some reason, his wife, Linda, doesn't care for it."

Couldn't imagine why not.

Carnie shook her head, which was missing a few spools. "There's no accounting for taste, Miss Glenda."

"Don't I know it?" She exhaled smoke.

"Franki," Bob approached the table and nodded a greeting at the others. "I'm afraid I have to leave early. Linda's got a migraine."

No doubt caused by the blue lights on Glenda's thread toga.

"But first, I wanted to thank you for warning me about that Tuaca bottle."

"Don't mention it, Bob. It's part of the job. But before you go, could you tell me what happened between you and Honorine?"

He shoved his hands in his pockets. "It has to do with that attempted murder trial. Like most attorneys in Austin, I followed the case. And the first time I met Honorine, I thought she was the spitting image of Dana Devlin, but I never imagined she was actually her after all these years. That day she asked me to meet her at the float den, I accidentally called her Dana. She seemed not to notice, but obviously she did."

Glenda dragged off her cigarette. "Well, Bob, even though you stabbed me in the back by coming out of retirement to do #krewecouture, I'm glad you're all right."

"It was never my intent to offend you, Glenda. Captain Claudine made me a one-time offer I couldn't refuse. Too bad I'll never see that fee."

Nadezhda's maroon spikes butted in. "I still not see tips."

I looked at Ruth, who was at the next table. She was still too soused on Jell-O shots to realize she hadn't gotten a float captain gift.

Glenda's eyes narrowed at Bob. "If the #krewecouture was a one-off, why did you agree to do #dragcouture for Miss Carnie?"

He shrugged. "To recoup my Clotho losses."

"Then I suppose all is forgiven."

"Oh, no—it isn't."

The dry exclamation came from a seventyish woman, whose face matched her dyed red hair, and the piazza lights had nothing to do with it. And based on Bob's reaction, the drive back to their home in Austin was going to be as rough as a ride in my mangled Mustang.

"Miss Linda," Glenda flipped her platinum Cher hair, "I was just about to ask Bob if he wanted to work with me on a #strippercouture collaboration."

"Bob's got a prior engagement."

"But," Glenda lowered her cigarette holder, "I haven't said when the project would start."

"Exactly." Linda's tone was as hard as her stare.

"Welp," Bob jingled the keys in his pocket, "this is the end of the road, everybody. I'm really retiring, unless Franki wants me to do her wedding dress."

Glenda huffed smoke at his nose. "I said I forgive you, Bob, but don't push it. If anyone's designing her dress, it's this Hucci Cucci Hot Couture mama right here."

The nonne crossed themselves, and I lowered my eyes to my too-tight tan toga, which, in the red-and green lights, was almost the colors of the Italian flag. Compared to one of Glenda's creations, an Italian flag wedding dress was looking good enough to make me rethink my other destiny proclamation— even if the dress came with Marcella's Leaning Tower of Pizza wig.

"Speaking of retiring," Chandra pranced to the table, dragging Lou behind her, "Mr. Toccato and I are back together, so I'm moving out of the singles' compound."

My joy was tempered by the charm bracelet on her wrist. If

her arm shot up to channel a spirit, I'd hop the next toilet out of town.

Bradley leaned close. "By the way, I think Lou and I might be related on my mother's side."

The pain in my body moved to my head. Linda's migraine was contagious.

Ruth bolted from her chair, holding an espresso cup. "I've got news too."

"No!" I slammed my palm on the table. "You are *not* moving in to the fourplex."

"Darn tootin' I'm not! Who wants to live next door to a ride reneger and rude interrupter?"

I rued whoever had given Ruth the caffeine to get her sober.

"What I was about to say is," she slipped on her cat eye glasses, "this parade has taught me that I can no longer deny my party girl side."

Chandra tightened her grip on Lou. "Not after that spectacle on Pinocchio."

Bradley looked at Ruth. "What are you going to do?"

"I was approached by a group of women who *appreciate* my Mardi Gras spirit." She paused to give us all time to wallow in guilt.

No one did.

Ruth sniffed and raised her chin. "These fine women want to meet with me about captaining a krewe next year, which means I'll need to go part time at Private Chicks."

"Well," Bradley sighed, "I'll be sorry to lose you for half the day, but we can work that out."

"Yes, you certainly can," I all but shouted. Although, my joy was once again tempered by the knowledge that Ruth could do a lot of damage around the office in a matter of minutes. Actually, seconds. *Milliseconds.*

Marcella brought her wine tote to the table. "Who wants

Chianti?" She threw back her hair curtain and laughed. "What a silly question, right? Everyone!"

She pulled out glasses and began pouring.

"Whoa, Franki," Wanda looked up from her phone, open-mouthed. "A journalist on the six o-clock news just reported that my weapon wig saved your life, and my email is blowing up with orders. Do you know what this means?"

"Hm, let me think." I tapped a finger on my chin. "An explosion of local crime involving sharp spindles?"

"Wrong. You get a big bonus!"

With any luck it would be enough to reimburse me for the more than four grand I'd lost on the throw package, van down payment, and cash bribes for Nadezhda and the COCKtail.

Nadezhda, who'd heard money, pulled up a chair. "I got idea, Vanda. Ve do new business. Ve call it, 'A Vax and a Vig.' I even got slogan. *Vax hair, put more zere.*"

The cringeworthy slogan made me think of a used-car dealer I wanted to forget. "That reminds me," I said to Bradley, "I've decided to have my Mustang towed from Carl Cash Cars before informing the police of his role in Anaïs's funny business at the Hotel Monteleone."

"Wise decision." He slid his arm around my shoulders. "But no more work talk tonight. We've got something far more important to discuss."

"Ruth's full-time replacement?" I asked dead serious.

He gave me a look.

Mom and Nonna arrived with the food, and I raised my brows to raise the alarm. "You know the pressure's only going to rachet up once we name a wedding venue."

Bradley flashed his signature dazzling smile. "Bring it."

I did—a kiss. It was amazing to be with a man who had his priorities straight.

My mother cleared her throat, and Nonna tugged at my arm. "Well-a? Where's-a the wedding?"

Which killed the kiss.

Bradley pushed back his chair and stood. "As you all know, Franki did me the honor of accepting my proposal exactly one year ago today." He took my hand and gazed into my eyes. "But she won't be single next Mardi Gras because I'm here tonight to ask her to marry me at The Driskill Hotel in Austin on January 11th."

Everyone cheered.

Except me. One reason was that Rosalie had wrecking-balled me, and I was struggling to overcome the blow.

"Brenda," Rosalie said, breathless, "we can have the bridal shower at the deli." She acted excited, but we both knew the body-check was payback for the fake shock pics of her with Glenda's Yardi Gras decorations.

Not to be outdone, Ruth stood. "And Veronica and I will throw Franki's bachelorette party here in The Big Easy."

Rosalie batted her eyelashes. "At GrrlSpot?"

I raised my phone, not to threaten her with the incriminating photos, but to delete the Find My Friends app—permanently. Come bridal shower and bachelorette time, I'd be in hiding.

"Well, babe?" Bradley asked. "What do you say?"

"Before I respond," I stood with my Chianti glass, "I'm grateful to each and every one of you for this night and your support during the investigation." I looked at Veronica, whose eyes had welled with tears. "I'm even grateful for the gratitude journal, which I'm going to burn after the office has been cleaned by hazmat."

She laughed, and we shared a silent toast.

Then I turned to the love of my life. "Now, as for marrying you at The Driskill Hotel, my answer is no."

Bradley blanched.

My mother screamed.

And the drag queens caught the nonne, who dropped like pasta over a pot.

"Calm down, y'all! I'm not done." I took Bradley's hands. "I want to get married in New Orleans at St. Mary's Catholic Church—"

"*Goooool!*" Nonna threw up her arms.

My mother grabbed Marcella's wine tote and drank straight from the spout.

"As for the reception," I glanced at the disembodied faces spitting water into the fountain where Naked Guy had bathed with a bar of Irish Spring, "I'd like that to be here at the Piazza d'Italia."

"*Viva gli sposi!*" Marcella spun—a behavior I hoped to break in light of our Clotho experience. She turned to two men with accordions—the Ragusa brothers?—"*Tarantella Siciliana,* boys!"

The nonne hit the dance floor, joined by David, The Vassal —and Wookiees.

Bradley pulled me into his arms and kissed me like we were behind closed doors. Then he leaned back and gave me a somber stare. "You had me worried there for a minute, Amato."

"Disappointed in my choices?"

He pushed a lock of my hair from my eyes. "I said I'd marry you here or anywhere. The place doesn't matter. But why'd you change your mind about Austin? It doesn't have anything to do with Honorine, does it?"

I debated whether to point out that The Driskill had *kill* in the name, which made it a nonstarter, but decided to keep that quiet. Neither the name nor Honorine were the reason I'd ruled out the famous hotel. "Let's just say that this case helped me get my priorities straight. Plus..."

"*Plus* what, babe?"

Resting my head on his chest, I watched my Mom and Rosalie serving stacks of pizza and pizzelle with gelato to guests, Nonna and the nonne teaching drag queens the tarantella, the Ragusa brothers dueling with their accordions, and my joy knew no bounds. "You can't escape your roots, Bradley. And with roots like these, why would I want to?"

FREE MINI MYSTERIES OFFER

Want to know what happens to Franki after *Limoncello Yellow*? Sign up for my newsletter to receive a free copy of the *Franki Amato Mini Mysteries*, a hilarious collection that contains "Prugnolino Purple" (Franki #1.5) and five other fun short mysteries. You'll also be the first to know about my new releases, deals, and giveaways.

Here's the blurb for "Prugnolino Purple:"

It's springtime in New Orleans, and Franki Amato's BFF and boss, Veronica Maggio, has dragged her to an art auction at one of the city's historic house museums. Up for sale, a provocative, not to mention peculiar, painting of their sixty-something ex-stripper landlady that is anything but priceless. Franki thinks the only crime at play is the image on the canvas until a cocktail waitress is found unconscious in front of an empty easel. After Franki finds a purple splotch on the presumed weapon, she and Veronica spring into action to ID the attacking art thief and locate the missing painting. But Franki's biggest surprise isn't the culprit—it's the "blooming idiot" who bought the portrait before the auction started.

And don't forget to follow me!

BookBub
https://www.bookbub.com/authors/traci-andrighetti

Goodreads
https://www.goodreads.com/author/show/7383577.
Traci_Andrighetti

Facebook
https://www.facebook.com/traciandrighettiauthor

BOOK BACKSTORY

I'm so relieved *Tuaca Tan* is DONE! Like many of my books, it has been rolling around my head (like a parade float) for years, waiting to come out. It was inspired by my experiences on two New Orleans Mardi Gras krewes, but I'll get to that in a minute.

First I want to say that Mardi Gras krewes are expensive, time-consuming, and hard work. But they're fun for adults and *magical* for children! Both times I participated, I saw kids who might not get many—or any—toys other than the ones they caught at the parades. And the krewes and dance troupes donate heavily to charity. So I applaud the people who participate on these krewes. They're not just about partying, they serve their communities.

Now, for the krewe-related parts of this book that are true. I was on an all-female goddess-themed krewe that assigned me to a pink-flowered Pinocchio float. I have never liked the Pinocchio story—the original book or a movie adaptation. I remember watching the Disney version as a little girl and thinking, What the hell is going on here? Where's the princess? The Prince

Charming? A wooden puppet and donkeys? Why would anyone want to watch this nonsense? I didn't even know any boys who liked the movie. I was therefore especially upset to get stuck on the puppet while other krewe members got to ride on goddess floats.

And, yes, the krewe captain told us members that we would be escorted out of a banquet by police if we touched the table centerpieces. To add insult to Pinocchio injury, everyone on our float had to wear long blue wigs and godawful headpieces with Blue Fairy wings (hence Glenda's costume). The foam cutouts were of a long-nosed Pinocchio, not Jiminy Cricket, but at least there were no drumstick noses on the front. And instead of wreaths they were top hats, which was worse. We looked like winged Abe Lincolns on a Pinocchio float in a parade cele-brating a Greek goddess. I won't even describe the costume, because I just can't go back there. Suffice it to say that one of my friends actually cut hers to shreds after the parade was over.

When I returned home to Austin from that parade, I dropped off leftover throws at some friends' house who were still in New Orleans (I decided to leave early that trip). And I'm not lying when I say that I left the Pinocchio cutout from my hat in their chiminea.

But onto more fun topics.

I went to the Greasing of the Poles in February of 2022, and I can't convey to you how fun it is. The audience often wears awesome wigs and hats (I saw a woman with a champagne bottle fascinator with fake bubbles). And like I mention in Chapter 2, there's a woman in a champagne glass in the hotel bar, and every year a group of tourists come from Switzerland who call themselves the "Greasing of the Poles Fun Club." Also true, a man from the Krewe of Bosom Buddies walked up to me, patted a sticker of the moon with the words *I'll send you to the moon* on my boob, and handed me a tiger-striped hat. Like Franki in the story, I was so excited about the hat that I didn't care about the pat on my breast. New Orleans is the *only* place in the world that could happen.

Wanda's wigs were inspired by the amazing Marcy Hesseling, who is the owner of Fifi Mahony's (in the French Quarter and the Bywater). Until I found her shop, I was not a wig person, and I had never liked dressing in costume. But something about Fifi Mahony's wigs draw you in—and hook you for life. I now own four: the Spaghetti Western, the Voodoo Saloon Girl, the Mardi Gras Christmas Tree, and the Creepy New Orleans Cemetery (I asked her to design all but the Mardi Gras Christmas tree). If you scroll through my Facebook author page photos, you'll see a few of the wigs—except for the cemetery one, which will make a grand and ghastly entrance on Halloween. Now that I have the cemetery wig, I'm thinking about asking Marcy to create a wig of Glenda's fourplex—maybe with miniature Yardi Gras decorations!

Another true tidbit: The door guy at Rouses Market in the Quarter actually read my body language and knew that I was leaving the store dejected because they were out of Hubig's pies!

Also, Bob Simpson and his wife, Linda, are my real-life aunt and uncle. He *is* a retired attorney, but he does *not* design couture for aging ex-strippers and drag queens. That is a figment of my twisted imagination!

Speaking of my twisted imagination, Lou Toccato's motorized toilets were not only inspired by the motorized La-Z-Boy recliners I reference in the story, but also the motorized clawfoot bathtubs I saw during the Krewe of Muses parade in 2022. The name of this delightful clawfoot tub krewe is Les Bonnes Vivantes. The Krewe of Comus is real too, and so conveniently similar to Commodus. I laughed out loud when I came up with that one!

Not a figment of my imagination: My dog Victor, aka "Tricky Vicky," "Vicious Vic," and "Vicolas (Should Be In A) Cage." He has behavioral issues, but I can't blame him. He was dumped by his owner—a stranger who approached me in a grocery store parking lot during the pandemic. Yes, he bites, so on the advice of a veterinarian, I only use a "positive tone" when I speak to him. This necessitated the creation of an upbeat language, e.g., "Vicky want a picky?" when I need to pick him up *and* avoid a blood-letting. I know he sounds bad, but Vicky is also super affectionate. And I adore him despite his tricky temperament.

Last but not least, I have personally used the book *Deadly Doses* many times for poison plot ideas, but I never planned to make the book itself the key to solving the mystery in *Tuaca Tan*. That just happened—like this book, really. All I know is, my husband gets nervous every time he sees me browsing the *Deadly Doses* pages!

Cheers!

Traci

COCKTAILS (LOL!)

FROZEN SOUTHERN MILK PUNCH

When I was looking for a Tuaca drink to use as a suspected murder weapon in this book, I was so excited to discover that the storied liqueur is in the frozen version of New Orleans' most popular brunch drink. Because wealthy society women definitely do brunch—just not like the Krewe of Clotho's empowerment version, one would hope.

Ingredients
  4 1/2 cups half-and-half
  1 3/4 cups brandy
  1/2 cup Tuaca
  1/4 cup powdered sugar
  1 teaspoon vanilla extract
  freshly grated nutmeg

In a large bowl or pitcher that will hold at least 8 cups of liquid, combine the half-and-half, brandy, Tuaca, powdered sugar and vanilla and stir well. Cover and freeze for at least 3 hours, until slightly frozen.

Just before serving, stir the mixture to make it slightly slushy. If it has been sitting in the freezer for longer than 4 hours and is more firmly frozen, use a metal spoon to scrape the top layer into a slush, breaking it up into small pieces. Let sit for 30 minutes, stirring occasionally, until the mixture softens to a pourable consistency.

TUACA MULE

Nadezhda would never drink this twist on the Moscow Mule, and after this book, Franki probably wouldn't either. But it's delicious! Incidentally, this drink is also called the Tuscan Mule, which reminded me of Franki's potential wedding venue in Texas City.

Ingredients
    ½ lime
    2 ounces Tuaca Liqueur
    4 ounces ginger beer or ale

Fill a copper mug or highball glass with ice. Squeeze lime into the glass, and then drop in the lime. Add the Tuaca and top with ginger beer or ginger ale. Stir gently, and drink up!

ALSO BY TRACI ANDRIGHETTI

FRANKI AMATO MYSTERIES

Books
Limoncello Yellow
Prosecco Pink
Amaretto Amber
Campari Crimson
Galliano Gold
Marsala Maroon
Valpolicella Violet
Tuaca Tan
Nocino Noir
Sambuca Scarlet (coming in 2025!)

Box Sets
Franki Amato Mysteries Box Set (Books 1–3)
Franki Amato Mysteries Box Set (Books 4–6)
The Franki Amato Mysteries Big Box Set (Books 1–7)

Short Stories

Franki Amato Mini Mysteries
(short mysteries free to newsletter subscribers only)

Franki Amato also investigates with the sleuths of Leslie
Langtry, Arlene McFarlane, and Diana Orgain in the

KILLER FOURSOME MYSTERIES

Books
4 Sleuths & A Bachelorette
4 Sleuths & A Burlesque Dancer
4 Sleuths & A Barnstormer

DANGER COVE HAIR SALON MYSTERIES

Books
Deadly Dye and a Soy Chai
A Poison Manicure and Peach Liqueur
Killer Eyeshadow and a Cold Espresso

ABOUT THE AUTHOR

Traci Andrighetti is the *USA Today* bestselling author of the Franki Amato mysteries and the Danger Cove Hair Salon mysteries, and she is a co-author of the Killer Foursome mysteries. In her previous life, she was an award-winning literary translator and a Lecturer of Italian at the University of Texas at Austin, where she earned a PhD in Applied Linguistics. But then she got wise and ditched that academic stuff for a life of crime—writing, that is. Get news of Traci's upcoming books and latest capers at www.traciandrighetti.com.

Speaking of capers, Traci and one of her Killer Foursome co-authors, Diana Orgain, take published and aspiring authors on writing retreats to Italy through LemonLit. If you're up for an Italian adventure, then *andiamo*! But be careful. Traci and Diana are a lot like their sleuths, so you never know what—or who— might go down on the trip...

SNEAK PEEK

If you liked *Tuaca Tan*, read the first chapter of:

NOCINO NOIR
Franki Amato Mysteries Book 9

by
Traci Andrighetti

CHAPTER 1

"Top secret, Veronica. We're going dark, completely covert." My tone was hushed to prevent the patrons of the Camellia Grill from hearing. "It's called Operation Black Swamp."

My best friend and boss laid her Chanel bag on the diner-style marble counter and spun her stool to face me. "This whole situation makes me so nervous."

"How do you think I feel? I'm the one who bears the brunt of it." I peered through the order window at a middle-aged cook in the kitchen, half checking on our food and half checking him out. Given our current predicament, no one in New Orleans was above suspicion.

Veronica chewed her bottom lip. "Do we have a list of names?"

"A *list*?" My head jerked backwards. As owner and CEO of the PI firm Private Chicks, she didn't get much fieldwork, but that was a shockingly novice question. "Any and all discussions of this operation must be spoken, not written. We can't leave a paper trail."

"Gotcha." She fanned herself with a menu. "But with this heat, why are we meeting across town when we could've gone to that new coffee shop by the office?"

"*NOLA Noir?* Does the name alone not explain it to you?"

"Honestly, no."

"It sounds suspect, which is precisely what we don't want." I glanced around to make sure no one was watching and shoved a Nokia Flip into her lap.

She blinked. "A burner phone?"

"Don't use it at home or at work, or even in your car. They could be bugged."

"Oh, Franki. Is this really necessary?"

"How can you even ask that?" I whisper-hissed. "We're dealing with professionals, Veronica. Hardened veterans. By the way," I nodded at a shopping bag on the floor between our stools, "I put together some disguises."

She leaned over and rummaged through the contents.

From the corner of my eye, I spotted the cook watching us. I met his gaze with a stare as steely as his spatula.

The guy didn't flinch. He simply turned back to the grill.

But I had his number.

"No way I can wear this." Veronica raised a black hoodie from the bag. "It's June, and the hottest on record."

I gave her blonde locks and bright look the onceover. "You

can't wear that Kelly green dress, either. You stick out like a leprechaun at a funeral, and odds are, we're being watched."

"Here?" She scanned the diner.

"They've got informants everywhere, like a modern-day Black Hand," I said, referring to the extortion rackets run by Sicilian immigrants and Italian gangsters at the turn of the twentieth century. "Hence the 'black' in 'Operation Black Swamp.'"

Her cornflower blue eyes held fear.

My jaw set. I was frightened too.

This operation was the biggest job of our lives, and there was no way to prepare for it. Sure, I'd taken on some criminal masterminds in my PI career and won. But now that my wedding was in the works, those crooks seemed like Sunday School teachers compared to the diabolical duo Veronica and I were up against—Brenda Amato, née Pavan, and Carmela Amato, née Montalbano.

A.k.a., my mom and nonna.

Ever since Bradley and I had picked the church and reception venue, those two had taken their master meddling tactics to mobster level. And according to my father, they'd rewatched *The Godfather* trilogy for pointers. Their intentions were good—get me hitched without a hitch. But like real mob bosses, they thought they called the shots. And I would rather *get* shot with a *lupara*, the Sicilian sawed-off shotgun favored by mafiosi, than submit to their wacky Italian wedding traditions.

A battle-weary sigh escaped my lips. "We'll get through this," I said, more to bolster my own resolve than hers. "All we have to do is neutralize Vito and Michael Corleone and freeze out the swamp animals."

Her lips parted. "The *swamp* animals?"

I didn't disguise my surprise that she hadn't grasped the other part of the operation name. "The ones who'll surface from the swamp's murky depths to darken or derail my wedding festivities."

"That's the list I just asked you for."

"Yeah, but do I really have to tell you who they are?"

Her chin rose. "As your maid of honor, it's my duty to make sure no detail is overlooked, especially not one that could ruin your wedding."

"Fair enough." I held up my hands to tick off the animals on my fingers. "The gator, the snake, the snapping turtle, the black bear, the common loon, and the turkey-necked ostrich, otherwise known as Glenda, Nadezhda, Carnie, Rosalie, Chandra, and Ruth."

"Cute. But ostriches don't live in the swamp."

My lips curled. "The turkey-necked variety does, and she wallows in its muck." I rested my elbows on the counter. "Now, as far as anyone knows, my bridal shower is in November. Our mission is to make sure none of them find out you're throwing me one this Saturday while Bradley's mother and grandmother are visiting."

She massaged her chest, clearly uneasy. "I'm not sure Bradley's family will appreciate the lack of notice, and I don't even want to think about your mom and nonna's reaction."

Neither did I.

"How will you get them to come here from Houston without them suspecting anything?"

"I'll say I've found the perfect wedding dress. My mom will fire up the Ford Taurus and make the five-hour drive in three-and-a-half."

"You do that," her gaze held a warning as she reached for her water glass, "and you'll open the door to more meddling."

"Veronica," I laid my forearm on the counter and turned to face her, "that door is not only open, it's off the hinges. And it's been thoroughly trampled, like my right to plan my own wedding."

She sipped some water. "Weren't you going to hire a wedding planner to help you manage your family?"

"Believe me, I tried. But everyone I've called is either unavailable or too expensive. Do you know what Delilah Delaire costs?"

"Gosh, eight grand, I'd imagine."

"Try twelve. That kind of wedding is out of my league."

"Pardon me, girls." An elderly woman a few stools down leaned toward us. She wore heavy makeup despite the humidity —foundation with white powder, dark-red lipstick, and black eyeliner on her upper and lower lids. Based on her deep wrinkles and sagging skin, she was ninety if she was a day, and she had the vintage lace-collared dress, rhinestone brooch, and black velvet hairbow to prove it. "I heard you mention Delilah Delaire. Are you talking about the Blain-Adair wedding?"

I shook my head. "Actually, n—"

"Shame they had to call it off," she fretted before I could finish my sentence, "but I can't say I'm surprised. Agata *was* one hundred and two."

And to think my nonna had been calling me a *zitella* since I was sixteen, the so-called "marrying age" back in Dark-Ages Sicily. "Uh, this Agata was getting *married*?"

The woman's watery blue eyes popped. "Heavens no. The bride-to-be is her great niece, Grace Blain. But Agata died the day before yesterday, the morning of Grace's wedding."

Veronica's fingers flew to her lips. "How awful. The family must be devastated."

"About postponing the wedding, yes, but not about Agata's death. They despised her." She scowled. "Agata lorded her wealth over them for decades, always threatening to disinherit them over some foolishness or other."

The waiter rushed up, sweating in his white jacket and black bowtie uniform, and frisbeed our plates—a pecan waffle for Veronica and a Mexican omelet with a side of bacon for me.

He was gone before I could ask for a bottle of Crystal Hot Sauce.

Veronica laid a napkin in her lap and looked at the woman. "By any chance, is Grace Blain the daughter of Edward Blain, the divorce attorney?"

"Why, yes." The woman's face brightened. "Agata was his wife, Lara's, great aunt. Last name was Villeré. She owned that rundown mansion on St. Charles, the one the kids avoid at Halloween."

I knew the place. It made the Munster's' house look inviting. "Not that it's any of my business, but if Ms. Villeré had so much money, why didn't she do the upkeep on her property?"

"She and her older sister, Pia, inherited the place from their parents, and they never took care of it. That was their family home, and they'd lived there together their whole lives." Her sparse brows rose in a panicked look. "Spinsters!"

I'd seen the same stricken stare on the faces of my mom and nonna—every time I had another birthday, and at thirty-two, I was less than one-third the age of Agata. "Their names sound Italian."

"Their mother was from somewhere near Naples. They had a brother, Lara's grandfather. Can't recall his name. There were so many Italians in New Orleans back then."

"And still today." Over three hundred thousand, and it seemed like they all knew my nonna, who'd immigrated to the city with my nonnu and raised my father and uncles in the French Quarter. While I was thinking about it, I took another look at the diner customers.

The cashier passed by, adjusting his bowtie.

"Excuse me, sir." I raised a piece of bacon to flag him down and then, tempted by the sight of it, bit off a hunk. "Have you seen our waiter?"

The man's nostrils flared. "He's back in de damn bathroom. Don' know what he ate las' night, but he's been in dere three times dis mornin'."

The bacon fell from my mouth. *No need for that hot sauce now.*

The old woman spread egg yolk on a slice of toast.

A taste preference? Or does she think it's butter?

She lowered the knife. "What Agata didn't spend on the house, she made up for in jewelry. Her collection rivaled Elizabeth Taylor's."

Veronica's eyes grew to the size of the Koh-i-nor diamond. "Do you mind if I ask what kind of jewels? My husband's a gemologist, and I'm a fan of gems myself."

"Her most notable pieces were an Art Deco tiara by Cartier, the canary diamond ring Bette Davis wore in the movie *Jezebel*, and the pièce de résistance, Marie Antoinette's pearls. She bought those from the 2018 Sotheby's auction."

My BFF sucked in her breath, transfixed by the mention of the guillotined queen.

Meanwhile, I couldn't get my mind off Bette Davis. I watched *What Ever Happened to Baby Jane?* with my parents around the time I'd graduated from college, and over a decade later the character still creeped me out. The movie was more disturbing than the fairy tales my mother had read to me as a kid. And it didn't help that the woman talking to us had a Baby-Janesque appearance.

Memories of the awful food scenes from the movie and my suspicion of the cook prompted me to look inside my omelet for unwelcome ingredients, even though I had zero intention of eating it.

The woman swallowed some toast. "Agata also inherited all

the family jewels after Pia was pushed down the elevator shaft in their home."

The cook shouted.

At first I thought he'd heard the woman's astonishing comment, but a fire had broken out on the grill.

Our waiter ran from the bathroom, as though fleeing a fire himself, and went to help the cook. The two men extinguished the flames, but a bad feeling spread like wildfire in the pit of my stomach.

I looked at the woman. "Did you mean that Pia 'fell' down the elevator shaft?"

"Oh, no." She smiled, revealing long teeth smeared with blood red. "Pia was murdered. Just like Agata."

A humid haze hung over the NOLA Noir sign, which was black except for the white neon outline of a coffee cup and some sort of symbol. *A fleur-de-lis? A puff of steam?* It was hard to tell from the third-floor lobby window of Private Chicks. Whatever the symbol, it was unsettling.

Like that elderly woman at the Camellia Grill.

Was she right that Agata and Pia Villeré had both been murdered?

Who is she, anyway?

And why in God's name was she dressed like Baby Jane?

A woman on the street distracted me from my thoughts. She wore all black, including a hat and sunglasses, and walked briskly toward NOLA Noir. She reached the door, pulled her hat brim low, and glanced behind her before slipping inside.

Her dark attire recalled the mourning dresses of my nonna and her nonne friends, who forever mourned the loss of husbands and other beloved family members.

A disturbing thought brought a frown to my lips. *Is she one of my nonna's Sicilian soldiers come to spy on me?*

I turned to Ruth Walker, who sat in the reception desk chair. "Something's not right with that new coffee shop across the street."

She spun, setting in motion the chains on her cat-eye glasses and the folds of her turkey neck. "What's the matter with it?"

"Looks shady, and the 'noir' in the name doesn't help."

Her lips went as tight as her graying brown bun. "You could be describing this office."

Bewildered, I surveyed the exposed-brick lobby and dark décor. "What are you talking about? 'Private Chicks' is a cool name, and this is a historic French Quarter building."

"I'm talking about the stark furniture and frosted glass door with the company name in black letters. Change the 'Chicks' to 'Dicks,' and you've got a detective agency from a 1940s noir movie," she hit me with a hard stare, "where they smoked and drank and got shot."

My index and pinky fingers pointed to the ground in an Italian *scongiuri* gesture my nonna had taught me to ward off bad luck—that Ruth's 'getting shot' remark had cast over me and the office. I doubted it would work, but given the questionable coffee shop, some superstitious backup couldn't hurt.

"Private Chicks has character, Ruth." My tone was defensive because Veronica owned the building as well as the business. "But from what I can see of NOLA Noir, it's sketchy. And in the month it's been open, there have been odd comings and goings."

"Wake up and smell the coffee." Ruth raised her Only-Judge-Judy-Can-Judge-Me mug adorned with the scales of justice. "That's The Big Easy."

I smirked at her—and her mug. "You make it sound as though every place in the city is corrupt."

"Not the buildings, just the people in them."

Good thing Ruth was Bradley's assistant and not a judge like her TV idol. Otherwise, half the town would be in Central Lockup, or the "hoosegow" as she called it.

My gaze returned to NOLA Noir.

A tall, slender man rounded the corner, and I stepped from the window. He wore a dark suit and fedora.

In the dead of summer.

Veronica breezed into the lobby from the hallway opposite the entrance. She went to Ruth's reception desk and picked up the mail. "Any calls?"

Ruth pursed her lips, emphasizing her fuzzy ostrich chin and turkey wattle. "Not even a telemarketer. And instead of going out and hustling business, Ace PI Franki Amato is worrying about that new coffee shop."

If I was worried about anything, it was the conversation with the elderly woman, but I couldn't tell Ruth that. She suffered under the delusion that she, and not Veronica, was throwing my bachelorette party, so word of my Camellia Grill breakfast could raise her swamp-animal sense and clue her in to the wedding planning. "I am *not* worrying about that coffee shop." To prove my point, I turned to face her—and stopped chewing my nail. "As for business, there's none to hustle. There haven't been any homicides in the city lately."

At least, as far as I knew for *certain*.

Nevertheless, my mention of murder brought me back to Pia and Agata Villeré, and I looked out the window.

Ruth harrumphed. "There she goes spying again."

I hated to provide evidence for her accusation, but a suspicious sixty-something male had just left the coffee shop in a round red wig and matching nose. "In my defense, their clientele is sketchy. The Thin Man went in a minute ago, and an old clown just came out. It's like something straight out of a noir film, except for that clown, who is pure horror flick."

Ruth glanced at Veronica. "Or it's a normal day in the French Quarter."

"She's right, Franki."

"About the Quarter, yes." I flopped onto one of the two facing couches in our waiting area. "But the 'no's' in 'NOLA Noir' speak for themselves."

"Anyway," Veronica picked up a letter opener, "since business is so slow, you should take a long lunch. It *is* Restaurant Week, and there are a lot of deals on prix fixe menus."

"Nah. I'm not hungry," I fibbed, hoping no one could hear my stomach, which was still grousing about not getting that omelet and bacon. Ruth had recently taken to inviting me to take her to lunch, and I wanted to avoid that scenario. "Besides, it's only ten thirty. I'm going to make a shot of espresso and reorganize my office."

Veronica grimaced. "Mr. Coffee died when I turned him on this morning."

"Ugh." I rested my head on the couch. "I need a caffeine boost. All this nothing-going-on has worn me out."

Ruth crossed her arms. "NOLA Noir's right across the street."

My stare was as intense as a triple espresso. "I'll stick with the established coffee houses, like Cici's or PJ's, thank you."

The door flew open, and we all jumped.

David Savoie, our part-time PI, entered with a Tulane backpack and a black go-cup.

Veronica pointed the letter opener at him, and his hands shot up. "David," she said, teeth clenched, "you break that glass, and I'll slice you open like an envelope."

"Sorry, I forgot." He edged his tall, lanky frame around the letter opener and went to his corner desk. "I'm in a hurry. I have to study for an exam."

I sat up. "I didn't know you were in summer school."

"It's not for my Comp Sci degree," he said, sliding the backpack from his shoulders, "it's a course on ethics and the law for my PI license."

"I'm free today, if you need help studying."

Ruth's eyes dropped on me like a gavel. Then she shifted to David, her glasses chains swinging. "I'd think twice before accepting that offer. Every time Franki helps me, I lose a job."

I refrained from comment. The judgmental Judy blamed me for all the ills in her life, and arguing with her was as futile as telling the real Judge Judy that you rejected your court sentence. "Is that coffee from NOLA Noir?"

David flipped his brown bangs to one side. "Yeah, it's the cappuccino the shop is named for."

"Watch out." I eyed the cup and noticed it had the same unidentifiable image as their sign. "No telling what the *noir* refers to."

"Oh, it's liqueur." He paled and gaped at Veronica, who gave him a look as dark as his cup. "Uh, not enough to get drunk or anything."

Ruth tsked in keeping with her I-don't-drink façade. "What kind of liqueur is it?"

"Vick, the owner, called it *nocino*."

"No-CHEE-no?" I repeated. "That sounds familiar."

David removed a black paper bag from his backpack. "You know how Italians drink Limoncello in the summer?"

I puckered—from the irony, not from the memory of the lemon liqueur. "I have some experience with that, yes."

"Nocino is the winter equivalent, made with walnuts."

"Why didn't you say so?" Ruth raised her mug, hoping for a sample. "It's non-alcoholic."

My eyes rolled like an empty liqueur bottle on Bourbon Street. Any alcohol derived from grain, fruit, nuts, or herbs—in other words, all of it—was non-alcoholic to Ruth, which was one of the reasons I didn't want to go to lunch with her. The last time

I did, she had so many cherry bounces that she bounced from her chair to the floor.

Veronica scanned the contents of a letter. "'Nocino cappuccino' is catchy. Why doesn't the owner call it that?"

Ruth shrugged. "It's a mystery." She smirked at me. "Or a noir."

I saw her smirk and raised her a sneer. "I think he's just a bad marketer. The indecipherable symbol on the sign is an indication."

"Either way, if you want coffee quick, it's the best option."

"You can stop trying to get me to go there, Ruth. It's not going to happen." I reached for my phone and saw I had a text message.

The contents of which made me shudder.

"What is it, Franki?" Veronica asked.

My eyes were glued to the display. "Delilah Delaire is at NOLA Noir, and she wants me to meet her about an urgent personal matter."

"It has to be your wedding."

"No, I think it's *her* personal matter."

"So?" Ruth shouted. "What are you waiting for?"

I hesitated. The woman at the Camellia Grill had implied that Delilah was the Blain-Adair wedding planner, and I was concerned that she wanted to see me about whatever had happened to Agata Villeré.

Ruth harrumphed. "Franki's probably afraid it'll be a case."

True, but not for the reason she thought. I couldn't explain it, not even to myself, but something told me not to go across the street.

David sat beside me on the couch. He opened the black bag and pulled out a flaky, layered pastry that gave off a heavenly buttery odor.

My stomach roared to life. "Is that...a *sfogliatella*?"

He nodded as he bit off a hunk. "Vick said his Italian grandma makes them."

I catapulted from the cushion. "I'd better go meet that wedding planner."

"Well, well, well," Ruth crowed. "That was such an abrupt about-face, I'm surprised you didn't fall."

Trying to save face, I raised my chin. "It's for investigative purposes."

"Mm-*hm*. While you're investigating the pastries—I mean the planner—get me a NOLA Noir and make it a double." She glanced at Veronica, whose eyelids had lowered. "Since it's non-alcoholic."

Although Ruth didn't fork over any cash, I agreed in hopes the booze would knock her out for a nap.

With my hobo bag in hand, I left the office and bounded down the stairs. The steamy air grew hotter and more suffocating with each flight, as though I was descending into hell instead of the French Quarter. Before exiting the stairwell, I tied my long brown hair into a knot. Then I looked both ways to avoid running into a passing tourist armed with an obligatory Hand Grenade, Hurricane, or Huge Ass Beer, all of which were murder on clothing.

As I stepped onto Decatur Street, the woman in the black hat exited NOLA Noir.

Our gazes met, and she removed her sunglasses.

Definitely not a nonna. "Delilah?"

She stepped into the street.

A black BMW careened around the corner and knocked her from her feet.

Horrified, I screamed as she landed in a crumpled heap a foot away from me. Before my frozen limbs would move, the BMW sped away, and an old black Buick Roadster with tinted windows came around the corner and screeched to a stop.

My traumatized eyes locked with those of a thirtyish woman in the backseat. She was dressed in red—a fitted blouse with shoulder pads and a wide-brimmed hat. Her jaw had dropped.

Mine had too.

Her driver hit the gas, and the car fishtailed.

I pressed myself against the wall of the building as the car swerved, narrowly missing the woman in the street, and sped away.

My limbs shook as I rushed to the woman's disturbingly still body, and when I realized it was too late to save her, my fingers struggled to dial 9-1-1.

But the hit-and-run wasn't the only thing that had shaken me.

It was also the woman in red in the Roadster.

Because she looked like a femme fatale who'd driven in from a 1940s movie.

A *noir* movie.